ECHOES OF FORGOTTEN MEMORIES

Court of the Underlings Book One

C Tarkington

Contents

Chapter 1

Prince Taliesin Dawen, Prince of the Golden and Dark Fae Courts

To Tal, nothing in his life ever seemed to make sense or fall into place. He blamed it on his heritage, a creature of two courts born to a mother of darkness and a father of light. His mother becoming the queen of the Golden Court had been the first great connection between the two Fae courts, much celebrated at the time. He could barely remember his mother, who never recovered from the birth of Tal and his twin sister and had died before their second birthday. To this day, he could still hear his father, the late king's laugh, bellowing through the halls of the Golden Palace long after his death. His oldest brother, who'd been known as the Golden Prince, now reigned over Brigant and the rest of the Golden Court as The Sun King.

Tal was fine with being the second son. He was just at home in the shadows as the sun, so he didn't mind spending much of the time in his mother's court, living in his uncle's palace. He usually wasn't too much of a nuisance for the Dark King, and when he did something to pique the old ruler's wrath, Tal visited the human lands.

If only he had been happily drinking at a tavern, talking to the wise old men in Callint, or paying attention to a lovely field maiden in Thiria, he could have been watching the mages at their trade in Illedria, but no, he had to be sleeping in the Obsidian Palace, passed out in his bed after a night of too much drink and flirting with too many women.

A knock at his door made him groan. His naturally fast-healing body usually meant he didn't experience too many effects from overindulgence, but he had been even more depraved than normal last night.

"Come back later," he mumbled from his bed, hoping it was loud enough for whoever disturbed his sleep to hear.

"It's urgent, Your Highness. Your uncle wishes to see you now," came a voice from the other side.

"Tell that prim and pompous old ruler that whatever father I pissed off, I'll make amends later. Now let me sleep." Tal put a pillow over his head, and all was quiet for a moment before a cold wind blew through his room, and his door banged open.

"You can tell this prim and pompous old ruler yourself."

Tal took the pillow off his head and sat up slowly. His uncle stood by his bed, arms crossed as his long fingers dug into his pale skin. He was dressed simply in a black shirt with dark trousers. It must not be a day that his courtiers would come to call.

"Whatever happened, it wasn't on purpose. If I dallied with some daughter of one of your lords, she shouldn't have been in that tavern to begin with."

His uncle rolled his eyes. "If it were that sort of place, then perhaps you shouldn't have been there either, Prince Taliesin."

Tal chuckled. "Why? Who am I to act high and mighty? Just a throwaway son with no position and no importance."

"I could remind you that I've offered you numerous positions in my court, and so has your brother, but you've refused each one."

"None of them sounded like much fun," said Tal, rubbing his head as he stood and stretched.

His uncle grinned; his black eyes lit up in amusement. "I think your days of choice might be over, nephew, but the good news is you'll no longer have to worry about being idle. Your brother has called you home and says he has a task for you."

Tal walked over to his dresser, took out a shirt, and pulled it on. "My brother can find someone else for this errand. I have no plans to return to Brigant."

His uncle's grin widened. "I don't think you understand. He's not asking as your brother." The Dark King snapped his fingers, and a scroll appeared in his hands. "Your king has commanded you to attend his court and perform a task for him."

"Fuck," said Tal, already feeling that tug of obedience in his chest. "Why now? After all these years, he decides to assert his dominance?"

"Must be of some importance."

"Then override it, Uncle," said Tal. "Give me a command to stay here."

"You know it'll do no good. You were born in Brigant. You are from his court. King Idris is your ruler."

"What if I knelt before you this moment? Declared my loyalty to this court?"

His uncle laughed. "You think I would take you?" He cocked his head, a wicked smile on his lips. "You do have some talents that could be useful, but not useful enough for me to annoy your brother into war."

"Why? You'd win."

"Flattery won't help you. I might win, but at what cost? We have peace now. Do you wish me to undo all your mother did to get us to this point?"

Tal sighed. "You make it sound like she was tortured. I hear she liked certain aspects of her life with my father."

"And yet, in the end, it caused her a short life," said King Adair. The room grew darker, blocking out the morning sunlight that had been pouring through the window.

Tal turned away; his uncle's implied message was clear. He was the reason his mother was dead. His birth had been the one that had weakened her. His twin sister came easily and quickly. She labored another half a day before he was born.

"Take the scroll, and go see what your brother has to say," said his uncle, stepping closer, the scroll in his outstretched hand. Tal took it slowly. "Perhaps it will give you a bit of direction. You could use it, boy."

"Over a half-century old is hardly a boy, Your Majesty," said Tal as he opened his message.

"Not when you still act like a spoiled child."

Tal ignored him, reading over his brother's words.

Brother,

It has been too long. You are needed back home where you belong. There is a threat in the human lands that has made its way into our court. I need you to take care of it. You are to come at once and appear before me this afternoon. My guards will meet you by the High Stream on the north edge of the village. I have a task for you, and you will do it. I command it as your king."

King Idris of Brigant

Tal practically bent over under the strength of his brother's command, even from so far away. He growled quietly, hating being chained to another, especially his half-brother.

He gritted his teeth. "I wonder what would happen if I ignored him and ran away to the human lands."

"You know how that would go for you. If he's forced to send his guards to look for you, they will find you. He could send enough to do away with you on the spot, but as his blood and mine, he would at least give you the courtesy of a trial."

"And I could expect no support from you. I'm sure you're glad to have a reason to get rid of me."

The darkness grew. "I've allowed you to live here though you offer no benefit to this court. I've ignored your depravity, slinking it off as youthful indulgences, and cleaned up your messes time and time again, hoping you would grow into your role and responsibilities. Don't act like I haven't shown you more mercy and hospitality than most. It goes against my nature, and still, I've done it."

"For my mother, I suppose."

"For her and because you're of my blood. My patience is at an end. Go to your court, serve your king, and perhaps you will finally grow up." The darkness left, letting the sun shine in again. "I heard only good things when you came here three decades ago. You were known as a clever and good-natured youth. I worried there would be too much light in you for my court, but I never imagined you would become this."

Tal shrugged. "I suppose my darker nature won out."

"Your connection to this court has nothing to do with your ways. Don't place the blame for your immorality on us. Even with our well-earned reputation, we still have rules we keep and some decency. You have been determined to break them all."

Tal chuckled. "And now it seems I will see how many I can break of my brother's laws. There are more there, so maybe I'll have more fun than I thought." Tal moved toward his bathing chamber. "I should prepare."

"You know, nephew, you could go to your brother's kingdom and actually try. Instead of seeing how many women you can bed or how much of your brother's wine you can drink, maybe you could focus on finding that young man you left behind when you came here."

Tal stopped at the door. "I hardly remember him, Uncle, so he could not be worth knowing."

Chapter 2

Tal

T AL STALLED AS LONG as he could, taking an abnormally long time to bathe and dress. When it was time for him to go, his uncle did not see him off. As he stepped out into the center courtyard, he saw his aunt overseeing two gardeners as they worked on her impressive garden. She spared him only a glance before turning back to point at something that displeased her. Tal didn't waste any breath saying goodbye to her as he called upon the darkness to transport him to his home kingdom.

Stepping into the warm, bright sunshine was disorienting after spending so much time in the muted light of Lironia. He took a deep breath, taking in the floral, sweet scent that hovered around the Golden Court. Though there were probably a hundred different flowers that grew along the edge of the forest near his home village, he could always pick out the smell of honeysuckle that grew thick between the trees, some climbing up the trunks. He stopped and picked a nearby bloom, bringing it up to his nose, resisting the urge to taste its nectar.

He hadn't stepped foot in his court in almost two decades. The last time, he came to celebrate the High Summer festival but left as soon as the sun rose. It was one of the rare occasions he had behaved himself, even managing to resist the charms of Lord Elgan's alluring daughter. It was difficult, but he did not wish to tangle himself with the lord, knowing he could be as good as betrothed to the young woman if her father found out.

Deciding he had stalled long enough, he walked into the bustling village. It was well-kept and whimsical—the kind of place human children imagined when they thought of a fairyland. Even the smaller homes were fine, with light stone walls and thatched roofs. The manors that housed the rich lords were almost as large as some of the human palaces, with vast lawns, elaborate fountains, and statues amongst the impressive landscaping.

Placing his hands in his pocket and keeping his head down, Tal walked through the village center, trying to avoid the stares of the Fae and creatures who inhabited the court. He knew he stuck out. The Fae around him were tan with fair-colored hair and light golden eyes. He looked much more like his mother's court with his dark brown hair and dark eyes. Still as small as he tried to make himself, it did no good. He was too tall to hunch enough, too graceful to hide his step well. Even his shadows seemed darker than normal, gobbling up the sunlight as they followed him.

A few whispers started, followed by the giggles of some young women outside a dress shop. Soon, most were bowing or curtsying as he walked by, well aware that he was a prince of their court. He glanced to his left and right, noticing a few didn't bother to notice him beyond a look. He didn't care and actually nodded his head at a woodland sprite as she sat on the edge of a fountain, her long brown legs crossed as she smirked at him.

"Your Highness, Prince Taliesin."

Tal turned his head but didn't stop. He blew out a puff of air, seeing his brother's head guard hurrying towards him, four others in his wake. Tal thought to speed up but knew it would do no good. He kept his gait steady, letting the man catch up with him. "Hello, Dyfan."

The man looked much as Tal remembered, though his sandy blonde hair was a bit longer than the last time Tal had seen him. It grew just past his arched ears. Dyfan's eyes were golden like most Fae from the Golden Court. He was a half head taller than Tal and, though more filed out than Tal remembered, still rather slim.

"You weren't where your brother commanded," said Dyfan.

Tal shrugged. "He commanded I come and appear before him. I took his idea of where I should arrive as more of a suggestion."

"You shouldn't walk through the village without protection." The four guards moved around Tal, surrounding him as he walked.

"Why? Do you know of some plot against me?"

"No, but you are a member of the royal family, and we don't always know who's within our borders. They might try to take you to get to the king."

"Most know holding me captive would mean nothing to the king. He would let me rot before making any effort to save me."

"That's not true," said the guard. "King Idris holds royal blood in high regard. He would do his duty."

"You're truly his man now, aren't you?" asked Tal.

Dyfan half smiled. "I serve the crown as I pledged to your father I would. That hasn't changed, though the ruler did."

"And how do you like your king these days?"

"It is not for me to have an opinion."

"But you do."

Dyfan said nothing, but he cut his eyes to Tal, giving him a look the prince remembered even being gone for so long.

Tal moved closer to Dyfan, keeping his voice so low he knew the head guard would have to lean in to hear him. "Do you know what my brother wants?"

"Trouble in the human lands has spilled into the court, angering an important lord. The king can no longer ignore it, not when Lord Elgan threatens to pull his support of the court coffers."

"Can't the king just command the use of the lord's gold?"

"Not with the old agreements still in place. Lord Elgan is powerful and important for a reason. There are things he can do that the king can't stop."

"And what could be so important to Lord Elgan in the human lands that he would go against his king?" asked Tal.

"Lady Eriana."

"Ah," said Tal. Lady Eriana was the niece of Lord Elgan and was known to be much loved by him. Some say even more than his own daughter. She was the only thing he had left of his much-beloved sister. Tal had a hard time remembering much about Eriana except she was beautiful and utterly unpleasant—not surprising since she was half-human.

"So, the lady's found trouble, has she? Taken in by some human rubbish like her mother?"

"If only that were it," said Dyfan darkly.

"More interesting then?"

"You'll see. I doubt I have the full story, so I'll let you hear it from your brother." He stepped back from Tal, probably because they had come to the palace gates, and no matter how softly they spoke, there was no guarantee someone might not overhear them.

Tal looked up at the familiar, impressive structure he once called home. Even though he wished he could call upon some pleasant memories from his youth to make the day a little more bearable, none would come to him. He rubbed his chest as he walked through the gates, the familiar empty feeling that plagued him daily even more noticeable. Whatever task waited for him inside, he sensed it could be nothing but torturous.

Chapter 3

Aven Mathias, Crown Prince of Illedria

T HE SMALL POND DEEP in the forest was his favorite place in the world. It was quiet and isolated, somewhere most could not find if they didn't know where to look. Even the stream that fed it was insignificant, drying up in times of little rain. Most would not think to follow it, and he had lucked upon it one day while riding.

Only in the early mornings could he escape the palace without any guards following him. He was sure his father knew by now of his little trips as the sun rose, but since he was grown and no harm ever came to him, his father appeared happy to let him be. It was during one of his first trips almost ten years ago as an adventurous ten-year-old that he found the thin stream and felt almost beckoned to follow it to its end.

He thanked the goddesses every day he had answered the call that led him to this place, that led him to her. Indeed, as he pulled up his gray stallion to the pond's edge, he caught a glimpse of her light red hair in the bushes on the other side.

"Come out, Silvie, and see what I brought you," he said before jumping off his horse.

Silvie stood up and hurried towards him as he held out a book to her. She took it, her long, thin fingers wrapping around the spine. She smiled at him, and he returned it. She was a pretty woman, though nothing out of the ordinary. In fact, everything about her was almost forgettable. Her gray eyes, small pink mouth, and straight nose were completely unremarkable. Aven had no idea how old she was, though she was already a grown woman when he first met her. She had not changed at all. If what he thought she could be was true, it was not surprising she had not aged.

"This isn't new," she said in her striking voice as she flipped through the pages. "It's been well read."

He nodded. "It's a collection of fairy stories I found in the back of our library. I thought you'd like it."

She stopped at one page and read for a moment; her eyebrows knitted together in concentration before she let out a beautiful, melodious laugh. "This is quite amusing." She closed the book. "A gift worth a new lesson if you'd like one."

"Do you still have things to teach me?"

She laughed again, placing the book in the pocket of her simple dark gray dress. "If you only knew the depth of my knowledge! Now come here to the water's edge and show me what you can do."

He happily joined her near the water, close enough that he got the tips of his boots wet. This is why he loved this place and her. He could be who he was meant to be with no judgment. He could freely use his magic without feeling guilty over his mother's worry or his father's disappointment.

He took off his gloves and placed them in his pocket, the chill of the autumn day hitting his exposed skin as the wind blew. Holding out his hands, he moved them back and forth, and the water stirred, mimicking his movements. Silvie nodded, and he raised a hand. A stream of water arched into the air. He raised his other hand, and another stream formed, extending the first, making the water hit in two places on the surface.

"Good," said Silvie. "Now show me more. The wind is blowing today."

Aven put down his hands, and the water went still. He lifted his face and closed his eyes, concentrating. The wind whipped around him, causing the leaves on the ground to rise and circle. He opened his eyes and threw his hands out, and the leaves flew in all directions.

Silvie laughed as she raised her hand, shielding herself from the onslaught. "Very good. Now the rocks."

Aven sighed. After all these years, he still wasn't steady enough to move any rock bigger than a pebble.

"Go on, Aven. Have you not practiced?"

He had when he had the chance, but it had to be done secretly. It was easier to explain a gust of wind or ripple in a fountain than a rock levitating. He tried to do as she asked.

He took deep breaths and raised his hand, keeping it in a fist until it was high above his head. He opened his hand, and the rock near him shuddered, rising a few inches off the ground.

"Now throw it in the water," said Silvie.

Aven grunted, pushing his hand out. The rock moved a few inches and fell to the ground.

"Try again," said Silvie.

So he did. He tried again and again and again, and he could not get the rock to move more than a few feet away into the shallows of the pond.

Silvie tutted as Aven sat on the ground, wiping sweat from his forehead. She raised her hands, and three nearby rocks rose, rotating around each other. "You still can't get the hang of anything solid. You're great with water and wind, but something stronger, well, you just aren't there."

"What if I'm happy with only being able to control wind and water?" he asked. "I'm decent with fire, too."

"If that's all you want to do, then fine. Never go any further, and be even less than your so-called mages," she said in disgust. "Think they're true magic-users with a little wind, water, and fire. Can't even lift a rock as high as you and forget mind control or calling down rain and lightning."

"And you can do all that?"

"I've told you before I can," said Silvie.

"And yet, in all our times together, you've never shown me."

"I'll show you when you've proved you deserve to see it. I don't perform parlor tricks, Aven," said Silvie.

"Then how can I know you're telling the truth?"

"You doubt me after all these years. Have I ever told you a lie?" asked Silvie.

"Not that I know of," said Aven as he played with some dead grass.

"Then trust me now," said Silvie as he raised his eyebrows. She shook her head. "Fine. I'll show you."

She stared at him and tilted her head. He couldn't help but meet her gaze, unable to look away. "Aven, you can move that rock with the gift you have been given. Now do it."

He opened his mouth to argue but found he had nothing to say. Instead, he stood up, keeping his eyes locked with hers, swearing they went from placid gray to deep blue for a few seconds. Without a thought, he raised his hand and lifted a rock to his waist.

"Now throw it," said Silvie, her voice all command.

He threw his hand out, and the rock flew into the air, falling into the middle of the pond. Silvie walked closer to him, her eyes locked with his. His head was quiet, every part of him locked onto Silvie, ready to do her will.

"Do not test me, Aven. I've come to care about you and have no wish to hurt you, but you should know the depth of my power. The things I could do with it would shock and scare you. Don't ask me to show you something you aren't ready to see." She looked away, and Aven bent over, his hands going to his knees as he took deep breaths.

He felt Silvie's hand on his back. "Are you alright?"

"Yes," he said, sounding breathless. "I just need a minute."

She pulled a small vial out of her pocket. "Here, drink this, and it'll fix you up."

He took it and saw it contained a liquid that almost looked like the golden wine served at the palace. "What is it?"

"Something to calm you and help you regain your strength. It won't hurt you." She pulled another vial out of her pocket, which was filled with the same color liquid. She took it in one drink. "See."

He nodded as he pulled the cork off the top and drained it. It was sweet and warm. Within a few seconds, his breathing became even, and he felt stronger.

"Better?" asked Silvie.

"Much."

"Sit with me by the water," said Silvie as she gracefully gathered her skirt and sat on the pond's edge. Aven sat beside her, and Silvie took his hand. "Moving something solid is not easy for someone who isn't grounded and sure of oneself. Tell me what's troubling you." She linked her fingers with his and stared over the water.

He was quiet for a moment, enjoying being there with his friend, listening to her gentle breaths, the lapping of the water, and the trickle of the nearby stream. "My father doesn't like me to use magic. My mother is terrified of it."

"Magic isn't cherished like it once was. Many in your line had the gift and used it to their advantage. Over the years, it has become treated with mistrust and as something to be used only sparingly by common folk."

"Do you know why? I've tried to find out, but there's nothing in our library."

"It was so long ago that history is lost in these lands. Perhaps the oldest of the Fae might know, but they have little interest in human affairs. They might've dismissed it and let it slip their minds. I'm sure it has something to do with the enslavement of humans five centuries ago."

"My father said it would be easier in time to bury my gift. Maybe he's right, but I don't want to keep it inside. It feels wrong."

Silvie leaned against him. "Your magic is very strong. I can feel it swirling inside of you. If you would ever completely trust in it and be who the gods made you, you would be beyond powerful."

"You sound so sure."

"I am." She turned and looked at him. "Is there anything else?"

He nodded. "Father says I should marry soon."

"Nothing surprising there. You're a grown man. Still very young for your kind, but if he wishes you to marry outside your kingdom, you can't wait too long. The other humans will be leery of uniting their young daughters with you if your age is too old, despite your long life."

"I know, and he has even said I can have time to choose, but it's just another step to becoming king one day. I know my father will likely live another fifty or sixty years, maybe a century, but..."

"Starting a family means you'll have more responsibility, something I'm sure your father reminded you. He probably wants you to take more interest in court business as well?"

Aven nodded. "He says there's a growing suspicion amongst the kingdoms of our lands. You must know of the rumored unrest, and so many kingdoms have never truly trusted us due to our mages and healers."

"They don't understand magic, so they're afraid of it." She squeezed his hand. "If war ever comes, you'll have to fight."

"I know, just like my father, so I need to have an heir soon. Of course, Kyra already has a son, but Darron wants him to be his heir over Moonhaven."

"Surely he would rather have a son as king than a lord," said Silvie. "Not that I want it to happen."

"He's a proud man," said Aven.

"It won't matter. You will be king, Aven. If I have to take down half an army myself, I will see to it."

He laughed. "I won't doubt you can do it, not if you say you can."

"I'm glad to see you aren't too old to continue learning." She let go of his hand and pulled her knees to her chest. "You need to leave soon. You can't miss breakfast with your father."

"Will I see you tomorrow if I make my way out here?"

Silvie shook her head. "I have some things to do. I'll be gone a couple of weeks at least."

"Where will you go?"

"Oh, here and there. You know I'm practically a bird, flying where the wind takes me, making little nests only for a time."

He smiled. "Surely you had a home once?"

She looked up at the sky and shrugged. "Maybe, but not now. I once had hope that I would find it again, but it fades with each year."

He hesitated and then said, "You could come back with me."

She looked at him sharply. "And do what? Do you think your father would let me live in one of his empty rooms? Or do you think I should be a servant in the palace?"

"You could go to the healers," said Aven. "I'm sure they would be happy to have your gifts and welcome you. I could visit you often."

She shook her head. "You think I would be happy as a healer?"

"It's a noble profession."

"Perhaps, but it's also a prison, a way to control those women and their powers, passing it off as the will of the goddesses, doing their work. The healers have been made to limit their powers to fit what others think they should be. I could never sit there and be made to stifle who I am, no matter how noble the profession."

"I was only saying I wish you to be safe and settled. I worry about you."

"Trust me, Aven, I'm the last person you should worry about. I'm more than capable of taking care of myself." She shook her head. "But I appreciate your concern. I didn't mean to snap."

Aven stood up and dusted off his pants before offering a hand to Silvie. "I have some sweet bread in my saddle bag. Would you like some before I go?"

Her face lit up as she stood. "Yes, please."

They stood by his horse and ate sweet bread together, Aven entertaining Silvie by describing the latest tournament where a young lord fell off his horse before he could even draw his sword.

"So, a few weeks?" asked Aven as he dusted off his hands.

"Maybe two, probably closer to three," said Silvie. "You should still come here to practice while I'm gone."

Aven smiled. "I will. I'll come here every day I can in hopes you come back early."

"I don't think I'll be able to cut my trip short, but I do promise I'll return."

"And you never lie to me, so I know it's true."

She smiled. "I'll have another thing for you to learn the next time I see you."

Chapter 4

Tal

THE GOLDEN COURT WAS just how he remembered it, except it seemed even more crowded. The area outside the throne room was bustling with well-dressed and beautiful light-haired Fae mulling around, drinking, talking, and laughing.

"Well, well, it seems the rumors were true," said a smooth voice to his left.

Tal glanced and held back the annoyed growl in his throat as he paused. "What rumors, Theo? I gather there are plenty around this place."

A man almost the same height as Tal with broad shoulders and long golden-brown hair tied back into a braid strode toward him. Almost everything about the man looked Fae, from his unnatural good looks to his pointed ears. His eyes were as golden as the lord of the Golden Court that had sired him, but Tal knew he wasn't full Fae. Theo didn't like to admit it. His father had found a young daughter of an Illedrian lord to woo and, once done with her, had left her with child. She died in childbirth, and since the golden lord's wife had given him no children, he took the son as his own to raise.

"That you would grace this court with your presence once again. I've heard it said periodically over the years, so I suppose at least once it had to be true," said Theo. He gave a half bow. "Are you glad to be home, Your Highness?"

"Would I have avoided it for so long if I was?"

Theo chuckled. "Yet you're here now."

Tal shrugged. "Can't ignore an order from our king. Can only hope that whatever it is he would have me do can be accomplished quickly."

Theo only hummed in response as he adjusted his open collar.

Tal started to move on when Theo said, "Your brother's task for you could be more than you bargained for. Might have been better to take your chances in the human realm."

"You know what my brother would have me do?"

"My father is close to the king. He hears things," said Theo. He looked over Tal's shoulder and waved. As he moved past Tal, he stopped and leaned in close to whisper. "If you do manage to find the lady, tell her I look forward to spending more time with her."

Tal narrowed his eyes, but before he could say anything, Theo walked away. Theo's words had sounded like a taunt, but why would he care if Theo had any interest in Lord Elgan's niece? Tal watched him go for a moment before heading to the door of the throne room, where he was met by another familiar person who put his encounter with Theo almost completely out of his mind.

She was a striking woman. Her golden, thick hair was pushed behind her arched ears and fell in neat waves over her shoulders. Her eyes were startlingly green, framed by dark lashes. She was dressed in a golden gown that seemed a little indecent for day wear even to Tal, but he couldn't help but admire her curves and generous cleavage.

"Welcome, Your Highness. It's been too many years." The woman curtsied low, giving Tal a good look down her dress.

"I see you're doing well, Lady Delphina." She rose and offered Tal her hand. He gave her a grin before taking it and giving it a soft kiss. "You look as lovely as always."

"Hmmm. I'd rather hope I had grown in beauty while you were gone, but I'll settle for not losing any."

"Perhaps you were already perfection, my lady."

She laughed in the restrained, pretty way high ladies were taught as she reached out and touched Tal's arm. "I'm glad you're here. Perhaps your presence will help calm my father. Let me take you to the king."

"Yes, I suppose we should go and get this over with. Whatever his order may be for me, I'm sure I'll have some time for myself. You might be able to show me a few places where I can find some amusement. I've been gone too long to remember."

"We're all to dine here tonight, but any time you're available, I would not be opposed to being in charge of your enjoyment, my prince." She cocked an eyebrow. "I've been told I'm quite good at keeping men well-occupied."

He grinned wickedly at her boldness, offering her his arm. "Take me to our king, my lady."

She took his arm, and the door was opened for them. Tal took the familiar trail through the room, following the gilded aisle toward the dais. He felt strange and out of sorts as he walked. He knew he had been in this room many times. Much of it was the same as when his father ruled, but there was something off. Were the stained-glass windows not as vibrant? Did the throne shrink in size? Had someone not washed the floors in a while?

He supposed he had seen the place before with youthful energy and fantasy. The place felt grander when he was younger. Once, it was a warm, magical place where he ran free with his sister and friends or sat by his father as those of their court came to call. Today, it felt cold despite the warmth in the air. Though the room was grand, it seemed almost dingy. Any air of hospitality it once had was gone, making Tal's stomach flop as he wished he was practically anywhere else.

As Tal approached the dais, his gaze landed on his brother. He had truly made the transition from Golden Prince to Sun King, though he looked nothing like the previous ruler. From what Tal could remember, his father had been a tall man, and Idris was a head shorter than Tal. Where Tal's father's eyes had been golden and warm, Idri's were deeper, almost brown, and appeared cold. In fact, everything about Idris, from his slender nose and full mouth, must have come from his mother, as Tal had a hard time finding one trait that reminded him of the previous Sun King.

Idris wore a white shirt and tan pants. The shirt was fitted and left open at the top to show off his strong, tanned chest, with a tattoo of a large sun spanning its width. Tal had a similar one on his back, and he felt a strange tingling sensation near it, which must have been in his mind playing tricks. Around the shoulders of Tal's brother was a golden robe trimmed in short white fur, and on his head was the Sun King's golden crown, catching the light from the overhead window just like it was designed to do.

Once he saw his brother looking just as Tal thought he would, he immediately looked to the king's left to see his sister. She was one of the only things he missed about this place. She gave him a small smile when she saw him looking at her. He felt guilty seeing her appear so welcoming. He should have written to her more and convinced her to come to see him in the Obsidian Place of Isel, but instead, he had only contacted her from time to time, letting himself be distracted to chase away the guilt.

Of course, she would welcome him. She had always been so good, inheriting their father's good nature and their mother's grace. She appeared to be in such a contrast to their kind, with her hospitable, open manners, but she was still shrewd and intelligent. She might first wish for peace and warmth but could turn cold and harsh if needed.

Tal reached the bottom of the dais. Lady Delphina let go of his arm and curtsied before leaving his side to stand by her father. Lord Elgan didn't even register his daughter's presence, keeping his deep green eyes on Tal and his arms folded against his chest.

Tal turned his attention to the king.

"Brother, how good of you to come today. It's been too long since you've been home," said King Idris.

"I've had things to do for my uncle, keeping our connection with the Dark Court."

"I wasn't aware you were an emissary," said Idris. "Or that any negotiations were needed to keep King Adair to his promises. Do you have something to tell me from the Dark King?"

"Only his good greetings," said Tal.

"I've offered you much better positions than emissary. While I'm sure you could serve well in the role, you have other talents to use for your court, and I ask you to do it now."

"Ask me? I was under the impression this was a command."

"Is it so wrong for your brother to miss you and use whatever he can to get you to visit?" said Idris with a wide grin. "The princess has missed you as well." He looked towards Tal's sweet sister. She nodded, her dark blonde curls bouncing against her shoulders as her light brown eyes shone from the sunlight coming through the windows. Dressed in her golden gown and wearing her golden leaf tiara, she looked like she fit perfectly in Brigant, not the creature of two courts that she was.

"It is good to see you, Prince Taliesin," she said. "I hope you will choose to stay here when your work is done."

"It's good to see you looking so well, Adalyn, and I suppose whether I stay depends on what the king will have me do." Tal looked back at his brother.

Idris stood, adjusting his robe. "Lord Elgan, come forward." The lord put down his arms and slowly walked to the foot of the dais. "Taliesin, I take it you remember Lord Elgan. He is much respected here, the highest lord in our court."

Tal looked at the lord, who stared coldly back at him. "Of course, I remember Lord Elgan. I appreciate you sending your lovely daughter to escort me into the room."

"I sent no one. Lady Delphina does what she wishes," said Lord Elgan with almost a hiss.

The king chuckled. "It seems all the women in your family share that trait." Lord Elgan glared at his king with such deadly hatred that it made Tal want to take a step back, but Idris ignored it. "Now, Lord Elgan's niece has gone missing in the human lands."

"She is part human," said Tal. "Perhaps she found her father's family and wishes to stay with them."

"Lady Eriana would never leave permanently without telling me," said Lord Elgan.

"Is she a lady?" asked Tal. "I thought her heritage wasn't settled."

"She's the daughter of my sister, who was a lady, and my sister told me Eriana was born legitimate in the human lands, so here she is a lady," said the lord.

"Then you know her father's name?" asked the king. "If so, this might make our task easier."

"Her father's name remains a secret, but I trusted my sister's word; therefore, I proclaim my niece as a lady. I would have her referred to as such."

The king waved his hand. "I'm sure the prince didn't mean to disrespect you or the lady. There's the worry that Lady Eriana has found trouble in human lands."

"And this trouble is?" asked Tal.

"Have you heard of the Court of the Underlings?" asked Idris.

"Court of the Underlings? Of course not. No such thing exists."

"But it does," said Lord Elgan. "They started as just a nuisance to the human lands, roaming from kingdom to kingdom to spread discord. This past year and a half, they have made a name for themselves, striking even human kings' properties."

"What is their purpose?" asked Tal.

"Who knows how human minds work?" said Idris. "They seem to love discord, so causing havoc is probably their only aim. They are quite good at it. Until lately, I've been happy to let them do it. Human problems are for humans to fix."

"We've helped before," said Tal. "Father sent out medicine and healers during the great plague."

"And what good will did that earn us?" asked Idris. "Many still died unnecessarily because some human kings mistrusted our medicines and threatened our healers who came in peace. No good comes of us meddling in human affairs."

"Yet, you will concern yourself with this Court of the Underlings?"

"For my loyal lord and friend, I will," said Idris, turning to Lord Elgan.

"My Eriana is a curious creature. She's always been interested in her human heritage, but I kept her here without problems until recently. Seeing as she was grown, I couldn't deny her some freedom, and she took advantage of it, often visiting the human realm. She always sent me messages about what she was doing, and she returned after a few weeks. Yet, this time, she's been gone for months, and I've received no messages until recently."

"Show the prince what came for you," said the king.

Lord Elgan pulled a scroll out of his pocket and handed it to Tal. Tal undid the small ribbon holding it together and opened it. On the scroll was only a symbol—a crow sitting on a branch with a red dahlia in its beak.

"That's the symbol for the Court of the Underlings. It's on the banners they carry and the shields they use in battle," said Lord Elgan.

"So, you think this means they have your niece?"

"Naturally," said Lord Elgan. "What other conclusion can there be? Eriana is missing in the human lands, and I receive this symbol."

"But there's been no call for ransom? No threats?" asked Tal.

"This is a threat," said Lord Elgan. "They've sent things like this to human lords and kings before and after they attack."

"I imagine they're hoping Lord Elgan will send his men to try to retrieve them, but I've asked him not to. Any Fae or faerie warriors from this court on human lands could lead to larger conflicts. I have no wish to start a war over one woman."

Lord Elgan stepped forward as though he would object, but the king held up his hand. "Still, this cannot be ignored. We need to find Lady Eriana, and if these renegades have taken her, she must be retrieved." The king walked forward toward his waiting guards. "Dyfan has volunteered to go with three of his guards, but as gifted as they are, I fear they will not be enough. Also, Dyfan has little knowledge of the human lands."

Tal blew out a puff of air, crossing his arms. "So, this is what you want me to do? Lead four of your royal guards out into the human lands to find a wayward woman?"

"Lord Elgan is important to this court, and Lady Eriana is an impressive woman," said King Idris. He cleared his throat. "One I have wished to court for some time."

Lord Elgan's head whipped towards the king, surprise and anger in his eyes.

"You wish to take a half-human woman as your wife?" asked Tal, stunned.

Idris smiled. "She may be half-human, but she is more Fae than many of those who reside in our borders. Her magic is strong. Lady Eriana's talents are numerous."

"She's also beautiful," said Tal's sister as she joined them. "Idris has always been one for collecting pretty things."

"Indeed, Sister," said Idris. "I cannot deny her attraction has numerous facets."

"You say you've wished to court her for some time? Has she been opposed to the idea?" asked Tal.

"Yes, Your Majesty. Have you spoken to my niece about your wishes? If so, I'm disappointed you haven't come to me asking for permission."

"I am your king, Lord Elgan. I don't need your permission even if she is of your house and under your protection."

"It's common courtesy."

Idris smiled at Lord Elgan. "I let her know my interest. She was flattered but did not want a husband anytime soon, as she liked her freedom. I told her I could change her mind. When she returned from her jaunt into the human lands, I planned to show her the benefit of becoming my queen. I'm in no hurry and happy to oblige her wishes for a time."

"But you don't wish to fight for her," said Adalyn.

"As I said, I was not ready to go to war for one woman. Her loss would be great, but I must look at the bigger picture. After thinking over the matter for a while, I decided I couldn't let her go and came up with a course of action."

"Scared of losing Lord Elgan's support and wealth," muttered Adalyn, loud enough for Tal to hear. If his brother did, he gave no reaction.

"So, you will go to the human lands, Prince Taliesin. You will seek out this Court of Underlings and retrieve Lady Eriana."

"You're commanding me?" asked Tal.

"I would rather you go willingly to serve your king and court, but if you will not, then yes."

Tal closed his eyes, the weight of his brother's command bearing down on him. "Fine. I'll go to the human lands and see what I can find out about these Underlings. Once I see the situation, I will gauge if retrieving the lady can be done."

"Oh, with your talents, it should be no trouble at all once you learn where she is," said the king.

"There are limits to my skills," said Tal. "As confident as I am in them, they are not without vulnerabilities."

"Not in the human world," said the king. "They will have no way to stop you. So tomorrow, you will go into the human lands. You can take whatever weapons you need."

"Yes, Your Majesty," said Tal, giving a mock bow. "And after I finish this task for you, you will let me be. No more commands."

"I'm your king. I will do as I see fit to serve my court and people." He studied Tal, his eyes roving up and down. "But if you're successful, I'm sure we could work something out to both of our satisfaction."

It was probably as good of a promise as Tal was going to get, so he nodded.

"Prince Taliesin, it has been some time since you've seen my niece. You might wish for a reminder of her appearance," said Lord Elgan. "I have a portrait of her in my home if you want to see it. I'm sure my daughter will be happy to host you and serve you some refreshments."

"Of course, Lord Elgan," said Tal. "We can go this instant if the king will release me."

"Go, but make sure you're back for supper. You will stay on the palace grounds tonight. You will need a good night's sleep, and I have no wish to hear of you causing a ruckus in my village."

"As you wish, Your Majesty." Tal gave another half bow and walked to Lady Delphina. "Will you escort me to your home, my lady? I look forward to your hospitality."

"Come back soon, Brother. I wish to have a chat with you before supper," said Tal's sister. He nodded toward her before escorting Lady Delphina from the room.

Chapter 5

Aven

AVEN KNEW IT WAS foolish to lament any part of his life. He had been born a prince of Illedria in a time of peace. His father was a good king, and his mother was a gentle woman who caused little problems. He felt as loved and cherished by his parents as could be expected. His mother often stated her love for him, kissing his cheek and squeezing his hand, but her nerves were not conditioned for motherhood. Until he was well into his adolescence, his mother did nothing more than see him twice a day and say what a healthy, handsome boy he was. Now, she was happy to sit in his presence and smile at him, but they had little real conversation.

His father had always been more involved in his life, teaching him about responsibility from an early age. His father was kind and never cruel, but he was not a jovial man. An air of melancholy and weariness hung around him at all times. Sometimes at night, Aven would find his father in his study, staring at the fire as he held a gold chain with a small locket. As a young man, he once asked where the locket came from, but his father gave a noncommittal answer, saying it was just a trinket from his youth he liked to fiddle with.

Aven had the normal duties of a prince—training to fight daily, reading reports on the kingdom, and sitting with his father in the throne room once a month to hear the concerns of the lords. It was, in truth, a good life. One many would trade with him in an instant, but Aven felt like satisfaction and happiness were out of his reach.

He felt guilty over it and tried to convince himself he was just being selfish, but no matter how hard he tried, he could not shake the feeling that he was incomplete. He was sure it had to do with the oppression of his magic. He had been born with it, which was no surprise. Several in his line had the gift, but like others before him, including his father, he was told to ignore it to make it go away. Those in the royal family could not use magic, not if they wished to gain the other kingdoms' trust and cooperation.

Aven had tried to keep it within him once he fully understood. As a very young child, he was excused for the magic that sometimes slipped out of him, making a room shake when he was angry or his bathwater wave. As he grew, he was punished when he slipped up and performed magic, whether to impress his friends or out of boredom. By his tenth year, he actively tried to keep it inside, no matter how much it wanted out.

It wasn't until he found the small pond and Silvie that he truly worked on his magic. He made his peace with it in that he did it in secret and that his lessons with Silvie helped him control his magic in public. Indeed, all these years later, no one knew of his abilities or his secret friend. When he could not meet with her, he still found time to work with his magic. Sometimes in his room late at night or in an empty space of the tallest tower. Most days, he would ride down early to the pond, even if Silvie wasn't there, to play with the water, sticks, leaves, and stones.

Today, there was no time for lessons or even a short ride. He had gotten up early to prepare for a long day of sitting on a hard chair by his father's throne as lord after lord came to the king with requests and news. Aven left his room as soon as his servants had dressed him and placed his crown on his head. He met his mother by the stairs, who smiled at him as she came close.

"Oh, my dear, Aven. How handsome you are this morning." She reached up and touched his hair. "Your hair is so dark, like your father's. Of course, your dear sister got my wretched hair, so dull and flat, but yours is so thick and wavy."

"Your hair is lovely, Mother, just like you."

"Hardly. I must look so old to you and your father. Only my father came from this kingdom. I do not hold my youth well."

His mother did look a bit older than his father though she was more than two decades younger, but she was still beautiful. Some said it and her complacency were her only good attributes. Aven would argue that kindness and gentleness were not traits to dismiss easily. Yes, his poor mother was a little simple, but she only wished good to everyone she met.

"You know you're still the most beautiful woman in this kingdom, Mother."

She laughed. "Don't let your sister hear you say it, or Lady Fischer. She thinks her daughter is quite the beauty. I suppose the dear is a pretty thing. Some say she is shrewd, but I never saw it. She knitted me the prettiest shawl, and she plays the harp like an angel. Lady Fischer mentioned she would be a good wife for you, but I'm not sure. You might like one a little taller."

"Perhaps," said Aven, half listening.

"And then there is the matter with Lady Beckons. Her son has run off somewhere, and she is beside herself with worry. I told her, dear, he is a young man and a second son. He probably went out to find a wife with a fortune, and all will be well, but she wouldn't listen, going on about the mages for some reason."

"Hmmm," said Aven as they walked down the stairs, letting his mother prattle on.

"Speaking of the mages, I'm afraid we will have fewer healers this year. Lord Farley told your father that, for some reason, many girls who were training are no longer available. I didn't hear why. Sad, though, I'd hate for us to have a bad winter with not enough healers."

"I'm sure there are plenty, Mother," said Aven reassuringly. "Will you join us in the throne room today?"

"Join you in the throne room? Whatever for? I have a tea scheduled after lunch and must prepare for it."

"Have a pleasant day, Mother," said Aven as they got to the bottom of the stairs.

"You as well, my darling," said his mother, taking his hand and giving it a squeeze.

Aven watched her walk away before heading to the throne room. He entered and found his father speaking with two of his advisors by the dais.

"Send word to King Marten that his invitation is appreciated, but the prince has no plans to travel at this time, even to Dewra. If he and his daughter would like to come here, they will be welcomed," said King Gavan.

"Very good, Your Majesty," said Marcus, the king's head advisor. He turned to Aven. "Good morning, Prince Aven. I hope today treats you well."

"Thank you, Marcus. I guess we'll see how discontent our subjects are."

Marcus chuckled as Aven's father shook his head. "The lords who come to speak with us are not discontent, Aven. They only want to be heard."

"It was only a joke, Father, nothing more."

"Court business is not something to jest, Prince Aven. What we hear today affects not just our kingdom but the whole land."

"I understand, Father." Aven smirked. "Though sometimes it's hard to see how Lord Lane complaining about Lord Farley's sheep eating his wife's prize roses as something that affects the entire land. You remember when Lord Farley came in complaining about being pushed in a bucket and having to have his servant cut him out of it? If the fate of our land comes down to the size of Lord Farley's ass, I'd be surprised."

There was a ghost of a smile on his father's face before it disappeared as he cleared his throat and adjusted the robe he wore. "Still, we must remember our subjects trust us to listen and rule fairly. Sometimes it might be tedious, but if our attention slips, we could miss out on something important."

Aven nodded. "Of course, Father."

They took their places on the dais, his father on the large gilded throne, a dragon etched on the high back. Aven sat in the smaller wooden chair beside him, trying to adjust himself into a halfway comfortable position, knowing it would be a long day.

The lords lined up at the appropriate time and were let into the throne room, taking their places on each side, awaiting their turn. The requests made and news told were tedious: commonplace land squabbles, announcements of births, marriages, and deaths, and not even a report of a behind being too sizable for a bucket to break up the monotony.

It wasn't until well past the midday meal, which Aven barely had a chance to partake, that a lord finally said something that made Aven sit up and listen.

A lord whose name Aven couldn't remember came before the dais, a torn dark banner in his hand. He threw it at the foot of the throne. Aven bent down to look at it as his father did the same. On the banner was a crow, a red dahlia in its beak.

"What's this?" asked Prince Aven.

"The symbol of the Court of the Underlings, Your Highness," said the lord.

"You've had dealings with them, Lord Melvins?" said King Gavan.

"They took two daughters from my servant quarters, Your Majesty," said Lord Melvins. "Both of them, not even twelve."

"Took them, my lord?" asked Prince Aven. "Took them where?"

"I don't know, Your Highness. No one knows why the Underling King does these things."

"Underling King?" said Prince Aven, looking at his father.

"Have you not been reading all your reports, Prince Aven?" His father asked him harshly. "The Court of the Underlings has been causing more and more havoc in the kingdoms surrounding us, though this is the first time they've struck our realm."

Prince Aven scratched his wrist. "It must have slipped by me when I was reading, Your Majesty. I have much correspondence to get through each day."

"A good ruler is careful, Aven. Remember it, and take time to read over your reports before you move on to other activities." He turned to the lord. "Was anyone hurt in this attack?"

"It was hardly an attack, sir. The girls were stolen away in the middle of the night," said Lord Melvins. "Came and left so silently that no one knew until the sun rose. The girls' beds were empty, and this banner was left on one of them."

"Why these girls?" asked Prince Aven. "Why take two servants?"

"The only thing they had in common is they were both marked by the healers as potential novices. They were to be tested later this year."

"And who knew this?" asked the prince.

"Me, my head of staff, and their parents." The lord adjusted his sleeves. "Who knows who else? It's a fine thing for a low-born daughter to be marked by the healers. The parents probably told everyone with ears."

"What course of action would you like me to take, my lord?" asked the king.

"I do not ask anything of you, Your Majesty. I know the girls are not worth the trouble of you or your forces. While the parents are distraught, they know better than to think you would send out anyone to retrieve them. I only came to alert you of the Underlings' doings in our court."

"What have you done, Lord Melvins?" asked Aven.

"What do you mean, Your Highness?" asked the lord.

"These are your servants. Those girls were under your protection, and now they are taken. Have you sent out men to look for them?"

"For two young servant girls?" asked the lord disbelievingly.

"Are their parents not loyal to you? Good workers?" asked Aven.

The lord shrugged. "The mothers work in my kitchens and the fathers in my stables. I know of no harm in them, but they are not irreplaceable. The girls were to leave me soon, anyway."

"So, their only worth is what they can do for you?"

"They are servants, Your Highness," said Lord Melvins as though that explained it.

"Thank you for your information, Lord Melvins," said the king loudly. "I appreciate the warning. I will see a sum sent to you and the girl's parents for their losses."

"It's not your fault, Your Majesty."

"Still, they were stolen from our borders. I will make amends." The lord bowed as the king turned to Aven. "You shall see what can be done about it, Prince Aven. You seem interested in this cause, and it will be something important you can do."

"You wish me to find the Court of the Underlings?" asked Aven. "I thought you wanted me to stay in Illedria."

"And for a time, I do, but you can ride out in our kingdom and see what you can find. We have spies and guards; send them out under your direction. Get as much information as possible about this Court of Underlings, and then present me with a course of action."

Aven studied his father. "This is your command?"

"Yes, as your king, and my wish as your father. You need direction and purpose. This could give it to you."

Aven held in his sigh, thinking of the endless hours of writing messages, riding out to small estates to seek out information that could not be found. It would be days away from his home, from his pond and Silvie. Practicing magic would have to be put aside.

"My king, I shall do as you wish and find all I can about this Court of the Underlings. My advice on how to proceed will be in front of you within two moon cycles."

Chapter 6

Tal

THE WALK TO LORD Elgan's manor was not far, as it was the closest building to the palace, practically on the grounds, so Tal was happy to walk with Lady Delphina. Lord Elgan did not follow, and Tal assumed he found another way to his home.

"I can't lament you coming home, Your Highness, but I do apologize for my cousin's trouble. I know it's an inconvenience," said Lady Delphina.

"My brother would've found some other pretense to practice his command over me at some point. I'm surprised he let me go on as I have for so long."

"You doubt your brother's intentions as king?"

"I think that would be too close to treason." Tal laughed. "You could be a spy for him."

She smiled. "Would it be too much to ask for a little trust? We've known each other for decades now."

He cut his eyes toward her. He supposed what she said was true, but he felt he didn't know the woman on his arm. His youth seemed long ago and was full of such foggy memories he could hardly string them together.

"It's been many years, my lady. Time changes us. I feel I hardly know you now."

She looked away. "Then I hope we have plenty of opportunities to remedy that."

"Hmmm."

"Is something wrong?"

"Of course not, Lady Delphina. You're being very proper, speaking as a lady of your station should speak to a prince."

"You don't sound like you're pleased."

"If your goal is for us to get to know each other, then these pretty manners will not do. There are several who reside close to my uncle's palace, which I have known for years, but I couldn't tell you much about them besides how much they smile when they say, 'Good morning' and if they look good in blue or green.

"But those I meet in a tavern or inn, even if it is just for an evening, I know them better than you can imagine. There are no manners or rules to stop the conversation."

"And plenty of spirits to keep it flowing," said Lady Delphina with a laugh. "So, you think I'm not capable of anything but pretty conversation?"

"Oh, I dare say you are good at dancing, maybe even singing, and perhaps playing an instrument. You can keep a good table and look beautiful and effortless doing it all."

"You make it all sound like an insult. Let me say you're being unfair. I've met many women who are just as you describe and intelligent and witty as well. They keep their homes and hobbies because they enjoy them, not putting on an act." She took her arm out of his. "You're wrong to dismiss them and act as though you are better because you refuse to play by the rules."

"I don't think less of anyone, only that they are not to my taste." He stopped as they came to the gates of her estate. "I know what I am, my lady. I don't pretend my way is proper or even the best one, only the one I prefer."

"And why do you think that is? Why ignore your duties and your court? Do you think I always enjoy decorum and batting my eyes at unworthy men to get information from them for my court and king?"

"So, you do play spy?"

"Spy?" She tilted her head as though considering. "I don't know if I would go so far as to call it that. I simply entertain those from our court and visitors from others. If I hear something useful to my king, I let him know."

"And my brother listens to you?"

"I hardly know. It's my responsibility to give information to him, and it's up to his discretion what he does with it."

"Even more reason for me to be careful around you. There are some words I wouldn't wish to get to the king's ears."

"It's still my choice what I tell the king." She touched the gate, and it opened. "There's some information I've received that I've kept to myself for my own uses."

Tal walked with her towards the house. "Still doesn't make me want to loosen my tongue around you. Perhaps it's more dangerous for you to keep my words to use later than to relate them to the king."

She laughed again. "Perhaps."

They came to the front portico of the handsome manor. The white stone and red roof looked new, as though it had been built within a month, but Tal knew it to be an ancient house. It was said that Lord Elgan's family had been there at the beginning when that Light God and the Dark Goddess joined and released their magic on the land, creating those to serve them.

"Welcome to Brightwood House, my prince. Perhaps you remember it?"

"A bit," said Tal, staring at the dark wood door. He did know the place and felt as though he had been there before, but there must not have been many meaningful memories for him between the walls, as he could recall none but one. "There was a supper here once, not long before I left. Your father invited me." He looked around the front. "I stood out here before going home for a long while. I didn't want to leave."

"Perhaps your father was angry with you," said Lady Delphina.

"Perhaps," said Tal, moving to touch one of the thick columns that held up the portico over the door. "Perhaps not."

"We should enter," said Lady Delphina. She opened the door to be met with an out-of-breath older servant.

"My lady, I'm sorry. Your father just told me you would be arriving with our prince. I tried to make it in time."

She pulled at her skirt. "Don't trouble yourself, Furrow. Our prince isn't one for proper decorum." She turned to Tal. "Come in, Your Highness."

He followed her into the grand entry hall, bright and cherry with a skylight overhead. Two staircases spiraled down, leading to the second floor. Portraits were hung, covering most of the wall, showing lords and ladies of the past.

"My father will be in the front parlor. It's where he keeps her portrait," said Delphina, her skirts swishing as she headed down the hall.

Tal followed her into a handsome room full of comfortable, cheery furniture. A low fire burned, giving even more warmth to the room. Lord Elgan stood before it, tending to it with a poker. All elegance and grace with one hand on the poker and the other propped on the mantle.

He turned when he heard them come in. "Welcome, Your Highness. It's been a few years since you honored these halls."

"I believe it has, though I'm having a bit of trouble remembering the last time. It was a supper, wasn't it?"

"I suppose it was," said Lord Elgan. "Can I offer you anything before we get down to it? Perhaps Delphina can arrange some tea and cakes." He looked at his daughter as he put the poker down.

"Of course, Father." She curtsied before saying, "Let me see to my duties, Your Highness, and I hope you won't think me simple for it."

She walked out of the room as Lord Elgan gave Tal a questioning look. "Delphina can be very expressive, Your Highness. I'm sure she meant no slight."

"I think it's I who slighted her, my lord, though it wasn't intentional."

"I'm sure it wasn't. Now come here, to the side wall, and you'll find what you're looking for." He moved over between the two tall windows in the room, both with their curtains open, letting in the sunlight.

Tal walked closer, seeing the two portraits hung there. They were well done and taller than the windows in matching gilded frames. Tal noticed there were no other portraits in the room. The one on the left was of a beautiful Fae woman with light brown hair and green eyes, much like Lord Elgan's. The smile on her full pink lips was somehow warm and inviting as it was teasing. The artist must have been a very skilled creature because it seemed her eyes sparkled, and her sun-kissed skin glowed.

"My sister," said Lord Elgan, seeing Tal looking at the portrait. "Lady Rhoslyn."

"I heard she was a great beauty, but I couldn't remember if I ever knew what she looked like. I'm sure I've seen this portrait before."

"You didn't know her. She died when you were still a babe. She lasted less than a few weeks after Eriana's birth. Came from the human lands, sick, malnourished, and tired. I wish she had come home before she was too far gone."

"But she managed to have a healthy babe here."

"She did," agreed Lord Elgan. "And you will see her here."

Tal moved over to the other portrait and was surprised it was not the first that caught his notice. As beautiful as Lady Rhoslyn was, her daughter eclipsed her in every way. Her hair was auburn, wavy, and long. Her dark pink mouth was even fuller than her mother's, her smile somehow bewitching. Yet it was her eyes that made Tal move even closer. They were startlingly blue and absolutely human. It was the only trait she must have gotten from her human father, as her skin was perfect, and her ears were as pointed as his own.

"She's lovely, isn't she?" asked Lord Elgan. "So much like her mother in looks and temperament."

"Your family has been blessed with attractive features."

Lord Elgan chuckled. "Yet, it is not Eriana's unnatural beauty that truly draws you in."

"Oh," said Tal, staring up at the picture.

"There is simply no one like her."

Tal waited for the lord to elaborate, but soon it became clear he wouldn't. "Is this portrait current?"

"Close enough," said Lord Elgan.

"Anything else I might use to identify her should her face be covered or...." He stopped himself, knowing if he went further, he would aggrieve the lord.

"She has a tattoo of a moon vine on her right arm. She got it to hide a rather nasty scar."

"How'd she get the scar?"

"She was cut," said Lord Elgan simply. "I believe she usually spends time in Uchel and Thiria. Though, she also travels to Iledria. The last time she was here, she talked of spending only two weeks out, ending with a visit to a friend somewhere on the border of Uchel and Iledria."

Tal nodded. "Do you know the friend's name?"

"No. Only that she lives in the Gethian forest. I believe she might be a forest witch."

"Very well, I'll check there."

"When you find her, Your Highness, tell her I agree with her last message. Tell her to hurry up so she can return."

"You think she's still alive? Even with the Court of the Underlings?"

"She is too valuable for them to lose. Your brother may not want to start a war over her, but I have no qualms about doing it. Protecting her was the last promise I made to my dear sister. I will not fail her."

"You didn't think to go out yourself?"

"I am ready to go at any time. Your brother has asked me to stay here. I had every intention of defying him until he told me he was calling you home for the task," said Lord Elgan as he looked at the picture of his niece.

"Why did that stop you?"

"Because I believe if anyone can help my dear Eriana, it's you." He turned to look at Tal. "I've always found you clever and discerning, much more than your brother. I also believe I can offer you something that you most want."

"And what would that be?"

"A way out of obeying your brother, a way to be released from his rule."

Tal half laughed. "You think you have a way to accomplish it? You can overrule a king?"

Lord Elgan smiled viciously, making Tal feel he should take a step back. The air practically crackled with magic. "You've heard a bit of the magic my family possesses, Your Highness. You should know you have only heard a small part of the truth. You find Eriana, and you will find what you seek."

Chapter 7

Tal

TAL HATED FORMAL DINNERS. He avoided them whenever he could at his uncle's palace, only showing up when his aunt demanded his attendance. It was never affection that called him to her table. She had no love for him, and he did little to earn her approval. The dark queen only sent a servant to summon him when an important guest from the Dark Court or one sent by the Sun King would visit.

Tal usually played the part of a well-mannered prince well, but there were times he slipped up, calling out the stupidity or ridiculousness of a guest. Usually, his particularly sharp barbs were saved for ones sent by his brother on the pretense of keeping goodwill between the courts, but Tal knew the real reason. Those from the Golden Court were told to spy on their runaway prince to see what secrets he may be giving to those who lived under the shaded trees.

The Sun King shouldn't have wasted the time of his lesser lords, as while Tal did not hate his uncle, he couldn't care less for court politics. Besides, any secrets he knew about the Golden Court seemed to fade from his mind like most of his memories before coming to his uncle's palace. He never knew why his mind didn't hold many images and thoughts of growing up in the Golden Palace of Brigant. He could remember some things, knew names and faces, places of interest, and the history of his land, but most personal experiences were as if they never existed. Perhaps his life had been so boring it hadn't been worth remembering.

Tal threw some water over his face before putting on a shirt, having told the servant assigned to him that his help wasn't wanted. He glanced at the golden crown sitting out for him on a low table before running his hands through his dark hair and leaving the room. The hall was quiet and empty, the setting sun pouring in from the windows and mixing with the candles lit along the walls. No matter the time of day or night, plenty of light was always found in the palace.

He made his way to the largest parlor, knowing his brother liked to show off even when the guests would be few and familiar. He found three servants waiting near the walls, plenty of liquor on the tables, and a blazing fire burning at each end of the room. It made the room much too warm for him, but he imagined those used to the bright sun and warmth of the Golden Court found the autumn nights almost unbearably cold. They lived their mild winters mostly indoors and bundled up in ridiculous furs.

One resident of the court sat in the middle of the room, as far away as she could get from both fires. Her short sleeves and long slit up her skirt suggested she did not mind the milder temperatures.

"Brother, I was hoping you would come in early so I could speak with you," said his sister as she rose.

"You said you wanted to talk with me. I came down early in hopes you would be here."

He walked up to her and put his hands on her arms as he leaned in and kissed her cheek. "It really is good to see you, Adalyn."

"It's been too long, Tal. Come and sit." She glanced toward the fire closest to him. "We can move closer to the flames if you wish."

"I prefer to stay away. As it seems you do," said Tal as she sat back down. He flopped into the chair next to her before pouring a glass of golden wine.

"I don't mind the heat of the fire or the coolness of the shadows. A gift from the gods and goddesses of our courts, I suppose." Tal made a noncommittal noise as she adjusted her skirt and studied him. "I suppose you look well, so that must be something. The news I've heard about you made me afraid I'd find you looking rough and ragged."

"What news is that, dear sister?"

"That you live a turbulent life, spending your nights and sometimes days drinking. You rarely stay somewhere for long, sleeping in our uncle's palace for a few weeks at a time before disappearing off into the human lands, going to the gods-know-where."

"I like to travel and try the local spirits; not much harm in that."

"Of course, there are the women too. You rarely sleep alone, I hear?" she asked, as though commenting on the weather.

"That's an exaggeration, as I'm sure you already know. Perhaps I do enjoy some female company, but not every night. Sometimes, I spend my days dallying with some pretty thing and keep my nights to myself."

"Hmmm," said his sister dryly as she poured a small glass of wine.

Tal drained his glass and poured another. "Addie, honestly, what you've heard. Some of it is true. I won't deny it, but it's been years since I was as wild as I once was. I enjoy traveling and speaking with others. I enjoy flirting with a pretty face, but I rarely take a lover these days. It hardly seems worth it."

"And you never thought of coming to visit us these past few decades? To not visit me? If you needed someone to speak with, why not your sister?"

Tal took a sip of wine as his sister stared at him. "It's not you that I've avoided. I'd have happily received you in the Obsidian Palace, and so would our uncle and aunt."

She looked away. "My time is not my own. I have commitments to our people, our court, and my ruler." She glanced at him. "Travel was impossible."

"You mean our brother commanded you to stay."

"Perhaps, but I'd never leave our court for longer than a day or two. I have a duty to protect all that is worthy within its borders."

"So, you're not a fan of our brother as king."

"I serve as a member of this court, same as you, Brother," she said carefully, looking towards the servants in the corners.

Tal leaned in and whispered, "They would report your words to their king?"

"He is the Sun King, Tal. What would you expect?"

Tal sat back and drained his glass. "So, you stay here and do your duty. What falls under your responsibility?"

"Officially? Greeting visitors, seeing to the daily functions of the palace, meeting with the lords our king has no time for and entertaining the ladies of the court when necessary. All the things the queen will do once she is chosen," said Adalyn.

"But it sounds as if our king has chosen his queen, so perhaps if I'm successful, you'll have less to do in the near future."

Adalyn grinned. "There are a few times our brother does not get what he wishes."

"Oh, you think Lady Eriana won't give in to our brother's charms? Or at least the position he offers her? A half-human woman facing the grandest opportunity of being the queen of a Fae court must be alluring. Of course, some of his lords might whine a bit, but what can they do, really?"

"I don't think Eriana cares for any position he can offer her."

"You know the lady well?" asked Tal.

"I do, and I'm one of the few. She's not always easy to get to know."

"I remember her as being very unpleasant."

"Why? Because she wouldn't fall into your arms? She's not unpleasant."

"You like her?" Tal stretched and refilled his glass.

"I do. She's one of the few I enjoy speaking with at court, an interesting woman."

"What do you make of her being taken by the Court of the Underlings? Is there any hope of finding her alive?"

"I have every hope you will find her alive and well. Not only is she too important to harm permanently, but I also can't see her being taken against her will. She is fierce, Tal, more so than even our greatest guard or lord. I've seen her spar with her father's guards and any young lord foolish enough to cross her."

Tal raised his eyebrows in surprise. "We don't know how many are in this group. Perhaps a large number attacked her. She couldn't face them all."

"But she is too clever to be ambushed," said Adalyn with something like admiration.

"You think she went willingly?"

Adalyn shrugged. "Maybe she had a plan." His sister leaned forward, placing her hand on his arm. "Maybe this Court of the Underlings isn't what you think. You should take all possibilities seriously if you truly wish to find her."

Before Tal could say anything else, the door opened, and a servant showed in Lord Elgan and his daughter. Tal and Adalyn stood, Adalyn grabbing Tal's wrist and whispering, "Watch yourself with Lady Delphina. She's not the gentle lady you think she is."

"She's let me know that already," said Tal with a smirk as Adalyn dropped his hand.

Tal greeted Lord Elgan, the lord saying little after bowing. He kissed Adalyn's hand and gave her a genuine smile before pouring a glass of wine and walking to the fireplace.

Tal poured a glass and offered it to Lady Delphina. "A peace offering? I never meant to offend you this afternoon, my lady, truly."

The lady looked at the glass before taking it. "You didn't offend me, Your Highness. I just couldn't let you go misinformed. We all have to play our parts at times, even you. Thinking of one as less than another is wrong and dangerous."

"Parts to play, my lady? Do you see life as a game?"

"Don't you?" she asked with a smirk before taking a sip of wine.

"Oh, I have my fun, but I'd like to think maybe there's some reason for all of it. I haven't found it yet, but I remain hopeful."

"Perhaps that's because we've created some idea that we were made for a reason to make us feel some importance."

"That's a rather sad thought, Lady Delphina," said Adalyn.

"Or a very freeing one," said the lady. "To think order and manners are only surface level to keep society going, while we can indulge our selfish delights underneath without consequence? Yes, please."

"Everything has a consequence," said Adalyn. "Even if it's not divine retribution." She walked away to Lord Elgan, smiling at the lord as she came near him.

"Your sister and I have never been good friends," said Lady Delphina. "She prefers my cousin."

"And how do you get along with Lady Eriana?"

"We were close once as young girls but have drifted apart over the years. I don't wish her ill. If she found some happiness in the human lands and stayed there, the only bother I have is it would grieve my father."

"He does appear to care greatly for her. He said he made a promise to his sister."

"Some of it does have to do with his closeness to my aunt, but he prefers Eriana over me in many ways. She's more like him than I ever could be. She bought into his idea of family duty while I tend to look beyond it."

"Yet, she is the one missing in foreign lands, and you stay here loyally with your father."

She grinned. "Perhaps staying here serves my purpose more than his." She smirked playfully at Tal as the king walked into the room with Theo and Theo's father following him. Tal couldn't help but roll his eyes, thinking of spending an evening in Theo's company.

"Good, you're all here," said Idris. "Taliesin, I'm sure you remember Lord Kerry and his son Theo?"

Tal nodded towards the lord as Theo stepped forward.

"I already had the pleasure of running into our prince," said Theo. "I believe he had just arrived."

"And I'm sure the prince is delighted to be reacquainted with you," said Idris. "Now, the benefit of having few guests for supper is there is less time to wait. Join me in the dining room, please." He walked forward and offered Lady Delphina his arm.

"Thank you, Your Majesty, but I already told the prince I would let him escort me into the room. You'll have to indulge him after being gone for so long." Delphina moved to Tal's side.

"Of course," said the king breezily, turning to exit the room as Lord Kerry followed him.

Lady Delphina hooked Tal's arm with her own. "See. I'm much more interested in doing what I want than what's best for my family."

"Are you saying you would deny the king a chance to court you if he turned his eyes from your cousin to you?" asked Tal as Lord Elgan escorted Adalyn out of the room. Theo glanced at Tal and Delphina before following them.

"When I have what I want in mind, Your Highness, nothing gets in my way." She winked at him before gently pulling him towards the door.

Lady Delphina showed little signs of her flirtatious attitude with Tal during dinner, except her hand would graze his at times, or her leg would lay against his for a moment. He couldn't tell if this was on purpose or accidental, so he did not comment. She focused most of her attention on speaking with the king or at least listening to him, as Tal's brother tended to dominate the conversation.

Tal took time during the meal to examine Lady Delphina more closely. She was beyond lovely, especially in the tight green dress she wore. Her golden hair was up, a few curls falling past her pointed ears to graze her long, graceful neck. His fingers itched to graze the soft skin by her collarbone to see if she would shiver at his touch. He hadn't been lying to his sister when he told her his wilder days were behind him, but spending an evening with a creature as lovely as Delphina was beyond tempting.

The last time he was here, her beauty had interested him. Now, with her added wit, he found it even harder not to be overcome by her charms. It was a good thing he was leaving in the morning, as he had no wish to be too entangled with such a high lord's daughter.

"I was hoping this mess in the human realms would stay there," said Lord Kerry as he motioned for a servant to refill his cup. "But of course, their simple-minded chaos would find its way here eventually."

"You don't find any importance in the human realms?" asked Adalyn.

"My princess, I'm sure you haven't spent much time there, if any. Let me tell you how uncouth you would find it. It's a dirty, ugly place full of stupid creatures with short lives. Sometimes, I wonder how kind it was to free them all those centuries ago."

"Surely not," said Adalyn. "Humans deserve their freedom, and I cannot find any hatred for them. I may not be as experienced in human relations as you, Lord Kerry." Tal snorted into his cup as he took a drink, his sister's lips curling up into a smile. "But the ones I've come across have always struck me as interesting and industrious. Besides, there may come a time when we need them more than we do now. Our numbers are not what they once were. Full Fae children come less and less, as I'm sure you're well aware." She picked up her cup and tipped it towards Theo.

"Perhaps, Princess Adalyn, some have their uses," said Lord Kerry.

Tal took a bite of his meal and leaned forward. "Was it an Illedrian woman who sired your son, my lord?"

"Taliesin, I'm not sure this is polite conversation," said Idris, though he had a wicked smile on his face.

"Why? It's not as if our friend's heritage is a secret," said Tal, giving Theo a small wink. "I suppose if you were going to breed a human woman, Lord Kerry, then you must have done some research. Illedrians would have the best chance to pass on mostly Fae features and magic, of course."

"Or maybe it doesn't matter what human woman is used," said Lord Kerry, "if the blood of the father is pure and strong. I come from an ancient line of Fae lords, ones your family probably owes its crown to."

Lord Elgan gave a soft chuckle. "History is always being rewritten to benefit ourselves, isn't it?"

"And how do you feel about having a half-human niece, Lord Elgan," said Lord Kerry with a look of distaste. "Your sister definitely had no qualms taking a human lover."

Lord Elgan looked non-bothered. "My niece is rather impressive, my lord, and I believe the king agrees with me. It wouldn't surprise me if, in the next century, there is more and more mixing between Fae and humans as there once was long ago. As our princess has stated, it might be a necessity if we want the Dark and Golden Courts to go on."

"True, my lord," said Idris. "But that is years in the future. We must focus on what is happening now." He turned to Tal. "You'll wish to speak with Dyfan tonight, Brother, about when you will leave and what you will need."

Tal nodded. "I'll find him after our charming company leaves. We should think about where we can get some horses out in the human lands. At some point, it might be hard to travel as I usually do."

"Do you plan to go in glamour?" asked Delphina.

"When it's necessary, I will. Other times, I like those I come across knowing what a threat I am. Depends on which form will help me get information."

Theo cocked an eyebrow as he grinned at Tal. "Stealth is usually better."

"I agree," said Idris. "You don't want to draw attention to yourself."

"I can stay hidden even without glamour, Brother, or have you forgotten I have skills from my mother's court?"

His brother's lips curled up in disgust, but before he could say anything, a wind blew through the room, blowing out every candle and fire, leaving the room lit by only moonlight. That light was soon gone as well, and an unnatural darkness swept through.

"Really, Taliesin, this demonstration is unnecessary," said Idris.

"This isn't me," said Tal, raising his hand and trying to spark the closet candle, but his magic would not respond, feeling trapped within him. "What in the dark hell?"

"If this is your idea of a joke..." Lord Kerry said as the sound of chairs scraping filled the room.

"I said this isn't me, and I meant it," said Tal. He felt Lady Delphina grab his arm as he stood up.

Another breeze blew by him as Delphina let go of his arm. He closed his eyes against the darkness, feeling untethered to the world around him as though the very floor beneath him had disappeared. He felt another breeze as a whisper buzzed in his ear. "Seek what you will, Prince, but we can only be found when we wish it."

He shook slightly as the whisper worked its way into his bones, chilling him. "How can you know what I seek?"

"You must think that's true, as you don't even know yourself." A teasing laugh caused gooseflesh to appear and his hands to ball into fists. "Do your duty and listen to your brother's command, but it is I who will find you." Another laugh. "Of course, I'll let you come of your own free will. I could take you this second if I wished."

"I'd like to see you try."

A hand rested on his shoulder, light and non-threatening, with another teasing laugh to accompany it. "You might, but it will be better to let you come to us. Sleep well, Prince Taliesin. Everything starts tomorrow."

The hand on his shoulder stayed for a moment longer with the feeling of someone behind him. Then it was gone. A breeze flitted through the room as the candles came back to life and the fire sparked. Tal leaned on the table, propping himself up with his hands.

"Your Highness," said Delphina, jumping up and putting her hand on his upper arm. Tal looked down at it, remembering the touch of the unknown on his shoulder. "Did it hurt you?"

He shook his head. "Something or someone spoke to me. I don't know what it was."

"I heard it too, and I know who it was," said Lord Elgan. He pointed to the center of the table. "Look."

Tal raised his head to see, just in front of him, a dark banner featuring a crow holding a red dahlia.

Chapter 8

Aven

THOUGH SOME HIGHER LORDS and ladies turned their noses up at an invitation to Mayfield, Aven had no qualms about visiting the grounds. He found the home interesting and the people inside engaging and intelligent.

Mayfield Manor was not what one would expect of a rich lord's home. It was large, but half was burned out from a fire a century ago. The current lord had more than enough money to repair it but saw no reason. He had a good parlor, more bedrooms than he could ever use, kitchens, a study, and excellent stables. To repair the east wing just to have more unused bedrooms, a ballroom, and a place to put another set of musical instruments for his wife and daughter seemed like an unnecessary extravagance.

So Mayfield Manor stood as it had since the great fire, half burned down and the rest with many of the stones stained black. The grounds were well kept, with a pretty garden tended by the lord's wife and daughter. The inside was clean, though a little outdated, but everything remained serviceable.

Aven knocked on the door, and it was answered by an elderly woman who did not curtsey as did servants in other houses. She smiled, tucking a gray curl back into her bun. "Prince Aven, it's good to see you. I was afraid you'd been convinced as the rest to avoid this house."

"Never, Meg. This is one of the dearest places to me in the kingdom. My schedule is the only thing that has kept me away."

"Master Quinn is in with his father, but I don't see why you can't join them. They'll both be glad to see you."

"Thank you, Meg. Any chance I can get some of those apple tarts you know I love so much? Even with the recipe you sent to the palace, no one makes them as well as you."

She laughed. "I'll send two for you just for your attempt at flattery. Go on with you."

He walked into the house and followed the well-worn blue rug that led to the lord's study. Aven knocked before opening the door to find Quinn and his father, Lord Dall, looking over something on the desk.

Quinn looked up, a bright smile lighting up his round face. "Aven! I haven't seen you in weeks."

"I've meant to stop by, but my father has kept me busy. I hope you don't mind me visiting, my lord."

Lord Dall stood up, pulling a handkerchief out of his pocket to wipe his perpetually red nose. "Of course not, Aven. You're always welcome here." He folded up whatever they had been looking at. "Let us go to the parlor, as I'm sure Prudence and Cara will want to see you."

"I'll happily visit with the ladies in a bit, but could we speak for a moment here? There is something I hope you both can help me with."

"What is it?" asked Quinn, eagerness on his face at being faced with a problem he could solve.

Aven cleared his throat, looking at the closed door. "What do you know of the Court of the Underlings?"

Quinn cocked his head and then looked at his father. "Funny you should ask."

Lord Dall nodded, tapping the paper he had just folded. "Quinn and I were just discussing them. Causing quite a ruckus in nearby kingdoms."

"And here as well," said Aven, moving closer to the desk. "Lord Mevins reported yesterday that two of his servants' daughters were taken, a particular banner left in their beds."

"The crow?" asked Lord Dall. "I've heard something about them taking it as their sigil."

"A crow with a red dahlia for some reason," said Tal.

Quinn went to one of the many bookshelves in the room and searched for a certain book. When he found it, he pulled it out and opened it, leafing through the old yellowed pages with dried flowers stuck in them until he came to the one he was looking for.

"Dahlia flowers grow in warm climates, usually in southern lands or the Golden Fae court." He glanced up at Aven and Lord Dall. "They bloom well into cooler months and have medicinal powers. They are sometimes used to treat those overcome with grief, have convulsions, or weak stomachs." His finger moved down the page. "Red dahlias have long been used to symbolize strength. The powerful Fae warrior Ryn used it on his shields and banners when fighting the great Fae War."

"Fae warrior," said Lord Dall with a grunt.

"Known to grow well in gardens in the Golden Court of the Fae," said Quinn as he looked over the page.

"So you think these Underlings are connected with the Fae?" asked Aven.

Lord Dall took the book from his son, and Aven peered over the lord's shoulder. "I'm not sure."

Quinn shook his head. "Wouldn't surprise me. They like to cause havoc on our lands and amongst our kind. It's why we had to temper magic in our kingdom so we wouldn't be associated with the wicked creatures. No one would trust us due to our connection."

Aven looked up from the book, surprised. "Our connection? To the Fae?"

"You didn't know?" Quinn asked as his father handed the book back. Quinn closed it and put it back on the shelf from which it came. "One of our first kings wed his daughter to a Fae from the Dark Court. It's where our magic comes from; at least, that's what legend says."

"Well, I don't know if it's where our magic comes from, but it's a fact that at least one of our earliest kings wed his daughter to a dark Fae," said Lord Dall. "We just call it legend to distance ourselves from our cursed history. No other human ruler would deal with us if it were believed real." Lord Dall crossed his arms. "Your father never taught you the connection of his family to the Fae?"

"No," said Aven. "But I had a hard time suppressing my magic when I was young. Maybe he was afraid to tell me too much about it."

"Maybe," said Lord Dall as a knock sounded at the door. "Come in."

The door opened, and a pretty, short, stout woman walked in. Her dark eyes twinkled as she looked at Aven. "Ah, Avie finally came for a visit."

Aven turned to the woman and bowed. "I've been gone too long, my lady."

"You have. Now, come give me a kiss before escorting me to the parlor. Whatever you're speaking about with my dear husband and son, you can share with me. I'm wiser than both of them put together."

Aven laughed as he moved forward and took the lady's hand. He kissed her cheek. "That you are, Lady Prudence." She kept a hold of his hand and pulled him towards the door. "Come along, Dall, Quinn, join us."

Aven walked with Lady Prudence into the comfortable parlor to find Quinn's sister sitting on the ground by the fire, a book in her hand and a quill behind her ear. Before noticing Aven, she grabbed her quill and dabbed it into an inkpot on the floor, making a note on the paper by her.

"Sitting in a mess, as usual, little scribe, I see. Planning your next great masterpiece?" asked Aven as Lady Prudence chuckled.

"Actually, I'm working on a spell and much too busy for a stuck-up prince," said Cara.

"A spell?" asked Aven. "What do you know of spells or magic?"

"More than you, which is a shame because you could actually do magic if you tried." Cara finished her note and placed the quill back behind her ear, leaving a few drops of ink on her cheek. She scratched her forehead and ran a hand through her messy, dark curls.

Aven crouched down beside the girl. "And what does this spell do?"

"It makes me appear as a man so I can write, fight, or travel as I wish without a husband," said Cara.

Aven laughed. "You don't wish you were a boy, Cara. You are much too pretty for that."

She blew at a curl that fell into her face. "What does being pretty matter? I want to write and see every kingdom and the Fae realms as well. If I were a second son, I could do as I wish."

"Perhaps we can find you a husband who can travel with you and let you do all those things." Aven offered the girl his hand. He saw Meg bring in a tray full of tarts and tea. "Come have some treats with me, and we can discuss it."

She narrowed her eyes and looked up at him. "You missed my birthday."

"You had another birthday? What was it? Your fifteenth?"

"Sixteenth, and you didn't even get me a present."

"Did I not?" He put one knee down and reached into his pocket, pulling out a bracelet shaped like a dragon and holding it out to her. "What's this then?"

She took it slowly, her eyes still narrowed. "Jewelry? You got me jewelry," she said, her voice dripping with disdain.

"This is not just jewelry," said Aven taking the bracelet back. It was gold and a perfect circle that looked like a dragon's head almost touching the tail. "This is an official piece of the royal jewels of Illedria. Queens and princesses have worn this. It is said it was once used to control dragons. It's said it could tame them." He took her small hand and slipped it on her wrist. "Perhaps it might tame you."

She tried to take her hand back, but Aven kept a hold of it. She finally laughed. "You should know that nothing could tame me."

"I do." He kissed her ink-stained hand and let it go. "More than you know."

He stood up and offered her his hand. She took it, and he pulled her up before she moved towards the tea and treats her mother was serving.

"You shouldn't give away something like that from your family line, Aven," said Quinn. "I can get it back from her. She'll understand."

"I want her to have it. She is as dear to me as any of you. We have several old trinkets just like it, and my mother doesn't care for any of them. She gave one to the local temple of the goddess to do with as they please." Aven smiled. "If anyone could tame a dragon, it would be Cara."

Quinn patted his shoulder. "Too true. It's too bad they never existed."

"What never existed?" asked Lady Prudence, taking her tea to sit on the sofa.

"Dragons, Mother."

Lady Prudence blew on her tea. "I wouldn't be so sure about that. The old books are full of tales of how they helped keep our kingdom secure."

"Probably just one writer after another finding another story and building off it," said Quinn. "If there were dragons, we would have evidence of them, bones or something."

"Depends on which legends you go by," said Lord Dall as he sat by his wife. "Some say dragon fire was so hot, it burned bones, so when a dragon died, another would see that no trace was left behind."

"But eventually, there would be one dragon left," said Quinn. "What of its bones?"

"Perhaps there are still dragons somewhere hiding," said Cara as she looked at her bracelet. "Maybe they are waiting to be called."

"Will you be the one to do it, little Sister?" asked Quinn, laughing.

Aven picked up two tarts and handed one to Cara. "Maybe she will. Then she can build the world to her will and live as she likes."

Cara smiled up at Aven, taking the tart. "I'll let you keep your crown, Aven. I'll be your greatest defender."

"Then my reign will be legendary."

"Overshadowed by the girl who called the dragons, though," said Lord Dall.

"A sacrifice I'm willing to make for my people and my friend," said Aven as he sat in a chair by Cara.

"So what were you discussing with my husband and son, Aven?" asked Lady Prudence, taking a sip of her tea.

"A threat to our kingdom and others, my lady," said Aven.

"Aven came to speak about the Court of the Underlings," said Lord Dall. "Quinn and I were discussing their attacks when the prince came in. We've been looking at the places they've struck on a map."

"Did you bring the map with you?" asked Aven.

Lord Dall nodded and pulled a folded-up paper out of his pocket. "Cara, clear the low table, please."

Cara sat her half-eaten tart on a small table next to her and moved the few books and cups on the table before her. Her father opened the map and spread it out over the table.

"The first known attack was in Cryfder," said Quinn, pointing to the kingdom on the edge of the forest that separated the human and Fae realms. "A mine was cleared out, several workers taken, and a few overseers beaten. One was killed when he fought back."

"The ones taken? Where they ever found?"

"One young man was found wandering outside a temple close to the mine, but he had no recollection of what happened to him. Besides his memory loss, he was unharmed," said Lord Dall.

"How do you know all this?" asked Aven.

"My brothers have settled in a few different kingdoms," said Prudence. "Connell is a knight for King Magnus of Callint, Harper married the daughter of a lower lord in Crfyder, and my youngest brother is a priest of the goddess Mayra. He travels from kingdom to kingdom. They've all written about different attacks, but it took us until very recently to put it all together."

"A few days ago, Connell wrote the Underling name and drew a rudimentary picture of the banner. I was working to get a report together to tell the king," said Lord Dall.

"There's no need for it now since he's placed me in charge of this. What other attacks have happened?" Aven bent down to look at the map.

Quinn and Lord Dall went through each attack they knew about with Lady Prudence's help. After getting a second tart for her and Aven, Cara also gave her opinions.

"And now you tell us that Lord Melvins has been targeted," said Quinn, pointing to the area of the Melvins estate.

"Is there a common factor?" asked Aven.

"I don't know," said Lord Dall. "I think the only way to find out would be to speak to those who were attacked, find out who was taken, and see if they all share a common trait."

"We can send out messages," said Quinn. "It will take some time, but if you and I do it together, Aven, we can get it done."

"I can help you," said Lord Dall. "Between the meetings I have with my steward and other obligations, I can see to a few letters."

"All I do is write correspondence some days," said Lady Prudence. "I don't mind adding a few more."

"You're all too kind. I hate to put work on you. I know you're not idle people," said Aven.

"If it helps our king and you, we will do it, Aven," said Lady Prudence.

Aven smiled at them in thanks before looking to his right. "Of course, I would feel better if the most notable scribe of your family pledged me her services."

Cara finished her tart and wiped her hands on her skirt. "I'll consider it, Your Highness. If you promise your next gift will not be some useless piece of jewelry."

"I guarantee it, my lady."

Chapter 9

Tal

THE MARSADAN FOREST WAS unusually dense, with a heavy fog that hung around it most of the time. It made it practically impossible for humans to cross over into the Fae realms, which was the point. With their unnatural vision and speed, Tal and his companions easily made it to the gate that separated the human world from the Fae realm. It was a gate wide enough to let in three horses at a time, grown up with dark ivy and made of iron.

Tal sneered at it, keeping his hands at his side. Dyfan came to stand next to him while the other guards waited behind him.

"This is it?" asked one of the guards, stepping closer to the gate, his nose flaring. "So it is iron."

"There are two, one here and one on the bank of the glass lake in the Dark Court. The humans insisted upon them being iron when they were first built. As soon as we cross, you will see a group of rowan trees on each side, full of their luring red berries." Tal glanced behind him. "Do not look to the left or right, only straight ahead. You will not even think of those berries if you keep focused. Don't be a fool."

Dyfan nodded. "Can you open the gate?"

Tal stepped as close to the gate as he dared, hovering his hands very near the iron bars, feeling the heat and poison coming off them. "May the Dark Goddess hide us from harm, keeping us in shadow. May the Light God guide our steps as we seek only the truth."

The gate glowed for an instant, and a hum came from it that made the birds in nearby trees scatter. A second later, the gate swung open. "Remember, look straight ahead, not to the left or right. Once we are a ways through, I will take us closer to the nearest village."

Tal walked through, keeping his head straight, ignoring the scent of the rowan trees and their poisonous berries, trying to ignore the siren song of the wind blowing through their branches.

"Gods, what is that?" asked the oldest of the three guards, cringing as he walked.

"It's the call of the rowan tree. Ignore it, don't turn your head, take no step towards it. We'll be past it soon enough."

The call became fainter, the smell of the berries almost drifting away when he heard the shuffle of feet and a cry. He glanced back to see one of the guards walking toward his right into a gathering of three rowan trees. Tal thought for a moment about letting the stupid, weak man meet his fate, but he wasn't sure what they would face in the human lands. They might need every sword they had with them.

He pushed past Dyfan and shoved the other two guards forward. "Keep going, don't look back." Dyfan nodded as Tal hurried to catch the guard. The smell of the berries was overwhelming, the song of the wind twirling through his mind, asking him to come see and taste. Tal shook his head and gritted his teeth, reaching out to grab the wayward guard just as the man almost touched a cluster of berries.

"You fool, you'll die within half a day of eating one cluster of berries," said Tal, bringing the man close.

The guard shook his head and looked at Tal with wide eyes. "I…I…I'm sorry, my prince. I don't know why."

"Because you're weak," said Tal as he pulled the man away, shoving him forward to fall in line with the other two guards. "Keep in between your fellow guards, and maybe they can stop you from being so stupid because the next time, I'll leave you to your fate."

Tal moved ahead, Dyfan hurrying to catch up with him. "Your Highness, the guard is young and has never left the court. He couldn't have ever come across a rowan tree."

"He'll see plenty more where we're going. The humans drink wine made from it. It's not as lethal as the pure berries, but just a few sips are stronger than any glass of faerie wine."

"You know from experience?" asked Dyfan with half a grin.

"A little," mumbled Tal. "That guard needs to know that stupidity will get him and all of us killed."

"He isn't stupid, Tal," whispered Dyfan. "He's a strong fighter and good man. He will serve you well. Perhaps some kindness and understanding wouldn't hurt?"

"I don't think either of those things has ever done me any good."

"You were both of those things once, kind and understanding. You were always a fierce fighter and a trickster like your father. You might have had a flair for drama, but you were never cruel. I suppose the Dark Court has changed you," said Dyfan.

"Time and experience have changed me. Whatever I was before my father died, I can't remember, so I must have been close to worthless."

Dyfan sighed. "You were not, not to me or anyone else. Almost everyone loved you, Tal. The people, the lords, the guards…" Dyfan paused and took a deep breath before moving even closer, his voice barely a whisper. "If you had said one word about passing over your brother as the next king, almost every guard would have fought for you. That's how much worth you had to the court."

"My father wished my brother to be king. I would never go against his word," said Tal.

"So instead, you abandoned us to your brother's rule, ran away, and became whatever you are now. Why?"

"Because this is who I want to be, and once I find this silly woman, I will go back to the life I've created," said Tal. "You say I've abandoned you to my brother's rule, but it doesn't seem too bad. The village looked like it always did. You and your guards seem more than happy to follow Idris."

"There are things you don't know," said Dyfan. "A rotting house usually looks fine and serviceable for years before it reveals its destruction."

"What are you talking about?" asked Tal.

"Things you don't care about, apparently," said Dyfan as he hurried his steps to walk ahead.

"Dyfan," started Tal, but he didn't know what to say. Whatever was going on in his brother's court was not his concern. The village appeared secure, and the people seemed as happy as always. Dyfan was always a worrier. He caught up with his old friend. "Let's just concentrate on finding Lady Eriana. Perhaps when she is safe and back with her uncle, we can sit down and have a drink."

"Perhaps," said Dyfan as they stopped by a fallen tree to let the guards catch up with them.

Tal wanted to say more to Dyfan. They had once been close, growing up on the palace grounds. Even with Tal being a prince and Dyfan the youngest son of a lower lord given to the king's guard to train, they had been as good as brothers. Much closer than Tal ever was to Idris. They trained together and snuck out into the village, and Tal was sure they had other adventures. He just couldn't quite remember them. When he left the Golden Court, he almost left a note for Dyfan to explain himself, but when he sat down to write out his thoughts, none would come. He left without even a goodbye.

The guards gathered around, the youngest one unable to look Tal in the eye. A bit of shame ran through him, but like most guilty thoughts he had over the years, Tal pushed it away.

"We are going to Farwarn first. It is a good-sized human village on the edge of the forest. Put your hoods up. Due to the number of people there, we can slide in easily without wasting any magic or strength on glamour. Keep your heads down, and don't speak with anyone; just follow me."

The men nodded. "Now, stay still, and don't say a word." Tal raised his hands as darkness gathered around them, blocking out the weak rays of sun that managed to get in between the trees. The youngest guard looked up but said nothing as the shadows surrounded them with a harsh wind. A moment later, the darkness was gone, replaced with the midday light of a mostly sunny autumn day.

Tal breathed in, relishing in the cooler weather of the human lands. The guards, including Dyfan, pulled their cloaks around them tighter.

"Bright god, it's cold enough to freeze a man's balls here," said one of the guards.

Tal chuckled. "Hardly. You should see how it is in midwinter. Sometimes up to your shins in snow and wind so harsh you swear your eyeballs will freeze."

"You couldn't have at least moved us with your light magic?" asked Dyfan. "Given us a bit of warmth before throwing us into this?"

Tal rubbed his head. "Haven't been able to do much with my light magic in a while."

Dyfan looked at him sharply. "How long?"

Tal shrugged. "Long enough where I've learned not to depend on it beyond sparking a small fire. Now come on. You'll get used to the weather. Until then, I'll find you some warmth and substance. There's a place I know up ahead."

They entered the village, going straight to the row of shops where the crowd was thick with men, women, and horses. Tal pulled his hood up, as did his guards. He led them through the crowds, stepping around a mess a horse made and moving to the other side of the street to avoid the beggars gathered by the temple. It took a little longer than he would have liked due to trying to maneuver five people instead of just himself, but they made it to the old tavern at the corner without drawing attention to themselves.

The room was dark, crowded, and warm due to the large fire in the corner. It smelled of sweat, mead, some kind of stew, and baking bread. Tal moved to the bar; a tall older woman with her graying hair pulled back at her neck looked at him as he approached.

"It's you," grunted the woman as she sat some filled mugs on the counter for a barmaid to take. "Thought maybe you finally pissed off the wrong man."

"I'm not so easy to take down, Mrs. Wesson," said Tal. He dug into his pocket and pulled out three coins, placing them on the bar. "Fetch Berg for me, will you?"

She looked down at the coins. "I ain't one of your servants."

"Which is why I pay you better than one." He added another two coins. "Tell him to come directly. Find us a room so we can talk. One that will accommodate my whole party and me."

She looked over Tal's shoulder and grunted again. "Brought nothing but trouble here as you always do." She picked up the coins and put them in her pocket. "These better be real and not some trick."

"I would never insult you in such a way, Mrs. Wesson. Not a woman of your station and contacts."

"Station?" She huffed. "All I have is this dirty tavern my drunkard of a father left me. My husband almost lost it with his gambling."

"Good thing he had that unfortunate accident then," said Tal with a small wink. "You seemed to be more graceful without him around as well. Haven't seen your face bruised in a while."

She narrowed her eyes at Tal. "There's an empty room to the left. It should be big enough for your purposes. I'll see if Berg is available."

"Thank you, ma'am," said Tal with a nod. "See that some stew and drinks are brought in as well. My men need something to warm them."

"I'll get you food, but no girls. I don't want you hanging around that long."

"As you wish," said Tal. He turned to Dyfan. "Follow me."

The room on the left was small, with only two tables and an empty fireplace. Two unlit candles sat on each table. Tal touched each one, the wicks igniting. "Put some of that wood in the fireplace," he said to the guards. The youngest one immediately moved to place a stack of wood in the fireplace. He said nothing as he raised his hand, and flames covered the logs.

"You can use light magic?" asked Tal, a little surprised.

The guard nodded. "My mother was an Eynon. One of the last ones. I have a cousin, but I don't know him well."

Tal glanced at Dyfan, who gave him a small grin. The Eynon family was known for its strong magic, some of the most powerful in the history of the Fae. If this young guard was one of them, he could come in handy.

"And your name?"

"Flint, Your Highness."

"Sit down, and rest a moment. Some food and drink will come shortly. Once we're done here, I imagine we'll have to travel elsewhere."

Mrs. Wesson entered with a tray of bowls, followed by a pretty barmaid with mugs and a pitcher. She looked around at the men, her eyes wide and her cheeks red. Tal couldn't help but smile at her, as she was lovely. Much too young and innocent for any immoral thoughts, but nice to look at. She blushed further and put down the mugs and pitchers before hurrying out of the room.

"You'll have no ideas about Tilla," said Mrs. Wesson harshly. "She's hardly a woman."

"You wound me thinking such ill of me, Mrs. Wesson. I was only admiring her pretty complexion. She reminds me of someone, though I can't think who."

"Hmmm. Your visitor will be in shortly. He had something to take care of first."

"I didn't realize he was such a busy man this early in the day," said Tal.

"Just woke him up, and he had to complete his morning routine. Usually, whatever vices he did the night before come to haunt him when he finds light again."

"We'll be happy waiting then," said Tal, sitting at a table with Dyfan and pouring a drink for himself and his friend.

The men ate and drank, Tal partaking a little of each. The stew wasn't bad, and the mead was more than serviceable, but he wasn't hungry. He was anxious to find the lady so he could be done with this. Perhaps Lord Elgan could keep his promise, and Tal could run as far as he wished without returning.

Eventually, the door opened again, and Berg stumbled into the room. He was a short man with a round belly. His clothes, while clean due to Mrs. Wesson, had many stains. His hair was a thick brown mess, falling into his eyes. Tal didn't know how old he was, and he couldn't guess. He thought the man had either some Fae or faerie in him or was originally from Illedria, those humans gifted with longer life.

"Your Highness," slurred the man as he moved towards the table. Tal poured him a drink as Berg fell into a chair. "It's been a while."

"How's life treating you?"

"Can't complain," said Berg, taking a drink as his muddy eyes flicked up to Tal. "Have everything I want, kept my head so far, and I never run out of drink."

"So, you're still in business then?"

"Depends which business you mean," said Berg. He looked at Dyfan. "Who's this fellow?"

"My brother's head guard," said Tal. "Dyfan, this is Berg."

Dyfan looked down at the man, a deep frown on his face.

"He doesn't look like much fun," said Berg.

Tal chuckled. "He is once you get to know him, but he's on duty now, as am I. We're on a mission from our king."

Berg put his mug down and wiped his mouth. "What does the almighty Sun King want in the human lands? I thought he wished to pretend we didn't even exist."

"He likes to keep you at a distance, but he's very aware of your existence," said Tal. "Especially now that some heathens amongst you have taken someone of our court."

Beg sat back in his chair. "A Fae? Some human took a Fae?"

"More than just a human, a group," said Dyfan. "One we hear is causing havoc all across your kingdoms."

Berg smiled, picking his cup back up. "We have several of those, some employed by kings. You need to be more specific."

Tal sighed, knowing this would not be simple, not with Berg. The man liked dramatics too much, but he always seemed to know everything, even if it took all day to pull it out of him. Still, it didn't hurt to try to push things along. Tall pulled out a pouch filled with golden coins and threw it on the table. "Tell me what you know about the Court of the Underlings."

Berg picked up the pouch and put it in his palm, feeling the weight. He pulled it open and looked inside. "You show your desperation, young prince."

"I'm not desperate; I'm impatient. It grows cold in the human lands, and you know how I like to spend my winters."

Berg laughed. "Usually curled up with as many beautiful women as you can find." He raised an eyebrow, putting the pouch down. "Is this one of your women that was taken? Maybe you finally found one you want to keep."

Tal rolled his eyes and tapped the tables with his fingers. "I know little about this woman beyond that she's a niece of an important lord in the Sun King's court. From what I remember about her, she isn't worth my time."

"Not much to look at then?"

"On the contrary, she's beyond what you can imagine as beautiful. Just not my type," said Tal.

Berg laughed again and looked at Dyfan. "Found one who wouldn't give in to his charms, did he?"

Tal growled. "I hardly tried with her. Asked her to dance, but she wasn't interested. Seem to think I was below her. I believe it was the other way around."

"So why do you care if she was taken?"

"My brother commanded me to find her. Her uncle is demanding her return. He could cause some problems for my brother should we not appease him. The king also believes she's more worth his time and effort than I do."

Berg threw the purse towards Tal. "Your future queen is missing, and this is all you offer me. I'm insulted, Prince."

Dyfan banged his hand on the table. "That's enough gold to set someone like you up for over a year. You're lucky we even offer you anything instead of stringing you up and poking you full of holes until you scream the information we want."

Berg looked at Dyfan like he was bored. "You think you're the first person to threaten me?" He glanced at Tal. "Your prince once thought as you do, but he soon learned how wrong he was." Berg snapped his fingers, and the fire sparked. He disappeared and reappeared behind Dyfan, a dagger in his hands pressed against Dyfan's throat.

"I could have already killed you should I wanted to," said Berg. "Perhaps I still will."

The other guards stood up, Flint pulling out his sword. Tal put both of his hands on the table. "Let him go, Berg. I don't want to explain to Mrs. Wesson why her floor is stained with blood."

Berg pressed the dagger slightly into Dyfan's throat, drawing a little blood before he let the Fae guard go. He chuckled as he walked back to his chair.

Dyfan put a finger on his cut. "He made me bleed."

"Barely," said Berg. "You'll be healed before we finish this conversation."

"Here," said Tal, not wanting to waste any more time. He threw out another pouch. "And if you give us good information that leads to us finding the lady, I will see more is sent to you with the king's thanks. Now, tell us what you know about the Court of the Underlings."

Berg picked up both pouches, opening up his cloak to put them in a hidden pocket. "I know a little about them. What precisely do you wish to know?"

"Where we can find them," said Tal.

"Well, that's a tricky question. They seem to be everywhere, and no one really knows if they travel and live out in the open or have a place to call home." He rubbed his chin. "I've heard rumors, of course."

"Tell us the rumors then," said Dyfan.

"It's not as easy as that. My memory isn't what it used to be, and I don't want to lead you astray." He stretched, his shirt coming up to show some of his hairy belly. "I do know someone, though—a young man who is practically still a boy. He claims to have been taken by the Underlings and dragged to their official court. Says they spelled him not to remember, but some things have come back to him."

"What things?" asked Tal.

Berg shrugged. "I can't quite recall. When I heard his tale, I was drinking some fine mead with a pretty girl in my lap."

"So we need to find this boy," said Tal. "Is he from here?"

"Mostly," said Berg with a yawn. "Like most young men, he tends to wander."

Tal huffed, opening his mouth to go with this game, when the sound of another coin pouch hitting the table made him look down. Dyfan leaned over the table. "Here, take this, and go find the boy. Bring him back here so we can speak with him. I'm tired of your games and even more tired of your smell."

Berg smiled, showing his brown teeth as he picked up the pouch. "I like you. Even more than your prince." He took four coins out and threw them back at Dyfan. "Get yourself some more mead. I'll fetch the boy and bring him back this evening."

Dyfan nodded as Berg stood up, but before he could turn away, Dyfan grabbed his arm and pulled him close, a sharp knife in his hand. "You betray us, and none of your little magic tricks can save you. You have that boy here before midnight, or I'll hunt you down." Dyfan moved his knife, slicing a spot on Berg's arm, a bright drop of blood forming. "I always pay back what is owed."

Berg pushed away and pulled down his shirt before pulling out two more coins and throwing them in Dyfan's direction. "Get yourself a woman while you wait. You need it."

Chapter 10

Aven

THE FIRE IN AVEN'S room needed tending, but he was too engrossed in his pile of messages to notice. Between him and Lord Dall's family, they had sent out hundreds of letters. Cara stated that at least they ensured the messenger carriers would have plenty of money to make it through the winter, though she worried about overworking the birds.

They had sent out messages to about every lord in their kingdom and several in other lands. The letters were sent by riders, birds, and even some, eventually going by ship to the sea kingdom of Dylen. Cara insisted on writing those, saying she had studied the most about the people and understood best what to say. No one wanted to argue with her, so she had her way.

Now, the answers had started pouring in, and Aven wanted to read each one himself, even those he had left at Mayfield Manor. The high pile on his desk was not even a third of what had been received. Most were short, stating they knew nothing about the Court of the Underlings, saying they had never heard of it. Aven wondered if it was true or if those who replied were too scared to tell the truth. Maybe they hoped if they ignored the problem, it would go away.

It wasn't going away, though. The few letters that were longer told of more abductions and a few houses being attacked. Another mine in Uchel had been attacked at night, taking away a dozen children who worked to help bring the rock out. Aven was concerned that an estate close to the border of his kingdom had been hit, the outer building burned, and the lord's family chased from their beds. His lady refused to return, and the family took refuge in her brother's estate.

Still, even with all the attacks, Aven had a hard time finding a connection. Perhaps Quinn or Lord Dall would think of something. They were better at puzzles than he ever could be. He threw down the letter he was reading, finding nothing interesting in it, and stretched before jumping up.

He was anxious and unable to stand still. His fingers tingled, and his stomach fluttered. It had been too long since he had practiced his magic, almost two weeks since that last morning with Silvie. He would need to wake up early and find time to ride out soon to see if she had returned. When she was gone too long, he became worried for her. The thought that this Underling King was out there made him even more fearful for her safety.

He paced for a moment before standing before his fire. He held his hand up to it, watching the flame bend towards him. It beckoned him to play with it and make it answer his will. He saw no harm in taking one moment for his magic as he closed his eyes. He concentrated as Silvie had taught him, bringing his hand up as he opened his eyes. The flame shot up where it was once dying.

He curled his hand in and out, and flame jumped into his palm. He held it before throwing it to his other hand and then back again. He added another and then one more to juggle the flames, smiling as he felt his magic dance within him. He was so distracted by it that he almost didn't hear the knock at his door or the opening of the latch.

As the door swung open, he threw the flames back into the fireplace. It roared and sparked as his sister walked into the room. Her head whipped towards the fire as Aven turned to face her.

"What on earth?" she asked, her hand coming up to her chest.

"I added a log, and it rolled too far back," said Aven. "Made it spark."

She stared at the fire for a moment. "Honestly, Aven, you're the Crown Prince. You should call for a servant if your fire needs tending."

"Why bother a servant with something I can do myself?"

His sister rolled her eyes. "You never have taken your position seriously. It's a shame the line usually skips females."

Aven crossed his arms. His sister always seemed perpetually displeased. He wasn't sure why, but she never smiled much unless it was at something unpleasant. He didn't understand the air of superiority she let linger about herself. She always seemed an unhappy, sour person to him, even with her gentle upbringing from both their parents. "I've heard you lament enough about being passed over to know how you feel, Kyra."

She pulled at her sleeves before walking closer to him. "I don't blame you, brother, or hate you for it. I'm quite happy in my position, actually."

"I'm glad to hear it," said Aven, raising his eyebrows in surprise.

His sister looked at his desk. "What's all this?" She picked up one of his messages.

He grabbed it out of her hand. "Part of the work you accuse me of not taking seriously."

"What work requires you to have so many messages?"

"Something father asked me to do," he said, piling his messages together and putting them in a drawer.

"And what is that?"

"My personal business," said Aven, rather harshly as he looked at his nosy sister.

She rolled her eyes again before going to his full-length mirror and examining herself. She ran a hand through her long brown hair and wiped at some imaginary speck of dirt on her nose. "Why hide anything from me, Aven? We're family."

"And yet you rarely come to visit. Why are you here tonight?"

"Mother kept sending me letter after letter asking me to come to visit. So, to appease her, I came. How I shall bear her prattle all night, I don't know. Darron can barely stand her."

"She's your mother and his queen," said Aven. His sister turned to look at him. "She's a good woman, Kyra. She may seem simple and, at times, silly, but she means well. There's not a bad bone in her body."

"Because she's not capable of serious thought. I wonder how father ever thought she would be an acceptable wife."

"You and I should be glad he did, or we wouldn't exist."

"True." His sister turned back to the mirror, putting her hair behind her ears and then moving it again. "I just know she'll ask a hundred times when we are going to have another child, as if there is any need. Darron has his boy. He's satisfied."

"Sometimes people have children because they love each other and want to share that love," said Aven.

"Is that what you think?" said Kyra with a sardonic laugh. "Children are necessary for advancing the family line, and that's all. It's time you found an acceptable wife and strengthened our family name, Aven. I have a few women in mind."

"I doubt you and I have the same ideas of what makes an acceptable wife."

"Maybe not, but you should listen to my council. If you don't watch out, you will be taken in and face a lifetime with someone like mother, or worse."

"I can think of many worse things than having a good, kind woman as my wife," said Aven.

Kyra nodded. "Mother is at least complying. You should watch yourself with that company you keep. I hear you've spent too much time at Mayfield Manor." She shuddered. "Such uncouth people."

Aven's hands curled into fists. "They are worthy people with manners and sense. More intelligent than any others in our court."

"They have a daughter, don't they? A wild creature who runs around the home, digging in the dirt. I hear she's a pretty little thing, though. You should be careful, Aven."

"Cara is barely sixteen," said Aven.

"Matches have been made at younger ages. They might trap you at some point, and then you'll be caught and forced to marry the feral girl."

Aven almost shook with anger. "Cara is not yet a woman. She is remarkable but very young. Her father or mother has no plans to wed her to anyone anytime soon, and they would never do anything to hurt me."

"Why are you angry with me? I'm only looking out for you, brother." She moved closer to him. "I care about you, Aven, and want you to succeed."

"I know what I'm about, Kyra. I'm not a child."

"No, but you're as naïve as one sometimes." She shook her head. "We need to go to supper. Mother will grow more anxious and nonsensical if we are late."

Aven walked to the dining room with his sister, surprised to see she and his brother-in-law weren't the only guests that evening. Two other lords and their wives were at the table. Lord Bowen lived just outside their village, and Lord Murphy's estate was on the southern coast.

"There you are," said Aven's mother as she came up to him and his sister. "I was about to send someone out to search for you two."

"We aren't even late, Mother," said Kyra, sounding annoyed. "You didn't need to worry."

"But I do worry." She took Aven's hand. "I hear more and more about complete chaos in our land. People have been taken, Kyra. What if someone managed to get into the palace and grab you or Aven? I don't think I could take it."

"The palace is surrounded by high walls and guards. No one could just waltz in here and take a member of the royal family," said Krya.

"But that's what's happening in other places. Maybe not palaces, but in grand homes and fortified mines." She squeezed Aven's hand and let it go. "Lady Boyle told me all about it at tea the other day. She said no one is safe."

"Mother, Lady Boyle is a gossip and an idiot. Why do you even let her on the palace grounds?" Kyra nodded to her husband, who started moving towards her.

"Because she's a high lady of our court," said Aven. "Mother always does her duty well." His mother smiled at him as she wrung her hands. "But you don't need to worry, Mother. I wouldn't be taken without a fight."

"And you are very strong, Aven," said his mother affectionately. "It's just all so awful."

"Come sit down," said Aven as Kyra's husband, Lord Darron, took his wife's hand. Aven led his mother to the table, pulling out her chair. She sat, causing others to take their seats. Aven signaled for a servant to pour her some wine before taking his seat across from his father.

The food was served, and the wine poured as conversation flitted around the table. At first, it was idle chit-chat. Children were asked after, new marriage agreements were brought up, and Aven said he had not found any woman he would like as his wife yet. He hadn't even looked. The ladies laughed at him and scolded him for denying the attentions and flirtation of such a handsome prince amongst the court. Aven smiled politely and said he would remedy it soon.

Aven's mother went on and on about Aven's good looks, talking much too long for Aven's liking about how clear and deep blue his eyes were and how his thick, wavy brown must have come from his father. "In fact, I think it might be hard to see any of me in Aven at all." His mother laughed. "He's so much like his father."

"He has your smile," said the king as he took the queen's hand for a moment. "And I know Kyra gets her loveliness and grace from you, my dear."

Kyra looked slightly horrified for a moment before steeling her features and nodding at her father.

It was oddly his mother who made the talk turn more serious. As she went on about trying to find a bride for Aven, she eventually said, "Of course, I hope you can find one here in Illedria. I hate to think of you traveling, Aven. There's so much chaos in the land. I can hardly sleep or eat when I think of it. I know you need a wife, and perhaps making an alliance with Dewra or Uchel might be beneficial, though I would prefer one of the beauties from Thiria. If you marry a girl from Callint, I'm afraid she will think me silly and dull." She stopped for a moment, taking a sip of wine.

"Be careful if you do go out to court a young lady, and take plenty of guards. This king of the underthings or whatever his name is scares me until I can barely function."

The king covered his queen's hand and turned to the servants to refill the queen's glass. "There is no need to upset yourself, Turia," he said gently.

"No, my queen, you don't need to worry for the prince," said Lord Bowen. "No one would dare touch him and risk our kingdom's wrath. We have one of the strongest armies and our mages."

"Of course, you shouldn't worry for Prince Aven, but the queen is right in that trouble is brewing in the land. Those heathens calling themselves the Underlings aren't the only problem," said Lord Murphy.

The king sighed. "There is always some unrest in the land, and there is not much we can do about it. Always someone unhappy with their lot or some young king thinking he can conquer new lands. It always piddles out in the end."

"True," said Lord Murphy. "But this time, the ambition of certain kings turns towards the Fae lands."

"What kings would be so foolish?" asked Aven. "There's a reason we have a dense forest and iron gate between us. They are deadly."

"Maybe in the past, but the Golden and Dark Courts aren't as strong as they once were. The Sun King is young and said to be foolish. He talks of invading the human lands, thinking we would be easy prey."

"Wouldn't we be?" asked Aven. "We were conquered once before. Only through the luck of having a benevolent Sun King over three centuries ago were we truly freed from their rule. The rest of the Fae lords see us as annoyances they let be as they don't think what we are worth stealing."

"But the rumors are this Sun King thinks differently. Some say it is he who has sent the Court of the Underlings to cause chaos, that it is not humans attacking mines and lords' homes but Fae soldiers," said Lord Murphy.

"All rumors," said King Gavan. "I've spoken with King Hugo, and he assures me the wise masters in Calliant all agree there is no plot against the human lands from either Fae king."

"I wouldn't be so sure," said Lord Bowen. "I'm sure the wise masters mean well, but they can't know everything. Cryfder has a new king, and King Abott is young and bold. He believes Uchel should have more power in the land."

"What else is new?" said Kyra, rolling her eyes.

"And think what you will about the power of the Fae, but they have never been more vulnerable. The Sun King is untested and young, and the Dark King is old and without an heir. There are whispers in his court about what will happen to the line," said Lord Murphy.

"Surely there's a nephew or cousin who can take it over should something happen," said Aven.

"The nephew was born in his father's court. The alliance between his mother and the old Sun King resulted in a boy and girl, twins. They both belong to the Golden Court," said Lord Murphy.

"I hear the nephew has no interest in ruling. He spends his days dallying around the human lands." Lord Bowen chuckled. "Must drive both Fae kings mad to think their kin prefers the beds of human women."

"He wouldn't be the first of their kind to find companionship with a human," said Aven's father. "It's not that unusual."

"Perhaps not, but usually it's a common Fae, not some true member of the court," said Darron.

"The point is that the Fae courts are unusually vulnerable, and some kings think they are ripe for conquering. They want to strike before this new Sun King can cause more havoc in our lands, weakening us," said Lord Murphy.

"Still sounds like just rumors to me, but we will listen and watch carefully as always," said King Gavan. "Aven is looking into the Court of the Underlings. Perhaps he will find something out before long."

Aven nodded as everyone at the table looked at him. "Whoever is the cause of this band of troublemakers, we will know soon."

Chapter 11

Tal

THE TAVERN BECAME EVEN more crowded as the afternoon turned into evening. Tal got bored sitting in the empty room with his guards, and he could tell they were fidgety. He eventually suggested they go out into the main room. Dyfan was hesitant, wanting to stay hidden, but Tal raised his hood and walked out of the room, letting the guards decide for themselves what they would do.

Tal moved through the crowd to the end of the bar as Dyfan followed him. There wasn't much room, only a small space between Tal and a large man animatedly talking while he sloshed his mead around, so Dyfan sat at a nearby table, keeping his eyes on Tal. The other guards came to Dyfan, who spoke to them in a whisper. They dispersed around the room, and Tal had no doubt their orders were to keep an eye on things and him.

Tal wasn't worried. He had been to this tavern many times without problems. It was popular and filled with travelers of various dress and stations, all with different motives, some good, some dubious. Most didn't even give Tal a second glance. He ordered a drink and turned to look around the room. There was nothing particularly interesting going on. No women were around who were more attractive than usual; they were just the normal crowd, drinking, eating, and playing cards.

Tal watched a moment before he turned back to the bar. He was surprised to see someone wedged between himself and the large man, as he hadn't noticed anyone walking towards him. The stranger was dressed in tight pants, a loose shirt, and a long black cloak with the hood up. He could tell by the figure that it was a woman next to him. Two thick braids of dark red hair peeked out from her hood, running down her chest. He caught a glimpse of a slender nose as she raised her head and hand to order a drink.

Her hand was elegant, even if it were a little dirty, her fingers long. He could see a few silver, faded scars along the back of her hand.

"It's rude to stare," she said in a steady, rich voice. She turned slightly, her hood still covering most of her face.

"Excuse me. I didn't see you come up. You surprised me."

She turned to look at the room, her braids swaying. "Are you looking for someone? I can help you. My eyesight is quite good, even in this dim light."

"I wasn't looking for anyone in particular. Just seeing who was about." Tal ordered another drink, pushing his empty mug forward.

"Looking for some company tonight?"

He smirked, his eyes taking in her slim figure, wondering what the oversized shirt was hiding underneath. "Why? You offering?"

She scoffed and turned back to the bar, picking up her mug. "I don't think getting involved with a Fae prince would be smart—even for one night."

He choked a little on his drink. "You think you know me?"

"I'm more than certain I do. The useless prince of two courts. It's not surprising you would be in some human slum of a tavern, drinking your night away." She took a long drink.

He moved slightly closer, causing her to draw back and bump into the man next to her. The man didn't seem to notice, carrying on with his boisterous conversation. "Have we met before?"

She laughed quietly. "You may have come across me in the past, but obviously, I'm not worth the trouble of you remembering me."

"I come across a lot of people. You shouldn't take it as a slight."

She picked up her mug again and drained it. "I've lived through too much to feel slighted by anyone, Prince Taliesin." She asked for another drink, and her mug was replaced with a full one.

Tal glanced at Dyfan to see him watching the woman. He gave a slight grin to Dyfan, letting him know there was nothing to worry about before looking back at the woman. "You know my name. It's only fair you give me yours."

"Why? You've met me before and don't remember. What good would it do to tell you my name just for you to forget it again?"

Tal leaned back. "Perhaps if I could see your face, it would jog my memory."

"Maybe I keep it covered because it's not worth looking at."

"Or maybe you keep it covered because you know it'll draw attention," said Tal.

She shook her head. "Is this your attempt at flattery? If so, I suppose you've had to depend on your looks and title to gain that reputation you have."

Tal leaned on the bar as he picked up his mug and sipped from it. "So you admit I'm handsome."

"I usually tell the truth. Your looks are more than passable."

"More than passable," he repeated with a chuckle.

"Hmmm, I didn't know vanity was amongst your many faults. Though it would explain the women and the fact you're dressed as you are in a place such as this."

He looked down at his simple black shirt and pants, his thick dark blue cloak free of any embellishments. "What's wrong with how I'm dressed?"

"Nothing if you're lounging around your brother's court, but the material and cut are a bit too fine for a seedy tavern. You might as well have announced your presence when you walked in the door." He pulled his cloak tighter to him, making her smile. "Do you see that man by the door, the one wearing an eyepatch and smoking a pipe? He's been staring at you for a while now, probably thinking of the best way to rob you."

"He'll have a hard time of it with my guards."

"You think he doesn't notice the four Fae guards with their pretty little heads covered?" She glanced towards Dyfan. "At least that one knows how to keep his weapons hidden. The others are flashing their swords and knives like they're trying to sell them."

Tal shrugged and said, "Why does it matter if they know who we are? They wouldn't dare try something. They know what Fae are capable of."

"Oh, but the idea that Fae are untouchable is waning in the human realms. Your Sun King is seen as weak, and your Dark King is believed to be beyond caring. He hasn't even been able to sire an heir. What would happen to your uncle's court if someone managed to do away with him? Would you take it over?"

"Who are you?" he asked.

She turned to him, her hands adjusting her hood, making her sleeve slip down, showing her arm on which a moon vine tattoo snaked up a raised scar that ran from her wrist to her elbow. She moved her hood back far enough for him to see her eyes as she gave him a twisted grin. "A pleasure to see you again, Your Highness."

"Lady Eriana," he gasped.

She tilted her head and opened her mouth to speak when the door to the tavern burst open just as the candles and fires went out. Women screamed, and men shouted.

"Shit," said Eriana as she grabbed Tal's arm. She pulled him behind her as she moved forward.

"What the hell are you doing?" he yelled at her through the chaos.

"Trying to keep you alive. Be quiet." He felt her turn. "We need to get to the back exit. Send three towards the door."

"Send three what?" asked Tal. "Who are you talking to?"

"Don't worry about it," she said harshly. "Move."

The room was so dark. It was as if every light in the town had gone out—as if the stars and moon had disappeared. Her grip on his arm was tight, pulling him along. He dragged his feet and worked to free his arm.

"Where are we going? And what are you doing here? We thought you were taken by the Underlings. Your uncle sent me to find you."

"No time now. Come on." She pulled at him again.

"Your Highness! Tal!" Dyfan called over the crowd somewhere from his right.

"I'm here," said Tal. He could almost see Dyfan coming towards him until a flash of light made him turn towards the room. More people screamed, some in fear and some in pain. It caused the room to erupt in full-out panic. Tables were turned over, and chairs scraped the ground. Eriana let go of him, and he looked down to see her pull a dagger out of a sheath on her thigh and a thin sword from her back under her cloak.

Another flash of light and more screams. "What is it? Is it the Underlings?"

"Keep moving towards the right. There is a hallway that leads to a door." Eriana glanced at him. "Are you armed?"

"I am, but I can just leave anytime I want."

"Are you so sure?" She pushed him to the right. "Can you not feel the wards set up? That first flash of light made it practically impossible to use magic."

Tal held out his hand, trying to spark a light or some fire. He called upon his magic, but nothing happened. His hand felt strangely cold. "How?" If the Underlings were humans, how could they stop Fae magic?

"No time, just keep moving, and if you have a weapon, pull it out."

He moved his cloak aside and took out his sword, wishing he had practiced with it within the past year, but he had let his usual sparring go for a while, believing he didn't need it. His magic always worked to get him out of any trouble. A little light shone in the windows from the moon, and a few lanterns lit outside. It revealed a room in chaos as many still tried to find an exit. The sound of windows crashing came next, and Tal saw several people lying on the floor, a few obviously dead, positioned awkwardly in pools of blood.

They kept moving through the crowd, Eriana pushing people out of the way until Tal saw a glint of silver in what little light there was. He didn't realize what it was until Eriana blocked the sword inches from his face. She pushed the attacker back and lunged toward him. In two moves, she disarmed the man and stabbed him in the chest. She turned to meet another sword, kicking this attacker away.

Tal couldn't get his bearings. He was paralyzed in shock, seeing the carnage and terror around him. He'd been in more than a few fights, but none so bloody and chaotic as this one. Dyfan came to his side as Eriana moved to slash at a man with her dagger and used her sword to block another.

"We have to get out of here," said Dyfan, yelling over the noise.

Tal jerked his head towards Eriana. "She says she's taking me to the back door." Tal looked behind him as Dyfan turned. There was another loud sound and blast of light, followed by masked men running down the hallway.

"Fuck," said Eriana as she came closer to Tal. "How in the name of the goddess did they know?" She glanced at Dyfan. "We'll have to fight our way to the front."

"My guards should be clearing a way now," said Dyfan. "Come on."

He moved in front of them as Eriana again grabbed Tal, pulling him along. He shook his head to clear it, wrenching his arm out of her grasp and meeting a sword slashed at him from his left. He was clumsy and unpracticed but, luckily, faster than the man he dueled. He managed to slash the masked man's arm and kick him away before returning to Eriana's side as they followed Dyfan.

Tal turned to the right to block a blade coming for him, not seeing the shorter man with the dagger to his left. As he pushed away the man he met, he saw the dagger coming toward his stomach. He pulled back, knowing it wouldn't be enough, prepared to feel the sting of pain, but a hand holding its own dagger met the blade first. Eriana hissed as the blade sliced across her hand, but she didn't pull away. She pushed and twisted her hand, burying her dagger in the man's gut. He fell as she pulled back.

She flicked her blade, blood flying from it and the slice in her hand as she cursed under her breath while looking up. Tal stared at the blood flowing from her hand for a moment, almost mesmerized by the red coating her fingers and dripping down to the floor. Everything went hazy for a moment as he continued to stare at her bloody hand. His sword felt too heavy. The room was too dark, the stench of blood too strong.

He stumbled, and Eriana caught him, putting the hand holding her dagger around his chest, her blood falling onto his dark shirt.

"Prince Taliesin!" A female voice called across the room. It sounded muffled as his ears were ringing. He tried to find its source, but his vision was too hazy. Eriana yelled something to someone nearby, but he couldn't understand what she was saying.

Her hand splayed across his chest. The dagger pressed harmlessly against his shirt. He felt her breath in his ear as she leaned forward and whispered, "I'll find you again. Stay close to Dyfan."

He tried to turn to look at her, to tell her to stay, that he had to take her back to her uncle, but the room faded around him. He felt her arm leave him as he sunk to the floor, the darkness covering him.

Blood, there was too much blood. He was screaming. It could not be happening, not like this. Pain raced up his arm into his chest, pulling out his very heart, taking everything he was away from him. He could see nothing but blood, blood that flowed down freely, never-ending. He blinked, looking down at his hands. They were completely red. He searched himself for any wounds, but he knew he would find none. The blood was not his own. What had he done?

He was going to be sick. His stomach clenched at the smell of blood and death around him. "Prince Taliesin, Your Highness?" A faraway voice said his name as someone shook him, making his stomach roil further.

He forced his eyes open, and blinding pain in his head made him close them again. "Your Highness, are you well?" That female voice again, a gentle hand on his shoulder, shaking him.

He shook his head before rolling to his side and pushing up on his hands to vomit. Feet scooted away from him as he retched, again and again, everything within coming up until there was nothing left.

"Tal?" Dyfan's voice was unusually gentle and quiet.

"What happened?" Tal choked out. "Where is she?" He moved to a sitting position, scooting away from the mess he had made on the floor to bump into a dead man, almost making him retch again.

"Where is who?" said the female voice. Tal slowly lifted his head to see Lady Delphina standing over him, dressed in dark pants and a red shirt, her hair braided over her shoulder.

"Lady Eriana was here," said Dyfan, holding out his hand to Tal. Tal took it, and Dyfan hauled him up.

"My cousin? She was here?"

Tal grabbed onto a nearby chair, steadying himself. He nodded. "We were speaking at the bar when everything happened."

"Did she explain herself? Why has she been missing so long and hasn't contacted my father?"

"I didn't get a chance to ask her. It all happened so quickly, and then I was just trying to stay alive." He pushed off the chair. "What happened exactly? Was it the Underlings?"

"My guess would be yes," said Delphina, "but there's practically no one left to ask." She looked to her right and left, her hands held out.

Tal looked around, seeing only dead bodies, a few dressed for battle in armor and leathers, but most looked to be travelers or local villagers. He walked further into the room, looking around until he saw a ripped piece of fabric lying under a man. Tal kneeled and pushed the dead man to make him roll, a bit of blood still flowing from his side. It coated the edge of the fabric before Tal could pick it up.

He looked over it in his hands before standing up and holding up the fabric towards Dyfan and Delphina.

"It was the Underlings," said Delphina as she moved closer. "They were here. They did all this?"

"It would seem so," said Tal.

"Why was my cousin here?" Delphina swallowed, her eyes shifting away. "She wasn't with them, was she?"

"No. I don't think so," said Tal. "She didn't try to harm me. She was trying to get me to safety. She saved my life at least twice."

"Then why did she run?" asked Delphina.

"I don't know. I passed out for some reason," said Tal. He looked at Dyfan. "Do you know?"

Dyfan shook his head. "I was too busy trying to keep anyone away from you. When I turned around, you were on the ground, and the lady was gone."

"But how did she leave? There was a ward put up, and the doors were blocked," said Tal.

Delphina walked around the middle of the room as though searching. "My guess would be whoever cast the ward was killed, though I don't see anyone who could do such a thing in the first place. Maybe they were just injured and left?"

"But if the Underlings are humans, who would have enough power to cast such a ward?" asked Tal. "It doesn't make any sense."

"There are humans that can use magic," said Dyfan.

"But at this level?" asked Tal, rubbing his head.

"Who knows?" said Delphina. "The question I want answered is what in the name of the goddess is my cousin up to? If the Underlings didn't take her, why hasn't she come home or at least sent word to my uncle?"

"I don't know," said Tal, his head aching. "Maybe she just got away from them, or maybe they're chasing her."

"Maybe," said Dyfan. "It won't do any good to stand around here and try to figure it out. My guards went to an inn across town to get us some rooms. We'd planned to take you there if you didn't wake up. You can come clean up and rest, and we can try to figure this out later."

Tal took a deep breath, the smell of blood and death making his head spin. "Fine." He started to walk away but stopped by Lady Delphina. "But why are you here?"

She gave him a small grin. "I felt bad about you coming out looking for my wayward cousin by yourself. My father said you would probably come here first, so I came in search of you. I didn't expect to walk into such a mess."

"Does your father know you came?" asked Tal.

She shrugged. "He's figured it out by now. I left him a note, saying I could not let the burden of my cousin's safety fall just on you. He'll let me be. He knows better than to try to stop me when I set my mind to something."

Tal wanted to tell her to go home, that she had no business following him, but his exhaustion was too much. His stomach was still unsettled, and all he wanted was to lie down and not think about what happened, about the blood that still sat in the back of his vision.

He waved her away. "Come along then. We can figure this out tomorrow." He turned to walk out the door when he saw someone come out from the back. It was Mrs. Wesson, looking beaten and hopeless. "Dyfan, go tell Mrs. Wesson we will send whatever she needs to fix what is broken. I'll write my brother's steward tomorrow to get the gold sent here."

Dyfan's eyes widened slightly before he grinned. "Very good, Your Highness. I'll see she's told."

"Oh, and Berg is supposed to meet us with someone," said Tal as he rubbed his head.

"I'll find him if he's around. Go get some rest," said Dyfan.

Tal put his hand on Dyfan's shoulder for a moment, squeezing it before letting it go. All he wanted was somewhere to lie down, hoping that no nightmares would come.

Chapter 12

Aven

THE POND WAS AS still as the cold, early morning air. No breeze blew that day, for which Aven was thankful. It was cold enough without the wind chilling him. He adjusted his thick cloak, looking in the trees to see if he could catch a glimpse of her. Perhaps it was still too early, but it had been nearly three weeks, and he was growing anxious for Silvie. He wasn't sure what he would do if she didn't turn up soon. It's not like he could go out and search for her. Where would he start? He didn't know much about her travels except that they were extensive.

He was about to mount his horse and leave when he heard a rustling in the bushes. A few seconds passed, and she walked from the edge of the forest, her light red hair falling down the shoulders of her gray dress.

"Silvie," he happily said as he walked towards her.

She smiled at him, but it was strained. Her eyes looked tired and sad, and she was even paler than usual.

"Good morning, Aven." She yawned before taking his hand as they met.

"Are you alright, Silvie?" He pulled her close, examining her for any signs of injury or sickness.

"I'm fine, just a little tired. I traveled far this time and haven't had much time for sleep."

"Where did you go?"

"Oh, here and there. Spent some time with a good friend and then went looking for an old acquaintance."

"Did you find them?"

She sighed. "No."

He waited for her to go on, but when she didn't, he asked her another question. "Did you run into any trouble out in the land?"

She shrugged. "There's always something that comes up, but nothing too bad. I'm here in one piece, as you can see."

He squeezed her hand. "Perhaps you ought to rethink going back out. I know you aren't interested in being a healer, but I have some friends who would probably let you stay with them. I don't think they would mind your magic as long as you didn't cause any trouble. I think you'd really like them, Silvie."

"I appreciated your concern, Aven, but there's no need. I'm more than capable of taking care of myself."

"But Silvie, things in the land are getting worse. There's a group causing havoc wherever they go."

"I know who you are speaking of, and believe me, they pose no threat to me."

"Silvie...."

"Aven, I'm fine. Now, enough about this. Have you brought me anything?" She smiled, looking towards his pockets and his cloak.

He chuckled. "I do have something for you, but I'm not sure how much you'll like it. I couldn't find a book I thought you'd enjoy, but one of the servants was cleaning out an upstairs room and came across some old family jewelry." He pulled a bracelet much like the one he had given Cara out of his pocket. "They found a couple of these, and no one seems to want them. I thought you might like it."

She gasped and held out a finger to brush the bracelet. "Aven, this is from your family?" Her eyes were wide with wonder as she touched the bracelet more firmly.

"Yes, but no one has worn them in generations. I'm not even sure how valuable it is. Perhaps if the gold was melted down, it might get a bit. The eyes are rubies, but see how small they are? They were all going to be given to the temple to see if they had any use for them, but I took a few to keep."

She looked at him and pulled her hand away. "I can't. This is too precious."

He gently took her hand and pressed the bracelet into it. "Silvie, I want to give you this. It's not as grand as you think. They have amusing lore attached to them, but they aren't that valuable. Please take it."

Her fingers slowly wrapped around the bracelet. She said, sounding breathless, "What's the lore?"

He laughed. "My family is rumored to have once had dragons. It is said whoever wore these bracelets could control the creatures." He let his hand drop as she held the bracelet in both hands.

She continued moving the bracelet around her hands, her fingers seeming to take in every detail. "It's been in your family that long?"

"Who knows how long? You know how rumors and stories grow, but it's been at least over two centuries." Aven shuffled closer to her. "Try it on. See if it fits."

She stopped fidgeting with the bracelet and held it in one hand before slowly sliding it over her hand onto her wrist. She took a sharp breath and pushed it up her arm before letting it go.

"Looks like it was made for you."

She raised her head, and he took a step back. Her eyes were wet with tears, and her lips trembled. A moment later, she launched forward and threw her arms around him. He stumbled back before putting his arms around her slim body.

"Thank you," she finally said after a few moments. It was a bit longer before she let him go.

"It's nothing, really, Silvie. I'm glad you're happy, but don't think you owe me anything. I actually gave someone else one much like it the other day."

"Who?" She asked without anger or accusation, only curiosity, as she positioned the bracelet on her arm.

"A young friend of mine. It was her sixteenth birthday. She's a fierce, inquisitive creature. I think you'd like her."

Silvie smiled. "I hope to meet her one day, then." She let go of her bracelet and put her arm down. "Thank you, Aven. You might not think it's much, but it means more than you can know to me."

He grinned. "You're welcome, and you could meet her if you came back with me. She's a part of the family that I think would give you shelter."

"I don't need shelter. I'm fine as I am. I said there would be no more about this," she said a tad harshly before taking a breath. "I'm sorry. I know you mean well, but Aven, I could never put people you care about in a position that could cause them trouble. Harboring me would come to the notice of someone, and it wouldn't go well, not with the way the world is now."

"But you are good, Silvie. I'm sure it would be accepted once it was known that you don't use your magic for evil use."

She took a step back and crossed her arms. "How do you know I'm good, Aven?"

"I can tell. You have shown me how to do magic all these years, asking for very little in return."

"What makes you think I don't have some motive for doing so? Aren't you worried I could be planning something to do with you?"

"It's been over a decade, and you've done nothing yet."

"You haven't come even close to your full potential, and I'm a patient creature," said Silvie, turning away from him.

"Fine, you say I should trust you, so do you have something awful in mind for me?"

She shook her head and looked at the water. "I could never stand to see you come to harm."

He moved to her side. "Then, that's enough for me."

She looked at him out of the corner of her eye. "You didn't ask if I had a motive for helping you."

"I didn't need to. I assume you have one. I'm not simple enough to think you accidentally came across me and decided to help me. Whatever your reasons are, I trust they're good ones."

She dropped her arms and sighed. "I hope they are, Aven. I hope everything I've done and am going to do has some good reason behind them. If not, I'll have a lot to answer for when I meet the gods someday."

"That's the hope of everyone, isn't it? That we aren't just deluding ourselves into thinking we are good people, but that we are actively trying to make our kingdoms and land a better place?"

She took his hand and squeezed it. "You call me good, Aven, but it's you who is truly good and wise. Whatever happens in the future, whatever injustice you are forced to see or even participate in unwillingly, don't lose who you are now. You will need it when you're king."

"I'll have to change a little. Father reminds me daily I need to mature. My sister has also been insistent lately. I'm unsure what to make of her sudden interest in me."

"She's your sister. Perhaps she only means to help guide you. You mentioned your mother isn't the best at giving advice," said Silvie.

"My mother is everything good and loving, but one would not call her wise." Aven let go of Silvie's hand and moved to the edge of the water. "Kyra is certainly intelligent but also cunning and manipulative."

"Those qualities are usually seen in a bad light, but they're not always nasty. Many great people throughout the history of our lands have had both of those traits and used them to make people come together."

Silvie lifted her hand, and water rose in a stream from the pond. "The Fae kingdoms were for centuries divided, almost always in some sort of conflict if not all-out war."

She raised another hand, and the clouds parted, a stream of sunshine coming down close to the stream of water. "The Dark King saw an opportunity when the Sun King's wife died. It was said while the golden queen was beautiful, she was also cold. The Dark King's sister was young, lovely, and kind. A strange creature to dwell in the shadowlands, to be sure, but beautiful flowers can bloom even in darkness."

Aven nodded. "My mother likes the moon vines that grow in her garden. Sometimes, my father takes her out after dinner to see them."

"So the Dark King wrote the Sun King asking for an audience to discuss a possible way to end their centuries of disagreements. The Sun King agreed to hear him out. The Dark King came not with his wife but his sister, claiming the Dark Queen was ill. Once in the Golden Palace, he claimed not to feel well, leaving his lovely, captivating sister to entertain the king. By the end of the visit, the Sun King was in love with the young woman and pledged his heart to her, asking for her unbreakable vow. She gave it to him immediately. They were completely bonded."

Silvie waved her hands, and the water moved into the sunlight, causing a rainbow to appear where they met. "So, the courts were united in a way that's hard to untie, especially after the new queen delivered a boy and girl to the Sun King."

"And she died not too long after that," said Aven.

"And yet the understanding remains. The bonds stay tied between the courts, even as the Sun King has changed. The prince and princess share the blood of dark and light for the first time in maybe forever."

Silvie put her hands down. "And all has been peaceful with the Fae since then, which also benefits the human realm. All because the Dark King saw an opportunity and took it. He was cunning and a bit manipulative, but it was for a good reason. He even secured his sister's happiness as she fell in love with her new husband."

"Or so they say."

"You don't believe the dark princess loved her king of light?" Silvie turned to look at him.

"It makes the story prettier, but we don't know if it's true. Perhaps she hated her new life in a strange court, or maybe she was ambivalent."

"They were completely bonded, which is not taken lightly by the Fae. There are those who live as husband and wife for centuries who don't take the unbreakable vow."

"Perhaps the young princess demanded it, knowing it would tie the Sun King to her in a way he could never take back," said Aven.

"I like to think it's true that the young Golden Queen was happy, even if it was for a short time. I like to think the prince and princess born of both courts were not a product of just a clever king but of love found between two very unlikely people."

They were quiet for a moment as two birds flew down and skimmed the water before Aven quietly laughed. "You're a romantic, Silvie. I would never have thought it."

"You sound like it's a bad thing," she said defensively. "With so much evil in the world, is it wrong to hope love is powerful enough to overcome anything?"

"No, of course. I just didn't expect it from you."

"I try to hold on to some hope for this word, though I will admit my views on love change daily. Perhaps if we had this discussion tomorrow, my thoughts would be different," she tried to say playfully, but it came off as sad to Aven.

"Have you changed much over the years of your life, Silvie?"

She took a moment to answer, watching the clouds move to overtake the sun once again. "In some ways, I hardly recognize myself from who I once was. In others, I'm the same fool I've always been."

"I don't know who you were ten years ago, but I can honestly say I am honored to know you and call you my friend. I'm not sure how I would have survived these past years without you."

"You would have been fine, Aven. You are the type to thrive no matter your situation, but I'm grateful I get to be a part of your life, even a small one." She turned and wiped her eyes. "Enough of this. We have wasted too much of the morning. Let's get on with your lesson, so you can return to your father."

Aven nodded and raised his hands, hoping his performance wasn't too poor after weeks of no training.

Chapter 13

Tal

Tal's head still hurt as they walked outside the village, the late morning sun barely peeking out from some clouds. He had fallen asleep as soon as his head hit the pillow, a fuzzy memory of Lady Delphina wiping his face and hands with a cloth. While he was sure his sleep was deep, it was not restful. His dreams were full of blood and a woman's scream mixed with his own. A deep pain in his chest seared through him as his hands scratched at his chest to tear it open and find what was plaguing him. Instead, the pain faded, but in its wake, there was nothing left inside of him. His chest felt empty, his once beating heart either still or absent.

He could scarcely open his eyes when he awoke to weak rays of light coming through his grimy window. It was as if they wouldn't cooperate with his will, wanting to protect him from facing another day. He forced himself awake, calling for some water and something to eat, hoping that going through the motions of getting ready for his day would wake him up.

It had worked in that he could walk downstairs to meet the others and show he was strong enough to leave, but his chest still faintly ached. His head pounded as though he had been beaten or perhaps in such great thought that his brain had shut down. They met the guards and left town, heading towards the edge of the forest.

He talked with Dyfan and Delphina about the night before, trying to make sense of what happened, but Tal could barely comprehend two words. He was able to understand

Dyfan when he told Tal that the young man they were to meet with was dead, though Berg had survived.

In the end, it was decided there was nothing to do but continue to look for Eriana, though Delphina thought it was foolish.

"We should just go home and leave my reckless cousin to her mess," said Delphina as they entered the trees of the forest. "Once we tell my father what she's up to, he will understand."

"I doubt it," mumbled Dyfan.

Tal glanced at him before saying, "My brother commanded I find her and bring her back to our court. There is no choice but to keep looking."

"But she's not being held by the Underlings or anyone else. Our king and my father thought she was in danger."

"She probably is in danger," said Dyfan as he unsheathed a dagger and looked over the blade. "If anything, last night proves it."

"What do you mean?" asked Tal.

"That attack on the tavern. Do you assume it had to do with you?" asked Dyfan.

"I haven't really thought of the reason."

"I doubt it was random. They didn't try to steal anything, and no one was taken. I checked after you went to sleep. It could be you they were looking for, but you just decided yesterday to go to that tavern and haven't been there in a while. Is that correct?"

"It's been at least a year," said Tal.

"And Lady Eriana has been traveling for months in the human lands. It would make more sense if someone were tracking her."

"Why would someone follow my cousin?" asked Delphina.

"I don't know," said Dyfan. "When we find her, we can ask."

"Where should we even look?" asked Delphina.

"Your father said she likes to visit a friend in the Gethian forest. After last night, she might be looking for somewhere to lay low for a while," said Tal.

Delphina huffed. "The Gethian forest is on the border of Uchel and Lledria. All the human kingdoms are practically unbearable, but those two are the worst."

"How so?" asked Dyfan as he put his dagger back in its sheath.

"Uchel humans think too much of themselves, always believing they should have more. They've built these horrid huge homes that are all starting to look alike, and I hear they have tried the oddest things like having warm water throughout the home or different ways to heat their house than wood because they hate the smoke."

Tal rubbed his temples. "That hardly sounds damning, my lady. Why shouldn't they want things to be better and easier?"

"Because they're starting to see themselves above everyone, including our people, Your Highness. These conveniences may seem harmless, but what about the weapons they're trying to create? Ones made out of iron, and swords tainted with rowan berries, even arrows with hollow tips that can contain a lethal dose for a Fae."

"You've seen these weapons?" asked Tal.

"Of course not. These are only rumors," said Delphina. "Things told to the king during his reports."

"And you heard them how?" Dyfan adjusted his sword and looked at Delphina.

"When you spend as much time in and around the palace as me, you hear lots of things."

Dyfan rolled his eyes before turning away. "Rumors and speculation then."

"I've heard enough to know the Uchel people are dangerous and unpleasant." She crossed her arms.

"And your complaints against Iledrians?" asked Tal. "They are the humans most like us. It's said they even have some Fae blood in their veins."

"Fae blood tainted with human," she said in disgust.

"Just like your cousin, then," said Dyfan.

She stared at him before shaking her head. "They are strange people, and their king is almost a recluse. He never leaves his borders, usually sending his daughter for official visits. No one outside of Illedria has even seen his heir. Perhaps the boy is deformed or stupid."

"Iledrians and those from Uchel are just like anyone else, my lady. There are very worthy people amongst them and those not worth knowing," said Tal.

"I'll take your word for it, I suppose. I rarely deal with humans. I've yet to find one worth more than a little of my time."

"A shame," said Tal as he stretched. "I've found plenty more than worthy."

She half grinned and moved closer to him. "Perhaps you spent too much time in the human realm and forgotten what the superior company of your own kind is like."

If he had been in a better mood, he might have continued the flirtation, but instead, he only half chuckled. "We better travel to Uchel. There's a small village at the forest edge, and maybe we can find some hospitality there."

"A small village?" Dyfan looked at his guards. "I suppose that means we need to be in glamour."

Tal nodded as Delphina loudly sighed. "Must we?"

"You don't have to do anything but go home," said Tal. "There's no need for you to travel with us."

"I told you I would help you find my cousin," said Delphina. "If you insist on continuing to track the wretched woman, then I'll go as well."

"Your father would probably prefer you stay home," said Dyfan. "I'm sure he's anxious for you to be safe with him while his niece is in danger."

Delphina's lip curled up as she looked at Dyfan. "My father stopped caring about what I did years ago. He'll probably barely even notice I'm gone. I'm going with you, and there's no arguing me out of it."

Dyfan looked at Tal, the annoyance on his face clear. Tal shook his head with a grin. "Fine, my lady. I guess there's no harm in you coming with us to Uchel, though you'll have to agree to go in glamour."

"If I must, then fine," said Delphina as she flipped her braid off her shoulder.

"Come now, my lady," said Tal with a laugh. "You aren't so vain to think your beauty would be dimmed too much by appearing human."

Delphina rolled her shoulders. "I hate how it feels like I'm not me. The last time I did it, I nearly screamed when I accidentally looked in a mirror."

"I'll remind you periodically how human you look if that helps," said Tal as he flexed his fingers, preparing to perform the necessary magic on himself and the guards.

"And how will you do that, Your Highness?" she asked aside with a smirk. "Will you treat me as you usually do attractive human women?"

He couldn't help but smile at her boldness before concentrating and glamouring the guards so they looked as human as they could. He didn't even bother using his light magic to try. He knew it wouldn't respond, but the magic he inherited from his mother did the trick. A moment later, he did the same to himself, taking a moment to adjust to his slightly shortened height and heavy-feeling limbs. Looking at his hands, he had to agree with Lady Delphina. It felt odd to be as he was like a shadow of himself in someone else's body. He was used to it, though, using it often to travel amongst the humans.

Dyfan was able to glamour himself, putting his hood down to show a handsome but human face, his ears no longer elongated. Tal looked at Delphina. She was definitely different, her hair not quite as golden, her green eyes almost hazel, and her skin no longer glowing against the overcast forest. Still, she was beautiful. Probably the most beautiful human any would ever see. He took in her body, looking even curvier than before.

"Do I pass your inspection, Your Highness?" she asked as she turned around. "Is there something that displeases you in my alterations?"

"You'll do," said Tal as he moved past her, his shoulder hitting hers, giving her a gentle shove. She stumbled before catching herself on a tree. "You have about as much grace as a newborn deer, it seems. I suppose that's how I'll remind you of your temporary body."

Dyfan chuckled as Tal turned to them. "Come close so we can get this over with." They gathered around him as a dark mist pooled out of his hands, covering the group. A moment later, they were in a new forest, this one darker than the first, the clouds overhead thick, gray, and heavy with rain.

Delphina shook her head and pulled her cloak close. "Fucking light of our god, it's colder than the Dark King's heart out here."

"Such language," said Tal. "And a slight to my beloved uncle. Has your human glamour extended to your manners, my lady?"

"Oh, don't act so offended. As if you don't spend most of your shitty days and nights around rough humans, probably saying much worse, or that you have any love in your heart for your uncle." She took some black gloves out of a pocket of her cloak and pulled them on.

"You told me I'd forgotten how much more preferable women from my realm were, but here you are cussing like a Thirian milkmaid."

She gave him a smug smile. "I was referring to other attributes of Fae women. The tales of us trapping men with our beauty and making them die in pleasure weren't just made up." She moved past him towards a town in the distance, giving him a shove this time. He stumbled slightly against Dyfan. "And yet there are no stories of human women dying from the love of a Fae male. Quite interesting, isn't it?"

Tal smiled at Dyfan, who huffed, saying under his breath, "Stay focused, Tal."

"I'm able to focus on more than one thing, Dyfan. A little amusement on this journey may make it more bearable."

"I'm not sure how trustworthy she is," said Dyfan. "We don't know where her loyalties lie."

"And where do you think mine do, Dyfan? Whatever her motives, I don't care as long as we find Lady Eriana and return her home," said Tal.

"She's still Lord Elgan's daughter no matter how human she looks at the moment. You should remember it before you find yourself trapped."

Tal kept his eyes on Lady Delphina before shrugging. "I suppose I have to settle down at some point. Might as well be with an interesting, beautiful woman."

"Tal..."

"I'm only joking, Dyfan. I know what I'm about." They started walking, following Delphina. "Why do you care anyway? Wouldn't you be happy if I married someone like Lady Delphina and settled in the Golden Court? It seems to be what you and everyone else want."

"Does it matter to you what anyone wants besides yourself?"

"You're angry with me."

"I have no right to be angry with you." Dyfan glanced behind you. "You're a prince, and I'm nothing but your brother's guard, a servant."

"You're more than that, and you know it. I would sooner call you my brother than Idris."

Dyfan stopped, the guards keeping their distance. "And yet you disappeared for years without even telling me. I've heard no words from you, only knowing you were alive by some idle chat I picked up at court."

"I...." Tal tried to think of the excuses he had for leaving the Golden Court—why he had left his friend, but whatever they were had slipped his mind. "I had to get away after father died. I didn't feel right being there anymore."

A light breeze shook some leaves off a nearby tree, Delphina getting further away. Tal started to follow her when he stopped at Dyfan's words. "I would have gone with you. Wherever you wanted to go for whatever reason, I would have stayed by your side and helped you somehow. All you had to do was ask."

"I couldn't do that to you, taint you with what I became. I'm not sure how, Dyfan, but I know I'm not who I was before. The things you've probably heard about me are mostly true."

"Whatever you've done, it's never too late to change. This might be the opportunity you're looking for to get back on track."

"If only I knew what I was looking for," said Tal.

"Are you coming?" called Delphina as she looked back at them.

"Of course, my lady," said Tal, walking quickly to catch up with her.

By the time they reached the village, Dyfan and the guards were just behind them. Tal looked around before turning to Dyfan and pointing. "There's a small stable over there. See if you can find us a few suitable mounts to borrow. It will be easier to get around the forest on horseback than walking. Two will suffice."

"Two, but there are six of us, Your Highness," said Dyfan.

"Your guards will wait here. I'll get a room or two for them and arrange for any food or drink. The Gethian forest is no place for young, inexperienced Fae."

"They are more than capable."

"My order is final, Dyfan." Tal looked at Lady Delphina. "You should stay behind as well, or even go back to your father and let him know what's happening. I'm sure he doesn't want you in the forest, not with its reputation."

"I'm not going home until we find Eriana. The forest or the rumors about it don't scare me. Even if you try to leave me behind, I'll follow you."

Tal rolled his shoulders, wishing his annoyance would roll away so easily. "Fine. Dyfan, see if you can get three horses unless you wish the lady to ride with you. Take your guards with you. I'll go see about rooms."

Dyfan hesitated before jerking his head at his guards towards the stables. They left, though Dyfan glanced behind him a few times.

"I suppose you're coming with me, my lady," said Tal. "Even if I don't wish it."

She grinned. "But you don't wish me away, not really. You can't act as though you don't want my company. Admit it gives you some amusement."

They started walking towards the inn located in the middle of the other end of the village. "I don't want amusement on this trip. I want it to be over, to fulfill my brother's command."

"I can help you do it and provide you with entertainment," she said with a laugh. "Come, you would grow bored and frustrated with only straight-faced and grumpy Dyfan to keep you company. You're more likely to complete your mission if you enjoy yourself." She moved closer to him, her hand on his arm. "You must admit finishing is always easier with an enjoyable partner."

He kept his face straight at her innuendo, though he had to admit a bit of desire built in his stomach at her smooth, lovely voice brushing his ear. "Do you have trouble keeping focus, my lady? Are you not always able to finish what you start?"

She smirked, her hand moving up his arm and then down. "I'm usually adept at choosing a task and partner that I know will give me success. I don't think I'll be disappointed on this adventure either."

They entered the inn, Tal bending down to go under the crooked doorway to find the first floor dark and warm. A few people sat huddled at tables over mugs of mead or tea. Though it was small, with only a few candles lit, and most of the light came from the fireplace, it looked clean. An older woman and a fresh-faced young woman stood behind the bar.

Tal took down his hood as he walked towards them, a charming smile on his lips. "Good day, ladies. My friends and I are traveling, hoping to arrive home deeper in Uchel before the winter comes, but I have business nearby. Are there a few rooms we could have for two or three nights?"

The young woman pulled some of her hair behind her ear and blushed, keeping her eyes down. The older woman wiped her hands on her apron and asked, "What business do you have nearby?"

"Our own," said Delphina, her lips twisted in a disgusted frown. "We have plenty of money to pay for any open rooms."

"We might not have any open," said the old woman, her lips curling as she looked at Delphina.

"You don't look busy," said Delphina.

"They're our rooms, and we let them out to who we like. You might want to move on to another village further into the kingdom."

"Now, now, please excuse my friend," said Tal, moving in front of Delphina. "Delphie is exhausted from our journey and not used to much company. Indeed, we keep her in the house usually because she's so unpleasant." Delphina gave a breath of annoyance, but Tal ignored her. "The rest of my party are very well-behaved men who will treat your place with nothing but respect. If you could give us three or four rooms, I promise to keep an eye on the lady to see she doesn't cause any mischief."

Tal smiled back at Delphina as he pulled out his last coin pouch and took out five coins. The old woman looked down at them before eyeing Tal. "I don't need any trouble. There's enough of it going around."

"I've heard. We'd like to avoid it as well," said Tal, placing the coins on the bar.

"I have four rooms. One is rather unpleasant, though. There's no window, and the bed is narrow and hard."

"A good one for my friend here, don't you think?" said Tal with a laugh.

The young woman giggled before clapping a hand to her mouth as the old woman gave her a stern look. "You'll be wanting food and drink and some baths at some point, I suppose?"

Tal nodded. "I can give you more money if that's not enough, though I would admit that even a charming establishment such as this can't warrant too much more."

"It's enough," said the old woman. She looked Tal up and down again. "Might not be as good as you are used to."

"My taste is quite simple."

"Hmph," said the old woman as though she didn't believe it. "I'll go fetch the keys. Melly, stay here and say nothing."

The old woman walked to the back as Melly kept her head down.

"Melly?" asked Tal. "Is that short for something?"

The young woman looked at him, a pretty blush still on her cheeks. "It's short for Melody. My mother thought it was a beautiful name, but my grandmother hates it. Says it's too fine for a girl as simple as me."

"Your mother was right. It's a pretty name and one that suits you," said Tal with a grin. The girl's cheeks became even redder. "What do you do around here for fun, Melody?"

She glanced at the door to the back before whispering, "In the summer, there's a stream not far in the forest where I sometimes go swimming with a few friends. My grandmother says the forest is dangerous, but we don't go too far within the trees."

"And now that it's colder, what do you do?"

"When my grandmother falls asleep, I'll go out to one of the fires they keep burning all night to keep the forest's evil spirits away. We drink, talk, and do other things." Melody turned away again.

Tal's grin grew. "Sounds interesting. Perhaps I'll find my way there before our stay ends."

Melody looked back at him, her eyes wide. "I can show you, but I suppose they aren't hard to find in the dark."

"That's kind of you." He glanced back at Delphina. "I didn't say it before because I didn't want to trouble you, but Delphie here is traveling for her health. We've been to the warm springs of Dewra and to a healer in Illedria, but nothing seems to get rid of the rash she has."

Delphina huffed, a snarl on her full lips.

"She looks fine to me," said Melody.

Tal leaned in towards the young woman and loudly whispered, "It's in a place you can't see. One we aren't supposed to speak about in mixed company. Poor Delphie, taken in by a pretty face, not knowing the hidden horrors."

"Oh!" Melody looked at Delphina with her nose scrunched up. "That's...unfortunate."

"So, we heard about a forest witch that lives somewhere in the Gethian forest. Have you heard of her?"

"A little, but we aren't supposed to talk about what's in the forest. It's said if we do, it summons the creatures that live there, even some banished evil Fae."

"Well, we can't have that," said Tal. "But maybe just a little about where she might live, in what direction."

There was a noise behind the closed door to the back, and Melody said quickly. "I don't know, but you should visit Mrs. Gall, the town's apothecary. She's close to the middle of the village. Some say she gets her remedies deep in the forest."

Tal nodded and pulled out a coin. "Thank you, Melody. Go buy yourself something pretty to wear to the fires the next time you go." He took her hand and put the coin in her palm, closing her fingers over it.

The door opened as Melody took her hand back. The old woman looked at her granddaughter, who put her head down and backed away. "Here are your keys," she said, handing them to Tal. "Straight up the stairs and down to the left."

They left the inn after securing the keys, Delphina smacking him on the arm once they were through the door. "You're awful, telling that girl I have some sort of disease on my... my..."

"Well, maybe if you weren't so unpleasant to where I had to scramble to sweet talk the old woman into giving us some rooms, I wouldn't have had to do it. Gods, Delphie, have you never had to interact with anyone besides brainless handsome lords and your servants?"

"Delphie?" she said, sounding enraged. "Where did you get that from?"

He shrugged. "I can't go around calling you my lady, and Delphina is clearly not a common name."

"But Delphie?"

"It suits you," he said with a grin.

He walked towards the center of town, stopping at what looked like a store. "Why are we going here?" asked Delphina.

"We need some different clothes. These make us stand out too much. I should have seen it earlier."

Delphina tugged at her top. "What's wrong with what I'm wearing? It's much simpler than my usual."

Tal moved closer to her, moving her cloak aside and placing his hand on her side. "This shirt is made with some of the finest cloth in Brigant." He rubbed his hand lightly against her side. "I doubt anyone here has seen anything like it." She shivered a bit, her breath catching. "So, you, Delphie, will need to change into something more practical." He leaned towards her a bit before taking his hand away.

She narrowed her eyes. "Fine, come along then. I'll buy you something that suits you as well, Tali. My treat."

"Tali?" he said with a laugh.

She huffed. "You shortened my name. Why can't I do the same?"

"Well, first, I already have a perfectly fine way to say my name." He reached out and touched the tip of her nose for a second. "And Delphie is adorable, while Tali sounds like some stupid lap dog."

"So you want me to call you Tal, then?" she asked, her face red with anger.

"You have my leave if you need it."

"Perhaps I'll just call you Jack since you enjoy acting like a jackass," she said as she opened the door and walked inside.

Tal laughed and followed her. Delphina chose a plain dark blue top and some slim-fitting black pants. She remarked about how rough they were against her skin but still changed into them in the backroom the man provided. Though she complained about the fit and cut, nothing could ever make her look anything but beautiful, and she knew it. Tal chose a black shirt and pants, much like he was wearing but made of rough, simple fabric. He bought some shirts for Dyfan and his guards.

Newly dressed, they met Dyfan and the guards in town. Dyfan had successfully gotten three horses to use the next day, though he wasn't pleased with their condition. Tal assured him they would do just fine. He sent Dyfan's guards to the inn with a key and their new shirts. He, Dyfan, and Delphina went on to find the apothecary. Dyfan stopped between two buildings and switched his shirt, seeing the wisdom in it.

They found the apothecary in a small building wedged between a temple and what passed for a butcher in the small village. Tal opened the door, a bell ringing as he stepped in, Dyfan and Delphina on his heels. The room was even darker than the inn, the only light being one lantern and a very small fireplace on the left wall.

"Good morning, or is it afternoon now?" asked a wispy voice from the counter at the end.

"Almost afternoon," said Tal. "About lunchtime. I'm glad to see you're still open. You are Mrs. Gall, aren't you?"

"That's what they call me around here, and it's always fortunate to catch me when you can. Time means very little to me. If you are here when I'm available, our meeting must be fated," said the voice.

Tal walked closer, unsure of what to say. He found a small woman standing behind a counter. She had on a simple light brown dress. Her hair was dark and loose down her back. She smiled at Tal, her face oddly beautiful with wide eyes, a mouth almost too large, and her nose crooked as though it had been broken. He wasn't sure of her age. She could have been as close to twenty as she was fifty.

"You came to me for a reason, so tell me," said the woman, her hands resting on her counter.

"We're looking for someone," said Tal.

"Oh, and is it someone in particular or someone who can do something for you?"

"Both, I suppose," said Tal. "We need to find someone who can point us in a particular direction to find someone in particular."

The woman's mouth curved into a smile, her wide eyes lighting up. "Maybe I could be someone then."

"I hope so," said Delphina, coming forward, her eyes soft and worried. "My dear cousin has gone missing, and I'm so worried about her. She's a traveler and enjoys this area, but we haven't heard from her in months. With all that's going on, I'm desperate to find her. She's as close to a sister as I will ever have."

The woman stared at Delphina, her eyes narrowed somewhat. "Your cousin is missing, and you think she's somewhere close by?"

"She has a friend in the forest she likes to visit," said Delphina. "One that perhaps isn't everyone's preferred companion, but dear Eri has always been a little different."

Tal looked at Delphina at her shortening of Lady Eriana's name. It struck him for some reason, and he tried to remember if he had ever heard anyone use it.

The woman chuckled, her hands going to her throat to play with a charm on a gold chain. "I'm guessing your cousin is Fae as well, then."

Tal shook his head to clear his thoughts, glancing down at his hands while Delphina touched her ears. The old woman chuckled again. "Your glamour is well in place. I've just been around longer than most and met enough Fae to know three when I see them. You tricked me for a second, but the faint glow you give off in the dimness tipped me off. Don't worry. Most can't see it, and I won't tell a soul."

"I suppose if anyone in town knows, it won't matter. We didn't want to cause problems," said Tal.

"And you know no one would even speak to you if they knew what you are," said the woman. "Well, you think I might know someone your cousin would visit in the forest." The woman moved to the table to the right. She picked up a pestle and smashed something in a bowl. "A few creatures might interest a Fae woman in the forest. Your cousin is Fae?"

"For the most part," said Delphina.

The woman stopped working and looked up. "Is she part something else? A woodland fairy? A water sprite?" She went back to grinding with the pestle. "I once knew a strange small man who was half-Fae, half-goblin. He had the most interesting skin, handsome too, strangely enough."

"She is half-human," said Tal.

Mrs. Gall ground a few more times before looking at her work. "A half-human, half-Fae? Can't say I've ever met one, though I've heard of it. Very rare, though. I assume her mother was Fae?"

"Why do you assume it?" asked Delphina.

"I believe a human woman would have difficulty carrying a Fae babe with the magic it must possess. I suppose a few from Iledria would be able to handle it, though it would be rough. I've heard even Fae women sometimes struggle with sickness and pain. Labor is sometimes difficult, isn't it?"

Tal closed his eyes, thinking of his mother and how she must have suffered with carrying Fae twins. She never recovered from it. "It can be."

Mrs. Gall nodded. "I've seen my fair share of childbirths gone wrong, yet we still go on with it."

"Not sure there is another alternative," said Dyfan.

"True." Mrs. Gall tipped the substance she ground into a jar.

"You said there might be a few creatures our missing friend might visit, but I believe she is particularly friends with a forest witch," said Tal.

"Ah," said Mrs. Gall. "Well, that narrows it down. There is Margred, of course. She lives deep within the forest, almost in the very center. There's another, but no one knows her name. It is said she can shapeshift and alter your memories, so you never remember what she looks like or even what she said. Some claim to have been healed by her but have no idea how it happened."

"And where does she live in the forest?" asked Tal.

"No one knows. I don't think she even has a home there. They just come across her as they travel through," said Mrs. Gall.

"Then we should start with the first. We have a name and an approximate location. If it's the other, then we might come across her as we look for the first," said Dyfan.

Tal nodded in agreement as Mrs. Gall grinned. "So you're going to visit the forest, are you? I trust you've heard the tales?"

"We know it has a reputation," said Tal. "But I doubt much in there can truly harm us. Probably just human thieves setting upon the unprepared as they travel through."

"There is some of that, yes, but things other than humans and benevolent witches haunt those woods, things that don't even have a form."

"What do you mean?" Tal crossed his arms as Delphina rolled her eyes, obviously not believing the woman.

"The forest is a living thing, old trees, tied together by roots and soil. They have been on this earth longer than even the oldest Fae. They have seen wars, sicknesses, celebrations, murders, and lovers. They know each of us and our natures, and they have no trouble revealing that to you. The wind speaks to you of your deepest thoughts and desires. You can lose your way amongst the roots and covers if you listen too closely and are unprepared for what you might hear."

Delphina smiled slightly. "An old tale, one told of many different places. I'm sure it's nothing but people's imaginations and fear of the dark paths. The old people of Iledria might have started them to keep enemies away."

"I wouldn't be so sure," said Mrs. Gall as she stared at Delphina. "Arrogance and dismissal of old legends will not help you. Even if you don't fully believe them, you should still be prepared when you enter a forest as old as Gethian." She raised an eyebrow. "Especially if you have secrets to hide."

Delphina watched the woman for a moment before turning to Tal. "We've heard all we'll find out from this woman. We should go and prepare to leave at first light, buy some food and supplies, perhaps."

Tal nodded. He reached in his pocket for a coin or two. "Thank you for your information and time, ma'am."

She held a hand up. "You don't need to pay me. I'm in no need of coin. I only ask that you and only you, young prince, come to see me after you return. I want to hear what you saw."

Tal physically started. "You know who I am?"

"I do," said Mrs. Gall.

"How?"

"Does it matter?" She laughed. "You should go. I have things to do. I wish you safe travels."

Tal had many questions he wished to ask the woman, but he got the feeling it would do no good. Dyfan looked at him as though he were troubled, but Tal only turned and walked to the door.

"Heed my warnings, all of you. The forest doesn't care who you are or the reasons for your quest. Be prepared to face your deepest fears, ones you might not even know."

Tal stopped and turned, looking at the woman over Delphina. He nodded before walking out the door.

Chapter 14

Aven

A VEN ADJUSTED THE STRAP on his bag as he walked down the palace stairs. Servants were bustling through the entryway towards the largest parlor, trays of tea, sweets, and other delights in their hands. Aven snatched a sweet roll from one maid as she stopped and gave him a small grin, offering another. He shook his head, and she curtsied and went on her way.

"Where are you going, Brother?" asked Kyra as she stepped out of the parlor, immaculately dressed in a dark blue gown, her curls piled on top of her head.

"Out doing my duty," said Aven. "Father has given me a task, and I mean to get it done."

"Perhaps you might pop into the tea for a moment? There are some lovely young women from very respectable families in attendance. You might see one that catches your eye."

"I don't want to disturb Mother's social event with my attendance. She gets great joy from playing court to all the women. I would interrupt her carefully laid plans," said Aven.

"Surely it won't distress our mother. Her tea will be a great success if her handsome, unmarried son comes into the room to charm the women. She'll be proud to show you off."

"Our mother doesn't do well when things don't go to plan. If you wanted me to attend, you should have told her earlier so she could give the invitation. It will only cause her worry and agitation if I enter the room. Besides, I have work to do. Give whatever ladies you wish my greetings, and if you want me to meet them, host an event yourself."

He thought his sister might stomp her foot as she did as a child. The anger on her face caused her to scrunch up her small nose, her eyes narrowing, making her look like some pinched-faced old woman and not the great beauty she was known as.

"Moonwood Manor is grand, but you know how far out it is? No one would travel there this time of year, especially with the rumors in the land. Why do you think we are residing in the palace at the moment? You think I like being around the ridiculous woman we call our queen? Sometimes, I'm convinced that she cannot be our real mother."

"So you want to take advantage of our mother's social calendar while showing her nothing but disdain and ridicule in front of your friends."

"I want to preserve some respect for our family. Mother is a joke to the realm, and father is hardly engaging."

"Our father is a good and just king. He rules fairly and cares about his people," said Aven harshly. "You have no idea all he does to ensure the kingdom's safety, so you can go on and have your pretty little parties."

"He is not loved, not like kings before him, and neither will you be, Aven, if you don't make better decisions. The company you keep will do you no favors."

"Lord Dall is a high lord of our kingdom and a wise, good man," said Aven.

"I still have reservations about that family, but they're not whom I'm speaking of." She moved closer to him, looking over his shoulder before whispering, "Who is it you go visit on your early morning rides? It must be someone very unacceptable to keep so hidden."

Aven's blood ran cold, and his hands shook slightly as he tried to reveal nothing to his sister. "I don't know what you mean. I take early morning rides to clear my head. I meet with no one."

She laughed lightly, a smirk on her face. "Just be careful, Aven. I'm sure many kings before you have dallied with lower creatures, even our father. Whatever your secrets are, keep them to yourself." She gathered her skirts and turned around back to the parlor. Aven took a moment to compose himself before walking out the door to mount his waiting horse.

By the time he arrived at Mayfield House, some of his anger had dissipated, but his worry about his sister discovering Silvie remained. He couldn't imagine giving up his lessons with her or the friendship they shared. Perhaps they could find a new place to meet, or maybe his sister would let it go if she assumed he was having some sexual liaison. It was better than her knowing the truth.

After giving his horse to a servant, Aven knocked on the door, which Meg answered promptly. She took his cloak with an affectionate greeting.

"The lord and Master Quinn are in the study. You should go right on in," said Meg.

"And Lady Prudence and Cara?"

"At the palace. The queen invited them to tea. I'm surprised you didn't know," said Meg.

"Mother doesn't usually tell me her guest list, but I'm glad she noticed Lady Prudence today. I would've greeted them had I known they were in attendance." His sister hadn't mentioned it.

Aven went on to the study to find Lord Dall behind his desk, a stack of messages by his side. Quinn was at a nearby table, a message in hand and a marked map next to him.

"Aven," said Lord Dall, looking up from his work. "Come have a seat by Quinn. We've got some things to show you."

Aven nodded and sat next to his friend. Quinn put down his letter and marked a spot on his map before grinning at Aven. "Maybe we can get this done today and go hunting tomorrow. Morton spotted a stag in our woods, and I'm dying to see if I can find it."

"Depends on what you show me. If I'm satisfied we've made headway into figuring this out, I don't think taking one day off would hurt."

"As you are well aware, we've received many messages," said Lord Dall. "You've read most of them, I believe."

"Yes, and a good amount gave us nothing," said Aven.

"True," said Quinn. "But in the few that are helpful, we've seen a sort of pattern, at least close to our kingdom. It was actually Cara who pointed it out last night."

Aven smiled. "Of course, it was her. So what did she notice?"

Quinn pointed to the map. "Here is every report we have of the Court of Underlings' doings. The ones marked with an 'x' are classified as attacks—actual violence and some destruction. The 'o's' are more covert operations, people being taken from their beds, things stolen, desks and rooms overturned with nothing gone, but a banner found to let those know who was there."

Aven looked over the map, making a point of checking each 'x' and 'o'. "So what's the pattern?"

"Well, the attacks are more random. Hard to see what's going on there, but the 'o's' have one thing in common," said Quinn. "Each person or thing taken has some connection to magic. Even the few missing objects have a history of magical use."

"The Clounds here at the edge of Uchel lost three young servants. All had a parent from our kingdom and were in the process of being sent here to see if they should be a mage or healer."

"The Thompsons moved to Uchel from here. Their eldest son is missing from his travels. They believe the Underlings took him. He had the opportunity to become a mage but decided against it. They moved to Uchel to get away from those who knew of his magic."

"The temple at Fortney is missing an old bracelet they had locked up," said Lord Dall as he pointed to a place at the north of Uchel. "It was said to have belonged to the goddess of song at one point, and anyone who wore it and sang could make someone do their bidding."

"Of course, you know about Lord Mevins's servant girls and their connection," said Quinn. "It goes on and on."

"But the attacks do not?" asked Aven.

"They are a bit tricker," said Lord Dall. "One is a mine close to the edge of the Gethian Forest. This was an old temple in a small village near Dewra. Nothing was taken, but the building was destroyed. A priestess was severely injured, though she recovered. No one really knows how, but she has made a full recovery in days. She believes it was a gift from her goddess, and she said she saw her while she was suffering."

"So, that leaves us with the non-violent incidents all having a magical tie. What can we do with that?" Aven continued looking over the map.

"They appear to be getting closer and closer to our kingdom with one strike within our borders. I think we need to prepare ourselves," said Quinn. "See about putting men on our borders, alert villages and lords to increase patrols. Tell them what to look for."

"There are some temples close to the forest. Maybe speaking with those priests and priestesses would help," said Lord Dall. "They house old objects connected with the lore of this land and your family, Your Highness. They might have some insight."

"Hmm," said Aven, looking where the lord was pointing.

"You could send someone," offered Quinn. "Surely you have some clever guards who could go and get a statement."

"I'm sure we do, but it will not be the same as myself hearing what they have to say or seeing the objects. I think the best thing to do is go myself."

"It's a two-day journey, Aven, with only a few small villages in between. It could be rough," said Lord Dall.

"I'm young and can handle a few uncomfortable nights. It's time I traveled and saw more of my kingdom. I'm sure my father will agree."

"Then I'll go with you," said Quinn. "I've spent more than a few nights in the old beds of questionable inns. You will need someone with you who knows what to look for. It should be me."

"Quinn, are you sure?"

"He is," said Lord Dall. "He should go with you. I would as well, but these bones are older than they look. More than a day in the saddle, and I would be nothing but an irritating old man complaining about my hips."

"I guess we should postpone that hunt." Quinn sighed.

"Maybe we will find some game on our way. We won't be gone long, a little more than a week. When we get back and rest, we can see about your stag," said Aven.

The door to the study opened, and Lady Prudence peeked in, dressed very finely, looking every bit the high lady she was. "We're back, darling." She dipped her head towards Aven. "Good afternoon, Aven. I didn't mean to interrupt anything."

"You know you could never interrupt anything I'm doing, my love," said Lord Dall. "How was the tea?"

She came into the room as Aven and Quinn stood. "Oh, very grand, and the queen was as kind and gracious as always." Lady Prudence put her hand on Aven's arm and squeezed. "She spends most of her time talking about you. She is so proud of the man you've become, Aven. I agreed with her on all accounts and was happy to sit by her side and let her go on and on about your wonderful attributes."

"Thank you for indulging her, my lady," said Aven.

"You don't need to thank me, Aven. She is a good woman, perhaps not the cleverest, but kindness is worth more than people give it credit."

"And how did Cara do?" asked Quinn. "Is she not with you?"

"She didn't say much coming home. I suppose she didn't really care for the younger ladies. I think your sister tried to cheer her, Aven, but it only made Cara retreat further," said Lady Prudence.

"My sister spoke to her?"

"For some time. I was too engrossed with your mother to hear what she was saying. I'm sure it was just idle chit-chat. Cara didn't look like she was saying much back. I will have to work on her small talk."

"Where is Cara now?" asked Aven. "Did she go to her room?"

Lady Prudence shook her head. "Said she wanted a quick walk, so she left the carriage and went towards the side of the house."

"I'll fetch her," said Aven. "I want to thank her for the work she did in figuring out the pattern. It won't take long."

"Yes, tell her to come inside. The wind is awful today, and I would hate it if she caught a cold."

Aven walked to the front of the house and out the door, not bothering with his cloak. He found Cara just where he thought he would, sitting in the old swing that hung off the largest tree close to the house. She looked older than her years, dressed as she was in a fine pink gown. Her hair was plaited and pinned up, and her cheeks were pink from the wind. She looked almost a woman, her girlish features seeming to transform a little each day. She held her head against one of the thick ropes, and her eyes were closed as Aven approached.

"I saw your horse and knew you were here. I came here to avoid you," said Cara, not opening her eyes.

Aven walked closer to her. "Why do you wish to avoid me? Have I offended you somehow?"

She shook her head against the rope. "I'm afraid my forwardness has made you uncomfortable." Her eyes opened, and Aven saw a tear fall down her cheek. "I never meant to try to trap you, Aven. It's never even crossed my mind."

Aven practically snarled, knowing this was his sister's doing. He would deal with her later, but for now, he wanted to make Cara feel better. He carefully sat down on the large swing with her as she scooted as close to the rope as she could.

"Why do you think you've made me uncomfortable?" She sniffed and shook her head. "Cara, tell me what happened at the palace today."

"I was with the younger ladies and girls in the corner when your sister came up and asked to speak with me. The other young ladies said how exciting it was to be singled out by the princess. I had no idea what she could want with me." Cara wiped a tear off her cheek. "She walked me around the room, talking of fashions and how well certain dresses would look on me. I think she might have insinuated that my dress was out of fashion, but I didn't really listen or care. When we got to the far window away from the others, she asked me about you."

"What did she ask you?"

Cara's cheeks turned even redder as fresh tears leaked out of her eyes. "She … She asked me if I thought you were handsome. I told her the truth."

"And what is the truth, Cara?" he asked gently.

"Don't make me say it, Aven. I was only answering objectively. If she had asked if I thought Lord Henley's son was handsome, I would have said the same thing."

He laughed slightly. "So you said yes."

"Of course I did. Any person with eyes could see that you're handsome. Besides, she's your sister, and you'll be my king someday. Was I supposed to insult your looks inside the palace to your kin?"

Aven carefully took her hand, holding on to it as she tried to take it away. "You've done nothing wrong, Cara."

"She went on and on about how I must dream of marrying you, a handsome prince, and being queen someday. She tried to make me say that my mother was pushing me towards you. She asked so many questions and made me answer. Do you often come to our house? Am I in attendance when you do? Am I allowed to speak or be alone with you?"

Cara's crying increased. "It was mortifying. She made it seem like I had done something awful, tried to flirt with you, and make it so you would be forced to marry me. She said..." Cara stopped and took her hand away, putting it on the rope with the other, her crying continuing.

"What did she say, Cara?"

"I can't say it, Aven. I can't. It's too awful."

"Please, tell me what she said. I promise you she was the one being uncouth and ill-mannered, not you. My mother and father would think the same."

Cara turned towards him but kept her head down. "She asked if I ever tried to...tried to...kiss you...or even touch you. If I had ever let you do things to me. Oh, Aven, don't make me say them."

White hot anger ran through Aven. His sister had gone too far, hurting such a wonderful, kind girl—one who was barely sixteen and probably had never had anywhere close to such thoughts in her head. Cara finally looked up at him, her eyes wide and wet, her face splotchy from crying. Perhaps it wasn't the smartest thing, but he couldn't help it. He took her into his arms, where she cried anew against his chest.

"I'm so sorry. I'm sorry," she said over and over.

"You have nothing to be sorry about, Cara, nothing. I can't believe she would say such horrible things to you. Did you tell your mother any of it?"

"No, I was too ashamed. I began to think perhaps I'd been naughty. I didn't mean to, but I do speak too freely with you. If I ever flirted, it was by accident. I have no idea how."

"Of course, you don't, and you've never offended me or made me worry. You've always been proper. Whatever has gotten into my sister's head is madness."

"You will never come to see us now. Quinn will blame me."

He pulled her back so he could look at her. "I'll come to see you as much as I always do, and I hope you won't avoid me. Your friendship means a lot to me, and because of you, I have hope of figuring out this Court of the Underlings mess. Quinn and your father told me it was you who saw the pattern."

She grinned through her tears. "It was obvious. You or Quinn would have seen it soon."

"But your wonderful mind works quicker than ours. You are invaluable to me and the kingdom. One day, you'll have to be my advisor and emissary. I'll send you out to all the kingdoms and have you charm everyone to learn their secrets."

She laughed. "I think I would like that. I want to travel someday."

"And you shall, but now, you need to come into the house. Your mother is worried about you catching a cold, and I think you need to tell your parents what happened."

"Oh no, Aven, I could never say it. They will be furious."

"They will be, but not with you." He stood up and held out his hand. "Come, let me escort you into the house. I'll help you tell your parents and assure them I will take care of it."

She wiped both eyes and stood up, taking Aven's hand. She smoothed out her skirts with the other and asked, "Do you think my dress is old fashion and ugly?"

"No, it is appropriate and lovely, just like you. Now come, I bet you barely had any sweets or tea at the palace. I'll ask Meg to make us some of those tarts we like."

She finally smiled fully, and Aven escorted her towards the house, knowing that as soon as Cara was settled and in better spirits, he would need to find his sister and let her know how displeased he was.

Chapter 15

Tal

THE ROOM ON THE first floor of the inn was hazy with smoke from the fire and the four or five pipes people were passing around the room. Mead and wine were being poured freely by Melody and another comely barmaid, both laughing as men tried to tug them into their laps.

"Would you like some more, sir?" asked Melody as she stood by Tal.

He pulled his mug closer to her. "Of course, I would. This is divine."

"It's a special brew. We make it ourselves, been in the family for generations."

"Well, it's very good," said Tal as he took a sip. "Looks like the whole village is here tonight."

"The hunters returned yesterday, which means the meat for the stew is fresh. The men come to celebrate, drink, and play cards. The ladies come in to see the men."

"Sounds like a fine way to spend an evening." Tal toasted his glass towards her before taking a long drink. She filled his mug again before offering Dyfan more. He covered his mug with his hand and politely refused.

"Oh, come on, Dyfan," said Tal as she walked away. "A few cups won't hurt you. It would take at least a dozen or more even to make you tipsy."

"Then you should be feeling something soon," said Dyfan as he pulled out his dagger, carefully looking at it and running it against his thumb.

Tal laughed. "Where are the rest of your men?"

"Two are on duty, watching the village, and young Flint is entertaining a pretty young thing in the corner near the fire." Dyfan pointed his dagger in that direction. "I should probably tell him to go to bed soon before he takes it too far."

"No, let him have his fun. The lady doesn't look like she's protesting." A young woman with wild blonde hair sat in Flint's lap, her arm draped over his shoulder. Flint had his hand on her thigh under the long slit of her dress, smiling before taking a drink.

"What about you, Tal? Do you see anything that piques your interest?"

"I need to stay focused, Dyfan. Finding our prey might be harder than I thought."

"Finding her didn't seem to be the issue, though. It's convincing her to go back home with you; that's the challenge." Dyfan laughed. "I suppose that's a new one for you. Ladies usually fall over themselves at the chance for you to take them somewhere."

"Perhaps I'll change my tactic the next time I see the lady. After being reminded of her beauty, seducing her wouldn't be too much of a chore."

"You think you can seduce Lady Eriana?" Dyfan laughed again. "You must not remember her at all."

"Are you well acquainted with her?" Tal drained his mug and raised it towards Melody, asking for another. He had lost count of how many he had. Human libations barely affected him unless he took in an ungodly amount.

"I am," said Dyfan, sheathing his dagger.

"Oh really?" said Tal, resting his head on his hand and grinning at Melody as she refilled his mug. "Just how acquainted?" He took the mug and raised his eyebrows at Dyfan while taking a drink.

Dyfan frowned. "You dishonor her and me by thinking such a thing. Lady Eriana is not the type of woman you use only for pleasure."

"No, I imagine not. She's very disagreeable. I do remember that."

"She is not," said Dyfan. "You could at least show a little appreciation for what she did back in Farwarn. Without her, you might be dead."

"True, and our conversation before that went better than the last time I spoke to her. I believe it was almost two decades ago. She would barely say two words to me and refused to dance with me. She left the whole party instead."

"She had probably watched you flirt and more with every beautiful lady in the room. Didn't want to end up as another nightly conquest by you."

"I don't see why not. I've never had any of them complain." Dyfan started to get up, but Tal put his hand on his arm, realizing he had pushed his friend too far. "No, stay with me a little longer. I won't say another bad word about Lady Eriana. I didn't know you were so fond of the woman."

"She's an old friend, almost as old as you. Whatever you might think about her, she has much to admire. Maybe you'll see it someday."

"Maybe, but I rather hope I'm not in her presence for long. I plan to deliver her to the king so he can make her his queen, then leave them be."

"You're so sure she'll want to marry your brother?" Dyfan asked after taking a drink.

"You aren't?"

"Suppose it's not my place to have an opinion, but I'll sprout wings and fly before she's his wife."

Tal laughed. "You're pretty enough to have some woodland sprite in you. Perhaps you'll show your heritage someday and gain some beautiful gauzy wings."

Dyfan shook his head with a small smile. It faded as he looked towards the stairs. "I think someone's looking for you."

Tal turned to look and saw Delphina searching the room. He waved his hand. "Delphie! Over here." She walked towards them and plopped down in the chair by Tal. "Glad to see you decided to join us."

"My room is practically unlivable. It's smaller than my closet, and the bed smells like feet."

"It's the one in the middle of the others, the safest place for you," said Tal. "We can all keep an eye on you."

"A true gentleman, a prince, would give the lady the better room," she said, blowing a piece of hair out of her eye.

"I'm afraid this prince is used to having his way, so you will have to stay where you are." He took a drink. "Of course, there's another alternative. My bed's big enough for two."

"Oh good," she said. "Then Dyfan can sleep with you, and I can take his room."

"Dyfan is rather fetching, isn't he?" said Tal, raising his hand to call Melody over. "But I imagine his feet are cold. He just strikes me as that kind of fellow."

Dyfan rolled his eyes. "You wouldn't be so lucky as to gain my presence in your bed. Besides, I might have other plans."

"Oh, has someone here caught your eyes?"

Dyfan only grinned before taking a drink as Melody came to their table.

"Ah, Melody, would you fetch a mug of mead for the lady?" said Tal.

Melody nodded and left, coming back quickly with a mug and pitcher. She put both on the table, leaning down to whisper to Delphina. "I hope you were able to take care of your little problem today. Must be awful."

Delphina turned bright red, her eyes cutting to Tal. "Oh, Delphie is quite on the road to recovery. Mrs. Gall said it was the worst she's ever seen, but all should be back to normal with time."

Melody quickly stood up and backed away. "I'm glad to hear it." She pulled another pitcher from the barmaid passing by. "Here, take this one too. That should last you a while."

"Cheers," said Tal. "To Delphie's health." Melody nodded before walking away.

"You are insufferable," said Delphina, smacking Tal on the arm.

"Oh, Delphie, relax and have a drink," said Tal as he poured Delphina a drink and then refilled Dyfan's glass. "What should we toast?"

"A successful mission," said Dyfan, raising his mug.

"Practical and boring. What about you, Delphie? Should we toast to the return of your cousin?"

Delphina picked up her mug. "Why not, or better yet, that Eriana gains some sense? What about you, Talie?"

"Hmmm, how about to finding what we're looking for? While searching has its amusements, it can be tiring after a while."

"I can drink to that as long as what you're searching for is worthwhile," said Dyfan.

"I hope it is," said Tal as he hit his mug against Dyfan's and took a drink. "And you, Delphie. May you get whatever it is you want. Though, I'm sure you're used to it."

She hit his mug with her own. "I do usually have my way." She drank, keeping her eyes on Tal.

"I should go see that young Flint calls it a night. He's had his fun, but he needs to be alert while we're gone." Dyfan finished his drink and left the table.

"Poor Flint, looks like he was getting somewhere," said Tal, watching Dyfan walk up to Flint as the young woman stood up off Flint's lap.

"And will you call it a night soon?" asked Delphina.

"I was thinking about it earlier, but now that I have charming company, I think I'll stay."

"Then I suppose I'll have another drink," said Delphina, picking up the pitcher.

They drank and laughed, watching the people around them. Tal speculated on what some might do for a living as Delphina remarked on those who appeared to be coupling for the night.

"Those two there," she said with a slight slur. "He doesn't know what he's getting into. I bet she's wild."

"Why do you say that?" Tal filled his mug again, losing count of how many pitchers they had gone through. Delphina's eyes were a little glassy, and her smile was lazy. He had recently started to feel a little of the effect of the mead and decided this would be their last pitcher.

"It's her eyes and the way she's gripping his hair as he kisses her neck. I doubt he'll be able to handle her."

"Are you so familiar with ladies in the bedroom that you can tell how they'll perform by sight?"

She shrugged. "Our lives are too long not to try everything available to us. That one there is rather alluring. I might put in the effort if I was in the mood." She took a drink. "Have you not tried the company of men?"

"I'm afraid not. I've thought of it but found I have no interest. It's a pity to have to eliminate half the population when looking for a partner."

"I doubt you've ever suffered from a lack of nighttime entertainment, Talie."

"Oh, you think so? What about me makes you think I can have my pick of women available?"

She snorted into her drink, putting her cup down and wiping her mouth with her hand. "As if you don't already know."

He leaned towards her. "Know what?"

She moved a little closer to him, her hand grazing his. "How devastatingly handsome you are, even in this form."

He grinned as he reached to move a piece of hair out of Delphina's face to put it behind her ear. "And you, my dear Delphie, are utterly tantalizing, especially in this form. I like seeing you so relaxed."

"You know," she said, putting her cup down. "I thought that night you came to the High Summer Festival, you and I might have spent more time together. I was ready to entertain you well into the evening."

"Hmmm," he said, looking over her lovely face. Her eyes were so beautiful, even in their muted state. Her full lips were just begging to be kissed. The drink and heat of the room had added a delicate flush to her cheeks. He reached out again and gently touched one cheek to feel her smooth, soft skin. "And how would you have entertained me?"

She leaned into his touch, moving as close to him as she could, their legs touching. "The forest outside the village is beautiful in summer. Not too far in, there is a small clear pond surrounded by the softest grass you've ever felt. I thought you might remember it and wish to be escorted there to see it again."

She tilted her head close to his, her lips slightly parted. All he would have to do was close the gap of mere inches between them. He could see how it would go. She was not so into her cups that she did not know what she was doing. He would claim her lips in a second, moving her into his lap. Soon, she would suggest going upstairs. He was sure the night would be a wonderful diversion, but then where would they be? Would they become steady lovers?

He could hardly set her aside for the rest of the trip and act as though nothing had happened. When they returned home, what would they be then? Would she expect something from him? It had been years since he had a steady lover, and even that had only lasted less than a few months. No one had been able to tempt him enough to capture his full attention. Every night he spent in a woman's arms had its enjoyment, but when it was over, he was left with the same hollow, empty feeling he had started with. About a decade into his antics, he learned that bedding a different woman almost every night had done nothing to cure his loneliness or sense of being lost. Perhaps things would be different with Delphina. Maybe he just hadn't found the right woman. He almost gave in to his urge to let her try when he thought about the pond in the woods she had described.

He pulled back slightly, able to see the area in his mind. It was summer, and the sky was full of stars. The air was warm and thick with the familiar smell of honeysuckle. A scent he always associated with the Golden Court. One that made him think of home. He felt more alive than he thought possible, his chest warm, his heart beating wildly underneath someone's palm.

"Did you ever visit the pond with me?"

"What?" asked Delphina, her half-closed eyes snapping open.

"That pond you described, did you and I ever visit it?"

"I don't think so," she said slowly. "I'm a bit younger than you. My father kept me close to the house when you lived in the Golden Court."

"I remember it, the pond." He leaned back further. "It's surrounded by thick trees. I think there is a trick to finding it."

She nodded. "There are vines hanging from the trees. You have to know the right words to get them to move. They have to be coaxed lovingly."

Tal closed his eyes, whispering, "The wind blows its sweet caress, leaving one wanting more. The stars, like my lover's eyes, shine like never before. Let me see your secret and dwell, to rest and know I am loved well."

"Yes," she said softly. "Those are the words." He could feel her breath against his face. It was sweet from the mead and her own scent. Her lips brushed his, full and soft.

He groaned, almost lost in his memories, as he leaned forward and pressed his lips firmly against hers. She sighed, her arms going around his neck. Her scent hit him. It was strong and sweet, almost overwhelming. It reminded him of the purple hyacinth his aunt grew close to the Obsidian Palace. It stung his nose as she parted her lips, and he had to push her away to turn his head and sneeze violently.

"Oh," she said, her eyes popping open as Tal sneezed again. "Are you alright?"

He nodded before sneezing again. "I'm sorry. I'm not sure what happened."

She smiled, moving forward and placing her hand on his thigh. "It's no matter. We can start where we left off."

"No." He took her hand off his thigh. "This isn't a good idea."

She leaned back, a pout on her lips. "Why?"

"We have a long, dangerous journey ahead of us, and we need to stay focused."

Her pout turned to a grin. "You think I will be so overcome by you that I can't concentrate the next day?"

"We wouldn't get much sleep, and that can affect anyone."

"Tal, I'm not worried about it. I'm sure you've done more on less sleep. We'll be traveling with Dyfan for a few days. Why not take advantage of a bed and privacy while we can?"

"It's not a good idea, not with who you are and who I am. Delphina, you don't want to get involved with me. I'm not a good man and have no plans to settle any time soon."

"You think I'll take this opportunity to trap you?" She sounded hurt as she crossed her arms.

He shrugged. "I can't discount who you are, who your father is. If we were to entangle ourselves further, he could expect me to make some sort of promise to you."

"So, you wouldn't have to listen to him. You're a prince, and he's just a lord."

"A lord who can cause a lot of trouble for my brother," said Tal.

"And you care? Why?"

"Because said brother has enormous control over my life at the moment." Tal drained his mug before standing up. "Come on, let's get to our rooms."

She turned her head, looking around the room. "Perhaps I'll stay down here a bit longer and try to find some other company."

He almost laughed at her attempt to make him jealous. If she only knew how devoid he was of any proper feelings. "You can do as you like, but I'll switch rooms with you if you come with me now. Mine has a soft bed, a window, and a washroom."

She turned her head to look at him. "We could still share if you wish."

"Not tonight," he said. "Come on, let's both get a good night's sleep. We don't know what we will face in the coming days."

She uncrossed her arms and took a deep breath. "Fine." She put her hands on the table and stood. They walked up the stairs together, saying nothing. When they got to the top, Tal took out the key to his room, offering it to her.

She took it slowly and fished out the one she had. "I suppose you think I'm some silly woman trying to seduce you for power."

He grinned, taking the key from her and then grabbing her hand, pulling her close. "I think you are probably one of the most tempting women I've ever met and one that knows what she wants. While tonight is not our time, my dear Delphie, perhaps another night will be different."

He leaned in and kissed the tip of her nose. "Good night." He turned and went to the small room, falling down on the hard bed, fully clothed. He expected to be kept awake thinking about Delphina, but instead, he fell asleep quickly, dreaming of a starlit pond and the scent of honeysuckle.

Chapter 16

Aven

I T WAS COLD AND misting when Aven and Quinn set off from the palace, two royal guards behind them, dressed as simply as Aven and Quinn to blend in. Aven would have preferred to travel without them, as he wanted no one on the road to know who he was, but his father was insistent, and his mother, in tears, wanted at least a dozen to guard her son. Aven relented, letting the two his father suggested join him and Quinn.

They left the village gates as the sun rose behind them, though it was hidden behind clouds, and headed west towards the Gershian forest to speak with the priests and priestesses of two temples a half-day apart. It would take two days to reach the first, and the ride appeared it would be dirty and wet. The roads were already muddy from earlier rains. With how cold it was, Aven wondered if they would eventually run into some snow or sleet.

Even with the biting wind and mist that turned into a light rain, they made good time, making it into the old, rounded Cianial Mountains a few hours after lunch. The rain let up just as they hit a valley. The grass still had patches of green, and it wasn't as cold as the mountains protected the area from the wind.

"We'll make it over the next knoll and to the Rian Valley before dark. There's a small inn in a village at the base of the next hill," said Quinn.

"So, a few more hours until supper then?" asked Aven.

Quinn slowed his horse and reached into a packet attached to his saddle. He brought out something covered in cloth. "Cara packed these for us, but I think they're mostly for you. Said you would want some to remind you of home on your journey." He handed the wrapped object to Aven.

Aven unwrapped the cloth to find two apple tarts, making him laugh. "Your sister knows me too well." He handed one to Quinn before eating the other in two bites. "How is she? I hope she recovered from that tea at the palace."

"She won't speak of it much, but she's been running around the house and writing in her journals as much as always. Father's still grumbling about it."

"As he should be. I can assure you I let my sister know exactly how I felt about it. I informed my father and mother, too. Father wasn't happy my sister insulted one of the highest lords in his realm. My sister was in his study for quite a while. My poor mother wouldn't eat supper after she heard. She wanted to go directly to your mother and apologize."

"My mother received an invitation to the palace yesterday evening. She's to have a private tea with the queen and was specifically asked to bring her charming daughter," said Quinn. "I know your mother meant it as a kindness, but I know Cara is dreading it."

"My mother will do all she can to make sure Cara is comfortable, though I'm sure your sister will find my mother silly and bothersome. She tends to prattle on when she's nervous."

"I suppose we'll find out when we return." Quinn finished his tart and pocketed the cloth. "I suppose you'll want to be careful around Cara from now on, not be in her company as much. She's getting rather old to be given as much freedom as she has, but my father insists his daughter is treated no differently than his son."

"I will not change how I interact with any of your family. Cara has never been anything but proper, and I hope you find no fault in my behavior," said Aven.

"No, of course not, but Aven, you must see how dangerous this could be. If Princess Kyra is saying such things to my sister, she must have noticed something that worries her. What if others have seen it?"

"My sister is paranoid and obsessed with position. She is also bitter that she is the firstborn but passed over for me. She doesn't understand why father didn't declare her his heir."

"He could have. We've had queens in the past. Usually, it's because there's no other child, but still," said Quinn.

"Father waited until I was sixteen to declare me the heir. He says I'm more suited for the role. Kyra married not long after. I thought she was satisfied with her place at Moonwood, but it would seem she still wishes for more power."

"And you, Aven, are you content with your fate? Will you enjoy being king?"

"I accepted being heir, didn't I?"

"But if you had a choice, if you could do anything you wished with your life, would you pick this?"

Aven shrugged. "I've never really thought about it. It was always said I would be king, so I just assumed it would be so. Perhaps that sounds prideful and pathetic, but it's the truth. My father trained me for years, even before officially naming me heir. I accepted it so long ago that I don't know any other way." He glanced at his friend. "Do you think I will not make a good king?"

"What? No, of course not. I have every faith in your ability to lead us. I just wondered if it's what you truly want."

"It is the hand life dealt me, so I will play it, Quinn, and I will do all I can to make sure I play it well. I do care about Illedria. I know how many depend on my family for their prosperity. My father is a man of duty, and he has spoken of it so much to me that it is the core of me as well."

As he said it, Aven believed it was mostly true. He was ready to do what was needed to lead Illedria someday, though a nagging voice in his head reminded him of his secret magic lesson and Silvie. Still, his father's death was far in the future. He had time to get the fascination with magic out of his system and focus on his future at a later date. For now, he would do the duties assigned to him and make time for his little indulgence.

They arrived in the village just before dark, and the inn was as small and dated as Quinn had said. Aven was too wrapped in the idea of staying somewhere other than the palace or a lord's home to care about the simple accommodations. As they ate a simple stew on the dark first floor of the inn, he was filled with curiosity, looking at the room half full of people.

"We should have found some local low lord to take us in. We could have waited a day or two and sent a message ahead. Any one of them would have been more than happy to host the Crown Prince," said Quinn, moving his spoon around his lukewarm soup.

"If we told one local lord I was around, then the whole village would know, and we couldn't travel as easily as we are." Aven looked towards the fireplace where two comely young women sat talking to a man who hovered over their table. "This place isn't so bad."

Quinn followed his gaze. "Aven, you could find twenty women more attractive than those two back home, and all of them would be jumping at the chance to do whatever you wish."

"Ah," said Aven with a grin. "But those girls don't know who I am. Perhaps I could practice my charm and see if it's enough to earn me any favors."

Quinn laughed. "Well, go on, then. Let's see what you can do."

"No, I should stay focused on our mission."

"Afraid to find out, eh?"

Aven put down his spoon and took a long drink from his mug. He cringed a little at the strong taste but steadied himself as he stood up. "Give me five minutes."

"Ha! I could give you ten, and the outcome will be the same."

Aven ran his hand through his hair and walked towards the two young women. One turned her eyes from the man in front of her and looked at Aven, her gaze sweeping him up and down. One corner of her mouth lifted as she leaned back in her chair, the bodice of her dress moving slightly down. Aven's mouth went dry, and he suddenly wondered what he was doing. The two women looked like they were holding court, queens of this small village, and he was nothing but a rugged traveler to him.

"I wouldn't take another step towards those two if I were you," said a voice to his right. Aven turned to see a small table in the shadows. A lone figure sat, a hood hiding her face. All Aven could see was two long dark red braids resting against her chest.

"Why is that?"

The woman leaned forward, her hood falling back a bit to show a pair of beautiful, clever blue eyes and a full pink mouth twisted into an amused smile. "Because they'll do nothing but cause you trouble and take at least half your money."

He crossed his arms. "Perhaps it would be worth it to spend a night with such beauties."

The woman leaned forward further and said in a dangerous, soft voice, "I would think the crown prince of the realm could do better than a couple of village harlots."

Aven's face contorted in shock as his arms fell to his side. The woman chuckled. "Sit down before you draw notice to yourself." He looked towards Quinn, who was watching him. "Call your friend over if you wish, but I won't keep you long."

Aven sat down on the edge of the chair across from the woman. "Who are you?"

"Does it matter?"

"You seem to know me. It's only fair I know your name as well."

She smiled, and it changed her fierce, beautiful face into something beyond lovely. "I have many names."

"Give me one then."

She laughed fully as she took a sip from her mug. Her laugh was as beautiful as she was, almost musical. "I'm afraid you'll have to be satisfied with only knowing I mean you no harm." She put down her mug and pulled back her hood further for a moment, showing pointed ears poking out of her auburn hair. She adjusted her hood back over them and picked her mug back up. "Giving any of my names is entirely out of the question."

Aven took a deep breath, wondering if he should be afraid or mesmerized. He had never met a Fae before, only read about them or heard tales of them from others. "So, it's true then if I get your name, I have some control over you."

"If it's true or not, you will not get my name. Besides, you already have some control over me. I wouldn't have stopped you from doing something stupid had you not some hold on me."

"How do you know me?"

"It doesn't matter. I want to help you. You're a long way from home, Your Highness, and I think I know why."

"I think I should get up, find my friend, and leave this instant," said Aven, half rising. "I don't know anything about you beyond that you're Fae."

Her eyes narrowed as she put down her mug forcefully on the table. "If you left this second, do you not think I couldn't track you? If I wanted to kill you, Your Highness, I already would've done it. I've taken a great interest in your kingdom and you, and the last thing I want is for any harm to come to you or Illedria. Now sit down and listen."

Aven wasn't sure it was wise, but he did as she asked, sitting down, keeping his hands on the table.

"You're headed to the temples close to the forest, and that is as good of a place to start as any. When you get there, warn the priests and priestesses that they will be attacked at some point. Tell them to give you the horn of Macha and the golden necklace of Mayra so you can take them to safety in the palace. Your old wards and mages will have better luck protecting them. The priestesses might resist, so you'll need a royal order." She pulled two small scrolls out of her pocket. "These will look like they come from the king. They're enchanted to make them do as it says."

Aven reached for the scroll, but the Fae woman held on to it. "Do not open them. Let the head priestess of each temple do it. They will give you the objects. The horn is in the northernmost temple, and the necklace is in the one to the south." She gave Aven the scrolls.

"Warn the priests and priestesses to evacuate the temple. Some will not comply, but others will. They cannot resist who's coming for them."

"Who's coming?" asked Aven.

"Those who only wish destruction on every good thing about our land," said the Fae woman darkly. "Do as I ask, Aven. I don't want to enchant you, but I will if I have to."

She said his name in such a familiar way that it threw him off guard. He stared at her, trying to remember if he had ever seen her before, but surely he would remember such a face. "Please tell me your name. I'll do nothing to use it against you."

"I cannot, at least not yet. One day, maybe."

"So we'll meet again?"

"I hope so," she said quietly. "There's one more thing you must do after the temples. Go into the forest and find a forest witch who lives there. Warn her that she must leave as soon as possible. She has a scroll that is invaluable. I don't know where she keeps it, but it must not fall into the wrong hands. I would go, but I think I'm being tracked outside your kingdom. The old wards give me some protection."

"What are these old wards you keep talking about?"

"It's too much to get into now. I need to be going, but I'm sure you know your people were once powerful magic-users, gifted the power by your goddess Seren. You were the one human kingdom that combined with the Fae, only increasing your power. This was before the dark times, of course, when the dark and light fell out of balance, and humans were seen as nothing more than chattel to do the wishes of the Fae.

"When it was made right by the good Sun King Elffin three centuries ago, magic was still mistrusted by the humans. Your kingdom muted its magic, keeping only to your mages and healers. I'm afraid the Light and Dark Courts are in danger of falling out of balance again. If it can't be stopped, this time might be worse than the last. Be prepared, Aven."

"How do I find this forest witch if I decide to go?"

"Walk towards the center of the woods. If you are looking for her with no ill intent, you will find her." She picked up her mug and drained what was left in it. "Be careful in those woods, and never be alone. If no one will go with you, forget what I said."

Aven tapped his fingers on the table, considering what he should do for a moment. He could ignore all this Fae woman said. It could be a trick, but why trick him? She was right. If she wanted him dead, he would already be so. And the part about the forest witch...

"Do I know this witch?"

"I doubt it, but how should I know everyone you've come across?" said the Fae woman.

"She's in danger?"

"I believe so. She is vastly powerful and won't go down without a fight, but I don't think even she can withstand them. It will take them some time to find her, but hopefully, you can get her to run. Tell her that her young mouthy friend wishes her to be safe."

Aven smiled. "And she will know what I mean?"

The Fae woman nodded. "Now, you should get back to your friend. I see him staring over here. Go get some rest so you can leave before first light. You need to make it to the temples as soon as possible. Do not spend too much time in one place. I don't think anyone is watching you, but I can't be sure."

"Is there anything else you can tell me? What is this threat? Is it the Court of the Underlings?"

She chuckled. "The Underlings aren't what you think, but be careful around anyone you meet." She hissed and looked at her wrist, where she wore a leather bracelet. "I have to go. Be safe, Your Highness. Do as I ask, and I will pray to the good goddess Macha for your success."

She pulled her hood to hide her face and stood up, backing into the shadows. A moment later, she was gone. Aven blinked, wondering if he really saw what he thought. He walked to the wall, touching it to see if there was some hidden door, but there was nothing.

He went back to Quinn, who stood up as he approached. "What was that all about? I thought you were going to speak to those women?"

"I got distracted," said Aven.

"I saw you talking to someone, but I couldn't see who. Was she even more comely than those lovely creatures?"

"She was something I've never seen before. Come on, we need to go to bed. I'll explain it to you in my room, but we must leave by first light."

Quinn's smile faded. "Aven, is something wrong?"

"If what I was just told is true, everything could be wrong."

Chapter 17

Tal

LITTLE LIGHT MADE IT through the thick trees on sunny days in the Gethian forest, so it almost appeared as perpetual twilight when it was cloudy. It was disorienting to know it was only mid-morning, yet it felt as though it could be well into the evening. Tal rode his old gray horse in between Delphina and Dyfan. His horse could hardly be called impressive, though it was tall and must have been more than serviceable in its younger years. Dyfan's wasn't any better off, being a bay stallion who looked like it would soon be done with its service. Yet, both their horses looked like prizes next to the small, sassy thing Delphina was currently riding.

"This is the best you can find me, Dyfan?" asked Delphina, jerking the reins to try to keep her horse on the narrow path. "She is practically a pony and not a compliant one at that."

"There wasn't much to choose from, my lady, and only your slight form is fit for that animal. I'm sure she's a good girl. You just need to become acquainted. Stop jerking her head around so much," said Dyfan.

"If I don't, there's no telling where I'll end up, and I'd rather not get lost in these trees." She looked to her left into the grown-up forest. "It must be almost pitch black in there."

"You aren't letting that woman's words get into your head, are you, Delphie?" said Tal with a teasing laugh.

"I don't know if what she said was true, but anything could be hiding in those trees. It feels different the further we ride in like something is always watching us."

"You're paranoid, Delphie."

"I'm not. It's true." She snapped her reins and rode a little ahead, her horse veering right until she jerked her back on the path again.

"You're not buying into this, are you, Dyfan?"

"That there's some mystical curse on this place?" He sighed. "I've seen stranger things, and I'm sure you have as well. I'm much more concerned about any old creatures or those wanting to cause harm that could be hiding in the trees. This place is old—older than any Fae we know, even your uncle."

"Then let's try to stay together," said Tal. He urged his horse into a fast walk. "Wait a moment, Delphie!" She slowed her horse as Tal and Dyfan caught up with her. "We need to stay together. Don't go off alone because you're displeased over some minor irritation."

"I wouldn't call you a minor irritation," she said with a huff.

He half grinned. "No one is forcing you to be here. We aren't very far into the forest. If you want to go home, I'm sure you have the means. We'll take care of your horse."

"I said I would go with you to find Eriana. We haven't found her yet. I won't go home until I do what I came here to do."

Tal bowed his head and said nothing. All was peaceful and quiet for a few minutes before Dyfan said softly, "Your worry for your cousin is commendable, especially since you don't seem to like her very much."

"What do you know about it?" she asked testily.

"I have eyes and ears, my lady. It is well known around the court that you have no love for your cousin. Some say it's because of envy, but to me, it seems to run deeper than that."

"Is jealousy not enough for you? The fact that my father openly shows more favor for his niece than his daughter isn't enough for me to have some anger towards her?"

"If your father really does show that much favoritism, perhaps your anger should be towards him. What fault of it is hers?" said Dyfan.

"If only my mother were still alive. She understood," said Delphina.

"When did she die?" asked Tal.

"Almost fifteen years ago, during the second great sickness. Some think it was the same illness that killed your father, but the king had the mercy of a quick death. My mother wasted away over months. I sat with her every day, hoping for something to help her."

"Your father sent in healers, I assume."

"He did, and when they could do nothing, my cousin consulted the healers of Illedria." Delphina turned away and spat, "As if those humans and their weak magic could do anything."

"And they didn't help?"

"Eriana was too late coming back with the medicines prepared by the healers. My mother died two days before she returned, so we'll never know."

"You blame her for your mother's death, don't you?" asked Dyfan.

"She was gone for weeks while my mother suffered. I doubt that human magic could have done anything, but it was our last chance. Eriana knew this, and she still dallied out in the lands. She tried to say she came as quickly as she could, but I know she didn't. She probably stalled on purpose to have my father's attention on herself."

"But your mother cared for Eriana as well. I hear your cousin saw her as a mother," said Dyfan. "Don't you think she would want to save her?"

"Eriana is a good liar, Dyfan. She's always been pleasing when she needed to be around my parents, but I've seen her true nature. She is devious and cunning, vicious even. Surely, you know. You've seen her spar with the guards. She shows no mercy."

"She is a cunning and fierce warrior, but I've seen her show great kindness. She is Princess Adalyn's greatest friend."

"My sister did say she liked her, even admired her, but also said the lady is hard to get to know. If that's my sister's intimate friend, then I'm sorry for her."

"Your sister is everything good, Your Highness," said Delphina. "Her soft heart makes it impossible for her to think ill of anyone."

"No," said Dyfan with conviction. "Do not make the princess's goodness sound like a weakness. She's the best kind of good because she knows that evil exists in the world and still chooses to be gentle and kind. She's not fooled by false manners and a pretty face."

Tal looked at his friend, surprised at the fierceness of Dyfan's defense of Adalyn, but he was the head guard and probably spent hours in her company. "I agree with Dyfan. Adalyn is probably one of the most cunning and intelligent creatures I know. If she likes your cousin, then there must be something that makes the lady worth knowing."

"What does it matter how I feel about my cousin? I want what both of you want: an end to this mission and my cousin back home where she belongs. That's the end of it."

"Very well," said Tal. "What then shall we speak about to pass the time?"

"Tell us about the Dark Court and what you've been doing over the past three decades," said Delphina.

"I'm sure you know more than enough about my exploits. I know I'm the subject of plenty of gossip," said Tal.

"I'd like to know how much of it is exaggerated. Some of it surely can't be true," said Delphina with a laugh.

"Is there a particular rumor you want me to address?" he asked with a sly smile.

"Hmmm, not today. I'm afraid your words wouldn't convince me."

"Oh, and what would?"

"Seeing for myself." She laughed wickedly. Tal turned to Dyfan with a grin.

He did not return it, only grunting slightly before saying, "We should focus on where we're going. I don't want to be in the forest any longer than necessary."

Delphina sighed. "All that lady in the village said was that this Margred is located in the center of the forest. Are we sure this is the way?"

"There are only three paths through the forest. One goes north, one goes south, and this one goes west, straight through the heart of the forest. This is the best chance we have of finding the place," said Dyfan.

"And if we go deep in the forest, we have a better chance of finding the other forest witch that is said to have lived here. Perhaps it is her who Lady Eriana goes to visit," said Tal.

"But this pash is so winding. Why does it not go straight into the forest? There must be an easier way," said Delphina.

"There is not," said Tal. "I looked at the maps yesterday, and Dyfan made inquiries at the stables. This is the only way."

"And we shall have to sleep out here, I suppose?" asked Delphina.

"Oh sweet, Delphie, are you too delicate for a night on the forest ground? Or perhaps you're worried about the cold?"

"I'm not looking forward to a night on the ground, but I've done it before. As far as being too cold, I know some tricks to warm myself up."

"Careful, Delphie, Dyfan will think you're quite wild. You might develop a reputation."

"She doesn't need my help," mumbled Dyfan.

Tal and Delphina both turned to look at Dyfan, Tal with delighted surprise and Delphina with barely controlled rage.

"Why, my Delphie, I thought you were a trained lady, full of decorum and proper behavior?"

"I have no idea what Dyfan is referring to." She pointed a finger at Dyfan. "You shouldn't listen to idle gossip of court ladies, probably brought on by jealousy."

"So it's not true then?" Tal made a great show of sighing in disappointment. "I'd rather hoped there was more to you than I thought, Delphie."

She growled, her usually calm, beautiful face contorted in rage and annoyance, her cheeks a bright red. "Stop calling me Delphie! And you, Dyfan, you have no right to speak about me as you do. I'm the only child of the highest lord to the king you serve." She pulled her horse to the left, aiming towards a clearing between some trees that might have once been a makeshift pass. "I'm done with you both for the time being, and I'm sure there is an easier way to get to the center of this forest. I will find one and come back for you." She snapped her rains, causing her horse to rear up slightly before taking off at a speed much faster than Tal expected.

Tal watched her go for a few seconds before turning to Dyfan. "I suppose we should go after her."

"Or not. She's not helpless, and she chose to go off on her own. We have a mission."

"Dyfan, her father will not be pleased if we lose her out here," said Tal.

"Lord Elgan told you to find his niece. His daughter came on her accord. He'll understand. He knows who Delphina is. She is away from home more often than you would think. She knows what she's about."

Tal shook his head and turned his horse down the old path Delphina took. "Come on, Dyfan. The sooner we find her and apologize, the sooner we can get back on track."

"Why? Why are you so adamant about pleasing her? If you want her as some conquest, it can wait until this is over, or we can find you another woman just as comely somewhere else. That might be better, actually."

Tal looked at his friend. He hardly had ever seen Dyfan discomposed. From what he could remember, Dyfan was usually calm and collected, even as a boy. Sure, he got mad from time to time, but nothing like this.

"Me liking her bothers you. Why?"

"So you like her?" Dyfan's eyes narrowed.

"She is beautiful, intelligent, and charming. What's not to like?"

"Plenty if you would just see it. She's not what you think she is."

"I know, and that's the best part. I have totally misjudged her, and I find myself wanting to know more and more." Tal moved his horse ahead, encouraging the animal to go as fast as he dared. He darted around trees, hoping the animal was more surefooted than he looked.

Dyfan called after him as Tal led his horse on the overgrown path, around old twisted trees, some with trunks so thick he couldn't see around to the other side. He assumed Dyfan followed him, but he didn't look behind him to check, keeping his eyes ahead to try to find Delphina.

Surely, she wouldn't go too far with her dramatics. He could see her riding off just out of sight to make a point, but as he got deeper into the forest, he began to wonder. First, he felt annoyed that she would be so hard-headed, but then the annoyance became worry as he rode deeper and deeper, the old path disappearing to become nothing but the grown-up ground and half-dead trees.

"Delphina?" he called into the growing darkness. "Delphina, there is no need for this. Come out so we can be on our way."

There was no sound in return save for a few birds fluttering their wings as they shot out from a nearby tree. "Delphina?" Still, nothing. He turned his horse, looking the way he came, hoping to hear Dyfan or see him riding out from the closet cover of trees. A few moments, and then something rustled the tall grass.

"Dyfan?" said Tal uncertainty.

Nothing came towards him as the grass moved again. The wind blew slightly, sending a shiver down his back. The forest was unnaturally quiet. The birds made no noise, and the trees' leaves did not rustle in the wind. Only in the tall grass did any sound come as it shifted like it was disturbed by something walking through it.

"Who's there?" Tal's horse took a few steps back as it tossed his head. It felt like something was staring him down, though he could see nothing around him but trees and low brush. "Dyfan? Delphina?"

His horse reared up suddenly, giving Tal only a moment to hold on. He managed to stay on despite his surprise, trying to control the animal. It came down on its legs, only to rear again, this time bucking as though scared senseless. Tal tried to control the beast, but it wouldn't listen to his commands or respond to his guidance. The third time, it twisted as it rose into the air, making Tal slip from the saddle. Though he tried to hang on, he was thrown to the ground.

Tal rolled as the horse stomped a few times in terror, barely missing its misplaced rider. The horse finally reared once last time before galloping off into the trees. Tal lay still for a moment, catching his breath and mentally checking over his body. The fall hurt, but he didn't think anything was wrong with him beyond a few bruises. The real problem was he was alone in the middle of a dark, cold forest with no horse or provisions.

Deciding he couldn't just lay on the ground all day, he raised himself into a sitting position, pushing his dark hair back from his forehead as he considered his options. He could try to go back the way he came, hopefully making it back to the path or meeting Dyfan along the way, or he could keep going further into the forest, trying to find Delphina. The smart thing to do was to go the sure way, finding Dyfan so they could find his horse and Delphina together.

Tal stood up and stretched his back, satisfied that nothing was broken. He had no cuts, only slight bruises that would be gone within the next few hours. He turned slowly around, trying to remember which way he had come. He thought he recognized the gnarled, dead tree to his left, so he walked that way, hoping he was right.

The forest around him grew darker as he walked. He wasn't sure why. It could not even be lunch yet, and though the sun was still obscured, the clouds had not thickened from what he could see through the dense trees. Tal pulled his cloak tight around him, the wind picking up, sending dead leaves swirling around as it whistled, blowing through the branches. He tripped a few times over mangled roots or dead limbs. It was a miserable journey, and it was one he was ready to be over.

After what must have been almost a half-hour of walking and cursing Lady Eriana, as it was her fault he was out here to begin with, Tal thought he must have chosen the wrong direction or gotten off track, stumbling through the woods. It would do no good to be out here alone for any length of time. The wisest thing he could do was use his magic to travel directly back to the village and see if Delphina and Dyfan had done the same. If they had not, he could quickly find the guards and more horses to look for his two companions.

He called upon the darkness as the magic he inherited from his mother always responded. The gift from his father grew more useless year after year. The darkness slowly started to gather around him, though it felt reluctant. He closed his eyes to concentrate when he heard his voice being called in the distance. His eyes flew open as he heard it again, still weak and a way off, but definitely to his right.

It was hard to tell, but he believed it was a female voice. "Delphina?" he called back. The wind blew harshly, causing him to tip his head down. As it died away, he heard his name again, this time clearer. "I'm coming! Stay where you are." He moved towards the voice as it said his name again.

The forest was even thicker in this direction, the trees growing so close together that many were thin and bowed. Low branches scratched his head and shoulders as he pushed against them, trying to get through. He thought it odd he saw no animals or even signs of one. Not even birds shot out as he slipped between the trees.

"Delphina!" he shouted again, hoping to hear an answer to let him know he was going the right way. A noise to his left responded as though someone had run by him, followed by a soft laugh. He grew agitated. "This is no time for games. I've lost my horse and Dyfan. Come this way, so we can figure out what to do."

Another laugh. The smaller trees behind him moved, making him turn. "Delphina, I swear!" said Tal angrily. "This is not fucking funny."

Laughter again, the same as before, but it was intertwined with another. This laugh was just as merry but most definitely male. He froze. Who was out here with him? "Delphina?" he asked softly. "Dyfan?"

He turned, hearing a sound behind him. A soft breeze flitted across his face, thick with the scent of honeysuckle. "What? Who's there?"

He felt a gentle touch on his shoulder and saw nothing but darkness.

Chapter 18

Aven

Aven and Quinn didn't talk much after leaving the inn before the sun rose, though Aven knew Quinn had many questions. Perhaps Quinn could read his mood and understood that Aven had too much going on in his mind to be attentive, or maybe it was the sharpness with which Aven answered any questions Quinn had late last night.

Perhaps Quinn was right, and he shouldn't follow the advice of some random Fae woman he came across in a small inn, but something within him said he should believe her. Why would she seek him out just to give him false information? If she wanted to harm him or anyone in his kingdom, there were probably a hundred more efficient ways she could do so.

"But the Fae are tricky and devious. What if she is leading you right into a trap to watch you suffer?" Quinn had said before they went to bed.

"Why would she do that? Why follow me, know my name, just to send me into some elaborate ruse to hurt me?" Aven shook his head. "It wouldn't make sense."

"When have the Fae ever made sense? They live in their own perfect realms and watch us suffer, probably for their own amusement. Most of them see us as nothing more than entertainment or property they believe has been stolen from them. Aven, this isn't wise."

"Either way, we have to go to the temples to see what's going on."

"We could turn around and tell my father and yours what happened. If the Fae are truly involved, this is bigger than the two of us can handle," said Quinn.

"I'm to be king one day, Quinn. If I can't handle this much, what business do I have managing my father's legacy? I'm going to the temples. If you want to go home, I won't be angry or blame you."

Quinn stood up from the small bed. "You know I won't leave you to do this alone, but we need to be careful. Any sign of anything suspicious, we leave directly, and if these objects turn out to be dangerous, we don't touch them." Aven nodded. "As far as going into the forest—well, let's see what happens at the temples first."

"Of course," said Aven.

"I'm going to bed. You should try to sleep, Aven. We need to get done with this and get back to our village as soon as possible. Whatever is happening in the kingdom, I don't want to get caught out here all alone with little help."

Aven tried to sleep, but his thoughts kept him awake. They led him down hazy paths, circling and circling as they went nowhere. He didn't believe the Fae woman meant him harm. There had been a desperation in her voice that made him think she needed his help. She radiated confidence and deadliness in almost all aspects but her eyes. They were soft and tired as they looked at Aven. They were earnest. Perhaps it would lead to his doom, but he believed her.

Still, he wondered who she was and how long she had been following him. She didn't look old, but that didn't mean anything. Fae could live for many years, forever, he supposed, if no injury or sickness fell them. And what was with these magical objects held in their temples? Why were they important and in danger?

He put his hand over the pocket that held the two scrolls. He wondered if they would be enough to make the head priestesses give up their precious items. A thought invaded, wondering if he should take these items at all. Perhaps if they were so wanted, they really were powerful and dangerous. What would he be bringing into his home, to his family and friends? But if this Fae woman wanted them safe, she must have thought his family and palace could repel any dangers.

"Quinn, what do you know about the old magic of our people?"

Quinn turned to Aven, blinking his eyes as if he had been engrossed in his own deep thoughts. "What exactly?"

"I don't know. That Fae woman said our people were blessed by Seren; she called her our goddess, but I don't know if I've ever heard of her."

"I'm sure you have, but you probably don't remember it or realize who you were reading about. She is not a part of the usual holy text, but she is more included in myths and occasional mythical stories told to children. She is sometimes called the Light Goddess or the daughter of the stars."

"That sounds more familiar."

"It should. It's a common story. Her mother, the goddess of night, caught the eye of a human prince. He was no ordinary prince, as he had power over the creatures of fire. He loved her cold, dark beauty and, in turn, earned her love with his passion and warm, open manners. The goddess of night was already bound to the Moon God, destined to exist together to keep the balance just as the Sun Goddess and Wind God dance with each other.

"Only when the new cycle came, and the moon disappeared to rest, could the Night Goddess meet her lover. She became with child, the moon thinking it was his heir, but when the babe was born, she had her mother's glowing skin but not her father's soft white hair. Instead, it was golden, and her eyes were the brightest blue you could imagine.

"The Moon God sought out the human prince to take out his vengeance on who would sully his partner. The Night Goddess found the human first and used her magic to protect him, giving it all away so that he could withstand the wrath of the moon. Then she turned and bowed before her vowed partner, promising to never stray from him again if he would spare this human and her daughter.

"The moon would only agree if she would join him in the sky permanently, never to walk the earth again. She gave her precious daughter to her love to raise, kissed him goodbye, and drifted into the heavens to stay there forever.

"The prince named his daughter Seren in honor of her mother. He gave her a dragon, and every night, they would fly together into the night sky and look at the stars. He told her each one burned to show Seren how much her mother loved her."

"And that prince was said to be of our people? Was he the start of our kingdom's magic?" asked Aven.

"That is the thought. It's all a myth, of course. Just legends and stories passed down, like the dragons."

"But some think the dragons were true," said Aven. "They are mentioned in the actual holy text and history of our people."

"Metaphors, probably."

"Maybe," said Aven under his breath. "So why would a Fae woman know about Seren? Why mention her to me?"

"Was she old? Perhaps she was around when the legend was more circulated."

"How am I supposed to know if she's old? She was Fae." He looked up at the cloudy sky, wondering if the sun would ever shine again. "I got the sense that she wasn't ancient. Older than us, but not centuries old like the Dark King."

"The Fae probably know more about the myths of the old gods, and I'm sure they're able to take in more information than us. Maybe she thought mentioning something from our people's legends would earn your trust."

They rode late into the night, stopping at a small inn close to the edge of the kingdom. Aven would have liked to make it to the first temple and take shelter there, but he could tell Quinn and his guards were exhausted. His body ached for sleep as well, and after taking a simple meal in his room, he fell asleep with no problems.

His dreams were as vivid as they were varied. Dragons, his father, the Fae woman, and even Cara danced through his mind. His father reminded him to do his duty as a black dragon stood behind him, his nose inches from his father's shoulder. The Fae woman stared at him, a small red dragon wrapped around her arm as she reminded him to keep his kingdom safe, and Cara laughed as she rode a dragon as big as two horses around him, teasing him for taking things too seriously.

By the time Quinn awakened him before the sun rose, Aven felt like he had spent years asleep, yet his body still ached with exhaustion. They made it to the first temple a few hours after sunrise, the building coming into sight as they crested a tree-covered hill.

"So, do we just go on and tell them why we came?" asked Quinn. "Or will you be more careful?"

Aven stared at the temple, seeing a few priests just outside the gate leading goats. Two priestesses worked not far from them, feeding a flock of chickens. "All appears as it should. We will ask to see the head priestess and discuss with her the horn the Fae woman spoke to me about."

"You will tell her about the Fae woman?" asked Quinn, sounding surprised.

"Priests and priestesses are more open to the Fae and magic than we are, but no, I won't say a word about the woman." He put his hand in his pocket. "I will ask to see the horn and then give her the scroll."

The priests had moved on as they rode up to the gate, but the priestesses and their chickens still lingered. A young one with pretty blonde hair and a bright smile stepped away from the flock to meet them.

"Greetings in the name of the goddess Macha. What brings you to our temple?"

Aven hopped down off his horse, and Quinn did the same. "Good morning. I am Aven Mathias, the Crown Prince of Illedria. I'm here on an errand from my father and wish to see your head priestess. I come on an urgent matter."

The priestess's smile faded as her eyes grew wide. "Prince? You are Prince Aven Mathias?"

"I am," said Aven as he took off his gloves. "I wear the signet ring of my position if you wish to see it."

She moved closer to him, her head lowered to look at his hand but quickly stepped back. "No, there is no need. Anyone who does not wish ill on the gods or their people is welcomed here. It does not matter who you are. I can show you into the temple and have Priestess Keeva sent for. She can decide if you are telling the truth or not."

Aven nodded before turning to his guards, telling them to look after the horses and keep watch. After they rode off, he and Quinn followed the young priestess into the temple. It was not a large building and looked like it had been built at different times. The darkest, most worn stone was a two-story square. Several rectangles of lighter stone came off the original, showing that new rooms were added as needed.

The priestess led them into the courtyard, where several priests and priestesses worked or prayed. Many stopped what they were doing for a moment to observe their guests, but no one said anything to them. They entered the building through simple wooden double doors, coming into a large, open, dim room.

"This is the worship space," said the young priestess. "You can wait here while I go see if Priestess Keeva will see you."

"If she wishes to see my ring or the letter from the king I carry, I will be happy to show her."

"I'll tell her," said the priestess before she turned and walked towards a door on the left side.

Quinn moved closer to the front of the room where a simple dark wooden table sat, three lit candles on the surface. He looked up at the portrait above them. "The goddess Macha is in the center. You can tell by her green armor and the horn in her hand."

"And I suppose that is Mayra to her left?"

Quinn moved a little closer. "I would say so. She is usually dressed in a golden gown, and that necklace with the emerald gives it away."

"And this is Cyerra, I believe. See the crow?"

"Three goddesses, Macha, Cyerra, and Mayra. One of war, one of protection and gifts, and one of beauty and peace." Quinn bowed. "We ask a blessing on our people, a time of peace, not war." He stood up and looked at Aven.

"I didn't know you were devout," said Aven.

"I attend services and observe feasts the same as you."

"Yes, but all of the court do. It would be odd not to," said Aven.

"When has my father or I done anything for fashion or because it's tradition? We both worship because we believe it is the correct thing to do. I study about the gods because I enjoy it," said Quinn, a bit of irritation in his voice. "Do you have no faith?"

Aven tilted his head, looking at the goddesses. "I haven't really thought about it. Honestly, if the gods and goddesses exist or not, it doesn't seem to affect me."

"Your family legends might say otherwise," said Quinn.

"True, but perhaps they really are just legends." He looked at his friend. "Don't be cross with me. I don't think less of you for your faith. Perhaps I should attend to mine more closely if I'm to be king."

"A wise thing to say, Your Highness," said a deep female voice from behind them. Aven and Quinn turned to see a tall, slim woman dressed in dark green robes. Her graying dark hair was braided down her back, which was the only thing that showed her age. She stood straight, and her face barely had any lines on it. Her eyes were a clear light green. Aven thought they looked a little shrewd but not unkind.

"Priestess Keeva?" asked Aven.

"Here to serve the gods and our king," she said as she bowed her head. "I understand you have something urgent to tell me."

Aven glanced at Quinn. "Yes, umm, I..." He put a hand through his hair. "I don't quite know where to begin."

She smiled. "How about with a question I can answer for you? You must have at least one."

"Have you heard of the Court of the Underlings?" The question came so quickly to his mind that Aven could not stop it before it popped out.

The head priestess's eyes narrowed a bit, and her smile faltered for a moment before she looked at the young priestess next to her. "Kalla, please leave us for a bit. Tell everyone not to come into the worship space so we aren't disturbed."

"As you wish," said Kalla. She bowed towards the front of the room before hurrying to the door.

"The Court of the Underlings? Is this what my king wished for you to ask me?"

"He put me on the task of finding out what we could about them. I have sent out letters throughout the kingdom, asking about attacks that have happened and people being taken. The answers we received led us to believe we should come here to visit and see what you might have heard. The attacks at temples have been numerous, and we're afraid you are next."

The priestess walked past them to the front of the room as Aven and Quinn turned to watch her. "I suppose you plan to visit the temple south of here as well?"

"We do," said Quinn. "They house a significant historical object there as you do here."

"That is true," said Keeva as she looked at the portrait above the table. "But it will do you no good to travel there."

"Why not?" asked Aven.

"They were attacked three days ago. Several priests and priestesses lost their lives, including the head priestess. The ones that survived made their way here." Keeva placed her hand on the table, bowing her head. "They brought their treasure with them."

"So you hold both items here?" asked Quinn. "You do realize how vulnerable you are?"

"We have more ways to protect ourselves than you think, young man," said the priestess. "There is a reason the object was brought here."

"What ways?" asked Aven.

The priestess smiled. "We have the goddesses on our side. They protect us."

Aven shifted his feet and crossed his arms. "You think that's enough?"

She turned to look at Aven, a small smile on her lips. "You don't, young prince?"

"Other temples have been attacked. You said yourself priestesses have been killed at one not far from here. What makes this place any different?"

"Our goddess, Macha, has assured me of our safety."

"How?" asked Aven.

"She came to me in a vision. Promised me safety from the Underlings and any other forces that might destroy us."

"A vision?" asked Quinn. "Like a dream?"

"No, of course not," said the priestess, sounding offended. "I was out praying not far from here, listening for the will of the gods and goddesses, when she appeared to me. Her hair was the sun. She wore green armor over a dark dress. Her eyes were like shining emeralds. I bowed before her, and she touched my head. I could hear her voice in my mind, though she made no sound. She told me to rest easy. To know no harm would come to my temple."

"Was that all?" asked Quinn.

"She asked me if I had any piece of hers that I watched over. I told her about the horn we held and said we kept it safe for her. She asked about her sister's necklace, and I let her know where it was. She said she would visit the other temples and keep them safe as well as long as they kept the faith."

"So why were they attacked then?"

"Priestess Vera has never been very devout, in my opinion," said Keeva. "Always talking about reason, and the gods gave us the ability to interpret their words and actions." She tsked. "Such blasphemy."

"Priestess, I think you might reconsider your position," said Quinn carefully. "I would hate for anything to happen to you and your people here. What if you were tricked?"

"Tricked by who and how? Don't you think I know the goddess when I see her? Nothing of this world could be as beautiful as Macha when she appeared before me."

"What about the Fae?" asked Aven, thinking of the woman in the inn. "They can be beyond what humans think is beautiful, mesmerizing even. What if one was playing with you?"

"I have met the Fae," spat the priestess. "A few came to me a year or so ago, asking me questions about the goddess and your family, Your Highness. I sent them away, called upon the goddesses to see that they were cursed as they left."

"And what did they do?" Quinn moved closer to Aven.

"Left, of course, just as my goddesses commanded them."

Quinn leaned towards Aven, his whisper barely above a breath. "Give her the scroll."

"What if it won't work on both objects?" said Aven, trying to keep his words secret.

"We have to try," said Quinn. "She has clearly lost her mind."

"What are you two whispering about? Do you doubt our goddesses?"

"No, of course not," said Aven. "I was only wondering if you would read the message my father, the king, sent. Perhaps it can persuade you." Aven picked the scroll out of his pocket and offered it to Keeva. "He asked for the necklace and horn to be brought to the palace for safekeeping. You can come with it if you like. I think it's best if you and the others leave this place."

Keeva rolled her eyes, grunting with disbelief. "Nothing the king says could change my mind. I'm sorry, Your Highness, but even he is not above the goddesses."

"True," said Aven. "But would you read it, so you can write a note back to him, answering it?"

"I am not obligated to do it."

"No, but perhaps you could tell him about your vision," said Quinn. "He could take it to the head priestess in the palace temple, so she could write it down in the Great Book."

Keeva put her hand to her mouth. "Do you think she would?" she asked reverently.

"I think it's a good possibility," said Quinn. "Read the king's message, and then we'll wait for you to write a reply."

"Very well," said Keeva as she took the small scroll out of Aven's hand. She opened it and turned away to read as Aven and Quinn looked at each other. Aven could hear her whispering the words, though he couldn't make out what she was saying. A moment later, her hand went slack, the scroll falling to the ground.

"You need the horn?" asked Keeva

"Yes, and the necklace," said Aven. "To keep safe in the palace."

"Then come with me," said Keeva. She walked between them, pushing them out of the way. Aven hurried to follow her, Quinn just behind them. She led them to a door on the right, opened it, and stepped through. Quinn and Aven were on her heels.

"It is in my personal rooms, locked in my chest. I put them together to watch over them."

"Of course," said Aven, not knowing what else to say.

Keeva's quarters were through another door. They were comprised of two simple rooms. The first held a fireplace, a desk, and a small sofa. The other was a bedroom that she led them to. It held a bed and a chest of drawers.

"We usually keep the horn in a glass case in the worship area, but I moved it here when the attacks started. I wanted to keep them safe." She moved the one picture in her room, an ordinary landscape. Behind it was a wooded door built into the wall. She opened it and pulled out a dark chest. "Here, they are both in there."

"Can I see?" asked Aven. She nodded, and Aven took the chest to her bed. He opened it to find a horn, probably made from a ram. It was hollowed out and yellow with age. Two holes were on each side, where a leather strap was attached. Aven carefully picked it up and saw the necklace. It was a gold chain with a large circular pendant hanging from it. The pendant had a rudimentary etching of a woman with a small green gem at the center.

"Here," said Quinn, holding out a cloth that once held some food. "Wrap the horn in this, and put it in your pack."

Aven did as he said and then picked up the necklace. He placed it carefully in his inner cloak pocket, the only one that buttoned closed. "We will keep good watch over these."

The priestess nodded. "You should go then."

"Will you not leave as well?" asked Quinn.

"No, we have the assurance of our goddess. We will stay here, keeping watch over the temple as we have for centuries," said Keeva, her voice still flat and dull.

"I really think you should leave, priestess," said Aven. "For your sake and those under your charge."

"I will do what I think best, Your Highness."

Aven went to argue further about it when all three turned, hearing a scream.

"What in the great mystery is going on?" said Keeva as she started towards the door. Aven adjusted his pack, glancing at Quinn before following Keeva out of the room.

They were met by the young priestess from earlier just as they entered the hallway.

"Head Priestess, it's awful, they've come," said Kalla, sounding out of breath. "They're here."

"Who?" asked Quinn, slightly shoving Aven to move forward.

"The ones who attacked the other temples. They're here, heading for our gates. The priest harvesting the last of the trees saw them and ran back to tell us. He says there are at least four dozen on horseback."

"And you are sure they are coming here to attack?" asked Aven.

"They have swords drawn, bows, and arrows. They are riding hard. Nothing else is out this way, no villages, no manors or palaces. They must mean to come here." Kalla sounded desperate, tears in her eyes. "What do we do, Priestess Keeva?"

The head priestess looked almost in a trance, her hands in tight fists as she only stared at Kalla.

"Is there a way out that is not noticeable, perhaps one towards the hills in the back, leading to the forest?"

Kalla stared at Keeva for a moment before nodding. "There is a way out under the original building. It leads to a door not far from the forest edge."

"Gather everyone you can, and tell them to leave now. Take nothing with them. There is no time," said Aven.

Kalla looked again at Keeva. "Priestess?"

Keeva shook her head. "Our goddess will protect us. We stay here and wait." She turned to Aven. "You should take the way to the forest. You came for the precious objects, and now you have them. Take them to the palace as the king commanded."

"We can all use the door," said Quinn. "Get into the forest and regroup. I'm sure we could get you somewhere safe, maybe even to our village. You can't stay here."

"I can, and I must. My goddess commanded it." She adjusted her robes. "Kalla, show the prince and his friend to the door. Then, gather our people and tell them to meet in the worship space. We will pray until our visitors arrive. Our goddesses will not abandon us."

"That's madness," said Aven. "We all must leave."

"Do your duty, Kalla. Take our guests away, now," said Keeva before walking towards the worship space.

"Priestess Keeva!" said Aven, starting to follow her, but Quinn took his arm.

"There's no time to argue with her, and it will do no good. Her mind is too far gone. We need to leave."

Aven watched Keeva go until she opened a door and closed it. He looked at Kalla. "Where are my guards?"

"In the courtyard, waiting for you."

"Send someone now, and tell them to leave and ride hard to the forest. They should wait just inside the tree line until I find them," said Aven.

"We can find someone as we walk to the stairs leading down," said Kalla. She turned and walked quickly towards the back of the building.

"Kalla, you don't have to do as the head priestess says," said Quinn. "You must see she is not well. You will be trapped here with no escape."

"We serve the temple and her," said Kalla. "We cannot disobey."

"You serve the goddesses," said Aven. "They would not want you to throw your life away."

"Keeva told us of her visions. We trust in her and our goddesses." She walked faster, calling for a priest to stop. He waited for her, and she whispered hurriedly to him. He bowed and ran past them. "He will see to your guards. Now follow me."

She led them to a door that opened to a narrow staircase leading down into darkness. "There is a room at the end with a door that leads to a tunnel. You will have to crouch to get through it, but you will both fit. I only hope it's all still standing, as it's as old as the original temple."

She picked up a lit candle from a nearby table and handed it to Aven. "Take this." She opened a drawer on the table and picked up several more thin candles. "And these as well."

Quinn took the bundle of candles and put them in the small pack he wore.

"Now go with the goddesses. May they have mercy on you and keep you safe," said Kalla.

Aven hesitated. "It feels wrong to leave. There's still time to gather most of the people."

Kalla smiled as she sniffled. "I would rather take my chances here than out in the world. Most of us would. We were either given to the temple as small children or found refuge here from a harsh world. There's nothing for us out there. If today is our end, it's the end we would want."

"But there is more..."

"Not for me, but you need to go. We are only humble workers for the gods and goddesses. You are the next king. If you were found here by those coming, well, I imagine they would have more interest in you than us."

"She's right, Aven. We have to go," said Quinn.

Though it still felt wrong and cowardly, he knew Quinn was right. He adjusted his pack and opened his cloak slightly, looking at the closed pocket. He swore he could almost feel the added weight of the objects, though he knew that was ridiculous. With a final look at Kalla, he stepped into the darkness, letting his small candle light his and Quinn's way as Kalla closed the door.

The room at the bottom smelled musty, and the floor was nothing but dirt. They searched for a moment before finding the door. It took Quinn a few tugs to open it as its rusty hinges creaked. Aven held up the candle, illuminating the tunnel. It was narrow and short. He could feel his anxiety grow, thinking of being trapped down there.

"Go on, Aven. It'll be alright. We'll hurry through, and it can't be that long. The forest isn't far off."

Aven nodded and moved forward into the darkness. They had to stay crouched the whole time, moving as quickly as they could. Quinn handed him a new candle every time the one he held burned low. It felt like an eternity in the small, cold space, but it was probably not more than half an hour when a door finally appeared before them. Aven turned the handle and pushed all his weight into it before it finally gave way and opened, the outside light making him momentarily blind.

When his eyes adjusted, he saw the forest before him, the trees thick and old, looking ominous. Everything about them said to turn away, not to enter. Aven rubbed his eyes and turned around, looking out upon the valley below.

"Quinn, look," said Aven, pointing in the distance. He could just make out where the temple stood. Great clouds of dark smoke rose from the spot, and on the wind, he could just hear screams in the distance. He felt an aching in his chest, thinking of all those they left behind.

"It'll do no good to dwell on it," said Quinn. "We need to find our guards and get back to the palace."

"How can I not dwell on it?" said Aven. "We left them to die."

"And we would be dead with them if we stayed," said Quinn. He patted Aven's shoulder. "I know...I know it's hard. I wish we could've helped, but all we could do was run. We need to get back and tell your father what's happened."

Aven took a deep breath and turned away, still hearing screaming in the distance. He looked at the dark forest before him. "We will find the guards, but we can't return home, not yet. There's something else we need to do."

"Aven, you don't mean the forest witch, do you?"

"We have to try to help her. The Fae woman said she was in trouble. After the temple, I can't leave her to the same fate, not if I can do something."

Aven kept his eyes on the forest, his mind wandering to early mornings with Silvie. She never told him where she lived or how she spent her time away from him. What if it was in this forest? "I have to see her. I have to try to help her." He looked at Quinn. "You and the guards can go back if you want, but I will go into the forest."

Quinn sighed. "Mother always said you had one of the best of hearts. I wish now that it was a little darker, and maybe mine as well. You know I'll go with you, but let's find your guards first."

Aven put his hand on Quinn's shoulder and squeezed. Together, they turned to the left to search the forest edge.

Chapter 19

Tal

BLOOD, THERE WAS SO much blood. He could feel it on his hands, smell it, taste it. It was not his, but it might as well have been. The pain it caused him made him cry; he was sure he would die. How was his heart beating when it was no longer in his chest? How was he still breathing when all reason to be alive was gone?

"Horrible," said a harsh voice above him. "You ruined it all with your cowardice. Left all you care about to rot."

He stood in the forest, though he could barely see. It looked to be nighttime, but he had no idea how. It was mid-morning a moment ago, but now it was as black as night.

"Who's there?" he asked as he spun around, trying to see anything, anyone.

"Someone who knows you, everything about you. I can see how black your heart is. What would your father say about you now?"

"I doubt he would give two shits about me. He never did."

"That's a lie. You are a liar, Prince Taliesin. A liar to all those you come across, and worse yet, a liar to yourself."

"What do you know about it?"

"Everything," hissed the voice. "I knew you before you were born, saw the future that was spun for you. All you had to do was grab it, to latch on and trust, but instead, you turned from it. You unraveled all that had been set in place because of fear. Now you destroy the very fabric of the world with your deviant behavior, running away from all you were meant to be."

"I was meant to be nothing," Tal said angrily. "Born a second son to the second marriage of a king. Besides playing a good little prince at court, what else is there? I chose something different."

"Liar," said the voice. "Not even a pretty liar. You're vile for what you have caused. The gods can have no mercy for you since you refuse to repent, refuse the very salvation offered to you."

"What salvation is that?"

"Home," said the voice.

"What home? I have no home!"

The voice laughed cruelly. "Liar. You know what I speak of. You've done your best to ruin it, but it waits for you. She waits for you."

"What?" Tal moved closer to a tree where he thought the voice was coming from, trying to see into the forest. "Come out, and let me see you."

The voice laughed again as Tal felt his world spin. How could the forest be turning around and around? But it wasn't the forest. It was him. He had fallen, and he was rolling and rolling until...thud, a tree stopped his progress. He lay still, trying to make his head stop spinning.

The blood came again. His vision was nothing but red, the scent overwhelming. He couldn't see anything, and he was sick, horribly sick, as his stomach lurched. He needed to vomit everything inside of him, to rid himself of all that was left because it was meaningless. It was agony as pain was all he knew. He had to get away from it. He had run from pain for as long as he could remember. He rolled to get up when he felt gentle hands on his shoulders.

"Shh," said a whisper close by. He tried to sit up, to open his eyes, but his body wouldn't obey. He felt his head lifted off the ground, and then he was lying in a soft lap as someone ran their fingers through his hair. "It's fine, Tal. Everything's ok. I'm here. I found you." The voice was sweet, the most beautiful thing he'd ever heard. He couldn't place the voice, but it was as familiar as his own.

He settled, focusing on the hand that kept moving soothingly through his hair. "You," he croaked out, his voice sounding hoarse. "You...found me."

"I'll always find you." A gentle kiss on his forehead and then his lips. "Rest, Tal."

His pain drifted away as his consciousness did. He was no longer on a hard, cold forest ground but lying in sweet, soft grass as a summer breeze blew over him, bringing with it the sweet smell of honeysuckle. A hand ran through his hair, and he grabbed it, giving it a kiss.

"We should get back soon," said that beautiful, precious voice he loved.

"What for?"

"You're expected to open the banquet with a toast. It's less than two hours until it starts, and I need to get dressed."

"You look fine as you are."

She laughed. "Dressed in a grass-stained gown with my hair in a horrible tangle?"

"You're more beautiful like this than anyone in this realm or any other," he said as he kissed her hand again.

"You only say that because you enjoy putting me in this state."

He groaned and raised up, opening his eyes to look upon his lover, but the blaring sun made it impossible to see her face. "Perhaps we have time for me to make you even more inappropriately attired."

An afternoon of loving her in the soft grass flashed through his mind, feeling her soft skin under his fingertips and lips and hearing her breathy moans as he kissed his way down her body. How wonderful she tasted as she reached her peak, and the overwhelming pleasure and completeness he felt when he seated himself fully inside her. He was so connected to this woman that breathing without her around was difficult.

She laughed and bent towards him as he raised further, wanting nothing more than to taste her lips once again. He kissed her, burying his hands into her thick hair. She gasped at the sensation, spurring him on further, his tongue running against her lips, asking for entrance. Her lips parted, and he deepened their kiss, his tongue slipping over hers. He pulled back to look upon her face, and the strong scent of hyacinth hit him, making his nose twitch.

"Your Highness," said a breathless voice.

Tal opened his eyes to see Lady Delphina staring at him with wide eyes, her lips slightly parted. He scanned her lovely face as he kept his hands in her hair, seeing a small smattering of freckles on her nose he hadn't noticed before. "It was you? You found me?"

"Yes," she said, not backing away from him. "You were unconscious and muttering. I was afraid you were ill."

"You found me?" he asked again.

She nodded. "I'm sorry I ran away. I didn't plan to go far, but then I got lost. I've been looking for you for hours."

He leaned forward, his lips brushing hers again. "Home," he whispered. "I want to go home."

Her hand went to his cheek. "You're not well. You need to rest. It's too dark to look for Dyfan or anyone else. You should rest, and in the morning, we'll figure it out."

He shook his head. "I'm fine. It's just... I'm tired of running, tired of it all."

"Running from what?" she whispered. Her breath smelled sweet and strangely alluring, pulling him in.

"From everything, from whom I need to be, where I need to be."

"Tal," she said quietly, and her pull became too much. He closed the small space between them, kissing her gently at first, waiting to see how she responded. She wrapped her hands around his neck and pulled him closer, giving him all the encouragement he needed.

He longed for something, something he had lost or perhaps never really had. Something that would make him complete. He had run from it for so long, but he could not avoid it forever. Maybe he had been shown a glimpse of the future. A time when he could be at peace with who he was. He wanted home, and perhaps he would find it with Delphina. He at least wanted to find out.

He kissed her again and again as his hands moved from her hair down her body. She was soft and warm, his hands eager to explore each curve. They broke apart to breathe, and Tal kissed his way down her jaw to her neck, sucking lightly and making her gasp.

She arched against him for a few minutes, seeming to enjoy his attentions until she pulled away, her hands returning to cup his cheeks. "You need to rest. We both do. We still need to find our way out of this forest."

"And Dyfan."

"I suppose," she answered.

He kissed her gently and then nodded. "You'll stay with me? You won't leave?"

"Of course, I won't leave you. Now, come with me. I have a small shelter set up. You can rest there for a while. I'll keep watch over you." She stood up and held out her hand. He took it, got up off the ground, and let her lead him to a small shelter she had created with sticks and leaves.

He bent down and entered with Delphina following him. They sat together for a while, his head on her shoulder as she stroked his hair and hummed a sweet tune. He breathed in deeply, her scent overwhelming him, making him feel peaceful and tired. He eventually sunk down into her lap, where she continued to run her hands through his hair.

He whispered something, a name or an endearment, but it was lost to him as he fell asleep. He wanted nothing but rest and darkness, but the nightmares came even with Delphina keeping watch over him. He smelled the blood before looking down and seeing it covering his hands. Screams that tore through him filled the room, but he could not see where they came from.

The pain hit, piercing his heart and forcing him to his knees. He would not let this happen. It was not who he was, but the pain became too much, and the smell of blood burned his nose, making him ill. He convulsed and wretched over and over until there was nothing left. He was purged of everything: his breath, purpose, and life. He was empty and unfeeling, and he hated it. Still, the hollowness was better than the pain. He could exist with it even if it were not really living. He would go on, knowing that though he would try, nothing would ever make him feel whole again.

When the early morning sun woke him, he felt as though he hadn't slept in a week. His body ached, his head pounded, and his tongue was so dry he thought he might die from thirst. Sitting up, he noticed he was alone in the shelter, though Delphina's scent lingered, meaning she couldn't have been gone long. He crawled out to see if he could find her.

As he stood and stretched his sore back, he saw a small, dying fire before him, but no Delphina. A canteen and two pieces of dry meat were close by. He picked them up, figuring Delphina had left them for him. He drank half the canteen in one gulp, trying to soothe his dry tongue and throat. After choking down one of the pieces of meat and taking another sip of water, he wondered where Delphina could have gone.

He turned slowly and searched the area, trying to see between the trees or listen for nearby footsteps. For many long moments, there was nothing but an occasional bird call or the rustle of leaves in the winds. He was about to walk into the forest and see if he could find some sign of Delphina when he heard a shuffle to his left. He turned just as he heard a small yelp followed by a thud.

"Delphina?" he called uncertainly, hoping she had not met some real trouble.

More noise came, followed by a frustrated sigh. Tal hurried towards the sound, moving past three or four trees and pushing a large bush aside to find a woman who was not Delphina sitting up on the ground, a thick briar tangled around her ankle.

She looked up at him, and her lips curved into a small grin as her gray eyes roved over him. "I tried to move past you without disturbing you, but the forest had other ideas."

She pulled up her gray skirt to examine her situation, revealing a toned, pale leg. Tal moved back a step, watching as she wiggled her foot back and forth and hissed slightly as the briar dug deeper into her skin. She tugged at the briar before pulling her hand away with a soft "Dammit" as she sucked on her finger.

"You need help?" he asked cautiously, unsure if he should move any closer.

She shook her head, pulling her skirt up higher and taking out a small silver dagger. Tal watched as she carefully cut away the briar, trying to avoid it digging anymore into her flesh. Whoever she was, she was a pretty woman, though not uncommonly so. Her light red hair was straight and loose, hanging over her shoulders. Her features, though not plain, were easily forgettable, and he doubted he could describe her to any discernible degree if someone asked him.

She freed herself from the briars and flexed her foot. The thorns had punctured a few places deep enough to cause her to bleed. Tal could not look away from a particular cut close to the top of her foot. Blood oozed out of it, puddling a little. He took another step back as the scent of it threatened to make him ill. The edges of his vision started to grow dim at the sight of blood starting to run down her skin.

The woman pulled down her skirt, using the edge of it to put on her wound. She held it down to stop the bleeding as she looked up at Tal. "You all right? I know you've probably heard some tales about forest witches, but I can assure you that most are exaggerated. I have no plans to attack you and drain your blood."

Tal blinked his eyes rapidly. "What?"

"You seem like you're ready to bolt. I promise I won't hurt you."

Tal glanced at the dagger in her hand. "Your use of a blade makes me think otherwise."

She laughed slightly. "Here, take it. In fact..." She dug a hand into the folds of her skirt, bringing out a slightly larger, older-looking dagger. "Take this one as well if it makes you feel better." She held the blades out to him.

"No, it's fine." He couldn't help but grin slightly. "Besides, who knows what else you have hiding in that skirt."

She laughed again, this time fully. It was rich and almost melodic. Warmth bloomed in his chest, calming him as he moved towards her. "Let me help you up."

"Unnecessary," she said as she gracefully popped up on her feet, adjusting her skirt. "Don't worry. I'm only putting away my blades." She turned from him and raised her skirt so quickly that she was done in a couple of blinks of an eye. "Of course, I doubt I would be any trouble for you, even glamoured as you are in your clumsy body."

Tal's breath caught in his throat, causing him to cough. "Excuse me."

She moved around him as he turned to watch her. "It's very good, your glamour. I doubt many can see through it, but I can. I can see exactly who and what you are."

"And you aren't afraid?"

She stopped and stared at him. "Should I be? Do you plan to do me harm?" Her head tilted as she looked him up and down. "I don't believe you do. Besides, I know this forest. I know its tricks and how to get around most of them."

"Yet, I found you on the ground."

"True," she laughed again for a few seconds, and he ached to hear more of it for some reason. "But I was caught off guard, trying to get away from you. This silly place decided to cause mischief. I don't know why. I suppose it grows bored and needs entertainment just like any of us."

"You speak as if this place is alive," said Tal.

"Of course I do. It is," she replied. "I'm sure you've been warned of this place."

"A bit, and I've heard another speak of it as if it has consciousness, but it's hard to believe. It's only a forest."

"A forest made of trees older than anyone alive in this world, even the oldest of your kind. The Dark King of yours is practically a child to these trees. These trees are as alive as you and me, and there are other things living in this forest."

"Animals, I suppose?" Tal moved a little past her, peering into the forest. "I'll agree there are living creatures amongst us, but to speak of the whole place as if it has purpose and reason seems a bit much."

She hurried to his side and grabbed his hand. "But why? Come here."

He let her pull him along as he looked at her determined face. He swore her eyes were practically shining, their dull gray mixing with something else. She placed his hand on the trunk of the thickest tree in the area and kept her own over his.

"Close your eyes," she said commandingly. He rolled his eyes slightly and glanced back at her. "Go on. Just for a moment."

He shrugged and closed his eyes as she moved so close to him. He could feel her body against his. "Now concentrate on the trunk, feeling the ridges of the bark." She moved his hands slightly against the roughness of the tree. "Can you sense it? The water as it moves through this great thing. It comes up through the roots under us, into the trunk and the branches. See if you can trace it as it moves."

Her breath was gentle and quiet against his ear. He suppressed the shudder it caused as he concentrated on her words, moving his hand up and down against the trunk.

"Imagine the water as it pulls up from the ground." Her voice was almost hypnotic, luring him gently into a feeling of peace he had not felt since he couldn't remember when. "It takes what it needs, but it also gives. Homes for small woodland animals, a place to hide their treasures. Birds nest in its branches, resting and producing new life. Its thick branches and leaves give shade for plants that can only grow here away from the harsh sun." She sighed, her chest moving against his back. "Listen to the wind. It's much like our breath, gentle at times but harsh at others. It moves the tree as our breath moves us."

He listened intently. "I can hear it. It's almost like a song at times as it moves through the dying leaves—the whistles through the branches."

"That's the trees speaking in their own language. They are truly alive and have seen and heard everything throughout our history. Wars, great times of peace, enemies, lovers, it's all written within their trunks, told by their scars and how they grow. Some gashes from battles, others marks from those who made their vows to one another. Life imprinted them as it does on all of us, Prince Taliesin."

His eyes snapped open as he turned to look at her. "You know my name."

"Yes."

"Then I should know yours."

She took a step back from him. "It would do no good to tell you. You don't know me."

"But you know who I am?" He turned to face her.

"Yes, I know who you are."

"Tell me your name."

She shook her head. "It's not worth knowing. I'm nothing to you."

"Let me judge for myself."

"You should go. Find your friend and keep him close. You're in a dangerous place, Your Highness."

"The forest means me harm? I don't believe that, not after what you just showed me."

"Not everything in the forest means well. Keep your eyes open."

She started to walk past him, but he caught her arm. "Wait, you're a forest witch. Maybe you can help me. We're looking for someone."

"I know you are."

"It's a lady from my realm. Her uncle and king are looking for her and sent me to find her. Do you know whom I speak of?"

The woman nodded.

"Have you seen her recently?"

There was a rustle behind them, making the woman turn. "Tal, is that you?" It was Delphina walking towards them.

"Keep looking for what you seek, Prince Taliesin."

"Tal! Please tell me that's you and you're alright," called Delphina.

Tal stared up ahead, seeing Delphina's golden hair between the branches. He turned to look at the woman to ask her to stay and found her gone. His hand still hung in the air where he held her arm, but it gripped nothing. He lowered it just as Delphina found him.

"Tal! Are you well? I saw you were gone and was out of my mind in worry." He turned slowly, looking for any sign of the woman, but she was gone. "Tal?"

He shook his head. "I'm fine. I just…" He went to explain what happened with the woman, but as he looked at Delphina, he didn't want to. Was what happened even real? It seemed like it was at the time, but now he was unsure. Was he having some strange visions? Perhaps he hit his head when he fell. "It's nothing. I just went looking for you, and now I've found you."

"I'm sorry I left. I just needed to take care of a few things and see if I could find anything useful for food or water sources. There isn't much here. We should keep moving and see if we can find Dyfan or this witch we're supposed to be looking for." She took a deep breath as she stared out into the forest. "I suppose we should still look for my cousin."

"Yes," said Tal instantly. "We have to find her, and I think if we keep looking, we'll find Dyfan as well." He took her hand. "Come on, let's get back and get your things, so we can keep moving towards the center of this place."

She let him take her toward the small shelter. "Fine, but we don't separate again. This place is strange. It sounds silly, but I feel like something is constantly watching me."

"I don't think it's silly. Something is definitely going on here; the sooner we are done with this place, the better," said Tal.

Chapter 20

Aven

THE FOREST WAS ODD and dark, keeping Aven on edge. His grip on his reins was tighter than normal, making his horse fidget slightly. He and Quinn found the guards after an hour of searching, waiting just out of the forest tree line and watching the smoke rise from the temple.

Aven couldn't get the priest and priestess who lived at the temple out of his mind. He even felt awful for the head priestess. She didn't appear well, as though something had caused her to lose all sense. No matter what Kava had told them about not wanting to leave, Aven felt guilty. Perhaps he should have stayed and fought for them or tried harder to get them to leave. No matter how many times Quinn pointed out that they would not have been able to stand against so many or that those of the temple could not be convinced, Aven still felt terrible.

It made him even more convicted to find the forest witch and see her safely somewhere, even more so if it was Silvie. He knew it was a long shot, but there was still a chance. Silvie was a powerful magic-user, and she had always been vague about where she spent her time. This strange, thick forest would seem just the place his odd friend would choose to settle down when she needed a rest. He would never forgive himself if something happened to her, and he had been able to stop it.

"I know you're feeling guilty, but there was nothing you could do, Aven," said Quinn. "You being there would have only gotten you captured and me killed with our guards at best. At worst, we'd all be dead."

"I know."

"But you're still fretting over it. It's why we're searching this damn forest, isn't it?" Quinn looked behind him at the guards.

"Partly, but also because I think it's the right thing to do."

"Because some Fae woman you don't know told you to?" Quinn sighed. "I don't like this place."

"Me neither," said Aven. "I'm also worried about what that group who attacked the temple will do next. We should alert our fathers so they can send out a warning."

"It would take us over a day to get to a village to be able to send a message, and I doubt it would be one that has reliable birds. We could probably move as fast as any other rider. Besides, I'm sure the kingdom is already on high alert. Rumors and warnings of the Court of the Underlings have been going around for a while now."

"You think it was truly the Court of the Underlings back there?"

"Who else could it be?" asked Quinn.

"Well, maybe not all the attacks are just one group. They all don't fit one specific pattern, do they?"

"Go on," said Quinn as he dunked down to avoid a branch.

"Some reports speak of attacks on estates, mines, or temples with people being killed, but others tell of only a few people taken from beds in the night. In a couple of attacks on mines, barely anyone was injured. The place was just destroyed," said Aven.

"True," said Quinn. "But that doesn't mean it's two separate groups. Maybe they have a reason for leaving some places virtually untouched and decimating others."

"But why? If they have the ability to destroy temples and estates, why use caution in some places? Why leave some people alive and well and kill many people in others?"

"So you think there is more than one group going around and terrorizing the land?"

Aven looked into the forest. "I don't know, but it's possible, isn't it?"

"I suppose it is. We can discuss it as we ride back home, hopefully soon?"

Aven nodded. "We need to get back as quickly as possible, but this is just something I need to do. Perhaps you should have ridden back with the guards."

"You think we can just leave you here unprotected?" Quinn chuckled darkly. "You're our next king, Aven. The guards could never desert you. You're also my best friend. I couldn't stand to leave you here alone."

Aven couldn't help but grin at Quinn. They had known each other their whole lives, being born barely a month apart. "I'll promise you this. We'll leave this forest within a day and a half. If we find nothing by tomorrow evening, we will leave the next day at first light."

"And if we do find this witch?"

"I'll tell her what the Fae woman instructed me to, and we'll be on our way. She can respond to the information however she likes. We will not wait around to see," said Aven.

They ate a hurried late lunch after finding a small clearing wide enough to give their horses a rest. The guards had thought well ahead, bringing plenty of water to last them and their mounts for the next few days. There was enough grass left on the ground for the horses to graze, and after a short rest, they were on their way again.

The forest grew even denser the further they traveled, the trees growing thicker, the brush on the ground wild. Whatever path they were following practically disappeared, and Aven began to worry they could not find their way back out.

"This place gets less and less appealing," said Quinn. "I feel like something is constantly watching me."

"I thought maybe I was the only one who felt it."

"No, but I suppose it makes sense. These trees are old, and the forest is wild. Who knows what could be lurking in here? I'm not sure I believe all the rumors and stories, but some may be true."

"You think thieves and the deviants of society lay in wait here, hoping to catch wayward travelers?"

"That would be more plausible than the scarier stories of Fae and faerie creatures being banished here from the faerie lands."

"What do you think gets you banished from the faerie lands?" asked Aven. "I didn't think they were much for rules."

"Oh, they have rules. They just might not make sense to you and me. Here, it's pretty black and white. If you kill or steal, it's a crime and must be punished."

"In theory," said Aven. "But there are those who get out of the consequences of their evil actions. More than one lord's atrocities have been overlooked in all kingdoms, even ours."

"Money and power are a good defense even amongst the most heinous acts, but for the most part, there is justice when someone breaks the law. In the faerie lands, it's not so obvious. Killing can be overlooked if it is done with the right reasons and possessions taken if one can show they are more deserving. It doesn't matter how hard the other person worked to gain it or how long it's been in their family's possession."

"Do you know how they decide such things?"

"Not really, and I think it's varied over the centuries as kings and lords change. Fae's minds are not like ours in some ways. Their ideas of right and wrong don't line up with ours. You have to be careful around them."

"So what would get one banished from the faerie lands?" asked Aven.

"Killing without reason and causing chaos. Of course, the first course of action would be to try to put something like that to death, but a few ancient creatures are too hard to kill. It's easier to curse them from the lands and send them to a place like this, where they can be held by old magical wards set up by our people centuries ago. That's what legends say, anyway."

"A time when we were a friend of Fae, I suppose."

"Yes," said Quinn with a teasing laugh. "When dragons roamed, and our rulers commanded them with a wave of their hand."

"So you really think it's just all legend, then?" asked Aven.

"What, that there could be old faerie creatures in this wood?"

"Well, yes, that and the dragons."

"I think faerie creatures in this forest are more likely. As you have heard, my father does not dismiss the dragons so easily, but until I see some evidence, I remain very skeptical."

Quinn looked away, appearing to search the forest to the right. Aven kept his eyes on the left, wondering if each shake of a leaf or strange noise was something to worry about. Perhaps he had made a mistake, and they should turn around. He worried about Silvie but didn't want to ignore the danger he was bringing upon his guards and, especially, Quinn. He thought to suggest leaving to his companions, but something stopped him.

The forest had a strange pull over him. He was wary at what could be hiding amongst the trees, but the place didn't scare him. It somehow made him feel more alive. His magic had become agitated as soon as they entered the woods. It swirled around his stomach and into his chest, making him feel jittery and anxious and yet not unpleasant. It gave him a feeling of expectation, as if anything could happen. He wanted desperately to do some magic. It was as if the forest was almost playing with him, asking to see something.

"I doubt we want to travel long after dark if we are even able to see a way," said Quinn. "We need to start looking for another clearing big enough for our needs."

Aven took a deep breath, trying to clear his head and attend to his friend's words when his horse suddenly whinnied and reared up on its hind legs.

"Easy," said Aven, working to control his mount. He had never had trouble with his horse. It was fairly young and known to be spirited, but it usually listened to commands.

The horse stamped its front feet and shook its head before rising again. Aven held on, not wanting to be thrown off. "Settle," said Aven, trying to get his horse to lower. The horse went down and then up again, Aven still trying to gain control.

"Aven!" said Quinn in alarm as he reached for Aven's horse's bridle, but the horse moved away, bucked up, and then took off into the trees. The reins ripped out of Aven's hands at the sudden movement, and he was unable to reach them. He gripped the horse's mane and shouted over the wind, "Halt! Stop!" Whether or not his horse could hear him, it didn't seem to matter. The horse continued his flight, spurred on by fear or madness.

Tree limbs whipped at Aven's face, scratching his forehead and cheeks. He flattened himself over the neck of the horse, trying to avoid any more cuts or bumps. Having no control over the animal was terrifying as they dodged trees and jumped over old logs. It seemed impossible his steed wouldn't hit something eventually.

"Please stop," said Aven, begging the horse. "Halt!" He wasn't sure how long they ran as Aven did all he could to hold on. He eventually had trouble keeping his eyes open as the wind and debris brought up by the horse's pace stung them. They rode deeper and deeper into the forest, the horse's pace not slowing, and Aven began to wonder if he would have to do something desperate and dangerous, such as jump off.

He began to look for some soft and clear area that would give him the best chance of survival when his horse suddenly shook his head and stopped. He halted so quickly that the horse half went down on his front knees, and Aven was thrown over the horse's neck.

He hit the ground hard, the impact taking his breath away, and the world was a blur as he tumbled and tumbled until a tree stopped his process, his back and head hitting against the trunk. Aven moaned as he fought to stay awake, but the draw from the darkness and trying to avoid the pain that would surely come was too much. He closed his eyes and saw nothing.

He wasn't sure how long he floated into nothing, only that he didn't mind. It could have been a few hours, a day, a week, or a lifetime, but it didn't matter. It was comforting. He felt as though the magic within him was let loose, surrounding him in some sort of protective shield. It sang quietly, a lovely song of the history of his people—of triumphs and defeats, of love and heartache.

However long he existed in the dark space, it did not last forever. Eventually, a light appeared, moving closer and closer to him until he was bathed in it. His feet hit solid ground, and as the light faded, he realized he stood in his father's study. It was different than he remembered.

The desk was on the wrong wall, facing away from the windows. His father liked to face the windows, so he could look out periodically. The chairs by the fireplace were covered in dark brown fabric instead of the pretty light blue Aven's mother had recovered them in a few years ago. The place even smelled different, full of smoke and leather instead of the fresh floral scent that was always present in his room due to the fresh flowers brought in daily.

"You must see this is madness, Gavan," said a voice by the fireplace, causing Aven to notice two men standing there. He realized one was his father, though he was much younger. His hair was longer than usual, and the gray flecks by the temples were gone. His eyes were bright and unlined instead of the sad, dimmed eyes the older version held.

The man speaking was the old king. Aven barely remembered him as he had died before Aven's eighth birthday. He was a tall, wide-built man with steely, cold blue eyes and dark gray hair. Aven had always been scared of him, though he wasn't sure why. He couldn't remember his grandfather ever saying a harsh word to him. He couldn't remember his grandfather talking to him much at all.

"It's not madness. It is the sanest I've ever been," said Aven's father. "I know what I want, Father."

"It's not about what you want, Gavan. It's what's good for our kingdom. She will never be an acceptable queen."

"Why not?"

The old king chuckled darkly. "You know why not. Whoever would accept her?"

Aven moved closer, seeming to be ignored by the two men. He was intrigued and surprised by the conversation. Had the old king not approved of Aven's mother as queen? While his mother was not the cleverest of women, she was still sweet and polite. She came from a good family, her father one of their lords.

"When they see how good, kind, and powerful she is, they will be happy to have her as queen."

"You are only seeing things as you wish, not as they are," the old king angrily said. "Gavan, I know this will be difficult, but you must stop before it goes too far. Tell the woman you can see her no longer."

"It's too late. I've already made promises to her." Aven's father smiled slightly. "She believes she might be carrying my child."

"Gavan, you aren't serious," said the king, half choking on his words.

"She isn't completely sure yet, but all the signs are there." He stood up straight. "So you see, it's done. She will be my queen, as she is probably already carrying my heir."

"This doesn't have to be this way. Our healers have ways of taking care of such things, especially if she isn't even sure yet. I can have something brewed you can give her," said the king quickly.

Aven's father's eyes narrowed. He moved closer to the old king, his hands in fists at his side, fire ringing his knuckles as a summoned wind ruffled Gavan's hair. "Don't you dare suggest such a thing. You are speaking of my child and the woman I love. If you threaten either one again, you will no longer be around to show your displeasure."

The old king stepped back, staring at his son's hands. "Magic? You've been using magic. Is this her doing?"

"No. I've been doing it since I can remember. It's nothing to be ashamed of."

"You're going to ruin this kingdom, Gavan. You must see it."

"I don't, and you won't change my mind, Father," said Aven's father as Aven felt a touch on his arm. He turned and suddenly was pulled away from the palace study back into the darkness.

Chapter 21

Tal

THOUGH HE HAD DOUBTED Delphina's horse when it was first brought to them, it turned out the beast was as steady and strong as they came. She was older and a little stubborn but was able to carry them both, which pleased Tal in two ways. One, he was still sore from his fall and was happy to be off his feet as they traveled. Two, the horse was small enough that Delphina had to ride very close in front of him. It allowed him to keep his arms around her as he maneuvered the horse and ample opportunities for him to drop small kisses on her neck and shoulder.

She gave him plenty of encouragement, making wonderful little noises each time his lips met her skin as she leaned back into him. She even turned a few times and kissed his lips gently, making him wish they had the time and place to stop so he could spend plenty of time drawing more of those tantalizing noises out of her.

All these thoughts of her pushed most of his other worries aside. Tal knew they needed to find Dyfan, but he was a capable man. Perhaps he was already out of the forest waiting for Tal and Delphina to appear. Tal even managed to push the idea of the forest witch he had met mostly out of his head. He didn't mention her to Delphina as he received no important information and wasn't even sure if it was real. She might have been some strange delusion he had from his fall and exhaustion.

"We aren't going to get very far today if you don't concentrate on where we're going," said Delphina as she put her hand on his arm wrapped around her waist.

"Are you in such a hurry to leave, Delphie?" he asked with a laugh. "Have I not kept you entertained?"

She turned her head to glance at him. "Perhaps I long for an appropriate place where you can show me all you have to offer for my amusement, Your Highness."

"Patience, Delphie," he whispered before nipping at her arched ear. "I'm in no rush since I have you at my disposal and your undivided attention. I rather like this leisurely pace."

"I'm not sure if I should take that as a compliment."

"You should, as there's simply too much of you to admire in one evening. I need plenty of time to get to know each lovely part of you."

She laughed as she leaned away from him. "Seriously, Tal, this forest already almost killed you once. Perhaps you might take this journey a bit more seriously, especially on this horse."

Tal took his arm off Delphina's waist and leaned forward to pat the horse's neck. "This old mare's a good girl. Been nothing but complying all day." He laughed. "Perhaps Dyfan was right about your inability to control her." He laughed again, kissing her cheek as she scowled.

"I'm not the one who ended up on the ground, though. You don't even know where your horse is."

"True, and I doubt we will come across him. I suppose I'll pay off the poor stable we took him from. It won't be much."

"I never thought I'd say it, but I'll be happy to see that small human village again. Even sleep in one of the inn's lumpy beds."

"You assume you'll get much sleep once we get back to the inn?" said Tal, putting his arm back around her.

"Maybe I'll make you wait until we get back home," she said with some attitude. "Make sure you have a proper bath."

Tal tried to laugh, but it caught in his throat at the thought of returning to the Golden Court and seeing his brother or Delphina's father. He was sure he wanted her, but he hadn't given much thought to the future. What would she expect of him? Perhaps he would do better to try to control himself. Just as he thought it, Delphina leaned back against him, her hand going to his thigh.

"I was only teasing, Tal. I'm in no rush to return home. When we find my silly cousin, we can see what she's about and send her to my father. There's no reason we must go too."

Tal didn't say anything, but he thought there was a very good reason for him to go back and see Lord Elgan. The man had offered a way to give him complete freedom. As much as Tal ached for Delphina at the moment, would he choose her over something he had wanted for so long?

She turned her head, her sweet breath falling on his face, making him smile lazily. "We'll figure it out as we go." She took her hand off his leg, grabbed the waterskin nearby, and took a sip. "Here, have some yourself. It's been a while since we stopped."

He nodded and took the water skin from her, taking a long drink. The water was cool and almost sweet, making him take another long swig. "Where did you get this?"

"A stream not far from where I found you. I filled up all three skins I had," said Delphina.

"Then you won't mind if I finish this one. It tastes divine. I must have been thirstier than I thought."

"Drink what you need," said Delphina. "Hopefully, we can find more soon."

Tal finished the waterskin and handed it back to her, so she could tie it back to the horse. Once she was done, she leaned back into him, and Tal closed his eyes for just a moment to relish her warmth. It should have been strange for him to want her this badly after such a short acquaintance, but he wasn't in the mood to question it. His senses were full of her, and though he talked of her having patience, he wasn't sure how long he could last before having her completely.

The forest started to grow dim as the day ended, and Tal thought they should find somewhere to set up a shelter before it got so dark they couldn't see. He could feel how weak his magic was in the forest and didn't want to depend on it for light or warmth.

"Tal, do you see that?" asked Delphina, taking him out of his thoughts.

"See what?" he asked, but he saw it when he looked where she was gazing. There was a light coming from between the trees to their right, one that must have come from a decent source because it didn't seem close.

"Do you think we should see what it is? Maybe it could be that forest witch's house."

"Or it could be something we don't want to come across," said Tal.

"We have to check it out, don't we?" asked Delphina. "Let's dismount and sneak up to see if we can figure it out without getting too close."

"You're right." He stopped the horse and dismounted, adjusting his shirt before holding out his arms towards Delphina as she slid into them. He couldn't help but give her a quick kiss before taking her hand and leading her into the forest.

They walked a wide circle, moving gradually closer to the light as it became brighter and brighter. As they approached it, Tal could feel the warmth coming from multiple fires and smell something wonderful cooking. He stopped behind a tree and peered around it as Delphina did the same, looking around the other side. He couldn't see much beyond a bright fire burning.

"What should we do?" asked Delphina.

Before he could respond, he felt a slight tug on his cloak. He turned to find a young girl with dark hair and large brown eyes staring at him.

"Who are you?" she asked.

Tal looked at Delphina, whose nose crinkled up as she stared at the girl. Tal raised an eyebrow before kneeling down to speak with the child. The girl was dressed simply in a light blue dress made for winter. It had a bit of dirt on the skirt and the edge of the sleeves. Her cheeks were red from the cold, and in her hands, she held a worn stuffed toy meant to look like a bear.

"We're just tired travelers. Who are you?"

"Nora," said the girl as she brought the bear to her lips and chewed on the ear.

"And what are you doing out here?"

"Mother had Peadar looking for wood for the fires. He was supposed to watch me and take me with him, but I got lost. I was following the light back to our tents like my mother taught me."

"Your home? Is that what's up ahead?"

She nodded. "I'm hungry."

"Well, you should scurry on back then," said Delphina, taking a small step closer as she gave the girl a slight grin.

Nora held out a dirty hand to Delphina, but Delphina didn't take it. "You're so pretty. Are you a princess?"

Delphina looked uncertain as she stared at the child, and Tal gave her a quizzical look. Did she not like children? He took Nora's small hand. "Delphie here is a little shy. She's not a princess, but you're right. She is very pretty." He gave her a mischievous smile. "Though I don't think she's as lovely as you."

The bear fell out of the little girl's mouth before she laughed.

"Nora! Nora! Is that you?" yelled a woman's voice behind them.

Delphina gave a small, surprised yelp as Tal stood up to greet a plump young woman with the same hair and eyes as the little girl.

"Oh," said the woman as she came to a stop, staring at Tal. She put her hands in her pocket, where Tal thought she probably had some kind of small blade. "What are you doing with my daughter?"

"Nothing," said Delphina, sounding irritated. "We want nothing to do with her. She found us."

"I'm sorry we disturbed you," said Tal, thinking of a quick lie to tell. "We've been traveling through the woods to get to Illedria and lost some of our party. We've been trying to get back on track ever since and stumbled upon you here. Your daughter found us on her way back home."

"You're traveling through the forest? Most take a boat to get to Illedria," said the woman.

Tal shrugged and built on his lie. "Boats are expensive. We could barely afford our horse, as sad as it is."

"I can understand that," said the woman as she took her daughter's hand. "Well, you found us, and it's our custom I invite you to join us. If you have any weapons, you'll have to leave them at our leader's tent in the center of the camp. They'll be returned to you when you leave."

"We have no interest in joining you," said Delphina sharply.

"You sure?" asked the woman. "It's almost dark, and people tend to get lost in these woods. All sorts are hiding out there. Most you don't want to come across."

"And yet you offer us hospitality?" asked Tal.

"It's custom, and if you intend us harm, you should know we're a decent size group. Though we prefer peace, we have ways of protecting ourselves." She held out her hand, and a flame appeared in her palm.

"Magic?" said Delphina as she moved closer. "You can use magic."

The flame increased in size. "My people have used magic for generations. We originally come from Illedria and have old Fae blood in us, though we don't like to claim it. People are leery of us enough as it is. Magic isn't trusted in the human lands."

"But you use it openly?" Tal stared at the flame as Nora held out her hand.

A small bit of the fire jumped into her tiny palm. "It's our way of life, and we refuse to ignore it or hide it away as those pompous Illedrians do." Nora's mother held her hand aloft, lighting the way. "Follow me to camp if you want a decent meal."

"Should we?" asked Delphina.

"I don't see the harm in it," said Tal. "A warm meal and shelter for the night sounds better than what we had planned."

"All right, but we need to leave early in the morning. I want to get out of this forest as soon as possible."

Tal took hold of their horse, and they hurried to catch up to the woman and her daughter. Nora looked back at Tal with her bear's ear in her mouth. Tal gave her a wink, and the little girl laughed. It wasn't a far walk to their camp, and the site was more than Tal expected. They had found a clearing in the woods and taken down a few smaller trees to make it bigger. There were at least four dozen rows of impressive canvas tents.

People and animals were all about. Three women chased a flock of chickens toward a gated area they had made. A man sat in a space with three goats around him. A group of women was gathered around a wooden tub in front of a covered wagon. They washed clothes as they talked and laughed. It was as if a small village had been set up in the woods.

Several smaller fires burned by the tents, with one large fire in the very middle in front of the biggest dwelling. It was at least twice as large as the other tents, with several rugs in front of it. A primitive chair was placed close to it in front of the fire, where an old woman sat with a group of children around her.

"Auntie Aghna is telling stories," said Nora happily, letting go of her mother's hand to run ahead and join the other children.

"Nora, there's no need to run. She has more stories to tell than you could imagine," said her mother.

Nora didn't listen, hurrying to the group of children and sitting between two older girls. One took Nora and placed her on her lap. Nora put her bear in her mouth and stared at the older woman.

"Love is strange, children. It often doesn't behave as we think it should, and it makes us do things we normally wouldn't. It turns us into fools and either cowards or heroes."

"How so?" asked an older boy close to the old woman's knee.

"I've heard of kings giving up their thrones for love. There have been women who have given their lives for their beloved and sometimes even more than that."

"What can you give up that's more than your life, Auntie?" said a girl as she stretched her back.

The old woman looked towards Tal and Delphina. She kept her eyes on Tal and said, "Plenty, dear girl. You can give up all you have that makes life worth living where death would be a relief." She smiled at the children. "But you'll have to wait to hear more. We have guests, and supper is soon. Go clean yourself up."

The children groaned, but the woman only laughed. "I'll tell you whatever you wish after supper. Now go."

The children hopped up, running off to various tents. A good-sized boy took Nora's hand and came to the woman next to Tal.

"Peadar, if you lose your sister again, I'll see that you're scooping up manure for a week."

He cringed and said, "Yes, ma'am," before taking Nora to a nearby tent.

"Who have we here, Dunla?" asked the old woman as she remained seated. Two well-built men came to her side, both staring at Tal and Delphina.

"Two travelers Nora found in the forest not far from here. They say they're on their way to Illedria."

"Come closer so I can see you. I'd rise to meet you, but these old bones work even worse than my eyes."

Tal took Delphina's hand and moved close to the woman, seeing her eyes were clouded over, and he doubted she could see much at all.

"State your names," said the old woman.

"I'm Tal, and this is Delphie," said Tal as Delphina rolled her eyes at his nickname for her.

"And where are you from?"

"Uchel, or at least that's the last place we stayed," said Tal.

The old woman looked up and down. "I suppose you're as good a liar as any I've met, but still a liar."

"Ma'am, what makes you think I'm lying?" asked Tal.

"The fact that you are," said the old woman. "It's no matter. If you mean no harm to us, I don't need to know what you want to keep secret."

"I don't mean you any harm," said Tal. "I'm just appreciative of a warm meal and place to rest."

"Hmmm." The old woman nodded. "And what of your friend, here? Is she a liar, too?"

"What good does it do to answer?" said Delphina. "You could call me a liar either way."

The old woman turned towards Delphina. "Those who tell the truth either say very little or answer simply. Your words betray you."

"You have weapons," said the man on the right. His dark brown eyes were wary, and the way he clenched his hands showed he was not comfortable. "You'll need to leave them here for the night."

"Of course," said Tal. He unhooked his sword and handed it to the man. The man took it as Tal took out a dagger and gave it to the other man.

"This is a fine sword for a simple traveler," said the man.

"It is," said Tal.

"Where did you get it?"

"I've had it for a while," said Tal.

The old woman laughed. "See, the truth takes very few words."

Delphina handed the men her sword, a bow and quiver of arrows she carried, and a small knife. The men took them without comment.

"That's all," said Tal.

"All the weapons you have," said the old woman. "But you could easily cause havoc in other ways."

"I have a feeling the same could be said of you, ma'am. You appear feeble and old, but I bet you still have a way to defend your people," said Tal.

The woman laughed again. "Truth. It becomes you, sir. Now, come and relax. You'll eat with me tonight. I could use your help walking closer to the fire for the meal. Perhaps your friend wouldn't mind going with Nora to help the others fetch the wine and food."

"Of course, Delphie wouldn't mind," said Tal with a grin at Delphina. "It's little to ask in exchange for your generosity."

Delphina narrowed her eyes, but then she brightened. "I wouldn't mind at all, happy to leave Tallie poo here at your service."

He leaned in closer to her and whispered in her ear, "You'll regret that later, Delphie."

She shuddered slightly but then recovered and said before walking off with Nora, "I'm counting on you to keep that promise, Tallie."

"Come help me up, young man," said the woman as she attempted to rise from her chair. The two men on each side tried to assist, but she waved them away. "Take my chair closer to the fire, and then gather the others. Our guest can handle anything else I need."

Tal moved closer to the old woman and took her arm as she rose. One of the men took the chair as they walked off together.

"It's hard getting old. My mind's as sharp as ever, but my body is falling apart. Becoming a burden on those you love is one of the worst things about this life," said Aghna. "You'll see one day."

He nodded, though he never would grow old like her. He might age slightly, and his body would eventually not be as spry as it was now. In the middle of his fifth decade, he was considered very young for a Fae. His uncle, who was well over six centuries old, showed little signs of aging.

"So, I know little about you, except you're good at lying. What else are you willing to tell me about yourself?" said Aghna as they slowly walked towards the fire.

"You want truth, I suppose."

"I'll take whatever you're willing. I'm sure any lies you come up with will be entertaining, though I'm not sure how in the mood I am for it. Something genuine would be welcomed."

Tal thought it over. "I'm a long way from home."

"From one of the northern kingdoms, then?"

"It doesn't matter where I'm from. The distance would still be the same."

"Do you have a destination in mind?"

"I have a task I must complete, but no, I have no destination," said Tal.

"Then you're lost," said Aghna.

"I suppose that's as good of a way to describe it as any," said Tal.

She patted his arm. "Don't sound so defeated. Many who are lost find their way eventually, and they discover wonderous things on the journey."

Tal half smiled. "Where is your home, ma'am?"

"Call me Aghna or Auntie, whatever you like, just not ma'am," said the old woman. "And this is home."

"You've lived in the forest your whole life?"

"Of course not," said Aghna. "I meant with my people. This is home. We take it with us as we travel."

"So you're travelers then?"

"We are. It's quite a life, you know. I've seen the best every land has to offer," she said as they arrived at the fire.

"I imagine you've seen the worst as well," commented Tal, taking her to her chair.

"Of course I have, but I don't like to dwell on it. It's the beautiful times I chose to remember. That's a lesson for you, young man, as you grow older. Choose to remember the good times, and let the bad ones go."

Tal sighed as he helped the old woman sit down, realizing he didn't have many memories, not ones he cared to recall. The past three decades had been a blur of dubious decisions, faceless women, and causing as much trouble as he could. Before that, he couldn't remember much about his younger self. "Sadly, I don't think much about my life is worth remembering."

"Oh, well," said Aghna as she settled into her chair. "You're young. You have plenty of time to make good memories. Vow to yourself tonight to start, young...Tal, isn't it?"

"Yes, ma'am," said Tal.

"Call me Aghna or Auntie." He nodded. "Now, Tal, is that short for something? Perhaps Taliesin?"

Tal almost started in shock, but he kept his ground and nodded. "It is Taliesin."

"Hmmm. An old name. Not one you hear anymore. A pity, really, when one of the very founders of this land had the same name. Quite a hero as well as a poet and singer. Are you able to spin verses and sing sweet songs?"

Tal smirked. "There have been times I've strung together a few worthwhile words to win over a lady."

"Ah, all young men become poets when a pretty face is involved," said Aghna. "I was once thought beautiful, and my dear husband wrote me some very nice stanzas. Nothing you would call profound, but they were dear to me because they were true to him."

Unsure of what to say, Tal merely nodded his head.

"Sit by me, Taliesin. Tell me any memorable prose or poems you managed to create."

Tal sat down on a well-worn leather cushion next to the old woman, planning on telling her there was none he could recall when a memory floated into his mind. It was a cool day in the Golden Court, the rain falling hard outside the windows. He sat in front of a fireplace, a warm body pressed against his.

"This flame is nothing compared to my love. It gives heat and can burn, but she is the one who can truly consume. Her beauty and goodness are like those above; her heart is only explainable as something new. She is settled yet excited, wise, although young. Everything that shouldn't be becomes what is about every song ever sung. What more can I say except without her, this fire cannot warm me, no other could enchant me, and my very heart sits within her flame."

Aghna was silent for a moment as she stared into the flame, and Tal sat back on his cushion. "Is this about the lady you travel with?"

"No," said Tal. "To be honest, I can't recall who was there when I spoke those words."

"Odd, as she must have been something to inspire such words." She turned her hazy eyes on him. "Did you lose her? Is that why you chose not to speak her name?"

"I tell the truth when I say I cannot recall, Aghna. I don't even know where exactly I was when I spoke those words. Probably just some evening conquest."

"No," said Aghna sternly. "Those were not words to a random woman you met for a night. Perhaps you think you don't remember, but your heart does. I only pray that one day you do as well."

A group of people came close to the fire, including Nora, with her mother, changed into a fresh dress with her hands and face clean. Dunla placed a jug of wine by the fire and turned to Tal. "Your friend said she had something personal to take care of and skipped off into the woods on the right side of camp. I thought she'd be back by now."

Men followed with the food, some sort of roasted meat, a few winter vegetables, and flatbread that had been cooked over a fire. The children took their places close to Aghna, Nora sitting next to Tal with a grin.

"We shouldn't eat until both our guests are present," said Aghna. "It would not be our way or the gods'."

"But it's a full moon, Auntie," said one of the men who served her. "We cannot worship and celebrate correctly until after supper."

"Even the great Moon God knows our ways," said Aghna. "He will wait with us."

Tal stood up as Nora watched him. "I'll go see what's keeping Delphie. She's not always the best with time."

Nora popped up off her cushion. "I'll go with you. I know all the good hiding places."

"Nora! You will do no such thing," said Nora's mother as she poured mugs of thick red wine.

"But he might get lost again," said Nora.

"It's alright," said Tal as he kneeled down. "Stay here and save my seat so I can sit by you. Keep one for Delphie, too. I won't be long."

Nora nodded and plopped back down onto her cushion. She placed her bear on one side and put her little hand on the other, looking around sternly at anyone who would dare take one of the cushions. Tal asked Dunla where she had last seen Delphie and hurried to that area of the woods.

The clouds had finally cleared enough to see the moon and some of the stars through the trees, giving Tal enough light to see. He held up his hand and concentrated, willing a flame, light, or something to appear in his palm. A small weak flame sprung up, and he shook his head, perplexed. It was true that he had problems with his light magic for a while, but he could usually still do simple things such as cast fire or light. Ever since he entered the forest, his magic felt weaker. His stronger dark magic wouldn't even respond. It was strange as it didn't seem to affect the travelers, and Delphie had made a fire.

Tal held up his hand as he entered the woods, the sounds of laughter and merriment coming from the center of the camp growing weaker as he moved into the trees.

"Delphie?" he called, holding his hand up higher to see.

"You're sure," said a whisper to his left. Tal turned, trying to see where it was coming from. A response came so quietly he couldn't make it out.

"We'll take care of it later. Do only what you came for and nothing more. That's enough," said the whisper again, sounding angry.

Another response, this one again so low, Tal couldn't hear it. He moved towards the noise, wondering who was out there with him. Perhaps it was someone from the camp, but it could also be someone unfriendly circling the travelers, intending to make trouble. Tal moved deeper into the woods, letting his palm drop to destroy his flame. The light from the moon was enough for him to see the trees before him. He silently came to one and leaned against the large trunk, peering around it.

"What on earth are you doing?" said Delphina, just behind him, making him jump.

Tal turned, his heart beating fast. "I thought I heard someone. I was checking who it could be."

"You heard someone?" asked Delphina. "Who would be out here?"

"Maybe just people from the camp, but I was afraid it was something worse, nefarious maybe. I thought they might attack the camp or have you."

She looked beyond the tree. "I don't see anything. I haven't heard anything either, and I've been around for a bit."

"Why are you out here?" asked Tal.

"I needed to take care of something," she said, looking away. "I have needs just like anyone else."

"I'm sure they have a place in the camp where you could have… freshened up," said Tal.

"I like my privacy. Can we not talk about this?"

"Fine, but no more going off by yourself. Every time I turn around, you're gone." Tal took her hand, bringing her towards him.

"Hardly," she said as she put her arms around him. "I get barely twenty feet away from you, and you don't like it? Already possessive, are we?"

"Not wanting you to be alone in a strange forest is hardly possessive, Delphie." Her mouth formed into a pretty pout, making Tal chuckle. "Come on, supper is ready, and everyone is waiting for you."

"You think their food will even be edible?"

"It didn't smell terrible, and hot food is better than the little dried bit we have in our packs," said Tal, pulling her towards the camp. "Now be the sweet, charming lady I've seen, and keep the spoiled, unreasonable creature you can be tucked away."

"Ugh, you speak of me as if I'm awful." Delphina tried to pull her hand away, but Tal kept it firmly in his.

"I do not. I enjoy both parts of you. I like it when you're a proper lady with your pretty smiles and manner." He stopped and turned to her. "I like it even more when you're a naughty little minx. I plan to draw that side out of you fully someday and take my time trying to tame it."

"You think you can tame me?"

"Not at all, but it'll be fun to try." He laughed as he turned from her and continued walking to the camp.

Supper was an interesting, loud event that fascinated Tal. He couldn't remember what banquets were like in his father's court, but he knew they were much different from his brother's or uncle's. His uncle's were quiet, dignified affairs with whispers and a little polite chit-chat. His brother's were loud but lacked the warmth of the simple feast in front of him.

The food wasn't bad. In fact, it was one of the best human meals he'd ever had. He saw that even Delphina cleaned the plate passed to her and had two glasses of wine. She smiled as she took his glass and filled it. "This isn't as bad as I thought."

"We haven't gotten to the best part yet," said Nora, clapping her hands.

"What? Is there dessert?" asked Delphina.

Nora shook her head, her dark hair flying. "It's a full moon! Auntie tells her story, and then there's dancing! Mama lets me stay up late to watch."

A few women and men came around and took up the plates while others put away the food and wine. Tal finished his cup before handing it to a man. Aghna cleared her throat as many of the children got up and moved closer to her. Some adults stood up and wandered over while others left the area.

"The Moon God watches over all of us. He gives us light at night and helps us tell our time and seasons. He keeps balance," said the old woman. "He takes over when the sun must rest. Just as the sun and wind dance together, so do the moon and Night Goddess.

"The Night Goddess is the Moon God's one desire, and though the Night Goddess may have wandered, she knew her destiny was to be his."

"Wandered?" asked Delphina, sitting back on her hands. "Where could she wander to? Her place is tied to the moon."

Agha tilted her head and appraised Delphia before answering. "But the moon has a time of growth and a time of rest, just like the land—perfect balance. Once the moon had turned away to rest, she wandered to our world. There are a few legends that tell what she got up to."

Aghna raised her hands. "Some say the Night Goddess came to this world and wandered around the empty lands. She was tired of looking down on nothing. She called to the moon, but he did not answer, as he was asleep. She kept traveling until she finally found someone. He was sitting on the only rock around, deep in thought."

Aghna's story continued in this way:

"Who are you?" she asked.

"Elfen," replied the man.

"Where do you come from?"

"I've always been here," he said as he raised his hand. Another rock appeared as he looked at the Night Goddess. "Would you like to sit?"

"How did you do that?" she asked. "How did you make that rock?"

Elfen shrugged. "I've always been able to make whatever's in my mind."

She looked around the land. "Then why not create something beautiful? Why stay in this desolate place?"

"I'm not sure what beauty looks like." He stood up and looked the Night Goddess up and down, taking in her dark skin and her eyes that sparkled. "Is it you? Are you beauty?"

"Perhaps I am a form of beauty, but there are others. Let me tell you."

Aghna put down her hands, leaning forward. "She spent the whole night and many others telling Elfen about beauty. She gave him glorious ideas, and every time they spoke, he created something new until this world appeared as it does now.

"Then, one day, Elfen and the Night Goddess decided to make beings like them. They took the Night Goddess's fine face and Elfen's long ears and strong body to make the first creatures. Do you know what they were, children?"

"The Fae!" yelled several.

"Yes, but they made others, men and women like you and me. All lived together for a time in cooperation. One young Fae asked the Night Goddess for magic. She asked him what he could give her in return, and he said a song and poem." Angha looked at Tal. "So young Taliesin sang her the most beautiful song she had ever heard and then wove together words about her beauty she could not imagine.

"She gave him magic, and he shared it with others, Fae and humans alike."

"Why do most men not have magic now, Auntie?" asked a young boy.

"Because along the way, some Fae and humans who wished for control spread ugly rumors about humans and magic, saying it was dangerous. It led to humans being used as chattel and many deaths. Though some wrongs have been made right, many still see magic as evil."

"Perhaps it is best magic is not used by many humans," said Delphina gently. "I've met some who couldn't handle it."

Angha stared at Delphina. "Perhaps it shouldn't be up to any of us what others can handle."

Delphina turned away, looking at her nails as Nora raised her hand. "There is another story about the Night Goddess!"

Angha smiled at the young girl. "There is, but it will have to wait until another night. I believe it's time for music."

Two men, one with a mandolin and the other with a fiddle stood away from the fire. A woman with a primitive flute came near them. The man with the mandolin nodded, and they started a simple jig. People cheered and hurried to circle up and dance. There was some rhythm to it, but each person moved their own way. Tal had seen much of it traveling in the human realms, but he imagined it looked very odd and primitive to Delphina.

He looked over to see how big the sneer was on her lovely face, but there was nothing but a slight smile and simple curiosity in her eyes. Tal stood up and extended a hand to young Nora. "Would you dance with me?"

The little girl giggled and left her bear on her cushion before standing up. They moved close to the music, and Tal took both of her hands. They twirled around, the little girl laughing continuously as they circled. He kept his eyes on the joyous girl, the light from the fire reflecting in her dark hair, giving a red hue. Her dark eyes were bright, with a few tears leaking out of them in laughter and joy.

For some reason, as he danced with Nora, he felt his heart clench in some sort of longing or sorrow. He didn't know why, but when the music ended, he found he didn't want to let go of her little, soft hands. She smiled fully at him before letting go of his hands and wrapping her whole arms around his waist, her head buried into his stomach.

"Thank you," she said gleefully. "No one ever dances with me since Father died unless Mama makes Peader do it."

She pulled back, her hair a mess, her face stained with tears, and Tal bent down and kissed her on her forehead. She laughed again and ran away to the cushion, where she sat down and picked up her bear.

Another song started playing, and this one was another raucous number. The crowd cheered again as they danced around the fire.

"You enjoy yourself with these people?" asked Delphina as she came close.

"These are the best people to lose yourself with," said Tal. "I've been all over the land, and humans such as these with not much to call their own are the freest. Why do you think I spend almost all my time traveling the human kingdoms?"

"Finding pretty girls to fuck?" she said softly. "I'm sure human women are easy prey for someone who looks like you, even in this form." She looked at the dancers and a few women nearby, drinking. "You could probably have your pick from at least a dozen here."

"I'll admit I've shared nights with more than a fair number of human women, but I have just as easily found conquest in the Fae lands. Maybe more easily due to who I am known to be there. The women are only a part of it. It's easy to forget who you are and what trivial problems you have when you are around such joyous creatures."

"Maybe," said Delphina. "But I can't help but wonder what they have to be joyous about. They have little, not even proper homes. Someone could easily wipe out this group even with their magic, whether to ravish the women or take their meager treasures."

"Dark thoughts on a night like this, Delphie," said Tal.

"Tal, you must admit..."

He held a finger up to her lips. "Hush. I won't hear it. Tonight, we only think of joyous things." He took his finger away. "Now you and I are going to dance, and all you are going to think of is how fine the music is, how good the wine has been, and what a handsome partner you have."

She grinned. "Fine. What else is there to do?"

He took her hand and led her closer to the dancing, bringing her into his arms to spin around. It took a bit for her to loosen up, but eventually, she threw her head back, her glorious hair spinning around her as they quickened their pace.

She was beautiful—one of the most beautiful creatures he had ever seen, even with her glamour. Her shirt shifted as she danced, revealing the top of her abundant cleavage. A bit of sweat formed there due to the fire and her exertion, and Tal couldn't look away. He eventually bent down and kissed her chest quickly as he spun her, not caring who might see.

She laughed at his antics and turned to find another man dancing nearby. She hooked her arm with his, and he turned her a few times before she found another man. A woman took Tal's hand, and he bowed before twirling her. Together, they moved through the crowd, each gaining different partners throughout several songs until, as the fire burned low, Tal took Delphina's hand again.

Most had gone to bed by then, and only a few young couples were left, now pairing up. Even Angha had left her post. Dunla came near them, yawning as she ran a hand through her hair. "There is an empty tent on the right edge of the camp. It's the one with the blue rug in front. You're welcome to it."

"Thank you," said Delphina before Tal could say the words. "For everything."

Dunla bowed her head before walking slowly back towards the tents.

"Are you ready to rest?" asked Tal.

Delphina shook her head, putting her hands around Tal's neck. "The music is still going. Could we not have one more dance? We will need to think of more serious things, but as you suggested, tonight, I only want to be free."

The music slowed down, and Tal put his arms around Delphina. They danced slowly as other couples either danced and spoke quietly together or slipped away into the shadows.

"When you are out on your adventures," said Delphina quietly, "and you see a woman you wish to bed, what do you say to her?"

Tal bent his head closer to hers. "I spend some time with her, getting to know what I can. I ask about her family and her situation. Believe it or not, it's not just to make her comfortable, but I find I enjoy most stories people have to tell. We usually have a few drinks together, and then I slip in how absolutely stunning she is."

"And are they usually as pretty as all that?" asked Delphina.

"I find that beauty does indeed come in many different forms, as the Night Goddess taught us. Some women have beautiful laughs and smiles. Others are so gifted with their words they draw me in. Of course, there are baser charms as well. I will admit to liking certain aspects of women." He kissed just below Delphina's ear. "How soft your skin is." His hand moved up her side. "The wonderful curves you seem to have." His hand continued up until it grazed the side of her breast. "And having such generous assets doesn't hurt."

Delphina turned her head with a smile. "And what would you ultimately find beautiful about me?"

He pulled her even closer, her body flush against his. "Everything, Delphie. I've been tempted by you for a while now. You have no idea how badly I do want you. You must know how fucking gorgeous you are."

"I've been told before."

"Then let me say it's not just your looks that intrigue me. Your wit, even your sass, draw me in. I can't count the times I've wanted to kiss that wicked grin you have off your face. Or throw you over my shoulder and take you to bed to erase your arrogance. Gods, Delphie, whether you have meant to or not, you have become irresistible to me."

She leaned forward and kissed him, her lips on his hard and demanding. She immediately opened up as soon as his tongue grazed her lips, and Tal knew that whatever was going to happen between them would soon not be appropriate in any public setting.

He kissed her for a moment more before pulling back and taking her hand. They silently moved quickly to easily find the empty tent a little away from the others. Tal entered it first, holding open the flap for Delphina. It was roomy, with cushions and blankets on the ground.

Tal turned to Delphina as she closed her eyes, letting her glamour fall. He sighed as he looked at her. She was glorious, her hair impossibly golden, her eyes the brightest green he could imagine, her lips the most delectable shade of pink. He wondered if other parts of her matched them.

"I want you to see me as I really am. I want to be with you as me, not some shadow I'm wearing as a costume."

He pulled her closer, wondering how she would take it if he kept his glamour up. He was comfortable wearing it, and it was as familiar to him as his own skin. She didn't say anything as he kissed her, his hands finding the hem of her shirt.

"You are so beautiful, Delphie," he said softly before kissing her again.

His hand moved underneath her shirt until it covered her breast. He squeezed it gently as he kissed her, unable to stop a moan from escaping him. She gasped as his fingers moved to her hard nipple to pinch it lightly.

He moved from kissing her lips to her jaw, then her neck, his hands now both under her shirt, gradually bringing it up. Before he could get it off, she pulled back and grabbed his shirt. She fell down on the cushions and brought him with her, so he hovered over her.

They kissed again, her hands moving down his back. "I've wanted this for a while," she said between kisses. "Wanted you."

He only groaned as one of her hands cupped him over his pants. She used his moment of inattention to flip him over, so she laid over him. He would usually admonish a woman for taking such initiative and control, but she was upon him before he could say or do anything. She kissed his neck as she pulled up his shirt, her hands lingering on his firm stomach for a moment before moving up to his chest, taking the material with it.

He closed his eyes as she moved down and brought his shirt up, feeling her lips and tongue on his chest, moving down slowly toward his stomach. Her hands moved so slowly that it was almost torture. He was lost in a haze of lust and need. Her lips were so sweet, the sweetest he had ever tasted. Her touch was maddening. He was surrounded by her scent, completely paralyzed by it as she continued her trek downward.

"You were right," she said, making his eyes open to look down at her. She stared at him with a small smirk. "Tonight was freeing, and I'm not sure if I'm in a hurry to get back to what I have to pretend to be."

She went back to kissing his stomach as her hands worked on the buckle of his pants. He thought over her words. Freeing, he had lived the last three decades trying to find some idea of freedom. Freedom over his brother's rule, over what he was expected to be, over his own strange grief and loneliness. Was this the answer? Was giving into Delphina's charms what he had been looking for, not just freedom but home?

He had a quick glimpse of what life might be like with Delphina. He saw the Golden Court, his brother standing behind his throne, and his sister behind him with an air of boredom. Lord Elgan was there, trying to keep his disgust and annoyance with the king off his face. Next to him was Delphina, glorious in a golden gown that hugged every curve. Her shining hair was free, curls running over her shoulders, and he was dressed in black and gold by her side, a thin golden crown on his brow.

To many, it would be a perfect picture. Two courts come together fully once again, light and dark. He would have passionate nights such as this one, but his days would be full of mindless duty and bowing to his brother. Everything within him revolted against it. His hands went to Delphina's face.

"Stop," he said suddenly. "Stop."

She looked up, her eyes blown wide with lust, suddenly confused. "Did I do something?"

Tal sat up and scooted away from her, refastening his pants. "No, not at all. I just...I don't think this is the right time."

"Whyever not?" she said, moving closer to him. "I thought you wanted me?"

The hurt and confusion in her eyes made him feel shameful. He put his hand on her cheek. "I do, dear Delphie, but not like this, not here in some cold tent." He rubbed her cheek. "I must complete this task before I can think about the future I want. I don't want to draw you so close to me and then pull back. It's not right."

She leaned back so his hand fell off her cheek. "You think if we have sex, I'll believe I own you? You think I'll expect something more than one night?"

"I do, and you should. Delphina, it's been easy to forget who we are on this journey, but we can't. You are the daughter of the highest lord of my brother's court, and I am a prince of two realms. You must have expectations of me, of us."

"We don't have to figure it out right now," she said as she again leaned towards him, her breath against his lips. "Let's just have tonight, Tal. I won't demand anything more." She kissed him, and he was almost drawn back in. It would be easy to put aside everything as she suggested, but he could not.

He pulled back, gently pushing her away. "No, not tonight."

She adjusted her skirt and threw her hair behind her, her lips coming to a pout. "This is ridiculous."

"No, it's wise." He rubbed his eyes. "This isn't a slight on you. I think...I think I care about you, Delphina, and to be honest, I haven't felt that way about anyone for a while, maybe ever."

Her eyes softened as she sighed. "I just don't see why we can't express what we feel now. I'm not...I'm not innocent, Tal. I'm not what you think."

"That doesn't change things." He stood up. "You sleep here. I'll find somewhere outside. We need to rest so we can leave early in the morning. I have a task from my king, and I need to complete it. We also need to find Dyfan."

She stared up at him. "You won't change your mind?"

"No, not tonight." He reached down and took her chin. "But this isn't over. Let me finish this, and then we will talk about us. I do want you, Delphina, but I need to be sure for the both of us."

She looked at him for a moment more before dropping her head. "Fine. Go then. Goodnight."

He probably should have stayed and tried to soothe her hurt, but he didn't want to push it. He wasn't ready to give up his chance at real freedom. Instead of consoling her, he walked out of the tent and straight to the edge of the forest, finding an old log to sit upon. The cold air soothed him as he stared up at the moon. The truth was he wasn't sure what he wanted. Not surprising as he wasn't sure who he even was.

Chapter 22

Aven

Aven groaned as he opened his eyes, seeing nothing but the tops of trees and a few stars in between.

"Stay still for a moment," said a familiar voice. "I need to make sure your injuries aren't too bad before I try to heal you."

"Silvie?" rasped Aven as he closed his eyes, the pain in his head and back almost too much.

"I thought I knew the horse I found, but I was still surprised to see you lying here. This is a dangerous place, Aven. You shouldn't be here all alone."

"I wasn't alone." He grimaced as Silvie lifted his head and then carefully rolled him on his side, looking at his back.

"Who were you with?" She rolled him gently on his back and rubbed her hands together.

"My friend, Quinn. I don't know if you remember me talking about him."

"I do, but this is a long way from home for both of you," said Silvie. She placed her hands over him. "Stay very still, Aven. Somehow, you escaped without serious injuries, but you have a nasty bump and broken ribs. Let me fix them for you."

"You can do that?"

"Yes, now stay still and quiet." Silvie hovered her hands above his chest, her eyes closing as she lifted her head. The wind picked up around them, making Silvie's straight, light red hair sway in the breeze. A moment later, a warmth emitted from her hands, covering Aven. He arched up slightly as his magic swirled inside of him, aching to get out.

He had no strength to stop it, so he let it have its way. It surrounded him, mixing with Silvie's, causing him to feel warm and light. The pain in his head started to fade away. His back felt better than it had since he left home. The long rides on horseback and sleeping in dubious beds had made it sore. Lastly, the pain in his side lessened, though it was still slightly there when Silvie put her hands down and opened her eyes.

"Your ribs will take a bit to heal completely, but not too long." She held out her hand to him, and he took it so he could sit up.

"How long was I out?"' he asked, rubbing the back of his head and looking around.

"I don't know. I came across you not too long ago," said Silvie. Aven shuddered slightly as the wind blew through the trees. Silvie leaned forward and pushed his hair back, feeling his forehead. "I don't think you're ill, but it's going to be a cold night with the clear sky. You can't stay out here."

Aven tucked his arms against his chest. "Where else is there?"

Silvie half smiled. "I know more about this forest than you can imagine. I have a place that will give you some shelter. It's a fair way from here but manageable if you can ride."

"I can ride," said Aven. He gathered himself and pushed up off the ground to stand. His back felt a little tight, but it didn't hurt. His side was painful, but nothing he couldn't manage. He put his hand against it as he moved towards his waiting horse. "Do you need me to help you up?"

Silvie laughed slightly. "As if you could, but I'm quite capable of mounting a horse. You go on first, and I'll get on behind you."

Aven patted his horse's neck. "Whatever it was, I hope it's out of your system. I don't want a repeat of last time."

His horse had the audacity to snort as if Aven couldn't understand what it had been through. He put his foot in the stirrup and prepared himself for the pain before jumping off the ground and pulling himself over in the saddle.

His breath left him for a second after he was mounted, his side aching anew. A moment later, Silvie mounted, graceful and with little effort, setting her thin form behind him.

"The place I'm thinking will work is through the trees to the right, probably about a half-hour ride."

"Have you seen Quinn or the two guards that were with me? I'd hate to leave them alone all night in the woods," said Aven.

"I haven't come across them, but I'm sure they can't be too far from here. They must be looking for you. If we don't find them on our way, I will see you settled and then go find them."

"Shouldn't you seek shelter for the night too?"

"I'm more than capable of spending a night in these woods. I've done it many times. I have ways of keeping myself warm." She leaned forward to catch his eyes. "You do, too, you know. Your magic must react strongly being in this forest since your people first set up its wards."

"I've felt it even stronger than usual. It's been hard to keep it within me at times," said Aven.

"Are you afraid of what your friend will think if he sees you use magic?"

"I'm more frightened of what the guards will think and say to my father. I think Quinn would understand, though I'm sure his advice would be to stop practicing with it and cut off all contact with you."

She was quiet for a few minutes before she asked, "Why are you out here anyway?"

"Quinn and I were traveling to the northern temples to see what we could find out about the Court of the Underlings and the mischief they've been causing. We barely managed to leave before the eastern temple was attacked."

Silvie gave an angry snort that tickled the back of his neck. "I know all about the attack. I went to see what I could do, but there wasn't much left when I arrived."

Aven swallowed, sorrow stinging his heart. "They were all dead?"

"There were plenty dead, but it looked like some had fled or were taken. The temple was burnt to the ground. I hate to say it, but I hope that horn they had burned with it and whoever did this didn't get a hold of it."

Aven sat up straighter on his horse and took one hand off the reins to pick up the small pack tied on the right. He opened it and sighed in relief. "You don't have to worry about the horn, Silvie. I have it and the necklace of Mayra."

Silvie gasped. "You have them both?"

He nodded. "Along the way, I met a woman, a Fae woman. She asked me to go to each temple and get the objects to take back to the palace. She spelled some document so each head priestess would do it, but when we got to the first temple, we found out the other was already attacked. The necklace was sent before the attack happened." Aven looked back and offered her the pack.

She pushed it back to him. "Keep that closed at all times until you get home. Now, what does all this have to do with you being in the forest? You could be well on your way back to the palace by now."

"The Fae woman mentioned a friend of hers in trouble in the forest, said she was a forest witch, and asked me to warn her that enemies were looking for her. She said this witch had some valuable scroll."

"And you just did as she asked? Aven, you don't even know her. What if this is a trap?"

"I felt like she was telling the truth, and if she wanted me dead, she could do it a hundred different ways more efficiently."

"Still, why come here for some random forest witch?" asked Silvie.

Aven looked away. "I thought maybe it might be you."

"Aven..."

"I don't know where you stay, Silvie, but I know you're a witch. Obviously, I wasn't too wrong in my assumptions since you're here."

"How many times have I told you I can take care of myself?" She took a deep breath, squeezing him gently. "I do appreciate it, though, you caring about me. It means more than you can know."

"I do care about you, Silvie," said Aven. "After all you've done for me, how could I not?"

"What I've done is land you in a heap of trouble, but I think no matter what, you would have found it eventually. I know you're scared of others discovering your use of magic, but you can't hide it forever, Aven. Things will happen soon where you might be the best chance of your kingdom surviving."

"Is it that bad? This group, this Court of the Underlings, are they large enough to cause so much trouble?"

"Things aren't what they seem. The court is the least of your worries. I'm afraid other kings in our land have exercised very poor judgment and been taken in. War is coming, and it will make these attacks we've recently seen look like children playing at battle."

"How do you know this?" asked Aven.

"I travel far and have lots of acquaintances. I hear things. It's all I've done for the last three decades: travel and listen. I knew something would happen. Eventually. I just hoped to accomplish more before now."

"Accomplish what?"

Before she could answer, there was a small commotion in the trees to their left. Aven stopped his horse and turned to watch the thick branches part, so a tired-looking Quinn could move through to the small path Aven was on.

"Aven!" said Quinn, sounding relieved and overwhelmed. "Thank all our gods and goddesses. I was about to give up looking for you tonight."

"I'm glad to see you too, Quinn, all of you. I was worried you'd be lost in the forest."

"I think we were," said Quinn, peering behind Aven. "At this point, we were just wandering, looking for someplace to set up camp where we could light a fire. Aven, who is that with you?"

Aven half turned in his saddle and grinned at Silvie. Her eyes were wide as she peered around Aven, looking at Quinn. "This is a friend of mine, one I've known quite a while."

Quinn moved his horse closer. "I've never seen her before. If she's from our village, I must know her. Or is she a daughter or ward of one of the lords close to your sister's home?"

"No, I am no daughter of a lord, sir," said Silvie. "I'm not from your village or even your kingdom. Well, not really."

"Then who are you?" asked Quinn, eyeing Silvie suspiciously.

"You know my name. What more do you require?"

"Plenty," said Quinn. "Where do you live? How do you know our prince?"

Silvie turned her eyes to Aven. He steadied his horse and looked at Quinn. "I'll explain later. Right now, we need to find some sort of shelter. Silvie says she knows a place."

"You think it's wise to trust her? What if she's leading us to someone who means you harm? Such as that group who destroyed the temple."

"I trust her," said Aven with certainty. "That should be enough for you." Quinn looked like he would argue, but Aven turned his horse. "I'm going on to where Silvie leads. If you want to follow, you are welcome; otherwise, you can do your best to find somewhere out here to rest." His horse stepped around Quinn's, and Aven moved him into a trot.

"Aven, you can't blame him," said Silvie quietly. "He should be leery of me. You must see how strange it appears."

"I know, and it's my fault. I should have told him about you and what we do at the pond ages ago. I'm not sure what I thought would happen eventually."

"I'm sure you thought you would have to quit coming to the pond one day, perhaps after you married."

Aven was quiet, hearing hooves hitting the soft ground of the forest behind him, letting him know Quinn was following. "I didn't want to quit coming."

"I know," said Silvie. "I'm not angry. It makes sense that one day you would have to forsake magic just as your father did."

Aven looked back at her. "Did he use magic? How did you know?"

"I've heard things for years."

"Silvie, are you...Fae? I know witches who fully use magic age even slower than Illedrians, but I don't think you've changed at all since that day we met."

"I do have Fae blood," she said carefully. "I won't deny it, but I have plenty of human blood as well." She looked down, taking a moment more to go on. "I would never hurt you, Aven."

"I never believed you would. I suspected you had some Fae in you for a while."

"Aven, wait," said Quinn as he caught up with them. "I didn't mean to anger you, but you disappeared into the woods. Then we find you with a strange woman. I mean no offense to either of you, but you must understand my suspicion."

"He does, and so do I," said Silvie.

Aven nodded. "When we get settled tonight. I'll explain it to you, but I ask you to withhold judgment until you hear everything."

Quinn's eyes grew wide. "Good goddesses and gods, you aren't married, are you?"

Silvie laughed louder than Aven had ever heard her. She shook as she put her hand up to her mouth. "We most certainly are not."

Aven half chuckled. "I'm not sure how flattering this response is. Am I so unmarriable?"

Silvie wiped her eyes with a finger. "Of course not, Aven, but the thought that you and me—no, no, it's too much." She laughed again.

"So that's not it," said Quinn. "She isn't some secret lover."

"Absolutely not," said Aven. "Now, if Silvie here can concentrate, perhaps we can reach this shelter before we all freeze."

Silvie steadied herself, putting her arms back around Aven's chest. "Of course, keep going this way until you come to another path. It's hard to see, but there is a rather large dead tree before it. Turn to the left on it, and it will lead us to where we need to go."

They rode on in mostly silence, though Aven could tell Quinn wanted to ask many questions. The guards rode closer to them, and Aven didn't dare breathe a word about Silvie to Quinn in case they overheard. He had no doubt he would have to think of something to say to his father about Silvie in case the guards told their king about the journey. Perhaps it was time to tell his father the truth anyway. Especially if what Silvie said about the coming of war was true.

They rode on until they came to the large dead tree and turned to their left. Eventually, the trees thinned a bit, not being as old as the rest of the forest, their trunks not as thick or as tall. The ground turned rocky with small pebbles and then several larger round rocks. Aven almost thought he was losing his mind when he saw what looked like a fallen tower up ahead.

"What is that?" he asked.

"Some ruins of an impressive fortress and palace," said Silvie.

"People lived here?" asked Quinn.

"Yes, a very long time ago. Surely you've come across this in your history lessons or at least a legend about it? Your people, those who would become the Illedrians, first settled here. They set up powerful wards around the woods, so powerful that some still exist today. Then they built a village within a fortress along with a palace for their king."

They rode past the tower and found ruins of walls and chimneys all around. Most were barely recognizable, the stones crumbling and covered in vines. Trees had grown up through some.

"Our people once lived here?" asked Aven as he stopped his horse by a large wall. "What happened?"

"The world changed," said Silvie. "Kingdoms grew, and hiding away became impractical. Your people needed to trade and make alliances. They moved south, closer to the sea, and lifted some of the wards on the forest."

"And left all this here?" Quinn circled his horse.

"After a time. It didn't happen overnight. It took years, decades, even a century for this place to become abandoned completely. Keep going. There is a building almost still standing. The walls can keep the wind from hitting you, and once you light a fire, it will keep you warm."

Aven did as she asked, walking his horse past the ruins and a small well with its round walls still standing until they came to what must have been once a small house. Three walls were still standing along with the chimney. Aven dismounted his horse, holding on to his side as his feet hit the ground.

"Aven, are you hurt?" asked Quinn.

"Not badly," said Aven as he stood up to help Silvie down, but she had already jumped off the horse. "I'm just a little sore. Silvie healed any wounds I had."

"Healed them?"

Aven glanced at the guards. "Will you both check the perimeter? Make sure no one else is around. We'll get a fire going and some food out, so you'll have warmth and food once you return."

One guard nodded before they rode off together. Quinn watched them for a moment before turning to Aven. "Now, tell me what's going on."

Silvie looked at Quinn, then Aven, and Aven took a step towards Quinn. "You know I, like my father and many others in my family, have access to the old Illedrian magic. I have told you that before."

"Yes, and like all others in your family, you were told to ignore it, so it would go away," said Quinn.

Silvie shook her head and scoffed. "As if it's that easy. Magic doesn't just go away, no matter how much you ignore it."

"So the king could still do magic if he wished?"

"It would take practice and time to use it proficiently, but he should still have access to it until the day he dies," said Silvie.

"But, yes, I was told to ignore it until I could forget about it, and that eventually I wouldn't feel unsettled all the time without using my magic," said Aven.

"That would never have happened," said Silvie. "Perhaps over time, it might have become easier to ignore it, but it would still be there, reminding you."

"I take it you haven't been ignoring it," said Quinn as he stared at Silvie.

"No. I've been meeting with Silvie for over ten years to practice my magic. We meet periodically by a pond in the forest behind the palace."

"Ten years...ten years, Aven!" Quinn turned away before glancing back at Aven. "How did you even meet her?"

"I came across her in the forest on one of my early morning rides. Once I reached the age of twelve and proved proficient on horseback, my father permitted me to ride behind the palace on my own without guards as long as I returned by breakfast. Not long after I started my rides, I came across Silvie by the pond."

"You just happened to come across her," said Quinn skeptically as he took a step toward Silvie. "How old were you? You can't be much older than Aven or me. Why were you out in the forest all alone?"

"I'm older than you think," said Silvie. "I was grown by the time I found Aven."

"And you just happened to find the young prince of Illedria out in the forest."

"I admit I knew who Aven was before I approached him. He knows I have certain motives for helping him," said Silvie.

"And what are they?"

"Only ones that mean to help him, protect him and his kingdom," said Silvie. "War is coming to the land. It has been for some time. Illedria has the tools to protect itself and others. You just need to use them."

"War? What war is coming? There hasn't been unrest in the land."

"There is, though," said Aven. "At least rumors of it. Uchel's king believes the Fae are vulnerable, and the young Sun King thinks it's time to put humans back in their place. The time of peace between our realms could be over. At least, that's what I've heard."

"You're not wrong, Aven, and you both know chaos has grown lately. You've witnessed an attack on a defenseless temple yourself," said Silvie.

"So who is doing the attacking then? The Fae or a band of humans?" asked Quinn.

"It appears to be both, as well as other creatures that reside in both realms," said Silvie. She ran a hand through her hair as she started to pace. "Which makes this harder to figure out. It seems some Fae have made allics with humans, but who and why?"

"How do you know all of this?" asked Quinn.

"I travel this land extensively. I have allies everywhere, those who keep me informed."

"And we should just trust you?" Quinn turned to Aven. "What if she's lying? What if she just wants control over you, over our kingdom?"

"I've known her for over a decade, Quinn. She could have caused me harm at any time, but instead, she has done nothing but help me," said Aven.

"Helped you? Helped you by making sure you defied your father's orders? Do you know why your father and your people demand you can't do magic, Aven? Why only our mages and healers are allowed limited use?"

"Because, unfortunately, your people, like most others, have a ridiculous fear of magic. Your fear is your weakness, one Aven can overcome," said Silvie.

"Or you know if Aven uses magic, it will isolate us from every other human kingdom, making us even more vulnerable. What if you are from Uchel or Cyrfder? You could be making sure we fail."

Silvie laughed as she raised a hand. A flame appeared in her hand. She raised her other one, a group of sticks rising off the ground and forming a pile in the middle of the space. She threw out her hand with the flame, and it shot onto the pile, sparking a fire.

"Do you see what I am, boy? Do you think either of those kingdoms would trust some forest witch? I would probably be put to death if they knew the things I could do. Of course, they would have to catch me, which is unlikely."

Quinn turned to the fire as Aven moved closer to him. "I trust her, Quinn. I know her, and she knows me. She wouldn't hurt me or our kingdom. I know she wouldn't."

"Aven..."

"Quinn, I would never let her near you if I thought she meant you harm. I could have died in the forest. I fell off my horse and had no idea where I was. She found me and healed me. Then she led us here, to shelter."

Quinn glanced back at Silvie. "I don't know."

"You don't have to trust me," said Silvie. "I don't blame you for having doubts, but at least for tonight, let's have peace. Stay here, and I promise no harm will come to you. As I said, there are old wards, and I will add some of my own. Rest here, and tomorrow, I'll show you how to find who you're looking for before we part. If you still want to find this witch, I know of only one other in this forest."

"You won't go with us?" asked Aven.

"I have somewhere to be tomorrow, but I'll make sure you know the way. You should be able to find her quickly and leave before midday if you choose to go."

"We should leave as soon as we can," said Quinn. "Forget this forest witch and return home."

"We are close, though," said Aven. "And after the temple, if we can help save someone, shouldn't we do it?" Quinn looked unconvinced. "The Fae woman mentioned a scroll as well. What if it's important? Something we don't want the wrong people getting a hold of. I say we should go."

"Fine, as long as we are on our way home by midday." He looked at Silvie. "You will stay here tonight?"

"I will if you allow it. I'll stay in a corner by myself, but if you prefer, I can seek shelter elsewhere."

Quinn glanced at Aven. "Quinn, she won't hurt us."

Quinn took a deep breath. "Stay here with us, but between the guards and myself. Someone will stay awake keeping watch all night."

"There is no need," said Silvie. "I promise you that you are quite safe here."

"Someone will keep watch, even if I must stay awake all night. Now, let me go get the guards so we can settle in for the night." Quinn looked at Silvie. "I'll only be gone for a moment. If you try anything..."

Silvie moved to the fire and gracefully sat down. "I assure you, my only motive tonight is to keep warm."

Quinn put his hand on Aven's arm. "Watch yourself."

Aven rolled his eyes as his friend finally walked away. He moved to the fire and sat by Silvie. "That could have gone worse, I suppose."

"Yes, I suppose he could have tried to kill me or taken you and ran." She picked up a small twig and twirled it. "You didn't need to send the guards away. I've made sure they won't remember seeing me. They won't remember much of this evening at all. If you wish, I can do the same for Quinn."

"You charmed them in some way?"

"I showed you how I can manipulate minds, didn't I? I suggested they forget what they've seen just before you found me and until I leave you. I can do the same for Quinn as well if you want."

"No, there's no need. If I ask him, he won't say a word about this. He'll see eventually you mean no harm."

"I'm glad he's suspicious of me and protective of you. It makes me happy you have such a good friend watching out for you. You'll need him and others with what's to come."

"I have you too, don't I?" asked Aven. "I could use a powerful witch who seems to know everything watching over me."

She took Aven's hand and rested her head on his shoulder. "I'll always watch over you, Aven. I promise, no matter what happens."

Chapter 23

Tal

I T WAS AWKWARD THE next morning as Tal and Delphina said goodbye to the travelers. Delphina was mostly silent, letting Tal do the talking as he bowed before Angha and bent down to accept a gift from Nora, a small, badly knitted blanket she had been working on with her mother for some time.

"It's so you won't get cold as you travel," said Nora, holding her bear tight. "Since mama says you can't stay with us."

Tal folded it up and smiled. "It's perfect. I'll keep it forever."

Nora beamed before looking over at Delphina. "I wanted to give my best hairpin to your friend to put in her pretty hair, but my papa gave it to me before he left."

"I'm sure Delphie wants you to keep it, Nora. She has plenty of pretty pins for her hair at home."

Delphina looked down at the child and gave her a real smile, nodding her head.

"She's so pretty," whispered Nora. "Are you sure she's not a princess?"

Tal laughed, leaning towards the child and whispering back, "She is not, but I'll tell you a secret if you want." The girl nodded her head vigorously. "She's not a princess, but I'm a prince."

She leaned away from him, her eyes wide. He grinned and put his fingers up to his lips. "Our secret, okay?"

"Yes," she said breathlessly before moving back to her mother.

They mounted Delphina's old horse, Delphina sitting in front of him, her arms crossed, leaning forward. They made their way back to the barely visible path leading deeper into the forest.

"You know this journey will be practically unbearable if you refuse to speak with me," said Tal after some time.

"I'm not refusing to speak with you. I just have nothing to say."

"Nothing? I doubt that, my dear Delphie. You haven't been able to keep your mouth closed for long since you joined me on this little adventure."

She kept facing forward, her arms crossed. Tal leaned forward, resting his chin on her shoulder. "You're cross with me, and I suppose you have every right to be. I didn't reject you last night. I was protecting you."

"Protecting me?" She looked back at him, jerking her shoulder, causing his chin to fall off it. "From what?"

"From me."

"You think I need protecting from you?" She shook her head. "I suppose you think I'm falling in love with you, that if I submit to you in that way, I won't be able to get over you." She uncrossed her arms and straightened some of the horse's mane. "You think too much of yourself."

"So, what? You only wanted me for one night? A one-time fling and that's it."

"I hadn't given it much thought. I told you I wanted you, and that was the truth. I never thought much about a future together." He wasn't sure what to say, though he couldn't help but feel the sting of her comment. "So if you were pulling back purely to protect me, you were wrong, but maybe it wasn't about me." She looked back at him. "Maybe it was about protecting yourself."

"You're insinuating I might want a future with you?"

"Is it so hard to believe?" she asked.

"No," he said truthfully. "But, Delphie, any future with me might not be one you want or could even have."

"I suppose you should let me decide that," she turned in the saddle, putting her hand on his chest. "Until then, why can't we have a little fun? I'm not trying to trap you."

He took her hand and held it while taking it off his chest. "We should concentrate today, see if we can find this witch and Dyfan. Get good information on your cousin. Once we get out of the forest and back to the village, then perhaps I won't need to spend another night in that objectionable room."

"Fine. I suppose you're right."

"Then you won't punish me anymore with your silence?"

Delphina laughed. "So you do like it when I talk?"

"As I've said before, you can be quite charming and intelligent when you want, and even when you're cross, you're still amusing." He leaned down further. "That little pout of yours about drives me out of my mind."

She blushed prettily before shaking out her hair. "Is that why you're so disagreeable? I thought it was just your personality."

"A little of both, perhaps."

She settled back into him, and they rode on in mostly companionable silence for a while. Tal hadn't gotten much sleep, and as Delphina seemed to be dozing against him, he had a feeling she didn't either. He placed one hand around her waist to steady her, enjoying her warmth against him as he looked down upon her.

She was ridiculously tempting, even in her slightly disheveled shape from a few days of traveling. Last night, when she transformed, she had been transcendent. Truly a dream come to life. He was beginning to think he had been foolish to leave the tent instead of taking the opportunity to spend the night with her, but what was done was done. Regret had never been his friend, so he rarely let himself feel it. The past could not be changed, and though he usually didn't use his past mistakes to make better choices, perhaps that was about to change.

He was tired of feeling out of place, exhausted from never truly feeling as if he had a real home. His uncle's court was not unwelcoming to him or uncomfortable, but he still felt like a stranger there. Even more so, in his brother's court, he felt like an outsider. If he had once belonged there, it was when his father reigned, and any sense of belonging had long gone away. He was beginning to wonder if it wasn't a place he was looking for but someone.

Maybe if he let himself become attached to another as much as he could, he could find a place. He wasn't sure about love, as he didn't know if it was real. People had told him his parents had been in love, but he had never witnessed it. He had heard rumors of it in both Fae courts and human realms, but it seemed impossible. To trust someone so much, you let them know you completely—the good and the bad and believe they wouldn't abandon you.

Delphina may have wanted him, but if she truly knew his dark thoughts, knew all he had done, and saw the hole where his heart should be, would she even wish to be in his presence? He had abandoned his court and his sister. He had left Dyfan without so much as a word. Humans and faerie creatures alike became nothing more than objects for his youth through the years.

She was warmth, light, and life; he was something less than death. A shadow of a man who possessed all the signs of life but had none of the qualities of real living.

Delphina adjusted in her sleep, snuggling further into his chest as her flowery scent invaded his senses. Was there still hope for him? Could he find some semblance of real living, and could it be with the woman in his arms? He wasn't sure but wasn't opposed to finding out.

They rode on deeper into the forest, moving well past mid-morning when Delphina raised her head and yawned. "Do you know where you're going?"

"About as well as I can. Did you have a good nap, Delphie?"

"You're at least warm, so you're good for something," she said, snuggling back against him.

He chuckled and was about to ask if she needed to stop when he saw something out of the corner of his eye. Before deciding whether to turn a different way or prepare himself, Dyfan rode out of the forest. Tal stopped as Delphina sat up. Dyfan sagged a little in his saddle with something like relief before his eyes narrowed.

"Where in the lowest hell have you been? I looked almost all night, only resting when the wind became too much," said Dyfan.

Tal rode up to him. "I ran into some trouble. My horse got spooked and threw me. Luckily, Delphina found me," said Tal.

"And you two have been riding around since then on that old horse?" asked Dyfan, sounding irater by the minute.

"Of course not. We found shelter with a group of travelers set up in the forest. They provided us with dinner and a place to sleep," said Tal.

"Warmth too, then, I suppose," said Dyfan. "Do you know how fucking cold it gets in the forest at night? I prayed to the Light God and Dark Goddess all night to deliver me and keep you safe, and the whole time you were guests at a damn feast with each other for company."

"I'm sorry, Dyfan, but I didn't know where to start looking for you. Finding shelter seemed the best option," said Tal.

"And how convenient that you found him, my lady," said Dyfan.

"I would say it was more fortunate than convenient, Dyfan. Unless you wanted to explain to the Sun King why you lost his brother in some woods of the human realm," said Delphina. "It seems I'm doing your job, keeping our prince safe."

"We should keep going now that we're all together and see if we can find this forest witch's house. Who knows, perhaps the gods and goddesses will shine down upon us, and Lady Eriana will be visiting," said Tal. "If not, we can only hope this witch might know her whereabouts."

Dyfan eyed Delphina a moment more before turning his horse to ride by Tal's side. "It can't be much further if it's in the center of the forest. We must be nearly there."

"Unless it's hidden by wards because this witch doesn't want to be found," said Delphina.

"The woman in the village seemed to think we could find this Margred if we didn't mean her any harm. I know I don't," said Tal. "What about the two of you?"

Dyfan shook his head as Delphina said, "I don't wish anyone harm, not really, though there are a few I'd like to give a good talking to, including my cousin."

"Hopefully, you can do that this evening," said Tal.

"I already have plans this evening, or have you already forgotten, Your Highness?" said Delphina with a laugh.

"Of course not, dear Delphie, but perhaps you will have time to speak with your cousin before more pleasant things."

Dyfan grunted but didn't say anything as they continued following a narrow path that let them ride side by side. The trees grew even wilder, the sky above them almost completely blocked out. Tal wasn't sure if it was his imagination or real, but the air seemed to grow thicker with something, maybe magic, or maybe it was going to rain or snow.

"Can we stop for a moment?" asked Delphina suddenly.

"Now? Here?" asked Dyfan incredulously.

"Yes, now and here," said Delphina, and she leaned up in the saddle. "I need a short break."

"For what?" asked Dyfan.

Tal stopped his horse as Delphina jumped off, catching herself as she hit the ground. "It's personal, but it'll only take a minute."

"You can't wait?" Dyfan stopped his horse and walked it around Tal's.

"No, I can't wait. We haven't stopped all morning, and I did drink quite a bit of wine last night and plenty of water this morning. I'll be as quick as possible."

She scurried off into the forest as Tal patted the old mare. "Must you be so hateful towards her, Dyfan?"

"I can't help but be annoyed by her, knowing her as I do. I would warn you again, but it doesn't seem you want my advice on the lady."

"I think you're biased for some reason. Did she reject your advances at some point?" asked Tal with amusement.

"It wasn't her that did the rejecting," said Dyfan with a frown.

Tal couldn't help but feel a bit of surprise and was about to ask what his friend meant when a scream came from the forest ahead of them. Tal looked at Dyfan, who moved his horse further up the path. Tal turned to where Delphina had entered the forest. "Delphina, hurry up. We need to go."

Another scream was followed by a blast of light. The ground slightly shook around them, leaves dropping from the trees. "What in the name of the Dark Goddess is it?" Tal moved his horse to be even with Dyfan.

"It's not far," said Dyfan.

"Should we run?"

"What if it's this Margred we're looking for, and Lady Eriana is with her?" Dyfan looked at Tal. "Come on. We have to go."

"Delphina isn't back yet."

"I don't think we can wait," said Dyfan. "She'll be safer back here."

"Delphina? Are you coming?" asked Tal. "I don't think we should leave her."

"We aren't going far, and it's not like she can't hear it for herself. Come on, let's see what's happening, and we can come back for her," said Dyfan. He urged his horse forward, trotting up the path.

Tal looked towards where Delphina entered the woods, wondering what was taking her so long. He was about to call out for her again when the area around them erupted in flame. Dyfan's horse reared in fear as Tal's old mare shook her head and stamped her feet. Dyfan regained control of his horse as a group of hooded figures made their way towards them, some carrying torches and others swords.

"What in the hell?" asked Tal as Dyfan pulled his sword from his back scabbard. "Should we run?" As he said it, he glanced behind him to see several other figures coming towards them, all with swords and torches. "Dyfan?"

"Can you get us out of here?" asked Dyfan.

Tal held up his hand, calling upon his dark magic. It responded but weakly. It might be enough to get them out, but... "We can't leave Delphina."

"She might already be a lost cause," said Dyfan, turning his horse around.

"No, we can't think that," said Tal.

The figures moved closer and closer as Tal held out his hand. He looked at where Delphina had entered the woods but still did not see her. He tried to decide if he should use what magic he could to deflect those coming towards them or use his power to take him and Dyfan out of the forest.

"Tal!" said Dyfan urgently, moving his horse close to him.

Tal's horse grew anxious, and the old mare tried to rear up but failed. Tal started to throw out his magic to get him and Dyfan out of there when there was a whooshing noise overhead, followed by dozens and dozens of arrows flying out of the trees, many hitting the hooded figures. A bright light followed as dozens of creatures of all sorts came out of nowhere wearing dark cloaks, their hoods down.

Tal could see Fae, humans, faeries, and even a goblin or two running toward him. Woodland faeries flew overhead, their effervescent wings fluttering. He scanned the group. Looking to be leading them was a female Fae with long red braids running down her front.

"Dyfan, cover the prince," she yelled in their direction as she threw up her empty hand. The other holding was a sword. Fire flew from her palm, slamming into three figures and pushing them back into the forest.

Dyfan stood his horse in front of Tal, keeping his sword out, ready to strike if needed.

"Dyfan, what's going on?" asked Tal.

But his friend didn't respond, keeping his eyes on the battle before him. "Eri, to your left!" he yelled over the melee. One of the hooded figures came close to them, raising his torch. The flame shot towards them, but Dyfan blocked it with his large sword, making the fire disperse. Tal's horse moved as Dyfan's backed up.

Lady Eriana turned, meeting her sword with one that had been swung at her. She quickly disposed of her opponent by thrusting her sword into his chest. The sounds of swords and magic were all around. The smell of blood and smoke hung heavy in the air, making Tal feel dizzy. Something in his mind told him to fight back and help, but he was beyond confused as more hooded figures came from the forest. He scanned them, gasping as he reached out toward Dyfan.

"It's Delphina!" he said urgently. "Dyfan, it's her. We have to help her." Delphina was between two of the tallest hooded figures, her eyes on Tal.

"We have to get out of here," said Dyfan, but he wasn't speaking to Tal. He was looking at Lady Eriana, who had run over to them. She nodded and pressed something on her wrist as Dyfan jumped off his horse.

"Grab the prince," said Lady Eriana harshly. "Be ready."

Dyfan hurried to Tal's side. "We have to go, Tal," said Dyfan as he grabbed the pack tied to Tal's horse. "Jump down."

"We can't. They have Delphina," said Tal over the ruckus around them. He looked for Delphina but had lost her in the crush of the fighting.

"Get down here now," said Dyfan angrily, "before you get us all killed." He reached for Tal and pulled on his arm just as a flame shot through the air. Tal ducked, his hair singing as the fire passed by. It knocked him off-kilter enough for Dyfan to yank him off the horse.

The smoke was so thick around them that Tal couldn't make sense of what was going on.

"Hold still so we can get out of here," said Dyfan.

"But Delphina, we can't leave her. They have her," said Tal, pulling at Dyfan's arm.

"How can you continue to be such a fool? Do you not see? They don't have her. She's one of them."

"What?" asked Tal, not understanding what Dyfan was saying, but before anything else could be said, there was a slight breeze, and the world dissolved around him.

Chapter 24

Aven

A VEN MANAGED A FEW hours of sleep in the ruins. He had a hard time getting comfortable, even with the warmth of the fire. He spent the first half of the night trying to get Quinn and Silvie to sleep. Silvie claimed she wasn't tired, and Quinn wouldn't let his guard down. He sat across the fire from Silvie, his eyes rarely leaving her.

They didn't speak much to each other. Quinn was irritable, giving only short answers to any question Aven asked or conversation he tried to start. Silvie looked in great thought, her gray eyes continually on the fire, filled with something that looked like sadness and worry to Aven.

Before Aven gave up trying to get either of his friends to sleep, he whispered to Silvie, "Are you alright?"

She slowly blinked, turning her head to look at him. "I told you I'd never lie to you, Aven."

"So you're not."

"There are some things I have to do that trouble me. I'd rather run away than deal with them," she said, looking back at the fire as she brought her knees to her chest.

"Maybe I could help you?"

"You have enough to deal with on your own. The fate of your kingdom and your people will be up to you soon. You need to get home and prepare."

"Silvie, I'm not sure my father will listen to me. Once I tell him what I've been up to with magic, he'll be furious," said Aven.

"Your father is a good king and man. He'll understand more than you think. Tell him the truth." She rested her chin on her knees. "I should have told you to tell him years ago, but I was a coward. I was afraid you would choose to stop coming to see me instead of facing your father."

Aven looked over at Quinn. He had rested his head against the wall, his eyes still open. The guards were at the other wall, far enough not to hear. Aven scooted closer to Silvie. "Why, Silvie? Why did it mean so much to you to help me?"

"We've been over this before," she said dully. "You're the best chance for your kingdom, and your kingdom is the best chance for the human realm."

"But that's not it, is it? It feels more personal than that. You could have found my sister or appealed to my father… and our lessons. You don't…you don't seem to mind my company."

A corner of her mouth ticked upward. "I don't mind it at all."

"Then why did you care so much about keeping our meetings?"

"I…I have few real friends, Aven. I'm often surrounded by groups of people, ones I even enjoy, but I feel lonely. Sometimes I'm so lonely it aches. Those early mornings with you, the ache would lessen, and I wouldn't feel so alone." She took a shaky breath, and Aven could see a tear fall down her cheek. "I should have told you by now you can learn on your own. You know enough about magic to do it, but I couldn't bear giving up our meetings."

Aven took her hand. "You've made me feel less alone, too. There are times I feel as if I've had to hide a large part of myself, one that feels important, but with you, there is no need. Thank you for giving me that."

She nodded. "You should get some sleep." She looked over the fire at Quinn, who was watching them. "You too. I'll keep watch."

To Aven's surprise, Quinn leaned back against the wall, folded his arms, and rested his chin against his chest, closing his eyes.

"Go on, Aven, lay down," said Silvie. "It won't be too long before the sunrise. Rest while you can."

Aven hesitated. "I'll see you again, won't I? This isn't goodbye?"

She laughed quietly. "No, this isn't goodbye, Aven."

He grinned at her before lying down. She added a few large sticks to the fire and then looked at him. "I told you I would watch over you and see you king one day. I meant it, Aven. I'll see your kingdom and you are safe."

"I want to keep you safe, too," Aven mumbled as his exhaustion started to overtake him.

"It's too late for me," she said quietly. "I left safety behind long ago."

Aven wanted to challenge her and ask her what she meant, but a deep sleepiness that seemed to go beyond normal exhaustion overtook him.

Aven awoke to Quinn gently shaking him. The day was gray with heavy clouds overhead. Quinn handed him some dried meat and a waterskin as Silvie put out the fire. The guards brought their horses over, and they all mounted, making their way out of the ruins of the forgotten Illedrian village.

"I'll have to ask my father what he knows about this place when we get back," said Quinn. "Maybe the library in the palace has some books on it, Aven."

"I've never come across any, but there are more books there than anyone could read in a lifetime," said Aven.

"And even more stored away in other areas." Quinn chuckled. "We can set Cara on the task. She loves spending hours searching through books and making notes."

"Who is Cara?" asked Silvie with curiosity.

"My sister," said Quinn. "She thinks herself a great learner and scribe."

"She is very clever," said Aven. "She was the one who noticed that the pattern of the abductions and stolen items in the land all had a link with magic."

Silvie looked at Quinn. "How old is your sister?"

"She turned sixteen not too long ago," said Quinn.

"Oh," said Silvie to Aven. "Is she your young friend you gave one of the dragon bracelets to? Like the one you gave me?"

Aven nodded. "I said you would like her."

"Who knows?" said Quinn. "The way things are going, you might meet her one day."

"I would like that," said Silvie. "I have a feeling your whole family is interesting and worthy of knowing, young lord."

"Not according to a good chunk of the lords of the kingdom," said Quinn angrily. "Many tend to avoid us."

"Why?"

"Because my father sees no use in needless finery and superfluous living. My mother keeps a comfortable, useful home, but it's not fashionable. My parents are kind and hospitable, but you won't catch them hosting grand balls. They prefer intimate suppers and teas with intelligent conversation."

"Then they are better off than most," said Silvie. "Perhaps they are shunned by some in the kingdom, but I'm sure it's those not worth knowing."

"And your parents haven't flitted away their fortune like others. They are richer than most in our kingdom, probably the realm," said Aven, "though most don't know it."

"No, and my father wants to keep it that way. Could you imagine what stupid young lords would already come calling for Cara if they knew?" said Quinn.

Aven made a face of disgust as Silvie laughed. "But she would have you two to scare them away. That poor girl, if she finds one she wishes to marry one day, he better have the patience of Madha and the perseverance of Mayra."

Quinn actually laughed. "Oh, he will if he wants to win Cara's heart. My sister has a list of things she wishes to accomplish, and I'm not sure marriage is even on the bottom."

"Good for her," said Silvie. "I hope she gets to accomplish all she wishes and that only the deepest, truest love ever lures her into marriage."

"Absolutely," agreed Aven. He felt Silvie tense behind him, and he turned to her. "What is it?"

"Stop," she said. "I need to leave you here."

"What? Right here?"

"Yes," she said as she let go of him.

Aven slowed his horse, and Silvie jumped off even before he could stop. She adjusted her skirt and turned to Aven. "This path will lead to another that turns right, going deeper into the forest. Follow it for an hour or so, and you should spot Margred's house. You don't need to be afraid of her, though she will seem a bit odd to you. Tell her whatever it is you need, and then leave. The easiest path to the south is this one. Come back to it and follow it out of the forest."

"What will you do?" asked Quinn. "We can't just leave you here alone in the middle of the woods."

"I know my way around, young lord. I'll be fine. Now, go find Margred and go straight home. Keep your prince safe and yourself as well. Your kingdom needs you both."

"I'll see you soon, Silvie?" asked Aven.

"I hope so, Aven. No matter what your father says, keep practicing your magic." She gave him one more slight grin before running into the trees.

"I'm probably a fool to say this, but if you don't want to tell your father about her, I won't say a word to anyone," said Quinn as they started walking again.

Aven noticed the guards rubbing their eyes and heads as though they were just waking up. "I need to tell my father everything. I'll face whatever consequences if there's a chance I can help save our kingdom."

"Then I'll back you up if you need it. Tell him what I've heard. I can speak to my father about it and ask his opinion if you like?"

"We'll see how it goes. Let's get to this witch's house so we can move on and get home. If there's someone or something out here that's a threat to a woman as powerful as Silvie, then I don't want to see it."

They rode on just as Silvie told them, taking the turn into the forest. It wasn't long before Aven could see a thin line of smoke rising over the trees.

"That must be it," he said, urging his horse to go faster. Quinn kept up his pace, the two guards following in their wake.

As they moved through a dense area of trees, they came to what looked like a small, wild lawn. An old wooden fence with a gate surrounded a simple cottage and well. In the back was a small orchard of twisted apple trees that held the last bit of their fruit from the season.

"What do you think?" asked Aven.

"I think I've read a few fairytales that started with a harmless cottage in the woods. It never turned out well," said Quinn.

"Silvie would never tell us to go somewhere we would be harmed. Come on. We won't stay long." Aven instructed the guards to stay close to the fence, hiding in the small orchard to keep watch.

Aven and Quinn rode to the gate and dismounted, tying their horses on the fence. Aven reached to unlock the gate when it swung open by itself as though inviting them in. Aven glanced at Quinn before walking through the gate and to the front door of the cottage.

He knocked, and just like the gate, the door swung open. Quinn peered inside. "Hello? Is anyone home?"

A small woman appeared in the hall, one hand raised and the other holding a dagger.

"Wait!" said Aven, holding up his hands. "We come in peace with a message."

The woman slightly lowered her hands. "A message from who?"

"I don't know her name, but she was a Fae woman. She said to tell you her young mouthy friend sent me."

The woman's hands lowered further, and she took a step toward Aven and Quinn. "Did she now? Where did you come across her?"

"In a small village in the valley of Cail. I was staying in the inn and about to make a fool of myself in front of two local women. She stopped me and asked that I come to see you."

The woman nodded. "Sounds like her. Come in, but make it quick. I need to be going, and you shouldn't be here."

Aven stepped into the narrow hall as the woman turned her back. He followed her to a space that was the strangest room Aven had ever seen. It looked like part sitting area, part library, and part dungeon. A fireplace that took up half the outer wall had a large fire burning with three different kettles hanging over it.

The woman walked over to a table where an open bag sat. She started throwing small books in it. Aven walked closer to her as Quinn came to his side. The woman was very small in height and figure. Her dark hair was streaked with gray and pulled up off her face in a messy bun. Her skin was not lined in any way, but something about her eyes made Aven think she must be quite old.

"Now, what's the message you came all this way to tell me?" said the woman as she placed another book in her bag.

"I'm Aven, and this is Quinn. We come from Illedria."

"I know where you're from. It's obvious," said the woman. "And I'm Margred, the dreaded forest witch of the Gethian forest. Now that's out of the way. What do you have to tell me?"

"Should we dread you?" asked Quinn.

Margred stopped putting books in the bag and looked up. Her dark eyes were almost black. "Do you mean me any harm?"

"No," said Quinn.

"Then you shouldn't dread me. What's the message? One of you better tell me quickly because I'm not planning to stay around here much longer." She put one more book in her bag and picked it up.

"Your friend said to tell you that you were in danger. She said that you should leave as soon as possible. She also mentioned a scroll. Said she would come to tell you herself, but she's afraid she's being tracked," said Aven.

Margred raised an eyebrow at this. "They've figured her out, have they?"

"I don't know," said Aven. "I don't know her. I've never seen her before that day or since."

Margred grunted. "You sure about that, boy?"

"I think I would remember if I saw her again. She wasn't exactly forgettable," said Aven.

"No, she's not, but she's clever. You could have come across her in a hundred different places and had no idea." Margred picked up a small jar and put it in the pocket of her skirt. "She needn't have sent you. I already knew it was time to leave. The forest told me so. Strange people in these woods now, those who do mean harm to me and many others."

"Is it the Court of the Underlings?" asked Quinn boldly.

Margred moved closer to Quinn, looking up and examining him. "You in training, boy? An apprentice somewhere?"

"An apprentice to who?" said Quinn, taking a step back.

"There are still a few old wizards around, one that lives somewhere near your southern coast. You've got the look and smell about you to be useful to him. Just his type, powerful and inquisitive."

"Powerful? What do you mean?"

"Magic, boy, your magic. It's practically oozing off you. Even more so than this future Illedrian king, though I believe he has better use over his. Probably always will. Ability and what's been given to us by the gods don't always correlate."

"I...I've never tried to use any magic," said Quinn. "My family suppressed theirs long ago until it was gone."

"Gone," laughed Margred. "I didn't think you were a fool, but you are young. You can't get rid of magic, even if you ignore it. Find a master, boy, soon if you want to become something." She turned and started to go to the fireplace when a loud noise shook the small cottage.

"Tits of Madha," Margred growled as she turned, "Already here? Damn old trees could have given me more of a warning. You two need to leave now."

"They're here?" asked Quinn, his voice quaking.

"Seems so," said Margred as the house was shaken again. A second later, two windows were broken out by large tree limbs on fire. The flames immediately caught one on a table and one on a chair, spreading so fast that it couldn't be normal.

"Shit," said Margred as she pushed past Aven and Quinn, running towards the front door. She cracked it open and gave an angry sigh before yelling, "Go to the back of the cottage. I'll get your prince out."

Margred closed the door and ran into the living room, throwing her hand out to push the fire to the walls. "Take down the flames in the fireplace," she said to Aven.

"What?" asked Aven, coughing as he followed her into the room.

"The flames in the fireplace, you can call them down, can't you? There's something there I need you to grab."

Aven felt Quinn's eyes on him as he moved to the fireplace, his eyes burning with smoke. The house shook again as another flaming torch came through one of the broken windows.

Margred cursed. "Hurry, boy."

Aven raised a hand and closed his eyes, trying to remember how Silvie taught him to concentrate and envision what he wanted. He moved his hand as he opened his eyes, and the fire flared before extinguishing.

"Good," said Margred, and she moved her hand, causing one of the torches to fly back out the window. "Now move that stone in the middle."

Aven hesitated. "I'm not good with stone."

"You can do it. You have everything you need inside you. You've been taught, haven't you?"

"I have, but..."

"Then do it, boy. No doubts."

Quinn came to Aven's side, looking at the fireplace. "Should we just go?"

Aven shook his head, putting up both his hands as he planted his feet. Silvie said he had to be sure and grounded, knowing he could do it. He took a deep breath and put his hands down and up. He heard the scraping sound before he opened his eyes.

"Now grab that scroll," said Margred. She moved a hand, and a window on the other side of the room shattered. "Escape out that window before they get any closer and see you. Damn cowards are trying to burn me out before they show themselves."

Aven knelt at the fireplace and looked into the space where the stone moved. A cylinder sheath lay there. His hand hovered over it, feeling something pulsing off it.

"It's old Fae magic," said Margred. "But it won't hurt you. Take it. Take it back to your palace, and keep it there behind your old wards. Those things are beasts and will not go down easily."

Aven took the scroll. It was warm in his hands. He stood up and looked at Margred. "What about you?"

"I'll fight them for a bit before I get out of here. If they see me, they'll think I have it. They'll never know where it went."

"What's on this scroll?" asked Quinn.

"The only hope for this entire land," said Margred. "Now go."

Aven felt bad leaving another person in trouble, but at least Margred seemed more than prepared for what was going to happen.

"When you see my old friend again, tell her I've gone to rest. If she needs me, she'll know where to look."

Aven nodded as Quinn grabbed his arm. "Let's go."

Aven gave one more glance at Margred, who held the fire at bay as she slowly made her way to the hall. He ran with Quinn to the window, carefully crawling out to avoid the broken glass. They found their guards and horses waiting for them, and Aven jumped up on his horse as it started moving, scared by the growing fire. He managed to find his seat just as they reached the tree line. Before he let his horse have his head to run through the woods, he placed the scroll in the same bag as the necklace and horn.

Chapter 25

Tal

T HE GROUND CRUNCHED UNDER Tal's boots, feeling rocky. A light mist was falling, and a harsh, cold wind blew. The air was filled with the scent of pines and oaks. They must still be in the forest, but he couldn't see. It was like some invisible, unfelt blindfold had been put over his eyes. His hands were bound with the same magic, and a familiar hand was on his back leading him.

"What the hell is going on, Dyfan?" said Tal through gritted teeth.

"Relax, nothing's going to happen to you. Your binds and blindness are only precautionary."

"Where are you taking me?"

"Somewhere safe," said Dyfan.

"Somewhere safe? You grab me, force me to leave, bind my hands, and blind my eyes, and expect me to believe you're taking me somewhere safe?" Tal struggled against his binds, calling upon his magic, but it still felt weak.

"You can't undo them, not in the state you're in. She's been covering your magic since she found us. I should've noticed earlier. I apologize," said Dyfan, grabbing Tal's arm as Tal slipped.

"Who's been covering my magic? That's not even possible."

"It was Delphina, and I'm not sure how. I grabbed your waterskin to see if one of the witches in the court can figure it out." They stopped walking, and Dyfan brought Tal to a stop. "I tried to warn you about her enchantment abilities, but you didn't want to listen.

I should've known you'd fall right into them. Either she is stronger than I believed, or you are weaker for a pretty face than I thought."

"Enchantment abilities?"

He felt someone stop and stand in front of him, but he couldn't pick up a scent, though he took a deep breath.

"Is he completely under her thrall?" said a tired voice he recognized.

"No," said Dyfan. "I don't think it went that far, Eri."

Tal felt a gentle breath against his face and then a soft touch against his cheek. "I think you're right. Still, it'll take a while to get her out of his head. Get him inside and settled. I'll meet with him after I speak with the others. I need to send some messages," said Lady Eriana.

There was a sound of stones shifting and a small cry. Dyfan's hand fell off Tal. "Eri," Dyfan said with worry. "You're not well."

"I'm fine," said Eriana before taking a deep breath. "Just need a moment."

"Eri..."

"I'm fine, Dyfan. Settle him in, and I'll check with you in a bit."

Dyfan sighed before saying, "Come on, Tal." Dyfan pulled him forward.

Tal stumbled but kept to his feet. As he walked, he felt something come over him, filled with powerful magic. It only added to his confusion, anger, and fear, making his stomach feel unsettled and his chest ache. What was Dyfan saying about Delphina trying to take his magic or enchant him? She would never hurt him. He had started to care about her and was sure she felt the same. She wasn't the one who grabbed him against his will. She wasn't who held him blinded and bound.

"Are you working against my brother, your king?" Tal tried to pull out of Dyfan's grip.

Dyfan grunted. "My king? Your brother is the last person I would ever claim my loyalty to."

"So where does your loyalty lie then?"

They reached some steps, and Dyfan helped him walk up them. There was a sound of a door opening on creaking hinges, and then Tal was pushed through a doorway into warmth.

"My loyalty is here to my fellow Underlings," said Dyfan with some amusement.

The darkness slowly faded away from Tal's eyes. He blinked against the bright entryway he found himself in. It was an open space lit by the largest chandelier he had ever seen. At least two hundred candles blazed overhead, not a drop of wax spilling.

Others pushed past him, one or two clapping Dyfan on his shoulder, welcoming him back. It was an odd assortment of creatures—humans, Fae, woodland faeries, and the goblins he had seen in the woods. Dyfan nodded to them all, even laughing as one whispered something to him.

"Come on, Your Highness, let me get you settled somewhere comfortable," said Dyfan.

Tal refused to move. "I don't want to go anywhere with you until you explain what's going on. You call yourself an Underling. Are you really a part of the Court of the Underlings? Is it you who's been causing havoc throughout the human realm? And what of Lady Eriana? I thought the Underlings took her, yet I saw her out there fighting with all these creatures, commanding you."

"Nothing is what you thought, Tal," said Dyfan. "I'm sorry to lie to you, but I had my orders. We tried to get you here earlier, but that incident in Farwarn spoiled our plans. It threw Eri off for her plan to go awry. It always does. She has big dramatic ideas, and when they don't go as she thought, well...at least you're here now. Once you were in the forest, she wanted to explain it all to you herself, but of course, it didn't go well again. Poor Margred. I only hope she got away. Eri will be devastated if she didn't."

"I don't give a fuck about Lady Eriana or what she wants," said Tal furiously. "I was sent out to save her, bring her back to her father, and I find the worthless woman has been pulling the strings the entire time."

"Watch how you speak about her," said Dyfan threateningly as he leaned towards Tal. "You have no idea what she's been through for our realm, for..." Dyfan half growled and turned away. "She is not the worthless one, Tal. What exactly did she drag you from? Wasting your days away with nameless women? Drinking all your uncle's good wine? She's spent the last three decades trying to figure out a way to keep this world together, to stop it from spinning out of control. You'll respect her within these walls."

"I don't want to be within these walls. Take me back to where I was or back to the village. I need to check on Delphina. We just left her there with whoever was trying to kill us. Her father will be furious, you know," said Tal. "I want nothing to do with whatever this is."

"You can't go until we say you can," said Dyfan. "There are things you need to hear first. As far as Delphina goes, she's fine. Haven't you listened to a word I said? She's been weakening you for days now, getting you under her thrall. It's one of her particular gifts.

I should have seen what she was doing when she disappeared into the forest. Once you stay here and rest for a few days away from her, you'll see it, too."

"I'm not staying here. I've not been enthralled. I know it. It's not possible for me."

Dyfan grabbed his arm and pulled. "Oh, and how are your hands bound by magic then?" He waved his hands in front of Tal's face, and the darkness appeared. "And how can I blind you?" Tal felt a slight breeze as Dyfan waved his hand again, and the room came back into view. "You've been weakened to the point your magic isn't responding. I hate to think what would have happened had she completed what she started."

Tal pulled at his magical binds, but his hands wouldn't budge. His light magic had not responded at all, which didn't surprise him, but even his dark magic was weak and slow. "How do I know it was Delphina and not you?"

Dyfan sighed in frustration. "You only feel so defensive about her because of her thrall. Trust me, Tal. It's me. Do you truly think I would ever bring you to harm?"

Tal looked at his old friend, seeing nothing but frankness on his face. "I don't know, Dyfan. I feel like a fool at the moment."

"Then don't make it worse. Come with me. If you cause any more ruckus, someone else might come and see to your hospitality. Everyone here has a common cause, but some are not as kind as others."

Tal saw there was nothing else he could do, so he nodded. Dyfan put his hand on Tal's back and guided him towards one of the two staircases in the massive entryway. "What is this place?" asked Tal as they ascended the stairs.

"The old palace of Illedria. It was abandoned centuries ago. Eri and some others found it a while back and have slowly worked to restore it. There are all kinds of wards on it. Some are ancient, and others were created by Eri and some witches who reside here. Anyone who doesn't know how to see it won't. They'll just see the ruins of the village that used to surround it."

"This place really exists?" They reached the second floor, and Tal looked up at the four floors above him. Others were walking along the corridors, some entering and exiting rooms. The stone underneath him looked worn, but a new-looking red rug was under his feet. "I thought this was just some old human legend."

"No, the Illedrians really first lived in the forest. They say it's because of the massive caverns found close to here. Places they could keep their great dragons. We've examined a few of the caves but found no signs of any dragons."

They stopped by a room not far down the hall. "Here. Most of the upper court is on the second floor. The higher floors are for some of the lower court and those who spend most of their nights elsewhere."

"You're putting me here amongst your upper court?" asked Tal.

Dyfan opened the door. "You're a visiting prince. I was told to give you a royal welcome."

Tal stepped into the room to find it large and well-appointed. A good-sized bed rested against the far wall. The fireplace was lit, and two overstuffed chairs sat in front of it.

Dyfan waved his hand behind Tal, and Tal's hands were finally free. "You have a washroom through that door. I'll make sure some water is charmed for you since you might have trouble doing it. Wash, and I'll see about some fresh clothes."

A young woman entered behind Dyfan carrying a tray. She had long brown hair and a face that would have been pretty had there not been a long red scar down the right side, causing her eye and mouth to droop.

"Thank you, Egrid," said Dyfan.

She put the tray down on a table by the fire. There was tea and a bowl of stew with steam rising off it. "Some t-tea and st-st-stew." She stuttered before curtsying prettily. "Y-y-you are w-wanted d-d-downstairs, D-Dy-Dyfan."

Dyfan smiled at the girl. "Your speech is improving. Thank you, Egrid."

She fully smiled and then curtsied to Tal before leaving the room in a hurry.

"Poor girl. She was seriously injured when one of the mines collapsed in Cryfder. Our healers did their best. Even Eri did what she could, but Egrid still has the scar, and it took her a year to start talking," said Dyfan.

"How many people call this place home?" asked Tal, walking toward the fireplace. He had to admit the smell coming from the stew was heavenly, and the fire's warmth was welcomed.

"We have about five hundred who live here and another three or four that check in periodically," said Dyfan. "Our number fluctuates a bit, of course, depending on who we lose and gain."

"And how long have you been a part of this court?"

"Since the beginning. I helped build it," said Dyfan.

"So you're its leader?" asked Tal.

"I have some under my command, but I'm no king if that's what you're asking."

"Who is then?"

"You'll find out soon enough. Eat and wash. Some clothes will be brought in. I'll come to fetch you in a while. You can ask what other questions you have," said Dyfan.

"And then what?" asked Tal.

"You'll be given a choice, whether you wish to join us or not," said Dyfan. "If you choose to join us, it will be decided how you can serve."

"And if I don't?"

"Then I imagine you will be sent back to Brigant safely unless we keep you as a hostage. It's unlikely, though. Not really our style. You will probably be returned with your memory altered."

Dyfan gestured to the food. "Go eat and get warm. I'll be back soon." He walked towards the door. "Don't try to escape. It'll do no good. I have guards watching each floor and staircase, and the exits are all warded. With your magic so weak, you won't have a chance." He put his hand on the doorknob. "It would also do me a favor if you would behave. I stood up for you amongst a few higher-ranked of the court. They wanted to take you and throw you in the lower cells until you proved trustworthy."

"You're not really selling your court, Dyfan," said Tal.

"I don't want to lie to you, Tal. This court has flaws like any other, but our motives and goals are worthy. I'll help you see it."

"I won't try anything. As you said, there's no use. Go do whatever you must, and I'll wait here," said Tal.

Dyfan left the room and closed the door as Tal sat in front of the fire. He felt exhausted as he closed his eyes, laying his head back. The warmth of the fire washed over him, and he tried to assess his situation. He was still angry to have been so taken in. A few weeks ago, he was perfectly fine with his life, lounging around his uncle's palace or slinking through the human lands.

He wasn't sure he would call himself happy, but it was better than whatever this was. He had been made a fool by Dyfan and Lady Eriana. He wondered if Lord Elgan knew what his niece was up to. It even seemed that Lady Delphina had not truly wanted him. If what Dyfan said was true, she was only using him for something.

Could it be true? He thought he was forging a connection with the lady. His heart had not been touched, as that was impossible, but he felt like he was growing fond of her. Fond enough that he actually considered for a moment or two what it would be like to settle with Delphina forever. To think she was only using him seemed impossible, but if it were true, it only strengthened his belief that he was not made for love or anything resembling it. He was beginning to think no one was, and it was a lie told over and over.

The delicious scent of the stew made him open his eyes. Besides the supper with the travelers, he hadn't had a decent meal in a while. He leaned forward and took a bite, finding the stew so good he almost moaned. It was like the food back home, not the bland things humans ate. He finished it quickly and poured a cup of tea. It was a rich brew that warmed him from the inside. When he was done with his meal, he thought he would like nothing more than to slip into the comfortable-looking bed and sleep for two days.

He couldn't, though, not with the million thoughts running through his head. He still didn't understand what was happening or what this Court of the Underlings was. He wanted to trust Dyfan. He had few friends, and he believed Dyfan was one of them. At the moment, it appeared he had no choice but to stay, so he decided to be as comfortable as he could while he was there.

The bath in his bathing chamber was full of hot, sudsy water. By the time he took care of his needs and bathed, clothes were waiting for him on his bed. They were a shirt and pants made of warm, fine fabric that was cut just the way he liked. After drying in front of the fire for a few minutes, he pulled them on as there was a knock at the door.

"Enter," he called as he buttoned his shirt.

Dyfan walked in. He, too, had cleaned and changed. Gone was the rough shirt Tal had bought him, replaced with a simple dark blue shirt. He had shaved, and his hair was still a bit damp.

Dyfan looked Tal over. "I thought we provided you with shaving supplies. Did you need someone to come in and help you with it?"

Tal rubbed the stubble on his chin. "I'm capable of seeing to all my own needs, but I like it as it is."

Dyfan shrugged. "Very well. You're wanted in the throne room."

"The throne room? Am I going to meet your king?" said Tal with a mischievous grin. "I suppose my fate will be decided quickly."

"It's not as serious as that. You aren't in any danger. Your fate, as almost always, is in your own hands. This is nothing but a welcome," said Dyfan.

Tal walked to the door and held his hands behind his back, looking at Dyfan.

"What are you doing?" asked Dyfan.

"Waiting for you to bind my hands."

"Is there a reason I need to bind your hands, or is it something you enjoy?"

Tal smirked at his friend. "Maybe it is, but not with you."

"Then, unless you're planning something, I see no reason to bind you," said Dyfan as he opened the door. "Your magic is still rather weak, and this is one of the rare times I have no doubt I could knock you on your ass. So, I might welcome a challenge from you."

"I won't give you the satisfaction," said Tal.

Dyfan chuckled. "Then come with me, Your Highness."

Tal walked Dyfan back to the first floor. They passed a few humans and Fae. Some looked like they were cleaning or stocking rooms. Others held books or weapons. None of them barely even glanced at Tal, though most nodded to Dyfan.

Once they reached the entrance hall, Dyfan took them down a wide hallway to the left. Torches lit it, and on the walls every so often was a dark banner bearing a crow with a red dahlia in its beak.

"Your standard is interesting," said Tal as he glanced at one of the banners. "Why the crow and dahlia?"

"Crows are intelligent birds and are often seen as a harbinger of change. Red dahlias are known to stand for strength and stability. It's also our queen's favorite flower," said Dyfan. "She's fond of them for some reason."

"Your queen?" said Tal, slowing a bit. "Not a king as reported, then?"

"Most people assume our leader has to be a man. We have a queen, not a king," said Dyfan.

Tal had a sinking feeling in his stomach. "Do I know your queen, Dyfan?"

Dyfan grinned at him. "You'll see for yourself. We're here."

Chapter 26

Tal

THEY CAME TO A set of wooden double doors at the end of the hall. Two Fae males stood guard, both wearing black shirts and holding long swords.

"We've been called by the queen," said Dyfan.

"Of course," said the guard on the right as he eyed Tal. "Is he armed?"

"I left my sword in my room," said Tal. "I do have my dagger still."

"Let him keep it," said Dyfan. "He's no threat."

"If you say so," said the same guard as the one on the left opened the door.

"After you," said Dyfan.

Tal glanced at his friend before stepping into the throne room, finding it was not what he had expected. It was dim, warm, and loud. The air was full of smoke, and the smell of the same stew Tal had eaten. The room was long and wide, with three fireplaces on each wall. There was a substantial fire crackling in each one. Tables were scattered amongst the space, all with a mixture of creatures around them: humans, Fae, woodland faeries, goblins, and everything in between sat together, eating, smoking, laughing, flirting, and playing cards.

A fiddler stood close to one of the fireplaces, playing a merry tune. A few couples danced nearby. Dyfan was offered a mug of something as they walked by a table, but he refused. A woman bumped Tal as she pulled a man from a chair and into her arms. She laughed at Tal before kissing the man.

As they came to the front of the throne room, the smoke cleared a bit, and Tal saw a dais with an ornately carved stone throne. It was cracked up top, but he could see it was meant to resemble a dragon head looking out over the room. The feet of the great seat were dragon claws, and the armrest was like wings.

Perched on that throne, looking more than comfortable as she reclined with her legs dangling over one of the armrests, was Lady Eriana. She was dressed as Tal had seen her earlier, in tight black pants and a matching shirt. Her long auburn hair was in two thick braids running down her chest. She watched Tal approach before stretching and propping her head up with her hand.

"So you've brought our honored guest, Dyfan," said Eriana, sounding bored.

"Just as you asked, my queen," said Dyfan with a bow.

She half grinned at Dyfan before looking at Tal. "How are your accommodations, Prince Taliesin?"

"Adequate," said Tal. "Do you know how long I'll be staying?"

"That's up to you, I suppose," she said. "Everyone who joins my court does so under their own accord." She sat up further and picked at one nail before continuing. "Of course, you're a little different than most brought before me. It isn't every day a prince of both Fae realms comes to call."

"Comes to call," repeated Tal with a laugh. "You had me dragged here against my will."

"Would you rather I left you in the woods at the mercy of those who were about to attack you?" She shook her head. "I suppose you think my sweet cousin would've made sure you were safe."

"I've had no reason not to trust Lady Delphina," said Tal.

"Oh," said Eriana as she jumped off the throne, landing gracefully on her feet. She knelt on the dais to be at eye level with Tal. "How's your magic working for you, Your Highness?"

"Am I supposed to take your word that it was her who muted it? What if it was Dyfan under your orders?"

"You accuse your old friend of such malfeasance?" She stared at Tal. "Or do you think I have such influence over him?"

Tal took a moment to examine Lady Eriana. She was beautiful, just as beautiful in the flesh as her portrait. Her astonishingly human blue eyes practically shone in the dim room, and the mischievous grin on her full lips only added to her attraction.

"It's been a while since I've spent much time with Dyfan, but you could very well be his type. I imagine you're most men's type, aren't you? A fact you've probably used to your advantage."

She sat back on her heels and raised her head to laugh. "You come to my court and accuse me of gaining my place by such dubious methods. Oh, my dear prince, have you forgotten all your manners during your travels?"

She suddenly jumped off the dais, landing by Tal. "Come with me, Your Highness. Let's take a walk, and I'll show you my court." She turned to Dyfan. "Get some food and have a drink, Dyfan. You've been gone too long."

"I'm not sure that's wise, Eri," said Dyfan as he looked at Tal. "I should go with you."

"It's unnecessary. Prince Taliesin is our guest, not a prisoner. Being such an exalted one, he deserves a tour given by a queen. Now go rest. That's my command."

"Eri..."

She reached out and took Dyfan's hand. "It's fine. It is."

Dyfan squeezed her hand and nodded. "If you need me..."

"Yes, yes, I know where to find you and everyone else. Go relax and enjoy yourself," said Eriana as she let go of Dyfan's hand. "Come with me, Your Highness."

Dyfan stared at Tal, a warning clearly written on his face. Tal scoffed at him, wondering what Dyfan thought he might do, what he could actually do even if he wanted to. Tal had seen this woman fight, and he wanted no part of her, especially when his magic wouldn't respond.

"You've been fed?" she asked as they moved around the tables, everyone standing as she walked past.

"Yes, in my room." He glanced at a filled mug, the smell of honey mead wafting from it. "I wouldn't mind some of what's in those mugs, though."

"I'll be sure there's some in your room when you return later this evening," she said as she came to the door and opened it. "After you."

He walked through, and she followed him, nodding to each of the guards. "I imagine you have many questions. Dyfan tells me you're angry. That's to be expected."

"I was called to my brother's court to look for you. Your uncle believes you're in danger."

She waved a hand. "My uncle believes no such thing. He knows where I am and what I do. He was only doing as I asked."

"He's in on all of this?" hissed Tal. "Working against his king."

"My uncle has never claimed allegiance to your brother, and he never will. The last king he served was your father."

"His loyalty now, I suppose, is with you," said Tal as they walked down the hall. "He calls you his queen, does he?"

"My uncle's loyalty is to his court. His family's duty has always been to serve the Golden Court in some way, once as rulers and now as servants."

"Rulers?" Tal stopped as they came close to the entry hall.

Eriana nodded. "Lord Elgan's family, my family, I suppose, were once the line of Sun Kings and Queens, but it was handed over centuries ago to your family." She gestured back towards the throne room. "That's the throne room, of course. I hold court there in the afternoons and evenings when I'm in residence. When I'm not, I imagine it's used as it is now."

"Wait," said Tal. "You expect me to believe that Lord Elgan's blood was once the line of rulers for my court?"

She nodded. "I do because it's true. Do you not remember any of the readings from your youth?"

Tal rubbed his head. "No. I have a hard time remembering anything beyond when I left for my uncle's court. I've never known why."

Eriana lifted her hand as though she would touch him in comfort but pulled back, taking a step away. "I'm sorry to hear that, as it must mean you have little memories of your father. It's a pity. He was a great man and king."

"So I've heard," said Tal. "But he wasn't destined to be king, according to you."

"No, he was." She started walking again, and Tal hurried to catch up with her. "The entry hall, of course. I try to keep it clear and inviting, but you'll usually find some matter of filthy cloaks and weapons lying around. Most put in their fair share of work, but keeping this palace clean is sometimes the least of our worries." She moved through the entry hall down a long hall. "This way."

This hall was narrower than the one that led to the throne room. It was well-lit with torches. Doors lined it, and some were open to show sitting rooms full of different creatures eating and relaxing.

"Some of our newer members relax and eat in these rooms, and some of our most trusted older members prefer the quiet of these areas. There is a library up ahead to the left. I have a few scribes from Thiria going through the old books left here and working to acquire more. It's rather pitiful at the moment, but you're welcome to use it as long as you're here. You used to be a great reader, but that was long ago."

"You knew me?" Tal asked, surprised. He supposed he shouldn't be. They were around the same age, and being of Lord Elgan's family, she would often be at court.

"I did," she said quickly. "Now, about your family's destiny to be the line of rulers. Your family once were only lords in the Golden Court, trusted allies of the original rulers. Though you were vicious fighters, your line also had a sense of fairness and balance. Your family was also known for their wisdom, which the original rulers depended on."

They passed many other rooms, including one that held some musical instruments. He could see a young woman playing a piano while another quietly strummed a harp in the corner. A few children sat on the floor before them, listening intently.

"You have children here?"

"We do—ones who most kingdoms have overlooked. They have lost their parents and have no families, so they were sent to the mines to work in dreadful conditions. I saved the ones I could and brought them here."

"A good way to build up your numbers," said Tal.

"We'll see. They will stay here as long as they need safety as they grow. Once they reach the age of maturity, they will be given a choice whether they want to leave or stay," said Eriana. "Everyone is given a choice here."

She stopped before two double doors on the end, and Tal looked at her. He noticed during their walk that she kept her eyes off him, and even now, she was looking at the doors, not him. "So my family became the line of rulers. How?"

"Oh," she said as she shook her head. "You'll have to forgive me. I've always been a bit scatterbrained. Someone once told me I had too many thoughts in my head to keep them all straight." She finally looked at him and grinned. "I suppose they were right."

Tal stared at her. He couldn't help it. Even in his annoyance, he saw how captivating she was. It was in a way he couldn't explain that went beyond simple beauty. It was no wonder she had managed to build such a court around her.

She looked away as she put her hand on the door in front of her. "The last king in my uncle's line had no worthy sons to carry on his legacy. His sons were known to be vile, caring only for themselves and power. Your family line had a young son the king was very taken with. He named him his heir, passing the right to rule to your family line.

"The boy and his father were flabbergasted by the act. They wanted to give something in return for such a gift. It was decided that the true heir from the original line would always be able to hold the line if necessary. Also, they would never be completely under the power of the new rulers."

Tal crossed his arms, still looking at Eriana. "That explains how Lord Elgan can do as he pleases, even against my brother's wishes."

She nodded. "Your brother is not worthy to wear the sun crown. My uncle knows it."

"Does he plan to take away the right to rule then? Has he already done it?"

Eriana sighed. "If only it were that easy." She opened the door and stepped in.

Tal waited a moment before following her. They came into what was obviously a ballroom, but no dancing was being done that evening, though it was full. In one corner, several humans lined up, and a human woman and a Fae woman led them in a lesson. Tal realized it was a magic lesson when several candles nearby went out and relit.

In another corner, close to a grand fireplace, were several tables. An older-looking woman and a young man bustled around the tables filled with young humans who chopped up herbs or read from books.

"We use this space to train with magic and potions, as you can see," said Eriana. "We have several humans here who are capable of it. Our head witches and wizards oversee them with help from our Fae members, who are comfortable around humans."

"Are all these Illedrians then?" asked Tal.

"Most are or have Illedrian blood, but lately, we've found more and more in other kingdoms. We've had to bring them back here before the forces sent by your brother and his allies found them."

"What?" said Tal, turning to her. "Are you saying my brother has soldiers hunting down children?"

"I am. He also has some human allies to help him. It's taken me a while to know which kingdoms are in his pocket, and I'm still trying to figure it out. He has some kings, but there are lords in other kingdoms. Idris is smarter than I bargained for, or he has placed the right people around him. It's tricky, slow work, and frustrating as we are running out of time." She looked over the room. "I've failed too many children and young men and women. I shudder to think what your brother has done to them."

"I'm sorry, but none of this makes any sense. Why would my brother care about what's happening in the human realms?"

"He cares plenty. He knows he's not the rightful Sun King, but he doesn't care and wants even more. He wants dominion over the human realms and even your uncle's court."

Tal half laughed. "He'll never get it. My uncle could turn him into dust with a glance."

"Don't underestimate your brother. I've done it, and it's cost me dearly."

Tal was quiet as he watched Eriana while she surveyed the room. "So why am I here?" he finally asked.

She turned to him. "Let's go into my study. It's not far from here." She walked from the room, leading him down the hall and into another until they came to a door. It opened into a room about a third the size of the throne room. Each end had a fireplace. Near one fireplace was a long table with various maps and books open on it. The other end had a sofa and two comfortable-looking chairs. A desk sat in the middle against the wall.

Eriana walked to the fireplace with the sofa and chairs, flopping down in one of the chairs and gesturing to the other. Tal sat cautiously on the very edge.

"I don't have any mead here, but I do have some wine," she said as she leaned forward and poured herself a cup from a pitcher. "Would you like some?"

Tal shook his head as Eriana took a long drink. She refilled her glass and sat back in her chair. "So you've seen much of this place and my court. There are, of course, some impressive stables and a blacksmith's forge out back. We have training areas for fighting and magic outside. Our kitchens are rather impressive, as you can imagine, since they have to be to feed so many."

"And I'll ask again. Why am I here, Lady Eriana?"

She looked at him as she took a sip of wine. Whether she was offended at how he addressed her or not, he couldn't tell. "Your brother will see this world destroyed. He will break the balance we've had for so long. Balance your uncle, mother, and father helped make. Idris has begun trying to eradicate any humans with magical abilities and allied with stupid, young, power-hungry human kings. He's made them piddly little promises while they've bargained away their kingdoms without knowing it. He wants total servitude from humans as it was in the dark times."

"You know this? How?"

"I've heard it from his own lips, Your Highness, and I've seen the fruit of his labor," said Eriana. "For every man, woman, and child we've managed to save, two or three more have been killed or taken by forces sent by your brother."

"You expect me to take your word on this?"

"You don't have to. You can stay here and ask everyone you wish. Listen to the stories of the creatures who reside here. Hear why each one is now a part of this court, and draw your own conclusions," said Eriana.

"You want me to stay?" asked Tal.

"Of course. I brought you here. It hasn't been easy convincing some members of my court that you're needed. They had other ideas of what to do with you."

"So you think I'm needed here? Why?"

She put down her glass and drummed her fingers against the armrest of her chair while staring at him. The silence stretched on.

"Are you going to tell me?"

"I'm trying to decide if you're ready for the full truth or just a bit of it," she said. "Whatever I tell you, I don't want to lie."

"You better give me the full truth if you want any chance of me staying here," said Tal.

She looked at the fire, resting her head against the back of the chair as she closed her eyes. They remained closed as she started talking. "It's a strange thing, holding great power inside of you but being limited on how you can wield it." She opened her eyes, and Tal leaned forward. She looked weary and sad, and he had a momentary urge to comfort her somehow.

"Your brother was never meant to be king."

"Someone should have told my father, then, before he made him his heir," said Tal with a dark chuckle.

Her eyes snapped to his. "Your father never made your brother heir. He named another, discussed it with my uncle, wrote it down, and sealed it with his blessing."

Tal rolled his eyes. "You know that can't be true. If it were, my brother would not be able to rule now. I wouldn't be under his command and certainly not here after this foolish mission I was sent on."

"Things happened." Eriana turned her gaze back to the fire. "Things that made it where the only possible thing to do was hand him a shadow of the power for a time. He now knows it's not permanent, but at the time, he was fooled."

"What things happened?"

Eriana opened her mouth, but no sound came out. She shuddered as if in pain before groaning. "Things I can't tell you, and no one else can either. It's a consequence of the false bargain made with Idris. Until I find a way to break it, I can't tell you much beyond that you're the rightful heir of your father's court and should be the true Sun King."

Tal couldn't believe what he was hearing. It couldn't be true. He would remember if his father made him heir. He didn't remember much of his younger years, but surely that would not fade away. And if not him, then someone would know beyond Lady Eriana.

"How can you expect me to believe this? Everyone acts as if Idris is king. He has ruled for over thirty years with no questions. If I were made heir, wouldn't more people know besides you? Wouldn't someone have done something about it, your uncle perhaps?"

Eriana rubbed her head. "My uncle has his reasons, and the bargain with Idris is tricky." She raised her head. "I'll be honest with you, Prince Taliesin, there was a time when I tried to find anyone else to give the right to rule. I thought of your sister or even my uncle, but only you can be the king because you were named." She looked away again. "I spent many years trying to find a way to release you from this burden."

"You knew my father named me, and you've tried to name another as ruler?" He wasn't sure why he was so angry. Did he even want to be king?

She half snarled as her eyes narrowed. "What did you expect me to do, Your Highness? You know how you've lived your life these past three decades. I've seen what you've done, how you've conducted yourself. I guarantee if your father saw what you've become, he would have more than second thoughts. I saw no other alternative, especially since..." She growled in frustration and leaned forward, her head in her hands.

It took a few moments, but she regained her composure and sat up. "I don't mean to cause you pain or offend you, but I want to be honest with you. This will only work if we are both completely truthful."

"Yet, you can't tell me everything."

"I cannot. It's out of my hands," she said. "I know this is a lot of information and hard to believe. I don't expect you to make any decisions right now, but soon. You need to think about what you want to do."

"You mean if I want to be king or not?"

She half smiled. "If you are king or not is not just up to you." She held up her hand, and a glowing ball of light appeared in her palm.

Tal leaned further forward as the light hummed. He could feel its warmth, hear its gentle call just for him. His hand raised on its own accord as he was transfixed on the light.

"You see, it seems my uncle believes I'm his true heir. It's just another thing that makes my cousin hate me, but she made her own bed. Anyway, I alone have the ability to pass the kingship on to you, and I will not do so lightly." She put her hand down, and the light went out.

Tal watched her for a moment before blinking his eyes and shaking his head. He took the pitcher of wine and poured a cup, drinking it in one gulp. "So, you brought me here to see if I can prove myself?"

"I wouldn't put it that way. I brought you here to see if you believe this world is worth fighting for. If you believe it is, I think the rest will fall into place. You have the ability to be a good king. I believe you do, but you seem to have forgotten it."

"And others in this court? You mentioned they had other ideas."

"Well," she said, shifting in her seat. "There appears to be only one way to take the right to rule from you, and it isn't something I would ever allow."

Tal couldn't help but give her a cold grin. "You mean to kill me, right?"

"Yes, but it isn't an option. You are here under my protection, and my command in this court is final." She dusted something off her pants. "You also will not be left alone. Either Dyfan, I, or a guard Dyfan deems adequate will keep watch over you."

"Which is why my room is on the second floor," said Tal, catching on. "You and Dyfan sleep there, don't you."

"We do, but I don't believe you have anything to worry about. Many terrible ideas are banded around in our meetings."

"I guess I should be comforted that you think killing me is a terrible idea," said Tal.

"Oh, I don't know how comforted you should be. Maybe I'm just worried about who fate would allow me to pass the line to if you perish. If I knew for certain it was Princess Adalyn or my uncle, I might give more thought to the idea."

Tal raised an eyebrow. "You've mentioned my sister twice. Is she in on all of this?"

"Of course, but not many know it, so keep it quiet. Adi is a valuable ally who gives us much-needed information about your brother's doings."

"So she's constantly in danger," said Tal.

"We're all constantly in danger. This world is teetering on edge, and I'm only trying to keep it from completely falling until everything is made right."

Tal stood up and walked to the fireplace. Several small portraits were on the mantle, one of her uncle and aunt. Another surprisingly looked like her with a young Delphina. The one in the middle was a smaller version of the portrait of her mother that hung in Lord Elgan's home. Next to it was a necklace holding a locket. Tal reached for it when Eriana's voice stopped him.

"It's not polite to touch someone else's things without permission. Your manners are atrocious, Prince Taliesin.

He put his hand down and turned to her. "What now? You want me to decide if I will stay here or…"

"No, not now, especially without you understanding what staying here means. If you choose to stay here in the Court of Underlings, you will be pledging your loyalty to the court and me. I will be your queen, your ruler for the time being."

"So I would be under your command."

"Yes, though I think you will find me a fair ruler. Perhaps more so than the one you must cower before now."

Tal perked up at this. "Are you saying if I pledge to this court, to you, it will take me out of control of my brother?"

"I have Fae blood, and I'm a ruler. I have a court, a throne, a palace. If you pledge yourself to me as your queen, you will no longer be beholden to your brother."

"But I will to you."

"As I said, I don't think you would find me an overbearing queen, but that is why I'm offering you time to decide. Ask around and see the court for yourself. I'll give you leave to go wherever you wish in the palace and on the grounds as long as you don't mind having a shadow. If Dyfan or I can't accompany you, a guard will be assigned to you, but they will not get in your way."

"But I can't leave the grounds."

"No, it's too risky as long as you are still under your brother's rule. He could call you home at any time. Here, under the old and new wards, he can't reach you. It's as if you've disappeared off the map, but once you step foot outside, he can find you."

"How much time will you give me?" asked Tal. The idea he could be out from under Idris's thumb was alluring, but he would be putting his trust in this creature in front of him. He needed time to decide.

"We can play it by ear as long as you behave," said Eriana.

"Behave? You mean no drinking or carousing with women, I suppose."

"I'm not your keeper, Your Highness, and anyone over the age of majority can do as they like. I'd like you not to go around drunk all day or take advantage of anyone. You can carouse with whoever you wish." Eriana stood and poured the rest of the wine into her and Tal's cups. "I meant if you don't try to run or go around without an escort. I wouldn't want you trying to push your brother's agenda either."

"I know nothing about what Idris wants, and even if I did, I'm sure I'd wish for the opposite."

"Then there should be no problems," said Eriana as she handed Tal his cup. "Now, let's have a drink to seal this little temporary deal." She raised her cup. "To possibilities."

Tal hesitated for a moment before clinking his cup against hers. "To possibilities."

Chapter 27

Tal

THE NEXT FEW DAYS went by quickly for Tal as he settled into the old Illedrian palace, though he remained wary. Dyfan was waiting for him each morning, accompanying him to breakfast. After breakfast, he encouraged Tal to train amongst the others to reacquaint himself with his skills. Tal knew he was pitiful amongst the most talented of them, especially Dyfan, but his speed still made him somewhat respectable as he sparred with the other warriors of the court.

Dyfan couldn't keep the smirk on his face as he managed to disarm Tal or push him down time and time again, though, by the end of the third day, some of Tal's old skills were returning to him. Dyfan even laughed when Tal was finally able to win one of their matches. Tal's magic started to recover, and he began to realize that perhaps some of Delphina's behavior had been suspicious.

She disappeared more than once without telling him, having vague answers about where she had been. He thought he was only drawn to her beauty and wit, but it was not like him to have such a pull towards any woman, no matter how alluring. He could look back and see that something more than simple attraction could've been at play.

When Dyfan was busy attending to other things, Tal was assigned a guard. He was surprised to see it was young Flint, though he shouldn't have been. It only made sense for the guards Dyfan brought with him when they left Brigant to be ones he trusted.

"I thought you hadn't been out amongst the humans before we left that day," said Tal after being at the palace for almost a week.

Flint followed him down the hall towards the throne room for supper.

"I hadn't," said Flint. "That was the first time I'd ever stepped one foot out of the Fae realms."

"Yet, you were already a member of this court?"

"I've spoken to our queen the times she stayed in her uncle's home. I came across her when she was visiting your brother's court. She was more open than most lords and ladies, but I thought it was due to her human heritage. I know now Dyfan had identified me as someone who might be sympathetic to the cause."

"And you were?"

"My family were once high lords in the Golden Court. Our magic was legendary until my great-great aunt fell in love with a human. It ruined our reputation, and we were shunned by many. By the time your father came to be king, it was too late. We had already fallen. It always seemed backward and sad to me that my family fell because of love and free will."

"Love seems to be the downfall of everyone," said Tal. "I wonder why people keep messing with it."

"You think you can control if you fall in love or not, Your Highness?" Flint moved to walk by his side.

"I think believing in love is a choice. I'm sure the idea is alluring, to be so connected with someone that they know the innermost things about you, that they can put you before anything. To be consumed by someone where you start to believe things make sense must be an attractive notion, but everyone I've seen try it has come to ruin."

"Perhaps my family fell, but my great-great aunt was not unhappy."

"For a time, I'm sure she was content with her human man, but what happened when he died?"

"I'm not sure. She disappeared into the human lands, and my family never heard from her again," said Flint.

"She was probably so miserable she let herself come to a sad end because it all ends the same, Flint. My mother was said to be in love with my father, and look what it cost her."

"You owe your life and your sister's to that love."

Tal stopped walking as they arrived in front of the double doors. "My sister's life, I'll give you. She's worth something, but it might have been better had I never been born. I seem to cause more and more messes the longer I live."

Tal nodded to the guards, and one opened the door for him. The room was already almost full, the smoke lingering over some tables. Two human women were setting out platters of food, and a woodland sprite flew around with a pitcher, filling mugs with mead. Tal's eyes automatically went to the dais, but the throne was empty.

He looked to the table next to it, where he usually sat with Dyfan, and saw his friend sitting there alone. Tal hadn't spent much time around the Queen of the Underlings since the night they shared a drink in her office. He caught a glimpse of her at times, but it almost felt like she was avoiding him.

"Hope you had a productive day," said Dyfan as Tal sat down, Flint finding another table to sit at.

"My dark magic has finally responded, though my light magic still won't even stir," said Tal.

Dyfan took a drink of his mead. "I gave your waterskin to one of the head witches, but I believe Eri might have grabbed it from her. She mentioned wanting to see what was done to you herself."

"Where is your queen, Dyfan? I've hardly seen her this week."

"Eri spends more time out in the land than most of us. She has certain informants who will only meet with her. She's gone so long that sometimes a few of us grow anxious," said Dyfan. "I expect she'll be back soon, though. She said she wouldn't spend too many nights night away until you made your decision."

Tal took a long drink, wanting to change the subject. "So, you've been coming out here while working for my brother?"

"I have. Your brother is not the most attentive king when it comes to those under him. As long as his guards were doing their duties, he never questioned me about my whereabouts. He assumed I stayed in the court."

"But now your days in Brigant are over," said Tal.

"For a time," said Dyfan. "Until the rightful ruler sits on the throne."

Tal took some chicken off the platter in front of him and placed it on his plate. "So, were you one of those who wished to off me and hope for the best?"

Dyfan snorted into his mug. "You know the answer to that question." He put his mug down and looked over the room. "Though someone is joining us who you might want to watch you back around."

Tal looked in the same direction and nearly stood up in shock. Berg had walked into the room, but he looked different than the small man Tal usually worked with. His face was ruddier, his forehead more sloped. His arms were not the thin, spindly things hidden under a cloak but broad and hairy.

"That's Berg?" Tal glanced at Dyfan.

"Yes, in his true form, and he is just as nasty as he looks. I swear his human mother must have been as horrible as his goblin father to produce such a son." Dyfan drained his mug before pouring another.

Berg walked up to their table and sat across from Tal. "Your Highness," he said with a nod as Dyfan passed Berg the pitcher. "Looks like you finally made it."

"I didn't mean to keep you waiting, Berg, but I didn't know this was where everyone expected me to go." Berg gave a short chuckle before drinking from his mug. "How long have you been a part of this little court?"

"Oh, I suppose it's over two decades now. Came across our lovely queen one night at a tavern in Uchel."

"And you, like all these others, fell for her charms?"

Berg eyed him, his muddy eyes narrowed. "You are dangerously close to insulting our queen, prince. I'd rethink that tactic in this room and especially around me."

"I meant no offense." Tal cut into his chicken. "Let me try again. She was able to convince you to join her cause?"

"It took a few glasses of good wine and some time to think on it, but in the end, I couldn't help but agree with her. If we don't do something, your shit brother and those weak human kings will muck up anything halfway redeeming about this world."

"Is that why you befriended me?" asked Tal. "On her orders?"

"Befriend you? Would you call us friends, prince?" The half-goblin shook his head, spearing a potato with a fork and popping it into his mouth. He continued with his mouth full. "You were a good source of keeping me in good liquor and even better women. This court gives me a home and a purpose, but I still have to pay for my hobbies."

Dyfan rolled his eyes as he put some food on his plate. Berg turned and pointed his fork at him. "We don't all hate fun as you do, Dyfan. You sure you're full Fae? Because you are the dullest fellow I've ever come across. Even humans know how to loosen up from time to time."

"Just because I don't drink myself to sleep every night or see how many women I can fuck doesn't make me dull," said Dyfan calmly. "I have goals and hopes for the future, and I won't piss them all away as the two of you have."

"Me? You're dragging me into this?" said Tal, feeling annoyed.

"You two have a lot in common. It's no wonder you found a purpose for each other," said Dyfan.

"Aye, you can't argue with that, prince. How many times did you see if you could drink me under the table? I've seen you with so many different women on your lap that I couldn't begin to count them." Berg laughed. "Perhaps I was hasty in telling the queen we should just do away with you. You might help me liven up this place."

"But it's that very reason you want me gone, isn't it? You think I'm not fit to be king," said Tal.

"I think you'll refuse even to try, which will make things much more difficult. Even if we manage to do away with your brother, what then? Do we put you on the golden throne and hope you have some bastard out there worth a damn who can claim his inheritance one day?"

Tal threw down his fork. He wasn't sure why he was angry. Berg wasn't completely wrong. Dyfan wasn't coming to his defense, and why should he? Maybe everything Berg said wasn't the full truth, but Tal had let the rumors run wild, wanting others to believe him completely depraved, and Tal wasn't even sure he wanted to be king. He'd never thought of it. He believed his father had chosen his worthless brother, the firstborn.

Tal drained his mug and stood up. "Where are you going?" asked Dyfan.

"For a walk. I need to get away from this dirty goblin smell."

Berg chuckled as Dyfan wiped his mouth. "I'll come with you."

"No, stay. Finish your meal. I won't leave the palace."

Tal turned and hurried from the room, dodging tables and everyone who milled around the space. The air was too heavy with food and smoke. The light was too dim. He felt trapped. Trapped with humans, Fae, and every other creature that all thought he was worthless. He saw the looks they gave him as he passed, ones of suspicion, even a couple of outright hatred. Even Dyfan didn't trust him fully. He saw that the first night when Eriana took him for his tour. Dyfan looked afraid to let Tal spend five seconds alone with her.

As he stepped out into the hall, paying no mind to the two Fae guards, he took deep breaths, walking towards the entry hall. The air was cooler out here, fresh and free of smoke. He met no one in the hall and was grateful. Supposing he would go to his room, he made for the stairs until he heard a small crying sound. It was coming from a child, a young one, he believed, and it made him stop.

It came from a half opened door just off the entry hall. Though it might have been wiser to walk past, he silently moved to the door and peeked in. The room was a small parlor, lit only by a fire and a few candles scattered around the room. In front of the fire stood a young girl, probably not even ten. Her long, wavy hair reached her waist, and much of it fell in her face as she cried.

Kneeling in front of her was Eriana. The queen was dressed as simply as always, her auburn hair in its two braids. The young girl shook with tears as Eriana gently moved the girl's hair out of her face. Tal should have walked away, but something kept him there to watch the tender scene before him.

"It's alright to be scared, Myfi. We all get scared sometimes," said Eriana.

"Mari doesn't. She says I need to grow up and stop crying all the time, but I miss Mama and Moren. Moren told me he would find Mama and come back, but it's been so long." The young girl's tears increased.

Eriana brought the girl into her arms, holding her and letting her cry. "It's alright, sweet girl. He'll come back. Your mother had to travel far to help your aunt, and there are a hundred different things that could delay her."

"What if he never comes back? What if he couldn't find Mama?"

Eriana pulled back and wiped some tears off the girl's cheek. "He will come back, and your mother will be with him. If they aren't back by the start of winter, I'll go look for them myself."

"But what will happen to me and Mari if they don't?" The girl's bottom lip shook as she spoke.

"I can promise you, Myfi, no matter what, you have a home here. You can stay here as long as you want."

"I never want to leave, even when Mama gets back. Moren says we might be able to build a house here someday. Everyone's so nice, and I get to practice magic."

Eriana nodded. "And let me tell you a secret. Madam Vorgell said you're one of her best students." Eriana lowered her voice. "Even better than your sister."

Myfi sniffed and smiled before she took a step back. "Oh, but Mari can't hear that I talked to you. She said I shouldn't bother you."

Eriana stood up. "You could never bother me, Myfi. I found you, but I won't tell her if you don't. Now, go on and eat. Your supper will get cold, and your sister will worry about you."

Myfi nodded and turned towards the door before Tal could back away. She froze and moved closer to Eriana. "Who's that?"

Eriana looked at Tal, her eyebrows slightly raised before she grinned at the young girl. "He won't hurt you, Myfi. He's a friend of mine. Would you like to meet him?" The girl nodded. "Then he should stop being rude and step into the room."

Tal slowly moved into the room, leaving the door half open. He walked up to the girl, careful not to get too close.

"Myfi, this is Prince Taliesin of the light and dark Fae courts. Your Highness, this is Myfi. She is from Dewra, though her father's family were Illedrian." Eriana gently pushed the girl closer to Tal. "Give a curtsey, Myfi."

The girl looked up at Tal with a finger in her mouth before taking her skirt in her hands and dipping into a clumsy curtsey. Tal gave her a small smile as he bowed. "It is a pleasure to meet you, Myfi. I should tell you that tonight's supper is excellent. You don't want to miss it."

"He's right, Myfi, and there is a pear tart for dessert. I believe that might be one of your favorites," said Eriana. "So hurry along to supper."

Myfi stared at Tal for a few more moments before he stepped to the side. She hurried from the room but turned at the door to look at Tal one more time.

"Poor thing. Her brother's been gone for three weeks. He went to see if he could find their mother. She was in Cryfder looking after her sick sister when their village in Dewra was attacked. They were looking for Myfi and her sister. They inherited their father's Illedrian magic. How it came to be known, I can't figure out." She turned back to the fire. "I can only hope their brother is successful."

Tal moved to stand at Eriana's side. "Do you know everyone's story here?"

"No, that would be impossible, but I try to get to know everyone I can, especially the children. Many of them are alone in this world, and you know how cruel it can be for those without parents."

"I suppose you're right." He watched her as she stared into the fire. "Did you experience any cruelty as a child, not knowing who your father is?"

"There were whispers, but I was well protected by my uncle and...others." She put her hand on the mantle and leaned forward. "Being half-human made me something of a curiosity in court. There were questions that hurt sometimes, made me feel less."

She reached out her right hand to raise the dying flames of the fire while holding on to the mantle with her left. Her sleeve slipped down so Tal could see the long, raised scar on her arm. It was covered with moon vine, starting at her wrist and disappearing under her sleeve.

"That's an impressive scar."

She looked at her right arm before letting go of the mantle and standing up. "For the most part, I look Fae, but my body doesn't quite heal as well as yours. It's one of many scars I've collected over the years."

"How did you get that one?"

"Same as almost all the others, I was cut." She flexed her hands in front of the fire before rubbing them together. "How have your days been since joining us?"

"Interesting," said Tal, sensing he would not get more of the story. "My magic's starting to respond again. At least my dark magic is working. My light magic remains silent."

"I'm glad to hear at least some of it is coming back. It's a wonder you haven't had any other effects. I've studied your water skin and found traces of rowan berries, herbs, and flowers known to cause drowsiness and weakness. Were you sick on your journey?"

"I don't think so," he said, thinking back over those days. "I was a bit more tired than usual at night, and my dreams were very vivid."

"I hope there are no long-term effects. I wanted to bring you here that first evening, but with the attack, it was impossible. I didn't know Delphina was involved. I thought she was just being the nosy spoiled brat she is. She's been curious about you for some time. I thought she was using the opportunity to get to know you very well."

"When did you realize she was working with my brother?"

"The day before we found you. I tried to take you then, but the circumstances weren't ideal. The forest can be a tricky place," she said, finally turning from the fire and looking at Tal with her arms crossed. "Have you spoken to others in my court?"

"I have."

"And what have you learned?"

Tal stretched and moved a step closer to the fire. "That everyone here practically worships you in some way."

She snorted. "I doubt that. I've made plenty of mistakes and enemies during my life. There are those here who stay in my court because they believe in the cause, not me."

"I haven't come across them, then."

"You will."

"I've asked other questions about your cause and why others have joined your court. Why they risk their lives," said Tal.

"And what have you found out?"

"You've done a good job spreading your message and making your mission personal for everyone. Humans want to protect their freedom. The Fae want balance and peace. Other creatures are frightened if the humans can be considered lesser, then they will be next."

"It's all true. Your brother wants to undo it all. Even Fae know they aren't untouchable. Once you start deciding that some are worth more than others, where does it end?"

Tal tilted his head, watching her. Her eyes were bright, and her cheeks red. She was obviously passionate about her court, more so than he could remember being about anything. He had to look away.

"Is it not enough for you?" she asked quietly. "You've lived mostly amongst humans the past thirty years. Do you have no friends? Have you no compassion for those who have shown you hospitality or shared a bed with you?"

He sighed and shook his head. "I'm afraid most of my relationships have been rather shallow. Especially with those I've shared my bed."

She huffed and licked her lips. "Still, you must have some affection for the human world. You've spent enough time in it."

"It's provided me with diversions I thought I needed. I'm not one to get attached to anyone or anything, my lady."

"Then think of yourself if you must. What will happen to you if your brother continues to grow in power? Do you think he will just let you keep on living, knowing your father named you heir?"

"Does he know you hold the power to bestow my right?" asked Tal.

"I believe he has some suspicions about me holding the power. I don't think he knows it has to go to you. I've done everything I can to keep that information from him."

She worried with one of her braids, her hands undoing the ribbon so she could reweave a part of it. "Still, he knows you're a threat to his rule. He's kept you alive to keep your uncle's wrath away and not offend a few lords, but once he has the human world in his grasp and the Dark Court under his control, what will stop him from doing away with you?"

"My uncle's court will not be easy to conquer," said Tal.

"You cannot be sure. Not when your brother has been doing all he can to get a hold of a few powerful objects, but even if it's hard to believe, play along with me. What happens to you if your brother gets what he wants and you are without any allies? Best case scenario, you become a hunted man, having to flit around from place to place, hoping you aren't found. Which you know is impossible if you remain under your brother's rule and power. Worse case, you're dead."

She had good points and knew how to be persuasive. "What if I went to my brother and swore to him my loyalty? That I would do all I could to help hunt you and your court down to give him what he wants? I have skills he could use."

"You do, and maybe he would keep you around for a while." She stepped closer to him. "But, Prince Taliesin, nothing you could do would erase the fact that you are the rightful king. You are the biggest threat to Idris, and he knows it."

"So then what if I throw my trust in you? What happens if I pledge to your court and you as my queen?"

"You start fighting for something worthwhile. You take the time to help us keep as much power as we can from Idris while experiencing more and more of this court. You take time to consider the worth of this world. You say you don't believe you can become attached to anyone or anything, but I don't believe it.

"Dyfan is your friend, and you know it. You've shown great loyalty to him and others, even if you don't remember it. You've spent too long only living for yourself. Maybe once you start worrying about things besides your own desires, your eyes will be open."

"Not sure I want to find out," said Tal.

"Fair enough. Let's keep it simple, then." She moved closer to him. "You pledge to my court and me, and you at least take yourself out of Idris's rule. You can finally hide from him. I'll have tasks for you, but they won't be anything you can't do." She slowly raised her hand and put it on his chest, her eyes staring into his. "You have great power, Your Highness, and you've been wasting it."

They stayed like that for a moment, Eriana's warm hand pressed against his chest, their eyes locked. Something swirled within him, and he realized it was his light magic. She gave him a small grin before putting her hand down. "It's all still there. It's just been sleeping.

"I'm glad Delphina's work didn't stop your magic permanently." She laughed lightly. "Haven't you been bored, Your Highness? You were made for more than what you've regulated yourself to the past three decades."

He was about to answer her when he heard Dyfan's voice outside. "Eri, Eri, where are you? I know you've returned."

"In here, Dyfan," said Eriana as she turned from Tal.

Dyfan walked into the room, his eyes widening seeing Tal. "I didn't mean to interrupt, but we've had news I knew you'd want to hear." He held up a folded piece of paper. "It just arrived from Eryk."

"Eryk? Isn't he in Illedria, near the palace?" She took the paper and opened it. Her lips moved slightly as she read the message, gasping as she came to the end. "How? The wards should have held."

"I don't know, but we have to do something, don't we?"

"Yes. Go gather our gold and green group. Tell them to be ready to leave immediately. We'll travel directly there. There should be enough who can do it in those two groups. I'll meet you out front in ten minutes."

Dyfan pressed a leather cuff he wore on his arm before hurrying out of the room.

"What is it?" asked Tal as Eriana waved her hand to extinguish the fire.

"Gwaednerth, the main village in Illedria, is being attacked. It shouldn't be possible with the old Illedrian wards, but your brother seems to have found a way. There are too many important objects and people there. The palace is there, and so many with magic running through their blood. I've got to go help them."

She started to walk from the room when Tal said, "Let me go with you."

She turned. "What?"

"Let me go with you. You said I need to start thinking of others. Let me see what my brother is up to. I'm a fair fighter, and some of my magic has returned. I can help you."

She shook her head. "If you leave these wards, your brother could find you."

"But you could do something, couldn't you? You made some of these wards. Could you not do the same around me, at least for a time?"

She blew out a puff of air as though she was considering it. "I could do it, but you would have to remain close to me."

"Fine," he said. "I can fight by your side."

"You really want to go?"

"Yes. I need to see for myself what's going on before I decide what I want to do," said Tal.

"If we do this, you must stay by my side and do all I tell you. If I command you to leave with Dyfan or someone else, you must do it. You can't go running off by yourself no matter what you see," said Eriana.

"Yes, I promise," said Tal as he held out his hand. "On my father's grave, I will do everything you say while we are in Illedria, or may the gods and goddesses curse me."

Eriana looked at his hand for a moment before taking it. Tal felt a warmth spread up his arm as his hand was locked with hers for a moment. Eriana took a shuddering breath before letting go. "Then go get your weapons and meet me in front of the palace."

Tal hurried from the room, running up the stairs. He couldn't deny that it felt good to be doing something. Eriana was right in that he had been bored for some time. Perhaps, finding some purpose was what he needed.

Chapter 28

Aven

The library of the Illedrian palace was vast, taking up half the south wing of the palace. It was two stories with wall-to-wall shelves filled with books. So many books that not even the most studious person could read a fourth of them in a lifetime. Some were in old languages long lost in history. There were some scholars who served the palace who worked to translate these works, but it was slow, painstaking work.

Aven feared the information he needed was somewhere in one of those books, the words beyond understanding. He decided to go through all the books he could just in case, asking one of the scholars there for the oldest books they had he could understand on kingdom history.

He had nothing better to do, being confined to the palace and the grounds for the most part. It was his fault. He had come home as fast as he could, stopping for little rest after the forest. He knew he looked a sight when he appeared before his father, not even checking to make sure his dear mother was not in the room.

She acted out of her mind with worry, seeing Aven in such a state that it alerted his sister, who was having her afternoon meeting with her son nearby. Then, instead of being able to speak to his father alone, he was made to account for his trip in front of all three of his family.

His mother cried, and his sister scoffed at his foolishness.

"After almost being caught in the temple, you thought it a good idea to scamper into the forest, Aven? What were you even looking for?" asked Kira.

He hesitated, not wanting to speak about the Fae woman, Silvie, or magic in front of his mother and sister. "We had word in the temple that another object lay within the forest. I thought it would be a good idea to find it. Which I did."

He then showed them all the objects he had brought back. His sister immediately picked up the necklace, which was not surprising since it was the most beautiful and looked the most valuable. His father put his hand over the scroll but stopped from picking it up. He then gently took the necklace from Kira and placed it back in Aven's pack.

"We will keep these in my study until the priestess of our temple comes back to examine them. She is out visiting other temples, bringing back any important artifacts and any priest or priestess that wishes to return with her. After the attacks, she could take no chances," said the king.

As far as the threat to the kingdom, Aven's father believed they were already well prepared. Mages were on hourly patrols, as well as the palace guards. Lords had been warned, and most estates were closed to all visitors. Aven didn't think it was enough, and he was desperate to talk to his father about magic, but to do so in front of his sister seemed impossible.

So, the items were taken by the king. His mother hugged him tightly, and his sister rolled her eyes and shook her head. His mother demanded that he not leave the palace for at least a week to rest. She was so adamant about it that his father said it was a good idea, so Aven relented, able to only send notes to Quinn instead of meeting with him. Though he had tried to get his father alone, he had no luck. He barely saw his father, and when he asked for a private meeting, the king was always unavailable.

Three days into his house imprisonment, and Aven had spent about every waking moment in the library, working to find out what he could about the history of his kingdom. He wanted to read about their start in the forest, their connection with the Fae, and when they started seeing magic as something beneath most of them.

He closed the book in front of him hard in frustration, dust rising to tickle his nose, making him sneeze. Aven put his forehead on the book with a groan. He wasn't sure what to think. There was definitely something going on out in the lands, and it had touched his kingdom. Still, he wondered if he was being paranoid to think Illedria was in trouble. The forest was far away from here. Should he trust some strange Fae woman he had never seen before?

"I don't think that's how reading works, Aven," said his father as he walked into the room. "Unless you've come up with a new way to absorb the knowledge."

Aven raised his head, surprised to hear his father's voice when he had been looking for him for over three days.

"Has your confinement been that bad, Aven? I thought you might enjoy a few days of rest after such a strenuous journey."

"I'm not one for staying inside," said Aven as he tracked his father's steps. He came before Aven and sat in front of him.

"I know, but it's only a few more days. Your mother's been worried sick about you."

"I'm grown and need to travel around our kingdom. If I'm to be king, shouldn't I know our people?" asked Aven.

"You're right. I should have taken you out to all areas of our kingdom and beyond as soon as you reached your majority, but things had started to come unsettled. I didn't want to risk you," said Aven's father.

"It's not like you don't have another who could take my place should something happen. My sister is more than willing to rule after you." Aven was surprised by the anger and hurt in his voice. He had felt for a while that while his father had tried to prepare him to rule, he had never listened to him.

His father looked at him sadly. "Is that all you think you are to me, someone to rule after I'm gone?"

"It's all you've ever spoken to me about," said Aven.

His father sat back in his seat and sighed heavily. "It was never my intention for you to feel as nothing more than a duty to me, Aven. I'm...I'm not very good at showing my feelings or expressing certain sentiments. I'm sure you've heard the talk amongst our court about what a cold king I am."

"I don't think you're cold. I think you're dedicated to your kingdom and people. Which is why I always thought you only spent time with me trying to make me a good leader," said Aven. "I have no right to complain, I know. Everything I could ever want has been given to me, and you have been more lenient with me than you had to be."

"But you want something else. I could always tell." His father put both his hands on the table. "Do you not want to be king, Aven?"

"I...I think I do," said Aven slowly. "While I certainly don't want it to be any time soon, I've never dreaded or feared the position." Aven fiddled with the cover of the book. "I'm just not sure I've been given all the information I need to rule well."

"What do you mean?"

"On my trip, I learned some things about our land. We took shelter one night in the forest amongst some ruins. Someone showed them to us and explained they were of an old village and palace set up by ancient Illedrians. This person said we first settled into the forest before moving here."

"I've heard something like it," mumbled his father. "But I was told it was only legend by my own father and my teachers."

"But I saw the ruins, father, and the person who told me...I have no reason to doubt her."

"Who showed you the ruins, Aven, and why do you trust her?"

Aven considered his father for a moment, taking a long breath. "Because I've known her for over ten years." His father raised his eyebrows and opened his mouth, but Aven held his hand up. "I'm going to tell you everything. All I ask is you listen to the whole story before saying anything."

His father blinked a few times and then nodded. It was not easy at first, but Aven started his story of finding Silvie out by the pond when he was twelve. As he talked about Silvie teaching him magic and getting to know her, it got easier to speak. Something in his chest lightened as he told his father all about learning magic and finding a friend who would listen to him. When he was done, he sat back and stared at his father, waiting.

"You've been practicing magic for over ten years?"

Aven nodded. "I have. I've gotten pretty good at working with much of it, except stone, but I think I'm figuring it out."

"All this time, you've been meeting with some strange woman behind the palace, working on your magic, and you haven't told anyone."

"I didn't want to lie to you, Father, but I knew how you'd react if I told you." Aven leaned forward, his arms on the table. "You have been excellent in teaching me about my duties for the kingdom. My mother is loving and kind, but there are times I've felt very alone. There is always something swirling inside of me, wanting to come out. I tried to push it down, I did, but it never felt right. When I met Silvie, and she showed me how to release my magic, it felt right.

"I thought it was a good compromise, working on my magic in secret and not burdening you with it. I hadn't planned to do it forever. I knew one day I would need to leave it behind, but now I think that would be foolish."

"What do you mean?"

"Silvie has told me there's more wrong in the land than we know. She says the Sun King is reaching out and looking for human allies and that he wants to control not just his court but everything, everywhere. The chaos growing in the kingdom is being caused by him and the foolish humans who would follow him. Silvie said the best chance for our land is Illedria, and we need to be ready."

"This woman has told you this? How does she know?"

"She says she has contacts all over the land, and she told me...well, she told me she has Fae blood, so she must know other Fae."

"She's Fae?" asked his father loudly before looking around the room and leaning towards his son, his voice low. "You've been spending time with a Fae woman?"

"She's not full Fae, Father. She doesn't even look Fae, and I know, I've seen one now."

"What?"

"I came across a Fae woman on our travels. She's the one who told me about the objects in the temples and the scroll in the woods. I know I shouldn't have trusted her, but she was right about the temples and the scroll. She told me the same thing as Silvie: that war is coming, and we must be prepared."

His father stared at him for a moment before rubbing his face and shaking his head. "Aven, I don't know where even to start."

"I wanted you to know everything. I'm sorry I kept my magic and Silvie a secret, but you know it all now."

His father stood up abruptly, keeping his hand on the table. He tapped his fingers against it before putting both hands behind his back as he grunted and turned away.

"I know you're angry at me. I don't blame you, but we have to move past it. I've been warned by those I don't believe meant me any harm. Either of them could have killed me at any time, but instead, they helped me and warned me about danger."

"Fae are tricky. You can't always trust them."

"But Silvie has been alone with me for years and has never hurt me. I trust her completely." His father turned to look at him. "The Fae woman, I don't know, but something about her...I think she only wanted to help."

"I'm not angry, Aven, not at you," said his father. "I'm angry at myself at how little I know my own son. I admit I've kept you at arm's length, but it's just hard after... well, it's not my nature to attach myself to others, not anymore. I should have watched you closely and spoken to you more. Then you wouldn't have felt a need to meet with some strange woman and trust Fae you meet on a whim."

"I'm not stupid or simple," said Aven angrily. "If you think you should have spoken and listened to me in the past, do so now. Listen to what I'm saying. We are in danger. The whole land is. We cannot keep hiding away our greatest means of defense. How many of our people could use magic if they wanted? Think if we let the mages fully examine their powers. Suppose we stopped seeing magic as something debased and lower. It is a gift from our gods and goddesses, and we should use it."

"And alienate every other human kingdom in our land. These women you've met say war is coming, specifically from one of the Fae courts, and urge you to use magic. What if they are trying to divide us from other humans? You know how magic is feared elsewhere. It's seen as so evil in other kingdoms that people can be put to death for using it. Our mages and healers are only tolerated."

"But other kingdoms are allying themselves with the Sun King, not understanding what will happen. He wants us back in chains, serving the Fae. We are being given a gift with this warning and time. We should use it."

"Aven, I understand what you are saying, but you must see how impossible it is," said his father.

"It's not impossible. You are the king. Your word is law."

"I am beholden to my people and have to do what is best for them with my best judgment."

Aven stood up. "And what's best for them is to use every tool given to us." Aven waved his hand, and a flame from a nearby candle jumped into his palm. He held it out, and it circled the room as Aven threw out both hands, pushing a wind around the bookcases and keeping the flame from catching fire.

The flame moved around the room a few times before jumping back into Aven's palm and settling. His father turned in a small circle, examining the untouched room as he pushed his hair back down after being ruffled by the wind. "I won't pretend that wasn't impressive, Aven."

"You can feel it, can't you, Father?" asked Aven as he held the flame in his hand out towards the king. "Your magic responded. I know it did. You want to take this flame, play with it, bend it to your will." His father only stared at him. "When I was in the forest, I had a dream or a vision. I think it was about you arguing with your father about something. I thought it was about marrying mother, but I don't see why the old king would oppose our mother."

His father's eyes misted over, his hand coming up to his side.

"What were you arguing about with the old king? Was it Mother or someone else? You mentioned using your magic, and he didn't want to hear it."

His father's hand came up further, close to Aven. His clenched fist slowly opened. The flame in Aven's hands danced. He could feel it ready to leap to his father's as the air practically crackled with magic.

The door flung open, causing them to turn and Aven to lower his hand, the flame flying back to the candle. Two guards came in with Marcus, the king's head advisor.

"Your Majesty, Your Highness, you must come into the inner chambers of the palace. The village is under attack."

"What? Attack? By who?" asked the king sharply.

"We aren't sure, sir, but our guess is there are at least some Fae with them. They have use of magic. Our mages are gathering as we speak, and the guards are doing what they can," said Marcus. "Now, you must come with me and get to safety."

"Hide away while our people suffer?" asked Aven.

"I will not," said Aven's father, "but you will, Aven."

"But I can help," protested Aven.

"You are the future of this kingdom and must be protected. Come on, I will see you to the inner courts with your mother and sister before I speak further with Marcus and my guards."

"Father, please," said Aven.

"Not now, Aven. I am your king, and my word is final. Come with me," said the king.

Aven, knowing arguing would do no good, followed his father from the room, the guards and Marcus surrounding them. They moved down the hall towards the entry hall, meeting Aven's mother and sister by the stairs. His sister was being handed her son by one of the servants as Aven's mother came forward.

"Oh, Aven, there you are. I was worried you were out and about even after you promised me you would stay put," said Aven's mother, taking his hand.

"I was in the library with Father. You didn't need to worry."

"But we are under attack. Guards came in just as I was finishing my tea and made me leave."

"We can have some tea or wine for you in the inner courts, Mother," said Aven. "We need to get you settled."

"Of course." She started walking with Aven down the right hall to where the stairs leading down led to the fortified inner courts. "I only hope poor Lady Prudence and her sweet daughter make it home. I would have had them leave thirty minutes earlier if I had known."

Aven stopped. "Lady Prudence and Cara were here?"

His mother turned to look at him. "Oh, yes. I loved their company last time and decided to invite them again. Lady Prudence is such a good listener, and her daughter is lovely and quite funny. I plan to make it a weekly thing. They even invited me to their home, which I am sure is charming."

"When did they leave?" asked Aven as his father and guards caught up with them.

"Less than ten minutes ago," said his mother. "Do you think they made it out of the village?"

He did not. If they had left the room ten minutes earlier, it would have taken at least five minutes to get their carriage and driver ready. Aven addressed one of the guards. "What's happening in the village?"

"You don't need to hear it, Your Highness," said the guard.

"I do. Tell me, now."

"Aven, we can do this once you're in the safety of the inner courts," said his father.

"Tell me now," said Aven again. "I need to know."

The guard still hesitated but then said, "Half the shops are on fire. They've been dragging out some of our people, especially younger ones, and rounding up a few, and umm... disposing of others."

"You mean they are..." He pushed past the guards. "I have to go help."

"Aven, what are you doing?" called his father as Aven started running.

He did not answer, knowing he had to do all he could. Lady Prudence and Cara were out there, and they were as good as his family. He owed it to them and Quinn to see if they were safe. He met more guards on the way to the entry hall, but they did not stop him as he ran through the open door.

Guards were streaming out the palace gates, while others gathered to fortify it once it was closed. Aven pushed through the guards, seeing a few recognize him, but none of them grabbed him or tried to stop them, seeming to be too shocked to act. He managed to make it out the gates at the end of the group, turning towards the way to Mayfield Manor, when he stopped, shocked by what he saw.

Fire was everywhere. Smoke was so heavy in the air that Aven could hardly recognize his home village. People were running, screaming, and crying. Some children wailed, wandering aimlessly until a man or woman would scoop them up or take their hand. They ran towards the palace gate, trying to make it within the walls before the gate closed.

Aven grabbed a guard near him. "Run back to the palace and tell them not to close the gate for a few more minutes. Tell them to let the villagers in so they can have safety."

The soldier shook his head before looking at Aven. "My orders are to make it to the center of the village and fight."

"I'm your prince, and I'm telling you to go back to the palace first. Tell them you have a direct order from me to keep the gates open. If they have a problem with it, then they can take it up with me later." He shook the man. "Now go, do it before it's too late."

Aven let go of the guard as he staggered backward. The guard looked at the villagers making their way towards the palace before nodding and running. Aven turned back to the village, trying to get his bearings. He could see fire shooting off in the distance towards the village center, so he turned the other way, hoping he would find the way clear and know that Cara and her mother got home safely.

He started to run down the road but stopped as a piece of stone from the nearby half wall flew at him. He dropped down to avoid it, the piece flying over his head. Another piece came towards him, and he threw his hand out in a panic. The stone blasted into pieces, covering him in harmless dust.

He got up, seeing a group of hooded figures walking towards him. Several threw fire at nearby structures, setting roofs ablaze. A few peeled off, moving toward a crowd of villagers trying to get to the palace. Aven held up his hands and closed his eyes for a moment. The wind whipped around him, and he threw his hands out. Three of the figures in the middle were pushed back.

He pointed his hand at the nearby well. Water gushed out of it, landing on a nearby home on fire, dousing the flames before they could catch further. Two of the hooded figures in front of him turned, examining him before throwing out their hands. Fire and stone flew at him as the wind threatened to push him back. He knew he could block the fire easily but was sure the stone would hit him.

He braced himself for the impact as he threw the fire aside. Before the stone got to him, it was thrown off course, hitting a large tree next to him. Aven looked to his right to see his father running up to join him, his hand out. A ball of flame came from the king's palm, pushing back one of the hooded figures. Aven watched his father for a moment more before thrusting a hand toward the stone wall. A piece of it broke free, moving towards the hooded figures, making them break apart.

He continued to work with his father, trying to push the enemy back, but more appeared behind them. Aven glanced at his father as he looked at him. They both threw out a blast of wind, knocking back half the line in front of them. Just beyond it, Aven could see a carriage on its side, one he recognized as belonging to Lord Dall.

He ran forward, hearing his father call after him, but Aven didn't stop. He threw fire and wind, trying to keep the hooded figures away. A blast of fire grazed his shoulder, singeing his shirt and burning the skin underneath. A large branch hit his leg, making him stumble, but he found his footing again.

He paused when he finally saw Cara helping her mother move towards a small home. Lady Prudence's leg looked to be injured, and Cara was doing her best to support her mother as they moved as fast as they could. One of the hooded figures noticed them, turning towards them, his hand outstretched. Aven tried to get closer to help but was cut off by more of the cloaked figures moving in front of him.

He called out Cara's name, trying to warn her, but he wasn't sure she would hear over the chaos. Just when he thought the figure would reach them, there were several disturbances all around. Humans, Fae, and all sorts of creatures appeared. Some had weapons. Others began throwing out spells and curses immediately, pushing back the hooded figures. The one moving towards Cara was struck down swiftly by some sort of creature with gauzy wings, flying over the crowd.

Aven's father caught up with him, breathing hard as he stopped at his son's side. "What is going on, Aven? Who are they?"

Aven put his hands on his knees, breathing deeply as he felt the sting from his injuries hit him. He shook his head, trying to keep his lunch from coming up. "I don't know, but I think they're trying to help us."

He looked up as his father gasped. Three Fae appeared in front of him. One was a tall, lean man with light brown hair and a handsome face. He held a silver sword in one hand and a dagger in the other. He immediately took off, moving towards a group of the cloaked figures, cutting them down one by one.

The other two were a man and a woman. The man was a bit shorter than the other Fae man but built more broadly. His hair was so black Aven didn't think it was possible. He pulled out a sword as he turned to the woman with him. She pulled down her hood, and it was Aven's turn to gasp as he realized it was the Fae woman he had met in the valley.

Chapter 29

Tal

Tal appeared with Eriana in the middle of chaos. The air was thick with smoke, and Tal could smell blood. Screams and cries came from all around. Dyfan arrived with them, weapons out and ready to fight. He nodded to Eriana before running off into the throng, meeting hooded figures and cutting them down with his sword while slashing others with his dagger.

Tal took out his sword as Eriana pulled down her hood, surveying the area. Several hooded individuals up ahead had a group of children surrounded. Eriana put her hand up, but before she could do anything, one of the figures grabbed a child and cut his throat, throwing the boy on the ground before grabbing another.

Tal nearly dropped his sword in shock, never seeing such a thing. As Eriana threw out a wall of magic, the bright light slashing through the hooded figures, Tal couldn't take his eyes off the still boy on the ground. He couldn't have even been ten years old. Eriana grabbed his arm, making him regain focus.

"Come on, we have to get deeper into the village," she said.

Tal didn't move. "Why are they doing this? Why hurt children?"

"I told you they want no opposition. Many children here are born with magic. If Illedria ever fully trained their people, they would be a strong force to stand up against any kingdom, Fae or human. Now, come help me."

They started to run towards the village when Eriana stopped as she gripped Tal's arm. She looked at two men standing nearby, both staring at her.

"What are you doing here?" she hissed at them. "Get back to the palace."

"It's you," said the younger man, taking a step towards Eriana.

"I warned you this would happen. Now, get back to the palace, and my people and I will take care of this. Go, now."

She pulled on Tal as he watched the two men. The young one took another step towards them as the older man stared at Eriana. "I can help," said the younger one.

"You want to help? Then get as many of your people within the palace gates as you can and stay there," said Eriana.

"She's right, Aven," said the older man. "Our responsibility is to our people."

Eriana nodded and pulled Tal forward towards the village. As they were leaving, he heard the younger man say, "I have to get Lady Prudence and Cara first."

The fighting intensified as they got further into the village. Tal barely glanced at the tall palace gates before Eriana threw him forward. "Be ready and stay by my side. Watch the left."

They moved into the heaviest of the fighting. Several Underlings had already made some headway, using magic, swords, daggers, and arrows to take down the cloaked enemy. Eriana pulled out her sword and threw out some magic with her free hand. A group of cloaked figures nearby who were trying to get into a village home were thrown in the air, landing far away in strange positions, obviously never to rise again.

One of the figures came towards Tal, his hood slightly falling to reveal a very human face. Tal met his sword, exchanging a few blows before burying his blade in the man's chest. He pulled it out and met another while seeing two figures approaching Eriana, who was busy fighting with another.

Tal took a breath, feeling his dark magic swirl inside of him. He glanced at the two men as his sword met the one in front of him. The men were covered in darkness for a moment, and then they were no more. Eriana glanced that way after taking out the man in front of her. She looked over her shoulder at Tal and gave him a slight nod.

They moved together almost as one, taking out enemies with magic and blades. Tal lost track of time and the faces in front of him. He became covered with blood and mud from the streets, the smell of death all around. He felt Eriana against his back several times as the enemies pushed in on them.

"You do this often?" he asked as he pushed a dying enemy off him.

"It's not usually this bad," she said, throwing out some magic. "They haven't hit anywhere else this hard."

"And you think this is all my brother's doing?"

"I'm worried his list of allies has grown. Once we take care of this, I'll have to see what I can find out."

Eriana sheathed her sword and moved forward. She threw out her hands as she yelled, and a bright light eclipsed the scene around them. Tal had to look away, his eyes not able to stand it. He heard screams and cries before he opened his eyes and saw someone familiar.

On the edge of the fighting, near a row of burned-out shops, stood Delphina. She was dressed much as he remembered her, wearing dark pants and a red shirt. Her golden hair was braided back, and she had a sword in one hand as she held the top of her leg with the other. Her wide, blue eyes filled with fear met Tal's, and her mouth opened in surprise.

He stopped and stared at her, feeling a pull toward her. He had been so sure they had formed a connection. It hadn't been some magic. It was real. To see her looking so scared and obviously injured stirred something within his chest. Before he knew it, he moved towards her as she retreated behind the shops.

He found her kneeling next to a tree as ash and smoke swirled around her. Tal carefully walked up to her. "Delphina?"

She looked up at him and smiled, slowly rising to her feet. He stepped closer, and she took his hand. "I'm so glad you're alright, Tal. When I discovered what Eriana was up to, I was scared she would hurt you. She hasn't, has she?"

Tal shook his head. "No, of course not. Why would she hurt me?"

"Because she hates Fae. All she cares about is protecting humans." Delphina threw her arms around him. "I'm just so glad to see you here, unharmed." She pulled back, holding his hand for a moment before she stepped away. "And so is your brother."

"My brother?"

There was a disturbance next to Delphina and then a flash of light. A moment later, Tal's brother, the Sun King, stood before him.

Aven

Aven watched the Fae woman run towards the village, grabbing the Fae man with her. He turned to his father, who still had his eyes on the retreating couple. "Father?"

"You know her?"

"She's the Fae woman I met on my journey," said Aven.

"Do you know her name?"

"No, she never gave it to me. We need to hurry and get our people to safety," said Aven. "I need to check on Cara and Lady Prudence."

Aven's father shook his head as if to clear it. "Where did they go?"

"In that small house over there," said Aven, pointing towards the dwelling not thirty feet from them. As he spoke, he noticed some fire from a nearby house grow as though fed by something unseen. It sparked and caught on the next building and the next until it hit the roof of the house Aven knew held Lady Prudence and Cara. Those who had shown up with the Fae woman tried to put it out with water and magic, but it continued to grow.

People streamed out of all the dwellings, and Aven moved forward, trying to see through the smoke. More hooded figures appeared, grabbing young men, women, and children. The others tried to help, rescuing whoever they could before the hooded figures disappeared. Aven and his father joined in, using their magic to try to shield certain groups and knock back those hooded figures.

Aven heard his name in a familiar voice. He turned as Cara ran towards him, Lady Prudence trying to keep up. Aven moved towards her as his father held the enemy back. Before Aven could reach her, one of the hooded figures appeared behind her and grabbed her around the waist. Cara screamed as the hood fell back on the figure, showing a Fae male with sandy blonde hair. The Fae took her arm and looked at it before getting in her face and sniffing. Cara reached up with her free hand and scratched the man's face, kicking her feet out to try to get free.

The Fae man snarled, blood running down his face. He wrapped his hand around Cara's neck as Aven tried to get to her. Aven threw out his hands, sending a blast of flame. The Fae male didn't even turn, throwing the flames away as he stared at Cara and lifted her off the ground.

Aven was ready to try again when the tall, trim Fae man from earlier appeared behind Cara with two others. He pushed out his sword, and Cara was thrown from her captor's arms, caught by some creature hovering nearby, her iridescent wings beating.

"Dyfan, watch it!" said the flying creature.

"Go," said Dyfan as he plunged his sword at the cloaked, blonde man. The blonde man met him with a flash of steel, pulling out his sword so fast that Aven barely saw it.

Aven ran towards the winged woman as the blonde man turned to Dyfan. "Such treachery, Dyfan. Fighting against your king."

"He's no king of mine," said Dyfan. "You're a fool to follow him, Iwan."

Iwan laughed at Dyfan, squaring up to fight him before he turned his head as though hearing something.

"Another day, Dyfan." Iwan glanced towards where the winged woman still held Cara. He grinned, showing his teeth before his hand whipped out, throwing a dagger towards them. Aven yelled, but the dagger never hit. The winged woman and Cara disappeared.

Aven turned his eyes to Dyfan, and he, too, was gone. All around him, the fighting stopped as the hooded creatures disappeared, the ones fighting them looking around before disappearing, some grabbing their wounded as they left. The fires died down as though called away as well, leaving half burned smoldering shops and homes. With the fighting gone, Aven could hear more of the wailing of the hurt and grieving.

Aven felt a hand on his shoulder and found his father beside him. "Aven, are you alright?"

Aven shook his head. "They took her."

Before his father could ask anything else, Aven heard Lady Prudence yelling his name. She limped towards him, holding up her ruined skirt so as not to trip. "Aven, Aven, where is Cara?" She stumbled before him, taking his hand.

He couldn't form words at first, not knowing how to tell the lady that her beloved daughter was gone.

His father took over. "My dear lady, your daughter was taken, but I don't think it was by those who would harm her."

"Taken?" Lady Prudence nearly sunk to the ground. "She was taken."

"Yes, but I'm sure we can get her back," said the king. "Come to the palace so we can see to your injuries, and we will discuss it further."

"Aven?" said Lady Prudence uncertainly.

"He's right, my lady. You need to come inside so we can make sure you're well. I'll contact Lord Dall and Quinn. I'm sure they're looking for you by now."

"But Cara? Oh, Aven, what will they do to her?"

"It'll be fine, Lady Prudence," said Aven with conviction. "No matter what, I will find her and bring her back to you. I promise."

Tal

Tal stepped back, not quite understanding how his brother was there before him. He looked so odd in the human lands, practically glowing in the fading light, dimmed by smoke.

"You're in one piece, after all," said his brother with a grin. "Thank the Light God. I feared the worst after hearing you were taken. I can't believe my head guard would betray us. I'm sorry for sending him with you, Tal."

Tal felt dumbstruck looking at his brother, who was smiling at him as Delphina took his hand again. "You need to come with us now," said Delphina. "We can get you back to Bringant and keep you safe. Poor Princess Adalyn is beside herself. I promised her I would bring you back."

"You promised my sister you would bring me back?" asked Tal. He wasn't sure why, but that didn't seem right.

"I did. She was angry when I returned without you, but she is such a dear. I know she will forgive me the moment I bring you to her," said Delphina.

No, it wasn't right. He had the impression that his sister didn't like or trust Delphina. Didn't she warn him about Delphina?

"Now come on, Tal. We need to leave before your absence is noticed," said Idris.

Tal took a deep breath, trying to take his eyes off Delphina, but he couldn't. He was so drawn to her, wanting to do as she asked.

"Yes. Come on, Tal," said Delphina, squeezing his hand. "It's time to go."

"He will go nowhere," said Eriana as she came from around the building, her hand up.

Tal blinked at Delphina before trying to take his hand away as he looked at Eriana. She was covered in ash and blood, a small gash on her cheek.

"Lady Eriana," said Idris with a small bow. "It's been a while."

"It has, and I've wanted to speak with you about some rumors I've heard. Is it true you've been telling people of your court that I'm to be your wife?"

Idris half smiled, crossing his arms. "Is it so bad that I wish to court you, my dear lady?" He moved past Tal towards Eriana, looking her up and down. "You and I could be something. Don't you wish to be a queen? I thought it was something you wanted."

Eriana moved closer to Tal as Delphina pulled him towards her. "I have no wish to be your queen."

"I can change your mind. I will, you know. You're too charming for me to let go, and you're so lovely." He growled in approval. "Especially like this."

"Oh yes," said Eriana with a half chuckle. "I'm sure it's my charm and beauty and not something else that draws you to me."

Idris laughed. "Oh, make no mistake. I have no qualms bedding you, even if there is something else you have that I want more." He reached towards her. "Lovely, wicked woman, give up this fight."

"I will never be your queen," said Eriana.

"You should listen to him, Eri," said Delphina. "Father will be so disappointed once he learns his sweet niece is betraying her king and court. I warned him your human nature would win out, but he wouldn't listen."

Eriana rolled her eyes. "Oh yes, because humans' tendency to be merciful and decent is so awful." She snarled at Delphina. "I suppose I should've been more like you, fucking anything I could halfway charm."

Delphina gasped, her eyes flashing in anger. Idris stepped closer to Eriana. "It sounds like you won't be persuaded today, so we will take my brother back where he belongs and be on our way." Idris pulled at the ridiculous green and gold jacket he wore.

"You will take him nowhere," said Eriana fiercely.

Delphina gave Eriana a mocking smile. "You have no control over him. He wants to come home with me."

Tal looked at Delphina, still feeling a pull towards her, but he turned as he heard Eriana's voice. "Your tricks won't work, Delphina."

"Tricks?" said Delphina with false innocence. "Dear Eriana, it's not a trick. The prince and I grew close on our little journey together. So much so, we made plans, didn't we, Tal?"

Tal kept his stare on Eriana, whose face revealed nothing but a small twitch of her lips.

"Enough of this. Tal, it's time to come home. You've done what I commanded. Now you are needed at the Golden Court," said Idris.

Tal bent forward at the strength of his brother's command, clenching his fist and baring his teeth. He tried to say he wouldn't. He didn't want to go with either Idris or Delphina. He looked at Eriana, trying to convey his feelings.

"If you wish to visit Prince Taliesin, Eriana, you may do so in my court," said Idris.

"He will not go to your court," said Eriana as she pulled out a dagger. "Not today."

Delphina laughed. "You think you can stop both of us, Eri? Not surprising, you always did think too much of your own abilities."

Eriana did not move toward Idris or Delphina. She held out her hand, a glowing orb resting in her palm. Delphina's hold on Tal slackened as she stared at the orb, and Idris shuffled slowly towards Eriana. Tal felt like his breath was stuck in his chest as he focused on the orb. He could hear it, calling to him with its alluring song.

"You do have it," whispered Idris.

Eriana raised her dagger to her throat, pressing the blade into her skin, making a prick of blood come to the surface. "Let him go, or I will do it."

Tal's focus left the orb as he stared at the knife at Eriana's throat. He felt like he should do something but didn't dare move.

Idris stopped moving towards her, his hand up as Delphina huffed. "Oh, let her do it, Idris. Then I'll control the right to choose our ruler and give it to you."

"You're so sure it would go to you, Delphina? Magic is tricky, especially one this old and intricate. Where will the right to rule go if it doesn't find you worthy? It could throw everything into chaos, and then you will never get what you want, Idris."

"Don't," Idris said softly. "Just wait."

Eriana pushed the knife deeper into her skin, causing her to flinch. The blood on her throat grew, and Tal couldn't keep his eyes off it. He wanted to slap the knife from her hand.

"The prince will come with me, and you will leave Illedria immediately," said Eriana. "Call all your little minions away."

"Oh, please, this is ridiculous. She won't do it," said Delphina. "Take the prince, and let's go."

Idris stared at the golden orb in Eriana's hand. Everything was still for a moment. Delphina's hand had completely fallen off Tal, but he was still scared to move, to cause anything to happen. Finally, Idris looked away, his eyes narrowing before he grinned. He grabbed Tal and pulled him close.

"Here, you can have him. We're done here." Idris leaned in and whispered in Tal's ear. "Enjoy your time with the lovely lady, but know she's hiding so much from you. You think you can't trust me, but Eriana is the one with all the secrets." He threw Tal toward Eriana, causing her to put down her hands and dagger as she caught him.

"Come along, dear Delphina," said Idris as the lady moved close to him. "I'll see you soon, my lady, and you too, Brother. I expect you'll both be in my court soon enough."

A bright light flashed, and they were gone. Eriana let go of Tal and swiped at the blood on her neck and then her cheek.

Tal looked at her in shame. "I...I'm...I." He tried to think of a way to explain himself but realized he couldn't do it.

Eriana sighed as she closed her eyes and put her finger on the leather bracelet she wore. "Come along, Your Highness. I need to get you back within our wards before I return here to clean up."

"Lady Eriana, I..."

She held up her hand. "We need to go. Come here." She took his hand and pulled him close. She refused to look at him as he stared at her. She looked sad and tired, and Tal felt a strange twinge in his stomach, something like regret, though he wasn't sure, as he hadn't felt the sensation in a long while.

Tal felt a breeze on his face as a white light surrounded them. A moment later, they were standing in front of the palace in the forest. Eriana let go of him. She swayed a bit, making Tal reach out for her.

"Lady Eriana? Are you ill?"

She shook her head and reached into a pocket inside her cloak. She took out a small vial and uncorked it, quickly drinking the contents. "I'm fine. Sometimes, certain magic drains me. Come on, get inside."

They walked through the door and were met by Dyfan.

Dyfan grabbed her arms and looked her over. "Are you alright?" He examined her face as she stared at the wall.

"I'm fine. I have to go back and see how I can help. Reset their wards and make them stronger. See if I can figure out how they were broken." She dropped her arms. "I'll go in glamour."

"You've been injured," said Dyfan, his hand coming up to Eriana's face. "Get cleaned up and seen by our healers, and then you can go back."

She shook her head. "It's nothing but a few scratches. They'll probably be healed by the time I come back."

"Then let me go with you," said Dyfan.

"I need you here, watching the prince," said Eriana. "Idris was there, Delphina too. He's vulnerable to her charms and Idris's command. Do not let Prince Taliesin leave the palace unless you're with him. He is not to step one single foot off the grounds."

Dyfan turned to Tal. "What happened?"

"I'll let the prince explain it to you. I need to go," said Eriana as she adjusted her cloak. "I'll try to be back tonight at some point. I need to see who we brought back. Make sure all the Illedrians are kept comfortable until we figure out what to do with them."

"Eri, I really think you should rest first."

"No, there's no time. Do as I ask." She finally looked at Dyfan. "Please, Dyfan, I need to go. I can't..."

His eyes softened into understanding. "Then go. Do what you need to, but come back tonight, or I'll come look for you."

"I'll try not to be gone long." She turned and started towards the door without looking at Tal.

"Lady Eriana," said Tal, stopping her. "I'm... I'm sorry. I don't know why I did it."

She stopped with her hand on the door latch. "Did you want to go with them? If you did, I can make it happen. I just couldn't let you go, knowing our location. I'll need to alter your memories before arranging your trip back to the Golden Court."

Tal felt Dyfan's eyes on him, but he couldn't look away from Eriana, from the pain, disappointment, and exhaustion on her face. "I don't want to go back. I don't want to be under Idris's rule."

Eriana turned her head to look at him. "And Delphina?"

"I think I misjudged what we had. I thought it had the chance to be real, to become something, but I was wrong. She's been using her powers to draw me in. I won't be fooled again."

"Then you can stay longer, but soon you'll have to make a decision. I can't have such a liability in my court amongst my people. Today shows Idris's ruthlessness."

Tal nodded. "I understand."

"And until you make a decision, you'll be under Dyfan's command. If you have any questions or requests, you will go to him. His word will be final," said Eriana. "I need to go."

Eriana opened the door, but Tal couldn't let her go without saying something. "Thank you for what you did."

"There's no need to thank me. I was only doing what was best for my court." She nodded at Dyfan and then left, closing the door behind him.

"Are you injured in any way?" asked Dyfan gruffly.

Tal watched the door for a moment and then turned around. "No."

"Tell me what happened."

The door opened, and several Underlings came in, a few being carried with gashes in their sides or on their legs and arms. A pretty wood sprite had a bleeding wing, her face pale. Tal waited for them to walk through, Dyfan clapping a few on the shoulder and reassuring the others the healers were ready.

"In here," said Dyfan as he grabbed Tal and pulled him into the same small parlor where he had found Eriana and the child. "Now tell me."

"I was a fool, Dyfan," said Tal. He proceeded to tell Dyfan everything from following Delphina to what Eriana did to get Idris and the others to leave with him.

Dyfan cursed when he was done and paced in front of the fireplace. "Fuck, Tal, do you realize what your weakness could have done? Eri has suffered enough for this court and more than enough for..." He stopped and shook his head as though in pain. "Why are you so drawn to that woman? Delphina is a viper, Tal. She'll do nothing but inject you with venom while dripping sweet words in your ear."

"I won't be fooled by her again."

Dyfan laughed cruelly. "You sure about that?"

"I am."

"And, your brother, he's still your ruler. You're under his command," said Dyfan.

"Not by choice," yelled Tal. "I want nothing to do with him. I never have."

"But you won't give your allegiance to this court, to the very woman who saved you today," said Dyfan.

"I...I'm still not sure. I need to think about it."

Dyfan stopped his pacing. "Fine. Then let me take you to your room. You'll stay there and take your meals there until I say you can leave." He grabbed Tal's arm.

Tal felt a faint tinge of anger as Dyfan dragged him up the stairs, but it was choked out by the guilt he felt. When Dyfan left him alone in his room, locking the door behind him, he couldn't help but feel his imprisonment might be justified.

Chapter 30

Aven

AVEN WORE HIS THICKEST cloak, but he could find no warmth as he stood by the small pond. Snow fell quietly around him, thick fat flakes starting to cover the ground. Three days had passed since the attack, and the village was finally in some sort of order. The dead had been rounded up, and the injured taken to the healers. Clean-up had begun, and the King's council had met with his father several times.

The night of the attack, a Fae woman with hair as dark as raven's wings came to see them, saying she was sent by the Queen of the Underlings. She spoke with Aven's father, telling him about her court and how they were misunderstood. She explained that the Sun King was behind the attack, but they had not figured out all his allies. She said she could strengthen their wards and keep better watch over their lands.

As Aven listened along with his father, he waited to see how the king would react. He asked fewer questions than Aven expected, thanking the woman and telling her he would make sure their village was patrolled at all times and would send out word all throughout his kingdom.

Before she left, Aven's father stopped her. "The Queen of the Underlings, she is your leader," said the king slowly.

The Fae woman turned, her dark eyes sweeping the king up and down. "Yes, for the time being."

"She was here, helping us, wasn't she?" The Fae woman nodded. "Who is she?" Aven looked at his father with surprise as he asked the question.

"Someone who wants the world to stay in balance, who sees all creatures as equal," said the woman.

"Her name. Can you tell me her name?"

The woman stared at the king and then at Aven. "She doesn't like it known for various reasons. I can only assure you that she thinks kindly upon your kingdom and will see to its well-being."

The Fae woman turned away as Aven moved forward. "Several of our people were taken. I think some were taken by your group, and many of them were children. What will happen to them? They need to be returned."

The Fae woman faced Aven. "The people taken were in danger from the Sun King and remain in danger. We will meet with each one and determine if their return is possible."

"Shouldn't their families have a say if they are returned or not?" said Aven. "One of our important lords is missing a daughter."

The Fae woman huffed, her voice impatient. "When we determine it's safe for your people to return, we will see to it. Their families will be notified." She ran a hand through her dark hair. "They were targeted because of their magic. Perhaps if you didn't have such a dark view on the subject, you and your people would be safer." Without another word, the woman turned and was gone.

Aven knew she had kept her word and strengthened their wards somehow. He could feel the magic surrounding him, pulsing through the air and making his own respond. His father had not spoken about magic yet, though Aven knew he met with the mages and healers.

When Aven left this morning, his father had stopped him. Aven had been afraid his father would ask him where he was going and forbid it. Instead, the king walked up to Aven and said, "You don't have that necklace you brought back from the temple, do you?"

The question caught Aven off guard. "No. I haven't seen it since the day I came home. I thought it was in your office."

"It was, but now it's gone. The horn and scroll remain untouched, but the necklace is missing. I was hoping perhaps you had taken it for a reason."

"I haven't," said Aven. "We need to find it."

"I'll ask Marcus if someone misplaced it. I'm sure it's somewhere in the palace. Not many have access to my study."

Aven nodded. "I'm going for a ride. When we get back, I'll help you look for it."

"I'm sure it won't be necessary. Take care on your ride." His father walked away towards his study.

Now Aven stood by his familiar pond, hoping Silvie may have heard of their troubles and would visit. He planned to come out the next few mornings to catch her. It appeared he was right in his assessment, as he didn't have to wait long before he saw her familiar light red hair through the trees.

Aven hurried to meet her as she came close to the pond. She took his hands. "Are you alright? You weren't injured at all?"

"No. I'm fine," said Aven. "Well, as fine as I can be with the state of my village."

"I heard," said Silvie, squeezing his hands and releasing them. "I was hoping to catch you one of these mornings. How awful is it?"

"It's terrible, Silvie. So much of the village burned in some way. At least two dozen were killed. Most were children." He looked away. "They hurt children. Why would anyone do it?"

"They must be evil," said Silvie. "Only someone completely vile could kill an innocent child."

"I thought it was the Court of the Underlings at first, but I think they were the ones who showed up to help. We would have been wiped out without them. An emissary of their queen came to see us, and she strengthened our wards."

"You don't sound very thankful, Aven," said Silvie.

"They took several of our people, mostly children." He pinched the bridge of his nose. "They took Cara, Quinn's sister."

"Oh, Aven...I'm so sorry, but you must know they won't hurt her," said Silvie. "I know a little about the Underlings. I don't think your friend will be in any danger."

"Try telling that to her mother, who won't stop crying, or her father, who feels he failed to protect his beloved daughter. Quinn is ready to leave the village and search the whole world to find her. Only his mother, who cannot bear to see him go, has made him stay."

Aven turned towards the pond. "I promised I would find her and bring her home. I don't break promises, Silvie. As soon as our village is secure, I'm going out there to find her."

"Don't do anything hasty, Aven. You're needed here with your people. I'm sure Cara will be home soon, or you'll at least hear something." Silvie moved to his side. "I have friends everywhere, even some who have contact with the Underlings. Let me see what I can find out for you. Don't do anything until you know more."

"I just feel like I have to do something. My village is in ruins. My father seems different, almost broken by what happened. He's still meeting with his council and trying to help, but it's like he's constantly distracted."

"I'm sure he feels guilty, Aven. Watching your people suffer is beyond difficult. Your father is a good king who cares. Give him a few days to recover."

"What...What if they come back?" Aven voiced the concern he hadn't allowed himself to say since the attack. "What if they break through the new wards and finish us off? I try to sleep at night; all I can hear are those awful screams. I can smell the smoke and blood. I can see the children lying still on the ground."

"Oh, Aven," said Silvie, pulling Aven into her arms. "I can't imagine how hard this is for you."

He leaned against her, his head on her shoulder as tears fell from his eyes. "I'm supposed to be king someday, but I don't see how. I don't think I was made for battle."

She rubbed his back. "None of us were truly made for battle, or we shouldn't be. What happened in Illedria was wrong, but I'm afraid it won't be the last of it."

"I can't take it, Silvie."

"I know it feels that way now, and I hope you're always appalled by such evil. You're stronger than you know." She took his face in her hands so he would look at her. "You will do what you must for your people, and you aren't alone." She wiped his tears with her thumbs. "I'll help you as much as I can. Let me find out everything I can about your friend while you stay here and help your village heal and prepare."

"My father hasn't said anything about magic. After what I saw, we need to be better prepared to fight. We can't be so helpless."

"Then talk to him about it. Don't let him dismiss your concerns or tell you you're wrong. Fight for what you know is right, even if it's with those you love. You'll get through this, Aven," said Silvie.

He stayed with Silvie by the pond until his tears dried. She promised him she would be back within a week with news about Cara, and he vowed he wouldn't give up. When he returned to the palace, he was ready to fight for his people.

Tal

Tal had never liked being still, and now he knew why. If he kept busy drinking, spending time with women, and traveling from place to place, he never had time to dwell on anything. Being confined to his room for over three days had given Tal nothing but time to think, and he hated it. For the last three decades, his life had been a waste, just like everyone had told him. He had known it but had never taken the time to care. Now that he had to face it, there was no escape.

As he lay in the dark, unable to sleep, he tried to remember what his life was like back in the Golden Court when his father was king. It had always nagged him why his memories were so fuzzy, but he pushed the feeling aside as he preferred to live in the now. For the first time in as long as he could remember, he really tried to find those memories.

He recalled times with his father, conversations they had, laughing with him, sitting in his study playing on his floor as a child. He remembered the times he ran around the court with his sister, the way her dresses swished around her feet as they raced each other to the back lawn. He could see in his mind sparring with Dyfan as a young man, pushing each other to the limit, knowing the scrapes and bruises would heal quickly.

Still, there were many fuzzy memories he could not access, things he felt he should have known but wouldn't come to him. He even spent time trying to remember Eriana. Surely, he would have known her back then. She was friends with his sister and important to Dyfan. If they spent time with her, shouldn't he?

When he wasn't thinking about what a waste he was or trying to remember his childhood, Tal tried to think of his future. Who did he want to be? He knew he didn't want to go back to the Golden Court or be under his brother's thumb, but did he believe what Eriana had told him?

Sure, in the back of his mind, he sometimes wondered what would have happened had his father named him the heir, but he pushed it aside quickly. His brother was the Sun King, and Tal had made peace with it. He even thought it was the better choice. His brother liked grandeur and surrounding himself with power. While Tal liked comfort, performing for a bunch of puffed-up lords or ladies was never his preference.

He had come to believe his father knew this and gave Tal his freedom while appointing a king over the Golden Court who would do his duty. But if what he saw in Illedria showed what kind of king Idris was, how could Tal just stand back and do nothing?

He had watched children being slaughtered in front of him. He saw homes of innocents burned to the ground. Humans had been attacked by Fae. Humans, who had no way to defend themselves and had done nothing to warrant such violence. Could he ignore what he saw and disappear into the human lands, knowing what was brewing around him?

He had only a few lasting relationships, none of which he would call friendly. They were mostly like what he had with Berg, all about what they could get from each other. Still, he had met plenty of what he would call decent people—those who in no way deserved what was done in Illedria.

It must have been almost supper three days after the attack on Illedria when his door opened. Tal stood up from his seat in front of the fireplace as Eriana walked into the room with Dyfan. She came to one of the chairs by his fireplace and sat down heavily as though exhausted. Dyfan stood close to the fireplace.

"Sit down, Prince Taliesin," she said with impatience as she fiddled with one of her braids.

"All I've done is sit the past few days," he said, sounding annoyed.

"I hope you've had time for some self-reflection as well," said Eriana as she propped her head on her hand. "I'm afraid you've about reached the end of our hospitality. If you aren't with us, ready to consider your future, then we need to find a way to move on."

"How would you do it?" asked Tal.

"Move on?" she asked, and he nodded. "I would keep trying to find a way to take the right to rule away from you if you don't want it. All while fighting your brother and trying to gain new allies in the Fae and human realms."

Tal swallowed. "And if you can't find a way to take the right to rule away?"

"I'm not going to have you killed, Your Highness. You're safe from my court and me. I can't say the same about your brother."

Tal glanced at Dyfan before staring at Eriana. "Can I ask you something a little more personal?"

Dyfan stood up straighter as Eriana lifted her head. "You can ask me whatever you want, and I'll see if I can answer it. I promise I won't lie to you."

Tal heard his brother's words in his mind about Eriana hiding many secrets. "You say you knew me when we were younger."

"I did."

"Were we... were we friends, or did you find me insufferable?"

She half smiled. "I didn't find you insufferable."

"So we were friends?"

"I wouldn't call us friends," she said shortly.

"So then it was easy to believe I was a no-good deviant when you heard the rumors."

"I didn't believe them until I saw it for myself." She sighed. "And I wouldn't use those words. I would say you are a man without purpose and maybe a little lazy. I believe you have potential, though, or I wouldn't even try to put you on the throne, right to rule or not."

"If I say I'm ready to pledge my allegiance to you, can you promise not to force me to do something I don't want?" asked Tal.

"I don't like to make promises I'm not sure I can keep," said Eriana. "I'd like to tell you I'd never force you to do anything, and I will do everything I can to make sure I don't. Things do happen beyond our control, and if I had to force you to do something to save yourself and others, I would."

Tal drummed his fingers against his chair. "Will I be able to leave the palace grounds?"

"Once I'm assured your magic has recovered and you are sufficiently trained, you will be allowed to leave for the right reasons. I'd rather you don't flit around the human or Fae realms unprotected only for pleasure. I still believe your life could be in danger."

"Fair enough," said Tal.

"But you will have free reign of the palace and grounds again. You will sit on my council, and I promise to listen to any complaints or ideas you have. I can't tell you I will act upon them, but I will consider them. You may be king one day, but if you pledge yourself to my court, you will claim me as your queen for now."

Tal stood up and wiped his hand on his pants. "How do we do it then? Do I kneel before you here and say some words?"

Eriana exchanged looks with Dyfan.

"There will be an official ceremony tomorrow to take new pledges into the court. We have a few who wish to join. You will kneel before your queen for all to see," said Dyfan.

Tal eyed Eriana. "You like a little pomp, do you?"

"I don't mind a bit of...ceremony," said Eriana, rising, "And I know the power of something being declared publicly. The court is more likely to accept you if they see you pledge your life to them and me. One day, if you choose to be king, you will need them all to follow you. I want them to see you as one of them."

"Fine," said Tal. "I'll do it."

"Good," said Eriana. "Then I'll see you tomorrow night, just before supper. Dyfan, you can do with him what you will until then. Let him wander if you wish."

"I think one more night of seclusion and reflection will do him good," said Dyfan as he followed Eriana. "I'll see supper is brought in tonight, as well as some clothes that should be sufficient for tomorrow night. If you change your mind, you let me know."

"I don't care what I wear," said Tal.

"I believe he was talking about your decision to join my court, Your Highness," said Eriana with a laugh. "Remember, you have a choice." She stopped at the door. "Even after you pledge to me, if you decide you don't want this, we'll work something out. As long as you are loyal to me and the other Underlings while you are a part of us, we won't have a problem."

Tal bowed. "Until tomorrow, then."

"Until tomorrow," she said softly, her eyes on him. "Good night, Your Highness."

She walked out, leaving Dyfan behind. "This may not be what you want, Tal, but I think direction and purpose are something you've needed for a while. Maybe you'll find them here."

"I hope so, Dyfan."

"There's one more thing," said Dyfan. "We're old friends, and even with our long estrangement, I still care about you."

Tal crossed his arms. "I never meant for us to become estranged."

"You're my friend, Tal, and that hasn't changed. But if you do anything to hurt this court or our queen, I will not hesitate to make you pay for it. You will respect your fellow Underlings, especially Eriana."

"I have no plans to betray any of you, Dyfan. I just want to figure out what's going on. I can't promise you I'll be king."

"I would never ask you to," said Dyfan as he held the door. "I'll see you tomorrow."

Tal was led by Flint and another young Fae male from his room to the throne room. When the doors were open for him, it was not like it was before. The tables remained, but everyone stood beside them, facing the dais. There was no music or conversations, though a few strains of laughter could be heard through the crowd. Tal stood at the back, watching as two Fae males and one human female kneeled in front of the dais, saying, "I swear my life to the Underlings. I will live as one, fight as one, and die as one if needed. I submit to the command of our queen, placing my life in her hands, my trust in her judgment."

Tal's eyes went from those kneeling to the throne on the dais. His eyes went wide, and his breath left him as he took in Eriana on her throne. Gone were her pants and loose tunic, replaced with a dress made of black with gold brocade. Its neckline was high, but her shoulders were bare. Her sleeves were long and fitted. Her magnificent auburn hair was free of its braids, the long waves falling over her shoulders down her back and chest. On her forehead was a thin golden crown with one red jewel.

She stood, looking down at those kneeling. "And I pledge to serve you well as your queen. What is mine is yours. I give you the hospitality of my hall and my protection. What I decide will be with your goodwill in mind. You call me queen, and I call you mine. Rise and join your brothers and sisters."

There was much applause and whooping in the room as several converged on the three new Underlings, hugging them or clapping them on the back.

"We have one more who wishes to join our number today, my queen," said Dyfan.

"Then let him come forth," said Eriana, standing in front of her throne.

Everyone went quiet, the new Underlings moving to the side as Flint gave Tal two pats on his shoulders before joining the crowd. Tal slowly walked to the front, trying to keep from pulling at the collar of his black shirt, his matching pants feeling tight and stiff. He kept his eyes on Eriana as he walked, unable to look away from the vision she was as queen.

He came just before the dais, his stare not breaking from her as he slowly knelt on the ground. He said his pledge as she stared down at him. When he was done, there was silence. Finally, Eriana gave her pledge to him. He stood up as Eriana took a deep breath.

She looked over the room and said, "We welcome Prince Taliesin, prince of the Dark and Light Fae Courts, to our number. He is now one of us and will be protected and respected as an Underling. Let us have a toast to him and all our newest members."

Mugs of mead were quickly passed out, Berg pressing one into Tal's hand. Eriana held up her mug to the crowd. "For the good of all."

The room repeated, "For the good of all," before taking a drink.

Before Tal could even taste his mead, Eriana was at his side. She whispered in his ear, "And to possibilities."

He took his mug away from his mouth and held it out to her. She clinked it with her own as Tal said, "To possibilities."

www.ingramcontent.com/pod-product-compliance
Lightning Source LLC
Chambersburg PA
CBHW040134160726
48006CB00014B/1490